The Wept of Wish-ton-Wish

A CHARLES E. MERRILL STANDARD EDITION

CHARLES E. MERRILL STANDARD EDITIONS

Under the General Editorship of
Matthew J. Bruccoli and Joseph Katz

Exact reprints, whenever possible facsimiles, of authoritative
texts of significant literary works. Each volume is introduced in an
appropriate manner by a major scholar, critic, or author.

James Fenimore Cooper

The Wept of Wish-ton-Wish

Introduced by

Richard Beale Davis
The University of Tennessee

CHARLES E. MERRILL PUBLISHING COMPANY
A Bell & Howell Company
Columbus, Ohio

This text of *The Borderers: or, The Wept of Wish-ton-Wish* is a facsimile of the edition published by Richard Bentley, 1833, from the copy in the Newberry Library (Case Y/255/.C 7966). For reasons he discussed in the Preface, Cooper was dissatisfied with the first edition (Florence, 1829) and so prepared this revision.

ISBN: 0-675-09298-X

Library of Congress Catalog Number: 75-127081

1 2 3 4 5 6 7 8 9 10 — 75 74 73 72 71 70

Printed in the United States of America

Introduction

by Richard Beale Davis

In the autumn of 1829 Cooper's eleventh book was published in five countries in four languages. In each language it had a different title, each emphasizing one among the several themes inherent in the novel. In Florence and in Philadelphia it appeared with what was undoubtedly the author's own choice of a title, *The Wept of Wishton-Wish*, suggesting that it is a tragically-ending Indian captivity narrative with a setting in a poetically and picturesquely named American valley. In London it appeared as *The Borderers*, stressing the symbolic struggle between European settlers and aborigines. In Paris the emphasis was quite different, for it was called *Les Puritains d'Amerique*, as though it presented a portrait of those religionists, perhaps at full length. In Berlin the French title was in part retained, but with additional suggestiveness: *Conanchet und die Puritaner in Connecticut*. Here are combined as subjects the noble Indian and one segment of American Puritans. Cooper, as any other nineteenth-century author, probably allowed rather than suggested these divergent labels, for they sprang from what the translator and his publisher saw in the book and what feature of the fiction they felt would appeal most to the readers in their particular language. What interests us is the number of quite different things these first readers saw in this novel, actually a greater variety than is shown in the titles of any other work by Cooper. Of equal interest is the fact that no one of the titles, or subtitles, suggests what many readers and critics today consider the most significant treatment and material in the book, its use of the regicide, or "Angel of Hadley," theme and characterization. These form a major element of the novel, and they represent along with Pocahontas–John Smith, Merry-Mount, and the Kentucky Tragedy the principal materials of American romance which have been used for artistic purposes for several centuries.

The Wept of Wish-ton-Wish is a tale of the character of the early Puritans, of King Philip's War against these people in Connecticut, of one of Charles I's judges in hiding, of archetypal border warfare, of a beautiful white captive and her noble Indian husband Conanchet, and of several other things, including Indian-white miscegenation. It is this variety or conglomerate of themes and materials which is the novel's strength and weakness, which has caused critics to view it on a wide arc of opinion from those who rank it above *The Last of the Mohicans* to those who dismiss it as a miserable failure to depict a people (the Puritans) Cooper was congenitally incapable of understanding. It should be placed or bracketed at neither extreme. It is by no means a perfect novel, but it does several things well and a few superbly. It is the only attempt by our first great novelist to portray the character of the early Puritan, though in other works he deals extensively with his decadent — in Cooper's eyes — Yankee descendant.

The novel apparently shaped itself in Cooper's mind in England in 1827, was continued in France and Switzerland in 1828, and completed in Italy in early 1829 [see James F. Beard, *The Letters and Journals of James Fenimore Cooper*, I (Cambridge, Mass., 1960), *passim*]. Its inception probably goes back several years, to W. H. Gardiner's critique of Cooper's *The Spy* in the *North American Review* of July 1822 (n.s, VI, 255-57), in which the reviewer points out three great epochs in American history which he considers peculiarly well fitted for treatment in romance — the times just succeeding the first settlement, the era of the Indian wars, and the Revolution. Gardiner goes on to suggest as most interesting the "fortunes of those sterner puritans, who did *not* rise in arms against their prince," which theme suggests Cooper's employment of the Heathcotes. *The Spy* had treated the Revolution, as had *Lionel Lincoln; The Wept* is concerned with the period just after the first settlement and the period of Indian wars.

Then there must be remembered Cooper's abortive project, once declared but abandoned after completion of the first unit, of writing a series of legends of the thirteen original colonies, with a novel to present a symbolic period and spirit for each. *Lionel Lincoln* (1825), concerned with Revolutionary Massachusetts, is the only openly-avowed contribution to the projected series. Yet *The Wept of Wish-ton-Wish*, with its entire setting and characters from the most critical moment in Connecticut's history, may well have been conceived as the representative fiction of that colony. Cooper's dedication in the first edition to an unidentified "the Reverend J.R.C." of Pennsylvania is almost surely to an individual of Connecticut and Indian origin. And sometimes even by open acknowledgment it is evident that Cooper employed John Winthrop's *Journal*, Thomas and Benjamin Church's *Entertaining Passages from King Philip's War*, Benjamin Trumbull's *History of Connecticut*, Ezra Stiles' *History of Three of the Judges of Charles I*, and Cotton Mather's *Magnalia*, all directly concerned with the Puritans in Connecticut, the regicides and their part in the Indian wars, and other matters noted above. Cooper's Indians, as one scholar has pointed out, speak three times out of four exactly as they do in his sources, and the sachems from Connecticut, including Uncas, Philip, and Conanchet, are no exception. As for the details of the two attacks upon the settlement, with their vivid violence and dramatic action, Cooper may have adapted them, as was his wont, from other localities, as the massacres at Deerfield in Massachusetts, Wyoming Valley in Pennsylvania, and Cherry Valley in New York. He almost surely used his favorites Heckewelder and Schoolcraft for some of the historical background of the Indians and the conflicts.

Cooper's novel, like a greater work by Hawthorne two decades later, is centered in a Puritan community. In other respects, except that both progress through a series of dramatic scenes, *The Scarlet Letter* and *The Wept of Wish-ton-Wish* are almost totally unalike. Hawthorne shows us his *personae* and their situation from inside, from the points of view successively of community, wronged husband, troubled wife and mother, and adulterous clergyman. Cooper tries rather successfully to keep his reader outside the action and the characters, viewing both as an onlooker. If the settlers or the Indians of Connecticut are admirable or despicable, they are to be judged so by their actions, or so the author intends. Cooper does pass judgments and display sympathy, but he tries to do so realistically through his presentation of events, so that the reader appraises them simultaneously with the author.

Though the majority of critics, perhaps unduly or unconsciously influenced by the devastating portrayals of later Connecticut Yankee character in other Cooper novels, have insisted that *The Wept of Wish-ton-Wish* is a distinctly hostile depiction of the colonial Puritan as Puritan, the careful reader will perceive that this really is not true. For Calvinist theology and its concomitant morality or moral judgment Cooper had no taste. He could see nothing good in what he calls the Puritans' metaphysical theological speculations. But intensely aware of New England's contribution to the forming of the republic he loved, the novelist here makes his most extended effort to understand it, admittedly as one who looks from without. His effort is made in terms of individuals influenced by the iron and subtle pieties of their creed. He sees them acting and feeling, perhaps not thinking, their religion and moral code. The novelist is not interested in Calvinist speculations for themselves. He does not write of covenants or Antinomian controversy but of primary elements of Calvinist Christianity under the pressures of the violent world of the American frontier. What Cooper found as he wrote was a series of ironies, or paradoxes, of men and of communities, a series of contradictions. Good and evil, pride and humility, genuine piety and self-righteousness, present in every human condition, Cooper sees existing in accentuated form among the Puritans, accentuated in varying degrees by their peculiar beliefs.

The portraits of individuals among God's elect are sometimes harsh but their colors hold and they seem basically fair presentations. Even the Reverend Meek Wolfe, often pointed out as a specific attack on the colonial Calvinist clergy, is by any historical standard seen to be a composite picture of scores of Puritan religious leaders. The long and intimate orisons addressed by the clergyman to his Maker, his even longer jeremiads directed at his congregation, his fear of witchcraft and of atheism and even the suspicion of either, his momentarily pitiless condemnation of

Conanchet, can all be documented in the histories Cooper had at his disposal. But too often has been overlooked the fact that Wolfe is a brave and resolute leader and a man moved to compassion by the suffering of his fellows. Cooper insists that "notwithstanding the veil which exalted theories and doctrinal subtleties had drawn before his judgment, the charities of the man were grounded in truth." If in part through Meek Wolfe evil triumphs in the valley of Wish-ton-Wish, it is not from any personal selfishness or religion-induced hypocrisy on the part of the man himself.

Obviously there is much to admire in the patriarch Mark Heathcote, who is wise and brave, just (he believes) even to the Indians, affectionate yet stoic in affliction, an old Puritan soldier whose prayers to the Almighty rise as often and linger as long as the frequent smoke from the settlers' cooking fires. Yet the theoretically resigned and humble sectarian can show a glow of pleasurable excitement at the prospect of armed combat, he gives many evidences of spiritual pride, and he is worldly enough to display his and his son's wife's family coats of arms over his great fireplace. These are among the ironies of fact abundant throughout the tale. Incidentally, Mark Heathcote's and his family's pride in ancestry does not support the contention of certain "social" critics that in the Heathcotes and the other settlers Cooper is instinctively or deliberately attacking the middle-class ideology they are said to represent.

Mark's son Content, drawn as truly but in less detail than his father, is by any count a sympathetic character. No subtleties of theology have obscured his judgment, and he is a man of discernment marked with compassion. Content's wife Ruth, who loses her only daughter in the first major Indian attack, is a true lady, a carefully drawn portrait of a woman who loses her beauty and her strength as the conviction of the finality of her loss grows upon her. The lesser folk of the community, the Dudleys and Rings, though they display Puritan fears of the black arts and belief in original sin and predestination, are ultimately only yeomen or rustics of the class Cooper delineates so well in almost all his fiction.

The regicide, one of the Cromwellian judges who had condemned Charles I, known throughout the novel only as Submission (with the suggestion that he has submitted to whatever fate God's Providence has prepared for him), clearly modelled on the historical and legendary figure of Colonel Goffe, is one of the two or three most important figures of the novel. The story begins with a household scene anticipatory of his appearance, and in the last pages the

reader is shown his gravestone. The regicide tradition Cooper must
have known at least since his student days at Yale (near which is
the Judges' Cave in which two regicides, Whalley and Goffe, were
said to have at one time been hidden) and even better through the
several historical, fictional, and dramatic treatments he had seen
and read. Scott had already depicted Goffe in *Peveril of the Peak*,
Hawthorne was to employ him later as the central figure in "The
Gray Champion," and James Nelson Barker had written a play
which Cooper had probably seen and one feature of which he certainly used. His historical sources mentioned above almost all contained a good deal on the two men. Though the regicides are most
frequently associated with Hadley, Massachusetts, their long-time
hiding place, they also spent considerable periods in Connecticut,
presumably in the sort of concealment Cooper depicts. Goffe especially became for American romantic writers one of the symbolic
figures of rebellion against British tyranny which anticipated the
Revolution. Here in Cooper his leadership, against the Indians,
presents him without colonial patriotic-rebellious overtones.

Submission, albeit a Puritan, is the stuff of which romances any-
where are made. Mysterious in his advent, in his manner, and in his
actions, his relationship to the other characters is made clear only
in the latter part of the novel. He is of course the Puritan militant,
the Calvinist man of action. Though his dramatic appearance to
alarm and to lead the Sunday congregation against the savages is
true to the novelist's sources, the plot hinges on the use Cooper
makes of him in connection with the Indian boy Conanchet and
the ultimate tragedy of that relationship.

The Puritans Cooper depicts, therefore, are zealous sectarians
who bring "their sublimated piety," among other qualities, with
them to the frontier. With the exception of Submission, they are
among those Gardiner noted as Puritans who did *not* kill their
prince. That is, the Heathcotes were among the first two generations who sought Zion in New England with unbloodied hands. The
wrong they do the Indians, and the suffering in turn inflicted upon
them, are much the same as the wrongs and sufferings of other
borderers along the whole Atlantic coast. The difference is that
the novelist attempts to show us how their peculiar ideology affected
them in their situation. What he saw and hopes his reader sees is
the Puritan, as in other novels he shows other times and people,
through the red glaze of the frontier.

Though in other tales Cooper had employed in brief sequences
various forms of the Indian captivity narrative, in *The Wept* he

gives it central focus and combines it with the problem of Indian-white miscegenation. The germ of the story of the younger Ruth Heathcote's captivity, marriage, and return to her parents may be found in a dozen chronicles. But here the novelist grafts it onto the stock of a major historical action, King Philip's War, and to historical personages such as Uncas, Philip, and Conanchet. Except for the youthful Conanchet's capture by the whites, his intimacy with Submission, and marriage to the grownup Indianized Ruth, the traits of his character and the events of his life are historically recorded as Cooper presents them. Leslie Fiedler and others read the novel as Cooper's denial of the rightness of miscegenation, and properly suggest that *The Last of the Mohicans* be reread in the light of what is here said on the subject. As usual Fiedler overstates his case, though it is probable that Cooper is unconsciously indicating his disapproval of red-white marriage or sexual union. But the reader should remember that Cooper was attempting to be and was here realistic, in showing actual historically documented white and Indian prejudice against the mixing of bloods, and that the elder Ruth's instinctive repulsion from her half-breed grandchild was valid for time and place. Exigencies of plot, not to mention the actual fact of Conanchet's execution in the manner described (though without any marital complexities), required that death dissolve the marriage. The younger Ruth (Narra-mattah) is the wept-for of Wish-ton-Wish because she was early a lost child and because after her recovery she was lost a second time through death, not because she has borne an Indian babe. Certainly the miscegenation, the love of white maiden and heroic chieftain and its fatal conclusion, heighten the sorrow. They do not cause it.

American readers as well as German might well see the novel as the story of Conanchet, one of the noblest in Cooper's gallery of noble Indians. In the earlier half of the novel he is probably entirely the product of Cooper's creative imagination, the author's conception of a fifteen-year-old son of a chief captured by whites. That the youth is haughty, strong, and comely are natural anticipations of what the historical Conanchet became as a man. When he reappears in the second half of the tale, he is the proud leader of the remnant of a great people, determined upon revenge upon the whites who have taken their land and their lives (including at least indirectly his own great father's life), yet capable of being moved by a kind of gratitude for his former treatment by the Heathcotes. As the author emphasizes in both his 1829 and later English 1833 prefaces, Conanchet as well as his father, Miantonimoh, and Metacom or Philip, and Uncas, were straight from the chronicles of New England. All except Uncas, the novelist observes, died "in a cause and in a manner, that, had it been their fortunes to have lived in a more advanced stage of society, would have enrolled them among the worthies of the age."

With Conanchet especially the author groped for an answer to the Indian question. When the regicide in his rocky hiding place, in conversation with his Indian friend, remarks that "The earth is large, and there is place for men of all colors and of all nations on its surface," all that Cooper permits Conanchet in reply is the dry, "My father has found but little." The continuing conversation allows no real conclusion. The invasion of the wilderness and the extermination of the Indian, Cooper implies as he did in *The Prairie*, is both right and wrong — morally and religiously wrong in any personal sense, morally and religiously right in the long view of the progress of civilization. Conanchet, according to his own and the white's philosophy, deserves only admiration. But it is inevitable, Cooper seems to infer, that he and his fellow chieftains and tribesmen must be displaced — or destroyed — if civilization is to advance. No more than in *The Prairie* is the Indian problem resolved, but perhaps more than in that better novel, in *The Wept* the novelist is in Conanchet demonstrating the epic and tragic elements inherent in the red man's lost cause. Along with that other Uncas of *The Last of the Mohicans*, Conanchet is Cooper's most heroic Indian.

The structure of the novel, along with its irregular pace, is perhaps its greatest weakness. Immediately upon its appearance Cooper wrote to his friend the sculptor Horatio Greenough that "You think better of Wish-ton-Wish than I do. There are detached parts of it that are not bad, and nearly all the last volume [of the three in the Italian-English edition], with a few chapters of the second will hold up their heads, but the book was written too much on the highway for the interest" (Beard, ed., *Letters and Journals*, I, 396). The author refers to the sporadic writing of parts of the novel during his European travels, a method of composition which for two-thirds of the work resulted in only a few fine scenes and characterizations connected by verbose descriptions and commentary, some of it significant to an understanding of Cooper the critic of America and the human race but little conducive to a sense of continuity or to rapidly accelerating action. That it improves in the latter part in vivid and continuous action and dramatic scenes is certainly obvious to the reader. Throughout there is evidence of the book's having been written "on the highway" in unexplained mysteries — as the conch shell warning — abrupt changes of scene and situation, and apparently unmotivated actions. The novel's joints are stiff.

Susan F. Cooper records [in *Pages and Pictures, From the Writings of James Fenimore Cooper* (New York, 1861), pp. 211-12] that

> Some time after the publication of the book, when revising his pages for a new edition, the writer expressed a regret that his plan had not varied in one particular; the leading idea, the abduction of the daughter of a Puritan family and her adoption by savages would have remained the same, but instead of bringing Narra-mattah to her old home again with the Narragansett Marauders, he would have carried the heart-stricken father into the wilderness on the trail of his lost child; he would have followed the parent step by step through the forest, as he was led onward — now deceived by some false rumor, then again guided by the right clue, wandering far and wide ... until at length, in some remote wigwam of the red man, he finds her as she is now drawn, a beautiful picture of sweet natural instincts and wild grace, appearing one moment in that subdued forest light which belongs to the red man's daughter, and then again brightening under some clearer ray of her earlier Christian nurture ...

Artistically as well as sentimentally this second-thought organization would undoubtedly have resulted in greater coherence, suspense, and final climax — if the story is entirely Narra-mattah's. It is more difficult to see how Submission's dramatic reappearance and Conanchet's great death scene would have fitted in. But Cooper's second thoughts on the structure of the novel seem aesthetically right, for the envisioned action would or should have made a dramatically effective main-plot thread.

Cooper made one other critical comment on the novel, this time an explanation of what he had attempted to do. It appears in the new preface he prepared for the British Bentley edition of 1833:

> It would seem that the writer has departed a little from the usual style of novel-writing in this work, his object having been to produce a familiar poem, rather than a common work of fiction. The motive for this experiment grew out of his communications with certain literary men on the continent of Europe, the style being better suited, perhaps, to translations than to the language in which the book was originally written. The result would seem to be what might have been expected, as it is believed the tale has had more success abroad than at home.

Cooper's terms here are unusual, and somewhat puzzling. What European writers may have influenced him is difficult to determine from the novel or from the few brief references to his reading or friendships to be found in his journals and letters of the period. *The Wept* is not the sentimental novel of a multitude of contemporaries nor the historical novel in the sense in which Scott wrote in that genre, and Cooper may mean this in referring to "the unusual style of novel-writing." "Familiar" may be a synonym for "domestic," but what British or continental writers he may have had in mind remains obscure. It is as stark a tragedy as Cooper was ever to write, and yet the roots of that tragedy lie deep in "family." But the poetry is here too, not only in the family relationships, but in the eloquent colloquies of Indian chiefs and white Puritans, in the frequent comparisons of the beauty of the American aborigine or his natural environment to the Pythian Apollo or a Swiss mountain range, in the tableaux of men in action against a somber or lurid background. Its greater appeal in translation, undoubtedly a fact, may also in part have been the result of the same qualities that have made Poe's tales tremendously appealing in French and other translations, qualities not yet fully analyzed.

Near the middle of the novel, as he sketches the changes that had taken place in Connecticut, as in all the other colonies, between 1661 and 1676, Cooper remarks that "To see America with the eyes of truth, it is necessary to look often; . . . " In the novels before and after *The Wept* and in such books as *Notions of the Americans* and *The American Democrat*, the author was obeying his own injunction. During his prolific creative career he spent all his time looking, directly and indirectly, at the people and institutions of his native land. From its history, including the individuals and groups who made it, he sought to show why it was what it was. In *The Wept of Wish-ton-Wish* he took a long look at early New England. Above all, he wanted to find out and to show how these particular white men's errand into the wilderness affected the American character.

The Heathcotes were convinced of their own innocence, and as we have seen both the novelist and the reader view them with sympathy. But as we have also suggested, Cooper was fully aware that their situation was ironic, for neither they nor any other white family were guiltless of robbing the Indian, however far removed from the initial act of transfer of land they may have been. Nor were they any less guilty of shedding the Indians' blood because they had personally never attacked them. Their zeal in religion, their desire to search for a peaceful haven, both good enough in themselves, at least on the surface, cause them to do evil. Their weakness, and their fault, lay in the self-delusiveness inherent in their religion and in human nature. That their designs prospered partially because of the feuds among the red men themselves makes them no less, perhaps even more, guilty, though again they saw all this as a divine dispensation in their favor.

But in all his other tales of the American past and of its present Cooper shows in other regions, among Christian people far removed from New England Calvinism, the use of evil to obtain apparent good, a conscious as well as unconscious rapacious acquisitiveness, a self-delusion, even frequently a spiritual pride, which he felt might bring about America's destruction. "To see America with the eyes of truth, it is necessary to look often": the hard look at Puritanism and the white man's treatment of the Indian brings him no comfort and no suggestions for improving his country's character. But in making or taking it he adds one more episode, pervasively ironic, slightly crude, and sometimes harshly presented but genuinely moving, to what he knew was a genuine epic, the story of the civilized European in the wilderness of the New World.

A Note on the Text

The first edition in English of *The Wept of Wish-ton-Wish: A Tale* was published by Molini in three volumes while Cooper was in Europe, in Florence, at the Dante's Head Press. The number of copies printed was apparently small, for Cooper seems to have designed it primarily as copy for editions to appear elsewhere. Though it seems to have had some personal supervision by the author, he later complained of the errors in punctuation and spelling. Copies were sent by Wells & Co., from Paris, on May 25, 1829 to Carey, to Colburn, and to Gosselin (the last for the French-language edition). With the Florentine title, Carey, Lea and Carey's Philadelphia edition, in two volumes, appeared November 9, 1829. The London edition, entitled *The Borderers: A Tale*, appeared in three volumes under the imprint of Henry Colburn and Richard Bentley in September 29, 1829.

The American edition was reprinted in two volumes by Carey in 1831 and in 1832, 1834, and 1836. In New York in 1849 Stringer and Townsend published it in two volumes in one (from the plates of the Carey edition) and reprinted it in 1852. The English edition was reprinted, with corrections, in "Standard Novels, No. 33" in October 1833 by Richard Bentley in London. A copy of the 1829 *The Borderers*, interleaved and containing a few notes and corrections in Cooper's own hand, now reposes in the Berg Collection of the New York Public Library. The Preface to the 1833 *The Borderers* suggests that this Berg copy was the basis for this corrected edition. In Paris *The Borderers* (3 vols.), published by Baudry (Galignani) appeared in 1829 in "Baudry's European Library," *Collection of ancient and modern British authors*, vol. 85.

The Wept of Wish-ton-Wish appeared also as No. 8 in the 26-volume *Novels and Tales* of Carey and Lea, 1835-1836, from the plates of the first American edition. In [1849] 1852-1854 Stringer and Townsend's *Cooper's Novels* (65 vols. in 33) included it as No. 21 (1852) from the plates Cooper had received from Wiley and from Carey but did not edit as he had done for Putnam, who had published twelve novels (this one was not included) in 1849-1851. For editions, all collected after Cooper's lifetime, and for further information on the individual issues noted above, see Robert E. Spiller and Philip C. Blackburn, *A Descriptive Bibliography of the Writings of James Fenimore Cooper* (New York: R. R. Bowker, 1934), pp. 58-60, 170-74. This bibliography also contains information on the various French, German, Italian, and Spanish editions.

STANDARD

NOVELS.

N° XXXIII.

" No kind of literature is so generally attractive as Fiction. Pictures of
life and manners, and Stories of adventure, are more eagerly received by
the many than graver productions, however important these latter may be.
APULEIUS is better remembered by his fable of Cupid and Psyche than by
his abstruser Platonic writings; and the Decameron of Boccaccio has out-
lived the Latin Treatises, and other learned works of that author."

THE BORDERERS.

BY J. F. COOPER.

COMPLETE IN ONE VOLUME.

LONDON:

RICHARD BENTLEY, NEW BURLINGTON STREET
(SUCCESSOR TO HENRY COLBURN):

BELL AND BRADFUTE, EDINBURGH;
CUMMING, DUBLIN; AND
GALIGNANI, PARIS.

1833.

LONDON :
Printed by A. SPOTTISWOODE,
New-Street-Square.

THE BORDERERS,

OR

THE WEPT OF WISH-TON-WISH,

BY

J. FENIMORE COOPER.

E. Pickering, pinxt.

W. Greatbatch, sculpt.

"Now look with an open eye; is there any
thing among these trees that seemeth like
an ancient tradition? Hast ever beheld
such a valley in thy dreams?"

LONDON:
RICHARD BENTLEY,
(SUCCESSOR TO H. COLBURN,)
CUMMING, DUBLIN; BELL & BRADFUTE, EDINBURGH;
GALIGNANI, PARIS.
1833.

THE

BORDERERS;

OR,

THE WEPT OF WISH-TON-WISH:

A TALE.

BY THE AUTHOR OF

"THE PILOT," "THE SPY," "THE PIONEERS,"

&c. &c. &c.

" But she is dead to him, to all:
    Her lute hangs silent on the wall;
    And on the stairs, and at the door,
    Her fairy step is heard no more."
                                    ROGERS.

LONDON:

RICHARD BENTLEY, NEW BURLINGTON STREET
(SUCCESSOR TO HENRY COLBURN):

BELL AND BRADFUTE, EDINBURGH;
CUMMING, DUBLIN; AND
GALIGNANI, PARIS.

1833.

PREFACE.

So much has been written of the North American Indians of late, that very little explanation is necessary to prepare the reader for the incidents and allusions of this tale. The principal aborigines that are introduced are historical; and, although the situations are imagined, they so nearly resemble facts that are known to have occurred, as to give a sufficiently correct idea of the opinions, habits, and feelings of a class of beings whom we are pleased to term savages. Metacom, or, as he was called by the English, King Philip, Uncas, Conanchet, Miantonimoh, and Ounawon were all Indian chiefs of great note, whose names have become identified with the history of New-England. The appellation of Uncas, in particular, appears to have belonged to an entire race among the Mohegans, for it was borne by a succession of Sagamores, and at a later day was found, among their descendants, united to the common baptismal names, such as John, Henry, Thomas, &c.,

having been regularly adopted as the surname of a family.

Metacom, or Philip, who figures in these pages as the most ruthless enemy of the whites, eventually fell in the war which he had been the principal agent in inciting. This was much the most serious contest in which the English were ever engaged with the native occupants of the country; and there was a moment when it threatened serious obstacles to their system of colonisation. The defeat and death of Philip finally enabled the whites to maintain the possession of New England. Had he succeeded in uniting all the hostile tribes in a common effort, secretly supported, as there is little doubt was the case, by the French of the Canadas and the Dutch of the New Netherlands, the realisation of his vast and noble plans was an event far more likely to prove true, than we may be disposed to admit at this distant day.

There is believed to be no exaggeration in the account of the temper and the practices of Indian warfare, as they are here presented to the reader. The traditions common to the whole of the western frontiers of the United States, the well-authenticated and printed accounts of the dangers and struggles of those who first peopled them, and all known circumstances, go to corroborate what there is an attempt here to delineate.

It will be seen that the writer has departed a little from the usual style of novel-writing in this work, his object having been to produce a familiar poem, rather than a common work of fiction. The motive for this experiment grew out of his communications with certain literary men on the continent of Europe, the style being better suited, perhaps, to translations than to the language in which the book was originally written. The result would seem to be what might have been expected, as it is believed the tale has had more success abroad than at home.

The work was originally printed as well as written in Italy, and the workmen employed on it were utterly unacquainted with the English language. So many errors are found in books which are printed under the most favourable circumstances, that the writer will be readily believed, when he ascribes very many of those which existed in the original edition of this work to the facts just mentioned. The punctuation was particularly bad, often so faulty as to destroy the sense, and, in many instances, words of the same sound were substituted for those that bore a different meaning. In the present edition care has been had to correct these errors; and it is hoped that the book, in these particulars at least, has been materially improved. Some redundancy has been curtailed; the style has been occasionally altered, it is thought for the better ; and such explanatory notes have been added as it was believed might help the European reader in comprehending the allusions and incidents of the book.   In other respects, the tale remains as it was originally conceived and written.

London,
September, 1832.

THE BORDERERS;

OR,

THE WEPT OF WISH-TON-WISH.

CHAPTER I.

I may disjoin my hand, but not my faith. — SHAKSPEARE.

THE historical allusions of this tale belong to a remote period of American annals. A colony of self-devoted and pious refugees, who fled from religious persecution, had landed on the rock of Plymouth less than half a century before the time at which the narrative commences, and they, and their descendants, had already transformed a broad waste of wilderness into smiling fields and cheerful villages. The labours of the original emigrants was chiefly limited to the country on the coast, which, by its proximity to the waters that rolled between them and Europe, afforded the semblance of a connexion with the land of their forefathers and the distant abodes of civilisation. But enterprise and a desire to search for still more fertile domains, together with the temptation offered by the vast and unknown regions that lay along their western and northern borders, soon induced bolder adventurers to penetrate more deeply into the forests, abandoning as it were all their ties and hopes of communication with what it was their practice to call the old world. The precise spot to which we desire to transport the imagination of the reader was one

B

of these establishments of what may be called the forlorn hope, in the march of civilisation through the country.

So little was then known of the great outlines of the American continent that, when the lords Say and Seal, and Brooke, connected with a few associates, obtained a grant of the territory which now composes the state of Connecticut, the king of England affixed his name to a patent, which constituted them proprietors of a country that extends from the shores of the Atlantic to those of the South Sea. Nothwithstanding the apparent hopelessness of ever subduing, or of even occupying a territory like this, emigrants from the mother colony of Massachusetts were found ready to commence the Herculean labour, within fifteen years from the day on which they had first put foot upon the well-known rock of Plymouth. The fort of Say-Brooke, the towns of Windsor, Hartford, and New Haven, soon sprang into existence ; and, from that period to this, the little community which then had birth has been steadily, calmly, and prosperously advancing in its career, a model of order and reason, and the hive from which swarms of industrious, hardy, and enlightened yeomen have since spread themselves over a surface so vast, as to create an impression that they still aspire to the possession of the immense regions included in their original grant.

Among the religionists whom disgust or persecution had early driven into the voluntary exile of the colonies there was more than an usual proportion of men of character and education. The reckless and the gay, younger sons, soldiers unemployed, and students from the inns of courts, early sought advancement and adventure in the more southern provinces, where slaves offered impunity from labour, and where war, with a bolder and more stirring policy, oftener gave rise to scenes of excitement, and of course to the exercise of the faculties best suited to their habits and dispositions. The more grave and religiously disposed found refuge in the colonies of New England. Thither a multitude of private gentlemen transferred their fortunes and their families, imparting a character of intelligence and a moral elevation to the country which it has nobly sustained to the present hour.

The nature of the civil wars in England had enlisted many men of deep and sincere piety in the profession of arms. Some of them had retired to the colonies before the troubles of the mother country reached their crisis, and others continued to arrive, throughout the whole period of their existence, until the Restoration, when crowds of those who had been disaffected to the house of Stuart sought the security of these distant possessions.

A stern, fanatical soldier, of the name of Heathcote, had been among the first of his class to throw aside the sword for the implements of industry peculiar to the advancement of a newly-established country. How far the influence of a young wife may have affected his decision it is not germane to our present object to consider, though the records, from which the matter we are about to relate is gleaned, give reason to suspect that he thought his domestic harmony would not be less secure in the wilds of the new world, than among the companions with whom his earlier associations would naturally have brought him in communion.

Like himself, his consort was born of one of those families which, taking their rise in the Franklins of the times of the Edwards and Henries, had become possessors of hereditary landed estates that, by their gradually increasing value, had elevated them to the station of small country gentlemen. In most other nations of Europe they would have been rated in the class of the *petite noblesse.* Notwithstanding the disparity in their years, the union had been happy, and the stern Christian soldier had reason to believe, now that he had reached a region in which civil and religious strife were unknown, that the tranquillity of his future life was to repay the hardships and dangers to which he had been exposed in his youth and earlier manhood. But the domestic happiness of Captain Heathcote was doomed to receive a fatal blow, from a quarter where, apparently, he had least reason to apprehend danger. The very day he landed in the long-wished-for asylum, his wife made him the father of a noble boy, a gift that was bestowed at the melancholy price of her own existence. Twenty years the senior of the woman who followed his fortunes to these distant regions, the retired warrior had always

considered it so perfectly within the order of things, that
he himself was to be the first to pay the debt of nature,
that this blow fell upon him with double violence for
being so unexpected. While the visions which Captain
Heathcote entertained of a future world were sufficiently
vivid and distinct, there is reason, too, to think that they
were seen through a tolerably long vista of quiet and comfortable enjoyment in this. The calamity cast an additional shade of seriousness over a mind that was already
more than chastened by the subtleties of sectarian doctrines, and from being grave and thoughtful, his character
gradually assumed a cast that approached to austerity and
melancholy. Still he was not of a nature to be unmanned
by any vicissitude of human fortune. He lived on, useful
and unbending in his habits, a pillar of strength in the
way of wisdom and courage to the immediate neighbourhood among whom he resided, but reluctant from
temper, and from a disposition which had been shadowed
by withered happiness, to enact that part in the public
affairs of the little state to which his comparative wealth
and previous habits might well have entitled him to aspire.
He gave his son such an education as his own resources
and those of the infant colony of Massachusetts afforded ;
and, by a sort of delusive piety into whose merits we have
no desire to look, he thought he had also furnished a commendable evidence of his own desperate resignation to the
will of Providence, in causing him to be publicly christened
by the name of Content. His own baptismal appellation
was Mark, as indeed had been that of most of his ancestors,
for two or three centuries. When the world was a little
uppermost in his thoughts, as will sometimes happen with
the most humbled spirits, he had even been heard to speak
of a Sir Mark of his family, who had ridden a knight in the
train of one of the more warlike kings of his native land.

There is some ground for believing that the great parent
of evil early looked with a malignant eye, on the example
of peacefulness and of unbending morality that the colonists of New England were setting to the rest of Christendom. At any rate, come from what quarter they might,
schisms and doctrinal contentions early arose among the

emigrants themselves ; and the men, who together had deserted the firesides of their forefathers in quest of religious peace, were ere long seen separating their fortunes, in order that each might enjoy unmolested those peculiar shades of faith, which all had the presumption no less than the folly to believe were necessary to propitiate the omnipotent and merciful Father of the universe. If our task were one of theology, a wholesome moral on the vanity, no less than on the absurdity of the human race, might be here introduced to some advantage.

Under the influence of this new impulse, and scrupulously believing in the wisdom and necessity of the change, Mark Heathcote announced to the community in which he had now sojourned more than twenty years, that he intended for a second time to establish his altars in the wilderness, in the hope that he and his household might worship God as to them seemed right. The authoritative and gravely communicated intelligence was received with a feeling akin to awe. Doctrine and zeal were momentarily forgotten in the respect and attachment which had been unconsciously created by the stern severity of his principles, united to the undeniable virtues of his practice. The elders of the settlement communed with him freely and in charity ; but the voice of conciliation came too late. He listened to the reasonings of the ministers, who were assembled from all the adjoining parishes, in sullen respect ; and he joined in the petitions for light and instruction, that were offered up on the occasion, with the deep reverence with which he ever drew near to the footstool of the Almighty ; but he did both in a temper into which too much positiveness of spiritual pride had entered, to open his heart to that sympathy and charity which, as they are the characteristics of our mild and forbearing doctrines, should be the chief study of those who profess to follow their precepts. All that was seemly, and all that was usual, were done ; but the purpose of the stubborn sectarian remained unchanged. His final decision is worthy of being recorded.

" My youth was wasted in ungodliness and ignorance," he said, " but in my manhood have I known the Lord. Near two score years have I toiled for the truth, and all that weary time have I passed in trimming my lamps, lest, like the foolish virgins, I should be caught unprepared ; and now, when my loins are girded and my race is nearly run, shall I become a backslider and falsifier of the word ! Much have I endured, as ye know, in quitting the earthly mansion of my fathers, and in encountering the dangers of sea and land for the faith ; and rather than let go its hold, will I once more cheerfully devote to the howling wilderness, ease, offspring, and, should it be the will of Providence, life itself !"

The day of parting was one of unfeigned and general sorrow. Notwithstanding the austerity of the old man's character, and the nearly unbending severity of his brow, the milk of human kindness had often been seen distilling from his stern nature in acts that did not admit of misinterpretation. There was scarcely a young beginner in the laborious and ill-requited husbandry of the township he inhabited, a district at no time considered either profitable or fertile, who could not recall some secret and kind aid which had flowed from a hand that, to the world, seemed clenched in cautious and reserved frugality ; nor did any of the faithful of his vicinity cast their fortunes together in wedlock without receiving from him evidences of an interest in their worldly happiness that was far more substantial than words.

On the important morning, therefore, when the vehicles, groaning with the household goods of Mark Heathcote, were seen quitting his door and taking the road which led to the sea-side, not a human being of sufficient age, within many miles of his residence, was absent from the interesting spectacle. The leave-taking, as usual on all serious occasions, was preceded by a hymn and prayer, and then the sternly-minded adventurer embraced his neighbours with a mien in which a subdued exterior struggled fearfully and strangely with emotions that, more than once, threatened to break through the formidable barriers of even his acquired manner. The inhabitants of every building on the road were in the open air to receive and to return the parting benediction. More than once the men who guided his teams were commanded to halt, and

all near, possessing human aspirations and human responsibility, were collected to offer petitions in favour of him
who departed, and of those who remained. The requests
for mortal privileges were somewhat light and hasty, but
the askings in behalf of intellectual and spiritual light were
long, fervent, and oft repeated. When the tongue was
wearied, and the mind was exhausted of all its immediate
stores of doctrinal subtleties, the aged traveller went his
way, followed by a train of those whose temporal fortunes
were dependent on his wisdom or caprice. In this characteristic manner did one of the first of the emigrants to
the new world make his second removal into scenes of
renewed bodily suffering, privation and danger.

Neither person nor property was transferred from place
to place, in this country, at the middle of the seventeenth
century, with the despatch and with the facilities of the
present time. The roads were necessarily few and short,
and communication by water was irregular, tardy, and
far from commodious. A wide barrier of forest lying
between that portion of Massachusetts Bay from which
Mark Heathcote emigrated, and the spot, near the Connecticut river, to which it was his intention to proceed, he
was induced to adopt the latter mode of conveyance. But
a long delay intervened between the time when he commenced his short journey to the coast, and the hour when
he was finally enabled to embark. During this detention,
he and his household sojourned among the godly-minded
of the narrow peninsula where there already existed the
germ of a flourishing town, and where the spires of a noble
and picturesque city now elevate themselves above so many
thousands of roofs.

The son did not leave the colony of his birth and the
haunts of his youth, with the same unwavering obedience
to the call of duty as the father. There was a fair, a
youthful, and a gentle being in the recently established
town of Boston, of an age, station, opinions, fortunes, and,
what was of still greater importance, of sympathies suited
to his own. Her form had long mingled with those holy
images which his stern instruction taught him to keep
most familiarly before the mirror of his thoughts. It is

not surprising, then, that the youth hailed the delay as propitious to his wishes, or that he turned it to the account which the promptings of a pure affection so naturally suggested. He was united to the gentle Ruth Harding, only the week before his father sailed on his second pilgrimage.

It is not our intention to dwell on the incidents of the voyage. Though the genius of an extraordinary man had discovered the world which was now beginning to fill with civilised men, navigation at that day was not rich in attainments. A passage among the shoals of Nantucket must have been one of actual danger, no less than of terror; and the ascent of the Connecticut itself was an exploit worthy of being mentioned; still, perseverance, resolution, and great caution, effected what is now readily performed by the aid of science, and all the obstacles were overcome, if not with facility at least without loss. In due time the adventurers landed at the English fort of Hartford, where they tarried for a season, in order to obtain rest and spiritual comfort. But the peculiarity of doctrine, on which Mark Heathcote laid so much stress, was one that rendered it advisable for him to retire still further from the haunts of men. Accompanied by a few followers, he proceeded on an exploring expedition, and the end of the summer found him once more established on an estate that he had acquired by the usual simple forms practised in the colonies, and at the trifling cost for which extensive districts were then set apart as the property of individuals.

The love of the things of this life, while it certainly existed, was far from being predominant in the affections of the puritan. He was frugal from habit and principle, more than from an undue longing after worldly wealth. He contented himself, therefore, with acquiring an estate that should be valuable, rather from its quality and beauty than from its extent. Many such places offered themselves, between the settlements of Weathersfield and Hartford, and that imaginary line which separated the possessions of the colony he had quitted from those of the one he joined. He made his location, as it is termed in the language of the country, near the northern boundary of the latter.

This spot, by the aid of an expenditure that might have been considered lavish for the country and the age, of some lingering of taste, which even the self-denying and subdued habits of his later life had not entirely extinguished, and of great natural beauty in the distribution of land, water and wood, the emigrant contrived to convert into an abode that was not more desirable for its retirement from the temptations of the world, than for its rural loveliness.

After this memorable act of conscientious self-devotion, years passed away in quiet amid a species of negative prosperity. Rumours from the old world reached the ears of the tenants of this secluded settlement months after the events to which they referred were elsewhere forgotten, and tumults and wars in the sister colonies came to their knowledge only at distant and tardy intervals. In the mean time, the limits of the other colonial establishments were gradually extending themselves, and valleys were beginning to be cleared nearer and nearer to their own. Old age had now begun to make a visible impression on the iron frame of the captain, and the fresh colour of youth and health, with which his son had entered the forest, was giving way to the brown covering produced by exposure and toil. We say of toil, for, independently of the habits and opinions of the country which strongly reprobated idleness, even in those most gifted by fortune, the daily difficulties of their situation, the chase, and the long and intricate passages that the veteran himself was compelled to adventure in the surrounding forest, partook largely of the nature of the term we have used. Ruth continued blooming and youthful, though maternal anxiety was soon added to her other causes of care. Still, for a long season, nought occurred to excite extraordinary regrets for the step they had taken, or to create particular uneasiness in behalf of the future. The borderers, for such by their frontier position they had in truth become, heard the strange and awful tidings of the dethronement of one king, of the interregnum, as a reign of more than usual vigour and prosperity is called, and of the restoration of the son of him who is strangely enough termed a martyr.

To all these eventful and unwonted chances in the fortunes of kings, Mark Heathcote listened with deep and reverential submission to the will of Him, in whose eyes crowns and sceptres are merely the more costly baubles of the world. Like most of his contemporaries who had sought shelter in the western continent, his political opinions, if not absolutely republican, had a leaning to liberty that was strongly in opposition to the doctrine of the divine rights of the monarch, while he had been too far removed from the stirring passions which had gradually excited those nearer to the throne to lose their respect for its sanctity, and to sully its brightness with blood. When the transient and straggling visitors that at long intervals visited his settlement, spoke of the Protector, who for so many years ruled England with an iron hand, the eyes of the old man would gleam with sudden and singular interest ; and once, when commenting, after evening prayer, on the vanity and the vicissitudes of this life, he acknowledged that the extraordinary individual, who was, in substance if not in name, seated on the throne of the Plantagenets, had been the boon companion and ungodly associate of many of his youthful hours. Then would follow a long, wholesome, extemporaneous homily on the idleness of setting the affections on the things of life, and a half suppressed, but still intelligible commendation of the wiser course which had led him to raise his own tabernacle in the wilderness, instead of weakening the chances of eternal glory by striving too much for the possession of the treacherous vanities of the world.

But even the gentle and ordinarily little observant Ruth, could trace the kindling of the eye, the knitting of the brow, and the flushings of his pale and furrowed cheek, as the murderous conflicts of the civil wars became the themes of the ancient soldier's discourse. There were moments, too, when religious submission and, we had almost said, religious precepts, were partially forgotten, as he explained to his attentive son and listening grandchild, the nature of the onset, or the quality and dignity of the retreat. At such times, his still nervous hand would even wield the blade in order to instruct the latter in its uses, and many a

long wintry evening was passed in thus indirectly teaching
an art, that was so much at variance with the mandates of
his Divine Master. The chastened soldier, however, never
forgot to close his instruction with a petition extraordinary,
in the customary evening prayer, that no descendant of his
should ever take life from a being unprepared to die, except in justifiable defence of his faith, his person, or his
lawful rights. It will be seen that a liberal construction
of the reserved privileges, would leave sufficient matter to
exercise the subtlety of one subject to any extraordinary
propensity to arms.

Few opportunities offered, however, in their remote
situation, for the practice of a theory that had been taught
in so many lessons. Indian alarms, as they were termed,
were not unfrequent, it is true; but as yet they had never
produced more than terror in the bosoms of the gentle
Ruth and her young offspring. They had also heard of
travellers massacred, and of families separated by captivity;
but, either by a happy fortune, or by more than ordinary
prudence in the settlers who were established along that
immediate frontier, the knife and the tomahawk had as yet
been sparingly used in the colony of Connecticut. A
threatening and dangerous struggle with the Dutch of the
adjoining province of New Netherlands, had been averted
by the foresight and moderation of the rulers of the new
plantations; and, though a warlike and powerful native
chief kept the neighbouring colonies of Massachusetts and
Rhode Island in a state of constant watchfulness, the apprehension of danger from this cause was not great in the
breasts of those so remote from the scene of strife as the
individuals who composed the family of our emigrant.

In this quiet manner did years glide by, the surrounding wilderness slowly retreating from the habitations of the
Heathcotes, until they found themselves in the possession
of as many of the comforts of life as their utter seclusion
from the rest of the world could give them reason to
expect.

With this preliminary explanation, we shall refer the
reader to the succeeding narrative for a more minute, and,
we hope, for a more interesting account of the incidents of

a legend that we apprehend will prove too homely for the tastes of those whose imaginations seek the excitement of scenes more stirring, or of a condition of life less natural.

CHAPTER II.

Sir, I do know you ;
And dare, upon the warrant of my art,
Commend a dear thing to you. — *King Lear.*

At the precise time when the action of our piece commences, a fine and fruitful season was drawing to a close. The harvests of the hay, and of the smaller corns, had long been over, and the younger Heathcote with his labourers had passed a day in depriving the luxuriant maize of its tops, in order to secure the nutritious blades for fodder *, and to admit the sun and air to harden a grain that is, almost considered the staple production of the region he inhabited. The veteran Mark had ridden among the workmen during their light toil, as well to enjoy a sight which promised abundance to his flocks and herds, as to throw in, on occasion, some wholesome spiritual precept, in which doctrinal subtlety was far more prominent than the rules of practice. The hirelings of his son, for he had long since yielded the management of the estate to Content, were, without an exception, young men born in the country, and long use and much training had accustomed them to a blending of religious exercises with most of the employments of life. They listened, therefore, with respect ; nor did an impious smile, or an impatient glance, escape the lightest-minded of their number during his exhortations, though the homilies of the old man were neither very brief nor particularly original. But devotion to the one great cause of their existence, austere habits, and unrelaxed in-

---

* The maize is the staple product of every American farm on which the richer plants, such as the cotton, tobacco, &c. are not grown. The grain is universally termed " corn,' *par excellence,* and it is said there is no animal, the purely carnivorous excepted, that will not thrive on it.

dustry in keeping alive a flame of zeal that had been
kindled in the other hemisphere to burn longest and
brightest in this, had interwoven the practice mentioned
with most of the opinions and pleasures of these metaphysical though simple-minded people. The toil went on
none the less cheerily for the extraordinary accompaniment,
and Content himself, by a certain glimmering of superstition, which appears to be the usual concomitant of excited
religious zeal, was fain to think that the sun shone more
brightly on their labours, and that the earth gave forth
more of its fruits, while these holy sentiments were flowing
from the lips of a father whom he piously loved, and so
deeply reverenced.

But when the sun, usually at that season in the climate
of Connecticut a bright unshrouded orb, fell towards the
tree tops which bounded the western horizon, the old man
began to grow weary with his own well-doing. He therefore finished his discourse with a prudent admonition to
the youths to complete their tasks before they quitted the
field, and, turning the head of his horse, he rode slowly,
and with a musing air, towards the dwellings. It is probable that, for some time, the thoughts of Mark were
occupied with the intellectual matter he had just been
handling with so much power ; but when his little nag
stopped of itself on a small eminence, which the crooked
cowpath he was following crossed, his mind yielded to the
impression of more worldly and more sensible objects. As
the scene that drew his contemplations from so many
abstract theories to the realities of life was peculiar to the
country, and is more or less connected with the subject of
our tale, we shall endeavour briefly to describe it.

A small tributary of the Connecticut divided the view
into two nearly equal parts. The fertile flats, that extended on each of its banks for more than a mile, had been
early stripped of their burthen of forests, and they now
lay in placid meadows, or in fields from which the grain of
the season had lately disappeared, and over which the
plough had already left the marks of recent tillage. The
whole of the plain, which ascended gently from the rivulet
towards the forest, was subdivided in enclosures by num-

berless fences *, constructed in the rude but substantial manner of the country. Rails, in which lightness and economy of wood had been but little consulted, lying in zig-zag lines, like the approaches which the besieger makes in his cautious advance to the hostile fortress, were piled ôn each other, until barriers seven or eight feet in height were interposed to the inroads of vicious cattle. In one spot, a large square vacancy had been cut into the forest ; and though numberless stumps of trees darkened its surface, as indeed they did many of the fields on the flats themselves, bright green grain was sprouting forth luxuriantly from the rich and virgin soil. High against the side of an adjacent hill, that might aspire to be called a low rocky mountain, a similar invasion had been made on the dominion of the trees : but caprice or convenience had induced an abandonment of the clearing, after it had ill requited the toil of felling the timber by a single crop. In this spot, straggling, girdled, and consequently dead trees, piles of logs, and black and charred stubbs, were seen deforming the beauty of a field, that would otherwise have been striking from its deep setting in the woods. Much of the surface of this opening, too, was now concealed by bushes of what is termed the second growth, though, here and there, places appeared in which the luxuriant white clover, so natural to the country, had followed the close grazing of the flocks. The eyes of Mark were bent enquiringly on this clearing, which, by an air line, might have been half a mile from the place where his horse had stopped, for the sounds of a dozen differently toned cowbells were brought to his ears, on the still air of the evening, from among its bushes.

The evidences of civilisation were the least equivocal, however, on and around a natural elevation in the land which arose so suddenly on the very bank of the stream, as to give to it the appearance of a work of art. Whether these mounds once existed everywhere on the face of the

---

* Hedges are nearly unknown in America, but each field is defended by a fence or a wall. This peculiarity distinguishes the landscapes of the country from any in the eastern hemisphere, where fences are sometimes found, but are never general.

earth, and have disappeared before long tillage and labour, we shall not presume to conjecture ; but we have reason to think that they occur much more frequently in certain parts of our own country, than in any other familiarly known to ordinary travellers, unless perhaps it may be in some of the valleys of Switzerland. The practised veteran had chosen the summit of this flattened cone for the establishment of that species of military defence which the situation of the country, and the character of the enemy he had to guard against, rendered advisable as well as customary.

The dwelling was of wood, and it was constructed of the ordinary frame-work, with the usual thin covering of boards. It was long, low, and irregular, bearing marks of having been reared at different periods, as the wants of an increasing family had required additional accommodation. It stood near the verge of the natural declivity, and on that side of the hill where its base was washed by the rivulet, a rude piazza stretched along the whole front of the edifice overhanging the stream. Several large, irregular, and clumsy chimneys, rose out of different parts of the roofs, another proof that comfort, rather than taste, had been consulted in the disposition of the buildings. There were also two or three detached offices on the summit of the hill, placed near the dwellings, and at points most convenient for their several uses. A stranger might have remarked that they were so disposed as to form, far as they went, the different sides of a hollow square. Notwithstanding the great length of the principal building and the disposition of the more minute and detached parts, this desirable formation would not, however, have been obtained, were it not that two rows of rude constructions in logs, from which the bark had not even been stripped, served to eke out the parts that were deficient. These rude primeval edifices were used to contain various domestic articles, and provisions ; and they also furnished numerous lodging rooms for the labourers, and the inferior dependants of the farm. By the aid of a few, strong, high gates of hewn timber, those parts of the buildings which had not been made to unite in the original construction, were sufficiently connected to oppose so many barriers against admission into the inner court.

But the building which was most conspicuous, by its position as well as by the singularity of its construction, stood on a low, artificial mound in the centre of the quadrangle. It was high, hexagonal in shape, and crowned with a roof that came to a point, and from whose peak projected a flag-staff. The foundation was of stone; but, at the height of a man above the earth, the sides were made of massive, squared logs, firmly united by an ingenious combination of their ends, as well as by perpendicular supporters pinned closely into their sides. In this citadel, or block-house, as from its materials it is technically called, there were two different tiers of long, narrow loop-holes, but no regular windows. The rays of the setting sun, however, glittered on one or two small openings in the roof, in which glass had been set, furnishing evidence that the summit of the building was sometimes used for other purposes than those of defence.

About half-way up the sides of the eminence on which the dwelling stood, was an unbroken line of high palisadoes made of the bodies of young trees firmly knit together by braces and horizontal pieces of timber, and evidently kept in a state of jealous and complete repair. The air of the whole of this frontier fortress was neat and comfortable, and, considering that the use of artillery was unknown to those forests, not unmilitary.

At no great distance from the base of the hill stood the barns and the stables. They were surrounded by a vast range of rude but warm sheds, beneath which sheep and horned cattle were usually sheltered from the storms of the rigorous winters of the climate.* The surfaces of the meadows immediately around the out-buildings, were of a smoother and richer sward than those in the distance, and

---

* The European obtains a very confused notion of the American continent, from the circumstance of its differing so much, in many particulars, from his own. Connecticut, the scene of this tale, lies in the latitude of Lower Italy, and yet its winters are as rude as those of the north of Germany, while its summers produce the fruits of a warm climate. The eastern shores of both the two great continents possess, in a greater or less degree, this peculiarity, while their western have a smaller range of the thermometer. It is not easy to account satisfactorily for the circumstance, but the fact seems certain.

the fences were on a far more artificial, and perhaps durable, though scarcely on a more serviceable, plan. A large orchard, of some ten or fifteen years' growth, too, added greatly to the air of improvement which put this smiling valley in such strong and pleasing contrast to the endless and nearly untenanted woods by which it was environed.

Of the interminable forest it is not necessary to speak. With the solitary exception, on the mountain side, and of here and there a wind-row, along which the trees had been uprooted by the furious blasts that sometimes sweep off acres of our trees in a minute, the eye could find no other object to study in the vast setting of this quiet rural picture, but the seemingly endless maze of wilderness. The broken surface of the land, however, limited the view to an horizon of no great extent, though the art of man could scarcely devise colours so vivid or so gay as those which were afforded by the brilliant hues of the foliage. The keen, biting frosts, known at the close of a New England autumn, had already touched the broad and fringed leaves of the maples, and the sudden and secret process had been wrought upon all the other varieties of the forest, producing a magical effect, which can be nowhere seen unless in regions in which nature is so bountiful and luxuriant in summer, and so sudden and so stern in the change of the seasons.

Over this picture of prosperity and peace, the eye of old Mark Heathcote wandered with a keen degree of worldly prudence. The melancholy sounds of the variously toned bells ringing hollow and plaintively among the arches of the woods, gave him reason to believe that the herds of the family were voluntarily returning from their unlimited forest pasturage. His grandson, a fine spirited boy of some fourteen years, was approaching through the fields, driving before him small flock, which domestic necessity compelled the family to keep at great occasional loss, and at a heavy expense of time and trouble, both of which could alone protect it from the ravages of the beasts of prey. A species of half-witted serving lad, whom charity had induced the old man to harbour among his dependants, was seen issuing from the woods, nearly in a line with the neglected clearing on the mountain side. The latter advanced, shouting and urging before him a drove of colts, as shaggy, as wayward, and nearly as untamed, as himself.

" How now, weak one," said the Puritan, with a severe eye, as the two lads approached him, with their several charges from different directions, and nearly at the same instant ; " how now, sirrah ; dost worry the cattle in this gait, when the eyes of the prudent are turned from thee ? Do as thou wouldst be done by, is a just and healthful admonition, that the learned and the simple, the weak and the strong of mind, should alike recall to their thoughts and their practice. I do not know, moreover, that an over-driven colt will be at all more apt to make a gentle and useful beast in its prime, than one treated with kindness and care."

" I believe the evil one has got into all the kine, no less than into the foals," sullenly returned the lad ; " I 've called to them in anger, and I 've spoken to them as if they had been my natural kin, and yet neither fair word, nor foul tongue, will bring them to hearken to advice. There is something frightful in the woods this very sun-down, master ; or colts, that I have driven the summer through, would not be apt to give this unfair treatment to one they ought to know to be their friend."

" Thy sheep are counted, Mark ? " resumed the grand-father, turning towards his de cendant with a less austere, but always with an authoritative brow ; " thy mother hath need of every fleece to provide covering for thee and others like thee ; thou knowest, child, that the creatures are few, and that our winters are weary and cold."

" My mother's loom shall never be idle from careless-ness of mine," returned the confident boy ; " but counting and wishing cannot make seven and thirty fleeces, where there are only six and thirty backs to carry them. I have been an hour among the briars and bushes of the hill-logging *, looking for the lost wether, and yet neither lock,

---

* After the trees are felled in clearing land, they are cut into convenient lengths to be rolled into piles, in order that they may be burnt. This process is called " logging," and a field while in this state is called "the logging."

hoof, hide, nor horn, is there to say what hath befallen the animal."

" Thou hast lost a sheep ! — this carelessness will cause thy mother to grieve."

" Grandfather, I have been no idler. Since the last hunt, the flock hath been allowed to browse the woods, for no man in all that week saw wolf, panther, or bear, though the country was up, from the great river to the outer settlements of the colony. The biggest four-footed animal that lost its hide in the muster was a thin-ribbed deer, and the stoutest battle given was between wild Whittal Ring here, and a wood-chuck that kept him at arms' length for the better part of an afternoon."

" Thy tale may be true, but it neither finds that which is lost, nor completeth the number of thy mother's flock. Hast thou ridden carefully through the new clearing ? — it is not long since I saw the animals grazing in that quarter. What hast thou twisting in thy fingers, in that wasteful and unthankful manner, Whittal ?"

" What would make a winter blanket, if there was enough of it ! wool ! and wool too, that came from the thigh of old Straight-Horns; else have I forgotten a leg that gives the longest and coarsest hair at the shearing."

" That truly seemeth a lock from the animal that is wanting," exclaimed the other boy. " There is no other creature in the flock, with a fleece so coarse and shaggy. Where found you the handful, Whittal Ring ?"

" Growing on the branch of a thorn. Queer fruit this, masters, to be seen where young plums ought to ripen !"

" Go to," interrupted the old man, " thou idlest, and misspendest the time in vain talk. Go, fold thy flock, Mark ; and do thou, weak one, house thy charge with less uproar than is thy wont. We should remember that the voice is given to man, — firstly, that he may improve the blessing in thanksgivings and petitions ; secondly, to communicate such gifts as may be imparted to himself, and which it is his bounden duty to attempt to impart to others ; and then, thirdly, to declare his natural wants and inclinations."

With this admonition, which probably proceeded from

a secret consciousness in the Puritan that he had permitted
a momentary cloud of selfishness to obscure the brightness
of his own faith, the party separated.   The grandson and
the hireling took their several ways to the folds, while old
Mark himself slowly continued his course towards the
dwellings.   It was near enough to the hours of darkness,
to render the preparations we have mentioned prudent ;
still no urgency called for particular haste in the return of
the veteran to the shelter and protection of his own comfortable and secure abode.   He therefore loitered along
the path, occasionally stopping to look into the prospects
of the young crops that were beginning to spring up in
readiness for the coming year, and at times bending his
gaze around the whole of his limited horizon, like one
who had the habit of exceeding and unremitted care.

One of these numerous pauses promised to be much
longer than usual.   Instead of keeping his understanding
eye on the grain, the look of the old man appeared fastened,
as by a charm, on some distant and obscure object.   Doubt
and uncertainty, for many minutes, seemed to mingle in
his gaze.   But all hesitation had apparently disappeared,
as his lips severed and he spoke, perhaps unconsciously to
himself, aloud.

" It is no deception," were the low words, " but a
living and an accountable creature of the Lord's !   Many
a day hath passed since such a sight hath been witnessed
in this vale ; but my eye greatly deceives me, or yonder
cometh one ready to ask for hospitality, and, peradventure,
for Christian and brotherly communion."

The sight of the aged emigrant had not deceived him.
One, who appeared a way-worn and weary traveller, had
indeed ridden out of the forest, at a point where a path
that was easier to be traced by the blazed * trees that lay
along its route than by any marks on the earth itself,
issued into the cleared land.   The progress of the stranger
had at first been so wary and slow, as to bear the manner
of exceeding and mysterious caution.   The blind road,
along which he must have ridden not only far but hard,

---

* A tree that has had a stripe of its bark removed by the axe is said to be
" blazed."   It is the usual manner of marking a path in the wilderness.

or night had certainly overtaken him in the woods, led to one of the distant settlements that lay nearer to the fertile banks of the Connecticut. Few ever followed its windings but such as had especial affairs, or extraordinary communion in the way of religious friendships, with the proprietors of the Wish-Ton-Wish *, as, in commemoration of the first bird that had been seen by the emigrants, the valley of the Heathcotes was called.

Once fairly in view, any doubt or apprehension that the stranger might at first have entertained, disappeared. He rode boldly and steadily forward, until he drew a rein that his impoverished and weary beast gladly obeyed, within a few feet of the proprietor of the valley, whose gaze had never ceased to watch his movements, from the instant when the other first came within view. Before speaking, the stranger, a man whose head was getting gray, apparently as much with hardship as with time, and one whose great weight would have proved a grievous burthen in a long ride, to even a better conditioned beast than the ill-favoured provincial hack he had ridden, dismounted and threw the bridle loose upon the drooping neck of the animal. The latter, without a moment's delay, and with a greediness that denoted long abstinence, profited by its liberty to crop the herbage where it stood.

" I cannot be mistaken when I suppose that I have at length reached the valley of the Wish-Ton-Wish," the visiter said, touching a soiled and slouched beaver that more than half concealed his features. The question was put in an English that bespoke a descent from those who dwell in the midland counties of the mother country, rather than in that intonation which is still to be traced, equally in the western portions of England and in the eastern states of the Union. Notwithstanding the purity of his accent, there was enough in the form of his speech to denote a severe compliance with the fashion of the religionists of the times. He used that measured and methodical tone, which was, singularly enough, believed to distinguish an entire absence of affectation in language.

---

* This bird is called the Whip-poor-Will by the people of America, from some fancied resemblance: to these words in its notes.

" Thou hast reached the dwelling of him thou seekest ; one who is a submissive sojourner in the wilderness of the world, and an humble servitor in the outer temple."

" This, then, is Mark Heathcote !" repeated the stranger, regarding the other with a look of long, and, possibly, of suspicious investigation.

" Such is the name I bear. A fitting confidence in Him who knows so well how to change the wilds into the haunts of men, and much suffering have made me the master of what thou seest. Whether thou comest to tarry a night, a week, a month, or even for a still longer season, as a brother in care, and I doubt not one who striveth for the right, I bid thee welcome."

The stranger thanked his host, by a slow inclination of the head, but the gaze, which began to partake a little of the look of recognition, was still too earnest and engrossing to admit of verbal reply. On the other hand, though the old man had scanned the broad and rusty beaver, the coarse and well-worn doublet, the heavy boots, and, in short, the whole attire of his visiter, in which he saw no vain conformity to idle fashions to condemn, it was evident that personal recollection had not the smallest influence in quickening his hospitality.

" Thou hast arrived happily," continued the Puritan ; " had night overtaken thee in the forest, unless much practised in the shifts of our young woodsmen, hunger, frost, and a supperless bed of brush, would have given thee motive to think more of the body than is either profitable or seemly."

The stranger might possibly have known the embarrassment of these several hardships, for the quick and unconscious glance he threw over his soiled dress, seemed to betray some familiarity already with the privations to which his host alluded. As neither of them however appeared disposed to waste further time on matters of such light moment, the traveller put an arm through the bridle of his horse, and, in obedience to an invitation from the owner of the dwelling, they took their way towards the fortified edifice on the natural mound.

The task of furnishing litter and provender to the jaded

beast was performed by Whittal Ring, under the inspection, and at times under the instructions of its owner and
his host, both of whom appeared to take a kind and commendable interest in the comfort of a faithful hack, that
had evidently suffered long and much in the service of its
master. When this duty was discharged, the old man and
his unknown guest entered the house together ; the frank
and unpretending hospitality of a country like that they
were in, rendering suspicion, or hesitation, unknown to the
reception of a man of white blood, more especially if he
spoke the language of the island which was then first sending out its swarms, to subdue and occupy so large a portion of a continent that nearly divides the earth in moieties.

CHAPTER III.

This is most strange : your father 's in some passion
That works him strongly. *Tempest.*

A few hours made a great change in the occupations of
the different members of our simple and secluded family.
The kine had yielded their nightly tribute ; the oxen had
been released from the yoke, and were now secure beneath
their sheds ; the sheep were in their folds, safe from the
assaults of the prowling wolf, and care had been taken to
see that every thing possessing life was gathered within the
particular defences provided for its security and comfort.
But while all this caution was used in behalf of living
things, the utmost indifference prevailed on the subject of
that species of moveable property which, elsewhere, would
have been guarded with at least an equal jealousy. The
homely fabrics of the looms of Ruth lay on their bleaching
ground, to drink in the night dew : and ploughs, harrows,
carts, saddles, and other similar articles, were left in situations so exposed, as to prove that the hand of man had
occupations so numerous and so urgent, as to render it inconvenient to bestow labour where it was not considered
absolutely necessary.

Content himself was the last to quit the fields and the
out-buildings. When he reached the postern in the palisadoes, he stopped to call to those above him, in order to
learn if any yet lingered without the wooden barriers.
The answer being in the negative, he entered, and drawing-
to the small but heavy gate, he secured it with bar, bolt
and lock, carefully and jealously, with his own hand. As
this was no more than a nightly and necessary precaution,
the affairs of the family received no interruption. The
meal of the hour was soon ended, and conversation, with
those light toils which are peculiar to the long evenings of
the fall and winter in families on the frontier, succeeded,
as fitting employments to close the business of a laborious
and well-spent day.

Notwithstanding the entire simplicity which marked the
opinions and usages of the colonists at that period, and the
great equality of condition which even to this hour distinguishes the particular community of which we write, choice
and inclination drew some natural distinctions in the
ordinary intercourse of the inmates of the Heathcote
family. A fire, so bright and cheerful as to render candles
or torches unnecessary, blazed on an enormous hearth in a
sort of upper kitchen. Around it were seated six or seven
hardy and athletic young men, some drawing coarse tools
carefully through the curvatures of ox-bows, others scraping
down the helves of axes, or perhaps fashioning sticks of
birch into homely but convenient brooms. A demure,
side-looking, young woman kept her great wheel in motion,
while one or two others were passing from room to
room, with the notable and stirring industry of handmaidens busied in the more familiar cares of the household.
A door communicated with an inner and a superior apartment. Here was a smaller but an equally cheerful fire; a
floor which had recently been swept, while that without
had been freshly sprinkled with river sand; candles of
tallow on a table of cherry-wood from the neighbouring
forest; walls that were wainscotted in the black-oak of
the country; and a few other articles, of a fashion so
antique, and of ornaments so ingenious and rich, as to
announce that they had been transported from beyond sea.

Above the mantel were suspended the armorial bearings of the Heathcotes and the Hardings, each elaborately emblazoned in tent-stitch.

The principal personages of the family were seated around the latter hearth, while a straggler from the other room, of more than usual curiosity, had placed himself among them, marking the distinction in ranks, or rather in situation, merely by the extraordinary care which he took that none of the scrapings that fell from the axe helve he was polishing, should litter the spotless oaken floor.

Until this period of the evening, the duties of hospitality and the observances of religion had prevented familiar discourse. But the regular offices of the housewife were now ended for the night; the handmaidens had all retired to their wheels; and as the bustle of a busy and more stirring domestic industry ceased, the cold and self-restrained silence, which had hitherto only been broken by distant and brief observations of courtesy, or by some wholesome allusion to the lost and probationary condition of man, seemed to invite an intercourse of a more general character.

" You entered my clearing by the southern path," commenced Mark Heathcote, addressing himself to his guest with sufficient courtesy to denote a breeding superior to that of most of those who dwelt in the wilderness, " and needs must bring tidings from the towns on the river side. Has aught been done by our counsellors at home, in the matter that pertaineth so closely to the well-being of this colony ? "

" You would have me say whether he that now sitteth on the throne of England hath listened to the petitions of his people in this province, and hath granted them protection against the abuses which might so readily flow out of his own ill-advised will, or out of the violence and injustice of his successors ? "

" We will render unto Cæsar the things that are Cæsar's, and speak reverently of men having authority. I would fain know whether the agent sent by our people hath gained the ears of those who counsel the prince, and obtained that which he sought ? "

" He hath done more," returned the stranger; " he hath even gained the ear of the Lord's anointed."

" Then is Charles of better mind and of stronger justice than report hath spoken. We were told that light manners and unprofitable companions had led him to think more of the vanities of the world, and less of the wants of those over whom he hath been called by Providence to rule, than is meet for one that sitteth on a high place. I rejoice that the arguments of the man we sent have prevailed over more evil promptings, and that peace and freedom of conscience are likely to be the fruits of the undertaking. In what manner hath he seen fit to order the future government of this people ? "

" Much as it hath ever stood; — by their own ordinances. Winthrop hath returned, and he is the bearer of a Royal Charter, which granteth all the rights long claimed and practised. None now dwell under the crown of Britain with fewer offensive demands on their consciences, or with lighter calls on their political duties, than the men of Connecticut."

" It is fitting that thanks should be rendered, therefore, where thanks are most due," said the Puritan, folding his hands on his bosom, and sitting for a moment with closed eyes, like one who communed with an unseen being. " Is it known by what manner of argument the Lord moved the heart of the prince to hearken to our wants ; or was it an open and manifest token of his power ? "

" I think it must needs have been the latter," rejoined the visiter, with a manner that grew caustic and emphatic. " The bauble, that was the visible agent, could not have weighed greatly with one so proudly seated before the eyes of men."

Until this point in the discourse, Content and Ruth, with their offspring, and the two or three other individuals who composed the audience, had listened with the demure gravity which characterised the manners of the country. The language, united with the ill-concealed sarcasm conveyed by the countenance, no less than the emphasis of the speaker, caused them now to raise their eyes, as by a common impulse. The word " bauble " was audibly and curiously repeated. But the look of cold irony had already passed from the features of the stranger, and it had given place to a stern and fixed austerity, that imparted a character of grimness to his hard and sun-burnt visage. Still he betrayed no disposition to shrink from the subject ; but, after regarding his auditors with a glance in which pride and suspicion were singularly blended, he resumed the discourse.

" It is known," he added, " that the grandfather of him the good people of these settlements have commissioned to bear their wants over sea, lived in the favour of the man who last sat upon the throne of England ; and a rumour goetn forth, that the Stuart, in a moment of princely condescension, once decked the finger of his subject with a ring wrought in a curious fashion. It was a token of the love which a monarch may bear a man."

" Such gifts are beacons of friendship, but may not be used as gay and sinful ornaments," observed Mark, while the other paused like one who wished none of the bitterness of his allusions to be lost.

" It matters not whether the bauble lay in the coffers of the Winthrops, or has long been glittering before the eyes of the faithful in the Bay, since it hath finally proved to be a jewel of price," continued the stranger. " It is said, in secret, that this ring hath returned to the finger of a Stuart, and it is openly proclaimed that Connecticut hath a charter ! "

Content and his wife regarded each other in melancholy amazement. Such an evidence of wanton levity and of unworthiness of motive, in one entrusted with the gift of earthly government, pained their simple and upright minds; while old Mark, of still more decided and exaggerated ideas of spiritual perfection, distinctly groaned. The stranger took a sensible pleasure in this testimony of their abhorrence of so gross and so unworthy a venality, though he saw no occasion to heighten its effect by further speech. When his host stood erect, and, in a voice that was accustomed to obedience, he called on his family to join, in behalf of the reckless ruler of the land of their fathers, in a petition to Him who alone could soften the hearts of

princes, he also arose from his seat.   But even in this act
of devotion, the stranger bore the air of one who wished to
do pleasure to his entertainers, rather than to obtain the
boon that was so ostentatiously asked.

The prayer, though short, was pointed, fervent, and
sufficiently personal.   The wheels in the outer room ceased
their hum, and a general movement denoted that all there
had arisen to join in the office, while one or two of their
number, impelled by deeper piety, or stronger interest,
drew near to the open door between the rooms in order to
listen.   With this singular, but characteristic, interruption,
that particular branch of the discourse which had given
rise to it, altogether ceased.

" And have we reason to dread a rising of the savages
on the borders ?" asked Content, when he found that the
moved spirit of his father was not yet sufficiently calmed,
to return to the examination of temporal things ; " one
who brought wares from the towns below, a few months
since, recited reasons to fear a movement among the red
men."

The subject had not sufficient interest to open the ears
of the stranger.   He was deaf, or he chose to affect deaf-
ness, to the interrogatory.   Laying his two large and
weather-worn though still muscular hands, on a visage
that was much darkened by exposure, he appeared to shut
out the objects of the world, while he communed deeply,
and, as would seem by a slight tremor that shook even his
powerful frame, terribly with his own thoughts.

" We have many to whom our hearts strongly cling to
heighten the smallest symptom of alarm from that quarter,"
added the tender and anxious mother, her eye glancing at
the uplifted countenances of two little girls, who, busied
with their light needle-work, sate on stools at her feet.
" But I rejoice to see that one who hath journeyed from
parts where the minds of the savages must be better understood, hath not feared to do it unarmed."

The traveller slowly uncovered his features, and the
glance that his eye shot over the face of the last speaker,
was not without a gentle and interested expression.   Instantly recovering his composure, he arose, and turning to

the double leathern sack, which had been borne on the crupper of his nag, and which now lay at no great distance from his seat, he drew a pair of horseman's pistols from two well-contrived pockets in its sides, and laid them deliberately on the table.

" Though little disposed to seek an encounter with any bearing the image of man," he said, " I have not neglected the usual precautions of those who enter the wilderness. Here are weapons that, in steady hands, might easily take life, or, at need, preserve it."

The young Mark drew near with boyish curiosity, and while one finger ventured to touch a lock, as he stole a conscious glance of wrong-doing towards his mother, he said, with as much of contempt in his air as the schooling of his manners would allow —

" An Indian arrow would make a surer aim than a bore as short as this ! When the trainer from Hartford struck the wild-cat on the hill-clearing, he sent the bullet from a five-foot barrel ; besides, this short-sighted gun would be a dull weapon in a hug against the keen-edged knife that the wicked Wampanoag is known to carry."

" Boy, thy years are few, and thy boldness of speech marvellous," sternly interrupted his grandfather.

The stranger manifested no displeasure, however, at the confident language of the lad. Encouraging him with a look which plainly proclaimed that martial qualities in no degree lessened the stripling in his favour, he observed that —

" The youth who is not afraid to think of the fight, or to reason on its chances, will lead to a manhood of spirit and independence. A hundred thousand striplings like this, might have spared Winthrop his jewel, and the Stuart the shame of yielding to so vain and so trivial a bribe. But thou mayest see by this weapon, child, that had we come to the death-hug, the wicked Wampanoag might have found a blade as keen as his own."

The stranger, while speaking, loosened a few strings of his doublet, and thrust a hand into his bosom. The action enabled more than one eye to catch a momentary glimpse of another weapon of the same description, but of a size

much smaller than those he had already so freely exhibited.
As he immediately withdrew his hand, and again closed
the garment with studied care, no one presumed to advert
to the circumstance, but all turned their attention to the
long, sharp, hunting knife that he deposited by the side of
the pistols, as he concluded. Mark ventured to open its
blade, but he turned away with sudden consciousness,
when he found that a few fibres of coarse, shaggy wool,
that were drawn from the loosened joint, adhered to his
fingers.

" Straight-Horns has been against a bush sharper than
the thorn !" exclaimed Whittal Ring, who had been at
hand, and who watched with childish admiration the
smallest proceedings of the different individuals. " A
flint for the back of the blade, a few dried leaves and
broken sticks, with such a carver, would soon make roast
and broiled of the old bell-wether himself ! I know that
the hair of all my colts is sorrel*, and I counted five at
sundown, which is just as many as went loping through
the underbrush when I loosened them from the hopples in
the morning ; but six-and-thirty backs can never carry
seven-and-thirty growing fleeces of unsheared wool.
Master knows that, for he is a scholar, and can count a
hundred ! "

The allusion to the fate of the lost sheep was so plain as
to admit of no misinterpretation of the meaning of the
witless speaker. Animals of that class were of the last
importance to the comfort of the settlers, and there was not
probably one within hearing of Whittal Ring, that was at
all ignorant of the import of his words. Indeed, the loud
chuckle and the open and deriding manner with which the
lad himself held above his head the hairy fibres that he
had snatched from young Mark, allowed of no concealment,
had it been desirable.

" This feeble-gifted youth would hint that thy knife
hath proved its edge on a wether that is missing from our
flock, since the animals went on their mountain range in

---

* " Sorrel " is a colour much known among the American horses. It is a
reddish chestnut. The word is old English, but has fallen into disuse in the
mother country.

the morning," said the host, calmly ; though even he bent
his eye to the floor as he waited for an answer to a remark
direct as the one his sense of justice and his indomitable
love of right had prompted.

" Is hunger, then, a crime, that they who dwell so far
from the haunts of selfishness visit it with their anger ? "

" The foot of christian man never approached the gates
of Wish-Ton-Wish to be turned away in uncharitableness,
but that which is freely given should not be taken in
licentiousness. From off the hill, where my flock is wont
to graze, it is easy, through many an opening of the forest,
to see these roofs ; and it would have been better that the
body should languish, than that a grievous sin should be
placed on that immortal spirit, which is already too deeply
laden, unless thou art far more happy than others of the
fallen race of Adam."

" Mark Heathcote," said the accused, with an unwavering tone, " look further at those weapons, which, if a
guilty man, I have weakly placed within thy power. Thou
wilt find more there to wonder at, than a few straggling
hairs that the spinner would cast from her as too coarse for
service."

" It is long since I found pleasure in handling the
weapons of strife ; may it be longer to the time when they
shall be needed in this abode of peace. These are instruments of death resembling those used in my youth by
cavaliers that rode in the levies of the first Charles and of
his pusillanimous father. There were worldly pride and
great vanity, with much and damning ungodliness, in the
wars that I have seen, my children ; and yet the carnal
man found pleasure in the stirrings of those graceless
days ! Come hither, younker ; thou hast often sought to
know the manner in which the horsemen are wont to lead
into the combat, when the broad-mouthed artillery, and
pattering leaden hail have cleared a passage for the struggle
of horse to horse, and man to man. Much of the justification of these combats must depend on the inward spirit,
and on the temper of him that striketh at the life of his
fellow sinner ; but righteous Joshua, it is known, contended
with the heathen throughout a supernatural day : and

therefore, always humbly confiding that our cause is just, I will open to thy young mind the uses of a weapon that hath never before been seen in these forests."

"I have hefted many a heavier piece than this," said young Mark, frowning equally with the exertion and with the instigations of his aspiring spirit, as he held out the ponderous weapon in a single hand; "we have guns that might tame a wolf with greater certainty than any barrel of a bore less than my own height. Tell me, grand'ther, at what distance do the mounted warriors you so often name, take their sight?"

But the power of speech appeared suddenly to have deserted the aged veteran. He had interrupted his own discourse, and now, instead of answering the interrogatory of the boy, his eye wandered, slowly and with a look of painful doubt, from the weapon, that was still held before him, to the countenance of the stranger. The latter continued erect, like one courting a strict and close examination of his person. This dumb show could not fail to attract the observation of Content. Rising from his seat, with the quiet authoritative manner which is still seen in the domestic government of the people of the region where he dwelt, he beckoned to all present to quit the apartment. Ruth and her daughters, the hirelings, the ill-gifted Whittal, and even the reluctant Mark, preceded him to the door, which he closed with respectful care: and then the whole of the wondering party mingled with those of the outer room, leaving the one they had quitted to the sole possession of the aged chief of the settlement, and to his still unknown and mysterious guest.

Many anxious, and, to those who were excluded, seemingly interminable minutes passed, and the secret interview appeared to draw no nearer its close. That deep reverence, which the years, paternity, and character of the grandfather had inspired, prevented all from approaching the quarter of the apartment nearest to the room they had left; but a silence, still as the grave, did all that silence could do, to enlighten their minds in a matter of so much general interest. The deep, smothered sentences of the speakers were often heard, each dwelling with steadiness and propriety on his particular theme : but no sound that conveyed meaning to the minds of those without, passed the envious walls. At length the voice of old Mark became more than usually audible, and then Content arose, with a gesture to those around him to imitate his example. The young men threw aside the subjects of their light employ- ments, the maidens left the wheels, which had not been turned for many minutes, and the whole party disposed themselves in the decent and simple attitudes of prayer. For the third time that evening was the voice of the Puri- tan heard, pouring out his spirit in a communion with that Being on whom it was his practice to repose all his worldly cares. But, though long accustomed to all the peculiar forms of utterance by which their father ordinarily ex- pressed his pious emotions, neither Content nor his atten- tive partner was enabled to decide on the nature of the feeling that was now uppermost. At times it appeared to be the language of thanksgiving, and at others it assumed more of the imploring sounds of deprecation and petition ; in short, it was so varied, and though tranquil, so equi- vocal, if such a term may be applied to so serious a subject, as completely to baffle every conjecture.

Long and weary minutes passed after the voice had entirely ceased, and yet no summons was given to the expecting family, nor did any sound proceed from the inner room, which the respectful son was emboldened to construe into an evidence that he might presume to enter. At length, apprehension began to mingle with conjec- tures, and then the husband and wife communed apart, in whispers. The misgivings and doubt of the former, soon manifested themselves in still more apparent forms. He arose, and began to pace the wide apartment, gradually approaching nearer to the partition which separated the two rooms, evidently prepared to retire beyond the limits of hearing, the moment he should detect any proofs that his uneasiness was without a sufficient cause. Still no sound proceeded from the inner room. The breathless silence which had so shortly before reigned where he was, appeared to be suddenly transferred to the spot in which he was vainly endeavouring to detect the smallest proof of human existence. Again he returned to Ruth, and again they consulted in low voices, as to the step that filial duty seemed to require at their hands.

" We were not bidden to withdraw," said his gentle companion ; " why not rejoin our parent, now that time hath been given to understand the subject which so evidently disturbed his mind ? "

Content, at length, yielded to this opinion. With that cautious discretion which distinguishes his people, he motioned to the family to follow, in order that no unnecessary exclusion should give rise to conjectures, or excite suspicions, for which after all the circumstances might prove no justification. Notwithstanding the subdued manners of the age and country, curiosity, and perhaps a better feeling, had become so intense, as to cause all present to obey this silent mandate, by moving as swiftly towards the open door as a never-yielding decency of demeanour would permit.

Old Mark Heathcote occupied the chair in which he had been left, with that calm and unbending gravity of eye and features, which was then thought indispensable to a fitting sobriety of spirit. But the stranger had disappeared. There were two or three outlets by which the room, and even the house, might be quitted, without the knowledge of those who had so long waited for admission, and the first impression led the family to expect his reappearance through one of these exterior passages. Content, however, read in the expression of his father's eye that the moment of confidence, if it were ever to arrive, had not yet come ; and so admirable and perfect was the domestic discipline of this family, that the questions which the son did not see fit to propound, no one of inferior condition, or lesser age, might presume to agitate.

With the person of the stranger, every evidence of his recent visit had also vanished. Mark missed the weapon that had excited his admiration ; Whittal looked in vain for the hunting knife which had betrayed the fate of the wether ; Mrs. Heathcote saw by a hasty glance of the eye that the leathern sacks, which she had borne in mind ought to be transferred to the sleeping apartment of their guest, were gone; and a mild and playful image of herself, who bore her name, no less than most of those features which had rendered her own youth so attractive, sought without success a massive silver spur, of curious and antique workmanship, which she had been permitted to handle until the moment when the family had been commanded to withdraw.

The night had now worn later than the hour at which it was usual for people of habits so simple to be out of their beds. The grandfather lighted a taper, and, bestowing the usual blessing on those around him with an air as calm as if nothing had occurred, he prepared to retire to his own room. And yet matter of interest seemed to linger on his mind. Even on the threshold of the door he turned; and, for an instant, all expected some explanation of a circumstance which began to wear no little of the aspect of an exciting and painful mystery. But their hopes were raised only to be disappointed.

" My thoughts have not kept the passage of the time," he said. " In what hour of the night are we, my son ? "

He was told that it was already past the usual moment of sleep.

" No matter ; that which Providence hath bestowed for our comfort and support should not be lightly and unthankfully disregarded. Take thou the beast I am wont to ride, Content, and follow the path which leadeth to the mountain clearing ; bring away that which shall meet thine eye near the first turning of the route toward the river towns. We have got into the last quarter of the year ; and in order that our industry may not flag, and that all may be stirring with the sun, let the remainder of the household seek their rest."

Content saw, by the manner of his father, that no departure from the strict letter of these instructions was admissible. He closed the door after his retiring form, and then, by a quiet gesture of authority, indicated to his dependants that they were expected to withdraw. The maidens of Ruth led the children to their chambers ; and, in a few more minutes, none remained in the outer apartment, already so often named, but the obedient son, with his anxious and affectionate consort.

" I will be thy companion, husband," said Ruth in a half whisper, so soon as the little domestic preparations for securing the fires and the doors were ended. " I like not that thou shouldst go forth into the forest alone, at so late an hour."

" One will be with me there, who never deserteth those who rely on his protection. Besides, my Ruth, what is there to apprehend in a wilderness like this ? The beasts have been lately hunted from the hills, and, excepting those who dwell under our own roof, there is not a man within a long day's ride."

" We know not. Where is the stranger that came within our doors as the sun was setting ? "

" As thou sayest, we know not. My father is not minded to open his lips on the subject of this traveller ; and surely we are not now to learn the lessons of obedience and self-denial."

" It would, notwithstanding, be a great easing to the spirit to hear at least the name of him who hath eaten of our bread and joined in our family worship, though he were immediately to pass away for ever from before the sight."

" That may he have done already ;" returned the less curious and more self-restrained husband. " My father will not that we enquire."

" And yet there can be little sin in knowing the condition of one whose fortunes and movements can excite neither our envy nor our strife. I would that we had tarried for a closer mingling in the prayers ; it was not seemly to desert a guest who, it would appear, had need of an especial up-offering in his behalf."

" Our spirits joined in the asking, though our ears were shut to the matter of his wants. But it will be needful that I should be afoot with the young men in the morning, and a mile of good measurement would not reach to the turning in the path to the river towns. Go with me to the postern, and look to the fastenings ; I will not keep thee long on thy watch."

Content and his wife now quitted the dwelling by the only door that was left unbarred. Lighted by a moon that was full, though clouded, they passed a gateway between two of the outer buildings, and descended to the palisadoes. The bars and bolts of the little postern were removed; and in a few minutes the former, mounted on the back of his father's own horse, was galloping briskly along the path which led into the part of the forest he was directed to seek.

While the husband was thus proceeding, in obedience to orders that he never hesitated to obey, his faithful wife withdrew within the shelter of the wooden defences. More in compliance with a precaution that was become habitual, than from any present causes of suspicion, she drew a single bolt, and remained at the postern, anxiously awaiting the result of a movement that was as unaccountable as it was extraordinary.

CHAPTER IV.

I' the name of something holy, Sir, why stand you
In this strange stare?   *Tempest.*

As a girl, Ruth Harding had been one of the mildest and gentlest of the human race. Though new impulses had been given to her naturally kind affections by the attachments of a wife and mother, her disposition suffered no change by marriage. Obedient, disinterested, and devoted to those she loved, as her parents had known her, so, by the experience of many years, had she proved to Content. In the midst of the utmost equanimity of temper and of deportment, her watchful solicitude in behalf of the few who formed the limited circle of her existence never slumbered. It dwelt unpretendingly, but active, in her gentle bosom, like a great and moving principle of life. Though circumstances had placed her on a remote and exposed frontier, where time had not been given for the several customary divisions of employments, she was unchanged in habits, in feelings, and in character. The affluence of her husband had elevated her above the necessity of bur-

D 3

thensome toil ; and while she had encountered the dangers
of the wilderness, and neglected none of the duties of her
active station, she had escaped most of those injurious
consequences which are a little apt to impair the peculiar
loveliness of woman. Notwithstanding the exposure of a
border life, she remained feminine, attractive, and singularly youthful.

The reader will readily imagine the state of mind with
which such a being watched the distant form of a husband, engaged in a duty like that we have described.
Notwithstanding the influence of long habit, the forest
was rarely approached, after night-fall, by the boldest
woodsman, without some secret consciousness that he
encountered a positive danger. It was the hour when its
roaming and hungry tenants were known to be most in
motion ; and the rustling of a leaf, or the snapping of a dry
twig, beneath the light tread of the smallest animal, was
apt to conjure images of the voracious and fire-eyed panther, or perhaps of a lurking biped, which, though more
artful, was known to be scarcely less savage. It is true
that hundreds experienced the uneasiness of such sensations
who were never fated to undergo the realities of the fearful
pictures. Still facts were not wanting to supply sufficient
motive for a grave and reasonable apprehension.

Histories of combats with beasts of prey, and of massacres by roving and lawless Indians, were the moving
legends of the border. Thrones might be subverted, and
kingdoms lost and won in distant Europe, and less should
be said of the events, by those who dwelt in these woods,
than of one scene of peculiar and striking forest incident,
that called for the exercise of the stout courage and the
keen intelligence of a settler. Such a tale passed from
mouth to mouth, with the eagerness of powerful personal
interest ; and many were already transmitted from parent
to child, in the form of tradition, until, as, in more artificial communities graver improbabilities creep into the
doubtful pages of history, exaggeration became too closely
blended with truth ever again to be separated.

Under the influence of these feelings, and perhaps
prompted by his never-failing discretion, Content had

ments weaker than common, had awakened some of the
lighter vanities, were gladly rid of gallants, who could not
soothe their ears with the unction of flattery without frequently giving great offence to their severe principles by
light and irreverent allusions to things on which they themselves were accustomed to think with fitting awe. Eben
Dudley could scarcely conceal the chuckle with which he
saw the party bury themselves in the forest, though neither
he, nor any of the more instructed in such matters, believed they incurred serious risk from their sudden
enterprise.

The opinions of the scouts proved to be founded on
accurate premises. That and many a subsequent night
passed without alarm. The season continued to advance,
and the labourers pursued their toil to its close, without another appeal to their courage, or any additional reasons for
vigilance. Whittal Ring followed his colts with impunity
among the recesses of the neighbouring forests, and the
herds of the family went and came as long as the weather
would permit them to range the woods, in regularity and
peace. The period of the alarm, and the visit of the
agents of the crown, came to be food for tradition : and
during the succeeding winter, the former often furnished
motive of merriment around the blazing fires that were so
necessary to the country and the season.

Still there existed in the family a living memorial of
the unusual incidents of that night. The captive remained,
long after the events which had placed him in the power of
the Heathcotes were beginning to be forgotten.

A desire to quicken the seeds of spiritual regeneration
which, however dormant they might be, old Mark Heathcote believed to exist in the whole family of man, and consequently in the young heathen as well as in others, had
become a sort of ruling passion in the Puritan. The
fashions and mode of thinking of the times had a strong
leaning towards superstition : and it was far from difficult
for a man of his ascetic habits and exaggerated doctrines,
to believe that a special interposition had cast the boy into
his hands, for some hidden but mighty purpose, that time
in the good season would not fail to reveal.

threw the body of its darkness on the trees, and a portion of its outline on the ground near the margin of the wood. Just at this instant the recollection that she had incautiously left the postern open flashed upon her mind; and, with feelings divided between husband and children, she commenced her return, in order to repair a neglect, to which habit no less than prudence imparted a high degree of culpability. The eyes of the mother, for the feelings of that sacred character were now powerfully uppermost, were fastened on the ground, as she eagerly picked her way along the uneven surface, and so engrossed was her mind by the omission of duty with which she was severely reproaching herself, that they drunk in objects without conveying distinct or intelligible images to her brain.

Notwithstanding the one engrossing thought of the moment, an object met her eye that caused even the vacant organ to recoil, and every fibre in her frame to tremble with terror. There was a moment in which delirium nearly heightened terror to madness. She fled instinctively and with the swiftness of the hind. Reflection came only when she had reached the distance of many hundred feet from the spot where the startling sight had half unconsciously crossed her vision. Then for a single and a fearful instant she paused, like one who debated on the course she ought to follow. Maternal love prevailed, and the deer of her own woods scarcely bounds with greater agility than the mother of the sleeping and defenceless family now continued her flight towards the dwellings. Panting and breathless she gained the postern, which she entered and closed with hands that performed their office more by instinct than in obedience to thought, and doubly and trebly barred.

For the first time in some minutes, Ruth now breathed distinctly and without pain. She strove to rally her thoughts, in order to deliberate on the course that prudence and her duty to Content, who was still exposed to the danger she had herself escaped, prescribed. Her first impulse was to give the established signal that was to recall the labourers from the field, or to awake the sleepers, in the event of an alarm; but better reflection told her that such a step might prove fatal to him who balanced in her affections against the rest of the world. The struggle in her mind only ended, as she clearly and unequivocally caught a view of her husband, issuing from the forest, at the very point where he had entered. The return path unfortunately led directly past the spot where such sudden terror had seized her mind. She would have given worlds to have known how to apprise him of a danger with which her own imagination was full, without communicating the warning to other and terrible ears. The night was still, and though the distance was considerable, it was not so great as to render the chances of success desperate. Scarcely knowing what she did, and yet preserving, by a sort of instinctive prudence, the caution which constant exposure weaves into all our habits, the trembling woman made the effort.

" Husband ! husband !" she cried, commencing plaintively, but her voice rising with the energy of excitement, " husband, ride swiftly ; our little Ruth lyeth in the agony. For her life and thine, ride at thy horse's speed. Seek not the stables, but come with all haste to the postern ; it shall be open to thee."

This was certainly a fearful summons for a father's ear, and there is little doubt that, had the feeble powers of Ruth succeeded in conveying the words as far as she had wished, they would have produced the desired effect. But in vain did she call ; her weak tones, though raised on the notes of the keenest apprehension, could not force their way across so wide a space. And yet had she reason to think they were not entirely lost, for once her husband paused and seemed to listen, and once he quickened the pace of his horse ; though neither of these proofs of intelligence was followed by any further signs of his having understood the alarm.

Content was now upon the ominous hillock. If Ruth breathed at all during its passage, it was more imperceptibly than the gentlest respiration of the sleeping infant. But when she saw him trotting with unconscious security along the path on the side next the dwellings, her impatience broke through all restraint, and throwing open the postern,

she renewed her cries, in a voice that was no longer useless
The clattering of the unshodden hoof was again rapid, and
in another minute her husband galloped unharmed to her
side.

" Enter !" said the nearly dizzy wife, seizing the bridle
and leading the horse within the palisadoes; " enter,
husband ; for the love of all that is thine, enter, and be
thankful."

" What meaneth this terror, Ruth ?" demanded Content, in as much displeasure, perhaps, as he could manifest
to one so gentle, for a weakness betrayed in his own behalf; " is thy confidence in Him whose eye never closeth,
and who equally watcheth the life of man and that of the
falling sparrow, utterly lost ?"

Ruth was deaf. With hurried hands she drew the
fastenings, let fall the bars, and turned a key which forced a
triple-bolted lock to perform its office. Not till then did
she feel either safe herself, or at liberty to render thanks
for the safety of him over whose danger she had so lately
watched in agony.

" Why this care ? Hast forgotten that the horse will
suffer hunger, at this distance from the rack and manger ?"

" Better that he starve than hair of thine should come
to harm ! "

" Nay, nay, Ruth ; dost not remember that the beast is
the favourite of my father, who will ill brook his passing a
night within the palisadoes."

" Husband, there is one in the fields."

" Is there place where One is not ? "

" But I have seen creature of mortal birth, and creature
too that hath no claim on thee or thine, and who trespas-
seth on our peace, no less than on our natural rights, to be
where he lurketh."

" Go to ; thou art not used to be so late from thy
pillow, my poor Ruth ; sleep hath come over thee, whilst
standing on thy watch. Some cloud hath left its shadow
on the fields, or, truly, it may be that the hunt did not
drive the beasts as far from the clearing as we had thought.
Come, since thou wilt cling to my side, lay hand on the
bridle of the horse, while I ease him of his burthen."

As Content coolly proceeded to the task he had mentioned, the thoughts of his wife were momentarily diverted from their other sources of uneasiness, by the object which lay on the crupper of the nag, and which, until now, had entirely escaped her observation.

" Here is, indeed, the animal this day missing from our flock !" she exclaimed, as the carcass of a sheep fell heavily on the ground.

" Ay, and killed with exceeding judgment, if not aptly dressed to our hands. Mutton will not be wanting for the husking feast, and the stalled creature whose days were counted may live another season."

" And where didst find the slaughtered beast ? "

" On the limb of a growing hickory. Eben Dudley, with all his slight in butchering, and in setting forth the excellence of his meats, could not have left an animal hanging from the branch of a sapling, with greater knowledge of his craft. Thou seest, but a single meal is missing from the carcass, and thy fleece is unharmed."

" This is not the work of a Pequod !" exclaimed Ruth, surprised at her own discovery; " the red men do their mischief with less care."

" Nor has the tooth of wolf opened the veins of poor Straight-Horns. Here has been judgment in the slaughtering, as well as prudence in the consumption of the food. The hand that cut so lightly had intention of a second visit."

" And our father bid thee seek the creature where it was found ! Husband, I fear some heavy judgment for my sins, is likely to befall our poor children !"

" Thy babes are quietly in their slumbers, and, thus far, little wrong hath been done us. I'll cast the halter from the stalled animal ere I sleep, and Straight-Horns shall content us for the husking. We may have mutton less savoury for this evil chance, but the number of thy flock will be unaltered."

" And where is he, who hath mingled in our prayers, and hath eaten of our bread ; he who counselled so long in secret with our father, and who hath now vanished from among us like a vision ? "

"That, indeed, is a question not readily to be answered," returned Content, who had hitherto maintained a cheerful air, in order to appease what he was fain to believe a causeless terror in the bosom of his partner, but who was induced by this question to drop his head like one that sought reasons within the repository of his own thoughts. "It mattereth not, Ruth Heathcote; the ordering of the affair is in the hands of a man of many years and great experience; should his aged wisdom fail, do we not know that One even wiser than he, hath us in keeping! I will return the beast to his rack: and when we shall have jointly asked favour of eyes that never sleep, we will go in confidence to our rest."

"Husband, thou quittest not the palisadoes again this night," said Ruth, arresting the hand that had already drawn a bolt, ere she spoke. "I have a warning of evil."

"I would the stranger had found some other shelter in which to pass his short resting reason. That he hath made free with my flock, and that he hath administered to his hunger at some cost, when a single asking would have made him welcome to the best that the owner of the Wish-Ton-Wish can command, are truths that may not be denied. Still is he mortal man, as a goodly appetite hath proven, even should our belief in Providence so far waver as to harbour doubts of its unwillingness to suffer beings of injustice to wander in our forms and substance. I tell thee, Ruth, that the nag will be needed for to-morrow's service, and that our father will give but ill thanks should we leave it to make a bed on this cold hill-side. Go to thy rest and to thy prayers, trembler: I will close the postern with all care. Fear not; the stranger is of human wants, and his agency to do evil must needs be limited by human power."

"I fear none of white blood, nor of Christian parentage; the murderous heathen is in our fields."

"Thou dreamest, Ruth!"

"'Tis not a dream—I have seen the glowing eye-balls of a savage. Sleep was little like to come over me, when set upon a watch like this. I bethought me that the errand was of unknown character, and that our father was exceedingly aged, and that perchance his senses might be duped, and how an obedient son ought not to be exposed —thou knowest, Heathcote, that I could not look upon the danger of my children's father with indifference, and so I followed thee to the nut-tree hillock."

" To the nut-tree! It was not prudent in thee.— But the postern?"

" It was open; for were the key turned, who was there to admit us quickly, had haste been needed?" returned Ruth, momentarily averting her face to conceal the flush excited by conscious delinquency. " Though I failed in caution, 'twas for thy safety, Heathcote; but on that hillock, and in the hollow left by a fallen tree, lies concealed a heathen!"

" I passed the nut-wood in going to the shambles of our strange butcher, and I drew the rein to give breath to the nag near it, as we returned with the burthen. It cannot be; some creature of the forest hath alarmed thee."

" Ay! creature, formed, fashioned, gifted like ourselves, in all but the colour of the skin and blessing of the faith."

" This is a strange delusion! If there were an enemy at hand, would men, subtle as those you fear, suffer the master of the dwelling, and, truly I may say it without vain glory, one as likely as another to struggle stoutly for his own, to escape, when an ill-timed visit to the woods had delivered him unresisting into their hands? Go, go, good Ruth; thou mayst have seen a blackened log; perchance the frosts have left a fire-fly untouched; or it may be that some prowling bear has scented out the sweets of thy lately gathered hives."

Ruth again laid her hand firmly on the arm of her husband, who had withdrawn another bolt, and, looking him steadily in the face, she answered by saying, solemnly, and with touching pathos—

" Thinkest thou, husband, that a mother's eye could be deceived?"

It might have been that the allusion to the tender beings whose fate depended on his care, or that the deeply serious, though mild and gentle, manner of his consort produced some fresher impression on the mind of Content, but instead of undoing the fastenings of the postern, as he had intended, he deliberately drew its bolts again, and paused to think.

" If it produce no other benefit than to quiet thy fears, good Ruth," he said, after a moment of reflection, " a little caution will be well repaid. Stay thou, then, here, where the hillock may be watched, while I go wake a couple of the people. With stout Eben Dudley and experienced Reuben Ring to back me, my father's horse may surely be stabled."

Ruth contentedly assumed a task that she was quite equal to perform with intelligence and zeal. " Hie thee to the labourers' chambers, for I see a light still burning in the room of those you seek," was the answer she gave to a proposal that at least quieted the intenseness of her fears for him in whose behalf they had so lately been excited nearly to agony.

" It shall be quickly done ; nay, stand not thus openly between the beams, wife. Thou mayst place thyself here, at the doublings of the wood, beneath the loop, where harm would scarcely reach thee, though shot from artillery were to crush the timber."

With this admonition to be wary of a danger that he had himself so recently affected to despise, Content departed. The two labourers he had mentioned by name, were youths of mould and strength, and they were well inured to toil no less than to the particular privations and dangers of a border life. Like most men of their years and condition, they were practised too in the wiles of Indian cunning ; and though the province of Connecticut, compared to other settlements, had suffered but little in this species of murderous warfare, they both had martial feats and perilous experiences of their own to recount, during the light labours of the long winter evenings.

Content crossed the court with a quick step, for, notwithstanding his steady unbelief, the image of his gentle wife posted on her outer watch hurried his movements. The rap he gave at the door, on reaching the apartment of those he sought, was loud as it was sudden.

" Who calls ? " demanded a deep-toned and firm voice from within, at the first blow of the knuckles on the plank.

" Quit thy beds quickly, and come forth with the arms appointed for a sally."

" That is soon done," answered a stout woodsman, throwing open the door and standing before Content in the garments he had worn throughout the day. " We were just saying that the night was not to pass without a summons to the loops."

" Hast seen aught ? "

" Our eyes were not shut, more than those of others ; we saw him enter that no man hath seen depart."

" Come, fellow ; Whittal Ring would scarce give wiser speech than this cunning reply of thine. My wife is at the postern, and it is fit we go to relieve her watch. Thou wilt not forget the horns of powder, since it would not tell to our credit were there service for the pieces, and we lacking in wherewithal to give them a second discharge."

The youths obeyed, and as little time was necessary to arm those who never slept without weapons and ammunition within reach of their hands, Content was speedily followed by his dependents. Ruth was found at her post, but when urged by her husband to declare what had passed in his absence, she was compelled to admit that, though the moon had come forth brighter and clearer from behind the clouds, she had seen nothing to add to her alarm.

" We will then lead the beast to his stall, and close our duty by setting a single watcher for the rest of the night," said the husband. " Reuben shall keep the postern, while Eben and I will have a care for my father's nag, not forgetting the carcass for the husking feast. Dost hear, deaf Dudley ? — cast the mutton upon the crupper of the beast, and follow to the stables."

" Here has been no common workman at my office," said the blunt Eben, who, though an ordinary farm labourer, according to an usage still very generally prevalent in the country, was also skilful in the craft of the butcher. " I have brought many a wether to his end, but this is the first sheep, within all my experience, that hath kept the fleece while a portion of the body has been in the pot ! Lie there,

poor Straight-Horns, if quiet thou canst lie after such a
strange butchery. Reuben, I paid thee, as the sun rose, a
Spanish piece in silver, for the trifle of debt that lay between us in behalf of the good turn thou didst the shoes,
which were none the better for the last hunt in the hills.
Hast ever that pistareen about thee ?"

This question, which was put in a lowered tone, and only
to the ear of the party concerned, was answered in the af-
firmative.

" Give it me, lad ; in the morning thou shalt be paid
with usurer's interest."

Another summons from Content, who had now led the
nag loaded with the carcass of the sheep without the postern, cut short the secret conference. Eben Dudley, having
received the coin, hastened to follow. But the distance to
the out-buildings was sufficient to enable him to effect his
mysterious purpose without discovery. Whilst Content endeavoured to calm the apprehensions of his wife, who still
persisted in sharing his danger, by such reasons as he could
on the instant command, the credulous Dudley placed the
thin piece of silver between his teeth, and with a pressure
that denoted the prodigious force of his jaws, caused it to
assume a beaten and rounded shape. He then slily dropped
the battered coin into the muzzle of his gun, taking care to
secure its presence, until he himself should send it on its
disenchanting message, by a wad torn from the lining of
part of his vestments. Supported by this redoubtable aux-
iliary, the superstitious but still courageous borderer followed
his companion, whistling a low air that equally denoted his
indifference to danger of an ordinary nature, and his sensibility to impressions of a less earthly character.

They who dwell in the older districts of America, where
art and labour have long united to clear the earth of its in-
equalities, and to remove the vestiges of a state of nature,
can form but little idea of the thousand objects that may
exist in a clearing, to startle the imagination of one who
has admitted alarm, when seen in the doubtful light of even
a cloudless moon. Still less can they who have never
quitted the old world, and who, having only seen can only
imagine fields smooth as the surface of tranquil water, pic-

ture the effect produced by those lingering remnants, which
may be likened to so many mouldering monuments of the
fallen forest, scattered at such an hour over a broad surface
of open land. Accustomed as they were to the sight, Content and his partner, excited by their fears, fancied each
dark and distant stump a savage, and they passed no angle
in the high and heavy fences, without throwing a jealous
glance, to see that some enemy did not lie stretched within
its shadows.

Still no new motive for apprehension arose during the
brief period that the two adventurers were employed in ad-
ministering to the comfort of the Puritan's steed. The
task was ended, the carcass of the slaughtered Straight-
Horns had been secured, and Ruth was already urging her
husband to return, when their attention was drawn to the
attitude and mien of their companion.

" The man hath departed as he came," said Eben Dudley, who stood shaking his head, in open doubt, before an
empty stall ; " here is no beast, though with these eyes did
I see the half-wit bring hither a well-filled measure of
speckled oats, to feed the nag. He who favoured us with his
presence at the supper and the thanksgiving, hath tired of
his company before the hour of rest had come."

" The horse is truly wanting," said Content : " the
man must needs be in exceeding haste to have ridden into
the forest as the night grew deepest, and when the longest
summer day would scarce bring a better hack than that he
rode to another Christian dwelling. There is reason for
this industry, but it is enough that it concerns us not. We
will now seek our rest, in the certainty that One watcheth
our slumbers whose vigilance can never fail."

Though man could not trust himself to sleep in that
country without the security of bars and bolts, we have already had occasion to say, that property was guarded with
but little care. The stable-door was merely closed by a
wooden latch, and the party returned from this short sortie
with steps that were a little quickened by a sense of an uneasiness that beset them in forms suited to their several
characters. But shelter was at hand, and it was speedily
regained.

E

" Thou hast seen nothing," said Content to Reuben
Ring, who had been chosen for his quick eye, and a sagacity that in its way was quite as remarkable as was his
brother's impotency ; " thou hast seen nothing at thy
watch ?"

" Nought unusual ; and yet I like not yonder billet of
wood, near the fence against the knoll.   If it were not so
plainly a half-burnt log, one might fancy there is life in it.
But when fancy is at work, the sight is keen.   Once or
twice, I have thought it seemed to be rolling towards the
brook ; I am not, even now, certain that when first seen it
did not lie at least eight or ten feet higher against the bank."

" It may be a living thing !"

" On the faith of a woodman's eye, it well may be,"
said Eben Dudley ; " but should it be haunted by a legion
of wicked spirits, one may bring it to lie quiet from the
loop at the nearest corner.   Stand aside, Madame Heathcote," for the character and wealth of the proprietors of
the valley gave Ruth a claim to this term of respect
among the labourers ; " let me thrust the piece through
the —— Stop ! there is an especial charm in the gun, which
it might be sinful to waste on such a creature.   It may
after all be no more than some sweet-toothed bear.   I will
answer for the charge at my own cost, if thou wilt lend
me thy musket, Reuben Ring."

" It shall not be," said his master ; " one known to
my father hath this night entered our dwelling and fed
at our board ; if he hath departed in a way but little wont
among those of this colony, yet hath he done no great
wrong.   I will go nearer to the knoll, and examine with
less risk of error."

There was, in this proposal, too much of the spirit of
right-doing which governed all of those simple regions, to
meet serious opposition.   Content, supported by Eben
Dudley, again quitted the postern, and proceeded directly,
though still not without sufficient caution, towards the
point where the suspicious object lay.   A bend in the
fence had first brought it into view ; for, previously to
reaching that point, its apparent direction might for some
distance have been taken under shelter of the shadows of

the rails, which, at the immediate spot where it was seen, turned suddenly in a line with the eyes of the spectators. It seemed as if the movements of those who approached were watched, for the instant they left the defences, the dark object was assuredly motionless, — even the keen eye of Reuben Ring beginning to doubt whether some deception of vision had not led him, after all, to mistake a billet of wood for a creature possessing life.

But Content and his companion were not induced to change heir determination. Even when within fifty feet of the object, though the moon fell full and brightly upon its surface, its character baffled conjecture. One affirmed it was the end of a charred log, many of which still lay scattered about the fields, and the other believed it some cringing animal of the woods. Twice Content raised his piece to fire, and as often did he let it fall in reluctance to do injury to even a quadruped of whose character he was ignorant. It is more than probable that his less considerate, and but half obedient, companion would have decided the question soon after leaving the postern, had not the peculiar contents of his musket rendered him delicate of its uses.

" Look to thy weapons," said the former, loosening his own hunting knife in its sheath. " We will draw near, and make certainty of that which is now so doubtful."

They did so, and the gun of Dudley was thrust rudely into the side of the object of their distrust, before it again betrayed life or motion. Then, indeed, as if further disguise were useless, an Indian lad of some fifteen years rose deliberately to his feet, and stood before them in the sullen dignity of a captured warrior. Content hastily seized the stripling by an arm, and, followed by Eben, who occasionally quickened the footsteps of the prisoner by an impetus obtained from the breech of his own musket, they hurriedly returned within the defences.

" My life against that of Straight-Horns, which is now of no great value," said Dudley, as he pushed the last bolt of the fastenings into its socket, " we hear no more of this red skin's companions to-night. I never knew an Indian raise his whoop, when a scout had fallen into the hands of the enemy."

" This may be true," returned the other, " and yet must a sleeping household be guarded. We may be brought to rely on the overlooking favour of Providence, working with the means of our own manhood, ere the sun shall arise."

Content was a man of few words, but one of exceeding steadiness and resolution in moments of need. He was perfectly aware that an Indian youth, like him he had captured, would not have been found in that place, and under the circumstances in which he was actually taken, without a design of sufficient magnitude to justify the hazard. The tender age of the stripling, too, forbade the belief that he was unaccompanied. But he silently agreed with his labouring man that the capture would probably cause the attack, if any such were meditated, to be deferred. He therefore instructed his wife to withdraw into her chamber, while he took measures to defend the dwelling in the last emergency. Without giving any unnecessary alarm, a measure that would have produced less effect on the wily enemy without than the imposing stillness which now reigned within the defences, he ordered two or three more of the stoutest of his dependants to be summoned to the palisadoes. A keen scrutiny was made into the state of all the different outlets of the place ; muskets were carefully examined ; charges were given to be watchful, and regular sentinels were stationed within the shadows of the buildings, at points where, unseen themselves, they could look out in safety upon the fields.

Content then took his captive, with whom he had made no attempt to exchange a syllable, and led him to the block-house. The door which communicated with the basement of this building was always open, in readiness for refuge in the event of any sudden alarm. He entered, caused the lad to mount by a ladder to the floor above, and then, withdrawing the means of retreat, he turned the key without, in perfect confidence that his prisoner was secure.

Notwithstanding all this care, morning had nearly

dawned before the prudent father and husband sought his pillow. His steadiness, however, had prevented the apprehensions, which kept his own eyes and those of his gentle partner so long open, from extending beyond the few whose services were, in such an emergency, deemed indispensable to safety. Towards the last watches of the night only, did the images of the scenes through which they had just passed become dim and confused, and then both husband and wife slept soundly, and without disturbance.

CHAPTER V.

Are you so brave ? I 'll have you talked with anon.
Coriolanus.

THE axe and the brand had been early and effectually used immediately around the dwelling of the Heathcotes. A double object had been gained by removing most of the vestiges of the forest from the vicinity of the building ; the necessary improvements were executed with greater facility —and, a consideration of no small importance, the cover, which the American savage is known to seek in his attacks, was thrown to a distance that greatly diminished the danger of a surprise.

Favoured by the advantage which had been obtained by this foresight, and by the brilliancy of a night that soon emulated the brightness of day, the duty of Eben Dudley and of his associate on the watch was rendered easy of accomplishment. Indeed, so secure did they become towards morning, chiefly on account of the capture of the Indian lad, that more than once eyes, that should have been differently employed, yielded to the drowsiness of the hour and to habit, or were only opened at intervals that left their owners in some doubt as to the passage of the intermediate time. But no sooner did the signs of day approach, than, agreeably to their instructions, the watchers sought their beds, and for an hour or two they slept soundly and without fear.

It was only when his father had closed the prayers of the morning, that Content, in the midst of the assembled family, communicated as many of the incidents of the past night as in his judgment seemed necessary. His discretion limited the narrative to the capture of the native youth, and to the manner in which he had ordered the watch for the security of the family. On the subject of his own excursion to the forest, and all connected therewith, he was guardedly silent.

It is unnecessary to relate the manner in which this startling information was received. The cold and reserved brow of the Puritan became still more thoughtful; the young men looked grave but resolute; the maidens of the household grew pale, shuddered, and whispered hurriedly together; while the little Ruth, and a female child of nearly her own age, named Martha, clung close to the side of the mistress of the family, who, having nothing new to learn, had taught herself to assume the appearance of a resolution she was far from feeling.

The first visitation which befell the listeners, after their eager ears had drunk in the intelligence Content so briefly imparted, was a renewal of the spiritual strivings of his father in the form of prayer. A particular petition was put up in quest of light on their future proceedings, for mercy on all men, for a better mind to those who wandered through the wilderness seeking victims of their wrath, for the gifts of grace on the heathen, and finally for victory over all their carnal enemies, let them come whence or in what aspect they might.

Fortified by these additional exercises, old Mark next made himself master of all the signs and evidences of the approach of danger, by a more rigid and minute enquiry into the visible circumstances of the arrest of the young savage. Content received a merited and grateful reward for his prudence, in the approbation of one whom he still continued to revere with a mental dependence little less than that with which he had leaned on his wisdom in the days of his own childhood.

" Thou hast done well and wisely," said his father;
" but more remaineth to be performed by thy wisdom and
fortitude. We have had tidings that the heathen near the
Providence plantations are unquiet, and that they are lending their minds to wicked counsellors. We are not to
sleep in too much security, because a forest journey of a
few days lies between their villages and our own clearing.
Bring forth the captive; I will question him on the
matter of this visit."

Until now, so much did the fears of all turn towards the
enemies who were believed to be lurking near, that little
thought had been bestowed on the prisoner in the block-
house. Content, who well knew the invincible resolution,
no less than the art, of an Indian, had forborne to question
him when taken; for he believed the time to be better
suited to vigilant action, than to interrogatories which the
character of the boy was likely to render perfectly useless.
He now proceeded, however, with an interest that began to
quicken as circumstances rendered its indulgence less
unsuitable, to seek his captive, in order to bring him before
the searching ordeal of his father's authority.

The key of the lower door of the block-house hung where
it had been deposited; the ladder was replaced, and Content
mounted quietly to the apartment where he had placed his
captive. The room was the lowest of three that the building contained, all being above that which might be termed
its basement. The latter, having no aperture but its door,
was a dark, hexagonal space, partly filled with such articles
as might be needed in the event of an alarm, and which,
at the same time, were frequently required for the purposes of domestic use. In the centre of the area was a
deep well, so fitted and protected by a circular wall of
stone, as to admit of water being drawn into the rooms
above, which served the double purpose of a communication
with the shaft, and that of an additional support to the
wooden superstructure itself. The door was of massive
hewn timber. The squared logs of the upper stories projected a little beyond the stonework of the basement, the
second tier of the timbers containing a few holes, out of
which missiles might be discharged downwards, on any

assailants that approached nearer than should be deemed safe for the security of the basement. As has been stated, the two principal stories were perforated with long narrow slits through the timber, which answered the double purposes of windows and loop-holes. Though the apartments were so evidently arranged for defence, the plain domestic furniture they contained was suited to the wants of the family, should they be driven to the building for refuge. There was also an apartment in the roof, or attic, as already mentioned, but it scarcely entered into the more important uses of the block-house. Still the advantage which it received from its elevation was not overlooked. A small cannon, of a kind once known and used in the forests under the name of grasshoppers, had been raised to the place, and there had been a time when it was rightly considered as of the last importance to the safety of the inmates of the dwelling. For some years its muzzle had been seen, by all the straggling aborigines who visited the valley, frowning through one of those openings which were now converted into glazed windows; and there is reason to think, that the reputation which the little piece of ordnance thus silently obtained, had a powerful agency in so long preserving the peace of the valley unmolested.

The word unmolested is, after all, perhaps too strong. More than one alarm had in fact occurred, though no positive acts of violence had ever been committed within the limits which the Puritan claimed as his own. On only one occasion, however, did matters proceed so far that the veteran had been induced to take his post in this warlike attic, where there is little doubt, had occasion further offered for his services, he would have made a suitable display of his knowledge in the science of gunnery. But the simple history of the Wish-Ton-Wish had furnished another evidence of a political truth which cannot be too often presented to the attention of our countrymen; we mean that which is contained in the maxim that the best preservative of peace is preparation for war. In the case before us, the hostile attitude assumed by old Mark and his dependants effected all that was desirable, without proceeding to the extremity of shedding blood. Such peaceful triumphs were far more in accordance with the present principles of the Puritan than they would have been with the reckless temper which governed his youth. In the quaint and fanatical humour of the times, he had held a family thanksgiving around the instrument of their secu-rity, and from that moment the room itself became a favourite resorting place for the old soldier. Thither he often mounted, even in the hours of deep night, to indulge in those secret spiritual exercises which formed the chiefest solace, and seemingly, indeed, the great employment, of his life. In consequence of this habit, the attic of the block-house came in time to be considered sacred to the uses of the master of the valley. The care and thought of Con-tent gradually supplied it with many conveniences that might contribute to the personal comfort of his father while his spirit was engaged in these earnest mental conflicts. At length, the old man began to use the mattress that, among other things, it now contained, and to pass the whole time between the setting and rising of the sun in its solitude. The aperture originally cut for the exhibition of the grasshopper was glazed, and no article of comfort, which was once carried up the difficult ladder that led to the chamber, was ever seen to descend.

There was something in the austere sanctity of old Mark Heathcote favourable to the practices of an anchorite, The youths of the dwelling regarded his unbending brow, and the undisturbed gravity of the eye it shadowed, with a respect allied to awe. Had the genuine benevolence of his character been less tried, or had he mingled in active life at a later period, it might possibly have been his fate to share in the persecutions which his countrymen heaped on those who were believed to deal with influences it is thought impious to exercise. Under actual circumstances, however, the sentiment went no farther than a deep and universal reverence, that left its object and the neglected little piece of artillery to the quiet possession of an apartment, to invade which would have been deemed an act bordering on sacrilege.

The business of Content, on the occasion which caused his present visit to the edifice whose history and description we have thought it expedient thus to give at some length, led him no farther than to the lowest of its more military apartments. On raising the trap, for the first time a feeling of doubt came over him, as to the propriety of having left the boy so long unsolaced by words of kindness or by deeds of charity. It was appeased by observing that his concern was awakened in behalf of one whose spirit was equal to greater trials.

The young Indian stood before one of the loops, looking out upon that distant forest in which he had so lately roamed at liberty, with a gaze too riveted to turn aside even at the interruption occasioned by the presence of his captor.

" Come from thy prison, child," said Content, in the tones of mildness; " whatever may have been thy motive in lurking around this dwelling, thou art human, and must know human wants: come forth then, and receive food; none will harm thee."

The language of commiseration is universal. Though the words of the speaker were evidently unintelligible to him for whose ears they were intended, their import was conveyed in the kindness of the accents. The eyes of the boy turned slowly from the view of the woods, and he looked his captor long and steadily in the face. Content now, indeed, discovered that he had spoken in a language that was unknown to his captive, and he endeavoured, by gestures of kindness, to invite the lad to follow. He was silently and quietly obeyed. On reaching the court, however, the prudence of a border proprietor in some degree overcame his feelings of compassion.

" Bring hither yon tether," he said to Whittal Ring, who at the moment was passing towards the stables; " here is one wild as the most untamed of thy colts. Man is of our nature and of our spirit, let him be of what colour it may have pleased Providence to stamp his features; but he who would have a young savage in his keeping on the morrow, must look sharply to his limbs to-day."

The lad submitted quietly, until a turn of the rope was passed around one of his arms; but when Content was fain to complete the work by bringing the other limb into the same state of subjection, the boy glided from his grasp, and cast the fetters from him in disdain. This act of decided resistance was, however, followed by no effort to escape. The moment his person was released from a confinement which he probably considered as implying distrust of his ability to endure pain with the fortitude of a warrior, the lad turned quietly and proudly to his captor, and, with an eye in which scorn and haughtiness were alike glowing, seemed to defy the fulness of his anger.

" Be it so," resumed the equal-minded Content; " if thou likest not the bonds, which, notwithstanding the pride of man, are often healthful to the body, keep then the use of thy limbs, and see that they do no mischief. Whittal, look thou to the postern, and remember it is forbidden to go afield until my father hath had this heathen under examination. The cub is seldom found far from the cunning of the aged bear."

He then made a sign to the boy to follow, and proceeded to the apartment where his father, surrounded by most of the family, awaited their coming. Uncompromising domestic discipline was one of the striking characteristics of the sway of the Puritans. That austerity of manner which was thought to mark a sense of a fallen and probationary state was early taught; for, among a people who deemed all mirth a sinful levity, the practice of self-command would readily come to be esteemed the basis of virtue. But whatever might have been the peculiar merit of Mark Heathcote and his household, in this particular, it was likely to be exceeded by the exhibition of the same quality in the youth who had so strangely become their captive.

We have already said that this child of the forests might have seen some fifteen years. Though he had shot upwards like a vigorous and thrifty plant, and with the freedom of a thriving sapling in his native woods rearing its branches towards the light, his stature had not yet reached that of men. In height, form, and attitudes, he was a model of active, natural, and graceful boyhood. But while his limbs were so fair in their proportions, they were scarcely muscular. Still every movement exhibited

a freedom and ease which announced the grace of childhood, without the smallest evidence of that restraint which
creeps into our air as the factitious feelings of later life
begin to assert their influence. The smooth, rounded
trunk of the mountain ash is not more upright and free
from blemish, than was the figure of this boy, who now
moved into the curious circle that opened for his entrance
and closed against his retreat, with the steadiness of one
who came to bestow, instead of appearing to receive,
judgment.

" I will question him," said old Mark Heathcote, attentively regarding the keen and settled eye that met his
long, stern gaze as steadily as a less intelligent creature of
the woods would return the look of man — " I will question him ; perchance fear will wring from his lips a confession of the evil that he and his have meditated against
me and mine."

" I think he is ignorant of our forms of speech," returned Content : " for the words of neither kindness nor
anger will force him to a change of feature."

" It is then meet that we commence by asking Him
who hath the secret to open all hearts to be our assistant."
The Puritan then raised his voice in a short and exceedingly particular petition, in which he implored the Ruler
of the universe to interpret his meaning during the forthcoming examination, in a manner that, had his request
been granted, would have savoured not a little of the mi-
raculous.   With this preparation he proceeded directly to
his task.   But neither questions, signs, nor prayer produced the slightest visible fruits.   The boy gazed at the
rigid and austere countenance of his interrogator while the
words were issuing from his lips ; but the instant they
ceased, his searching and quick eye rolled over the different
curious faces by which he was hemmed in, as if he trusted
more to the sense of sight than that of hearing for the information he naturally sought concerning his own future
lot.   It was found impossible to obtain from him any gesture or sound, that should betray either the purport of his
questionable visit, his own personal appellation, or that of
his tribe.

" I have been among the red skins of the Providence Plantations," Eben Dudley at length ventured to observe ; " and their language, though but a crooked and irrational jargon, is not unknown to me. With the leave of all present," he continued, regarding the Puritan in a manner to betray that this general term meant him alone, — " with the leave of all present, I will put it to the younker, in such a fashion that he will be glad to answer."

Receiving a look of assent, the borderer uttered certain uncouth and guttural sounds, which, notwithstanding they entirely failed of their effect, he stoutly maintained were the ordinary terms of salutation among the people to whom the prisoner was supposed to belong.

" I know him to be a Narragansett," continued Eben, reddening with vexation at his defeat, and throwing a glance of no peculiar amity at the youth who had so palpably refuted his claim to skill in the Indian tongues ; " you see he hath the shells of the sea-side worked into the bordering of his mocassins : and besides this sign, which is certain as that night hath its stars, he beareth the look of a chief that was slain by the Pequods, at the wish of us Christians, after an affair, in which, whether it was well done or ill done, I did some part of the work myself."

" And how call you that chief ? " demanded Mark.

" Why he had various names, according to the business he was on. To some he was known as the leaping Panther, for he was a man of an extraordinary jump ; and others again used to style him Pepperage, since there was a saying that neither bullet nor sword could enter his body ; though that was a mistake, as his death hath fully proven. But his real name, according to the uses and sounds of his own people, was My Anthony Mow."

" My Anthony Mow ! "

" Yes ; My, meaning that he was their chief ; Anthony being the given name, and Mow that of the breed of which he came, as I understand the matter," rejoined Eben, with confidence, satisfied that he had finally produced a sufficiently sonorous appellative, and a perfectly lucid etymological explanation. But criticism was diverted from its aim by the action of the prisoner, as these equi-

vocal sounds struck his ear. Ruth recoiled, and clasped
her little namesake closer to her side, when she saw the
dazzling brightness of his eyes, and the sudden and expressive dilation of his nostrils. For a moment, his lips
were compressed with more than the usual force of Indian
gravity, and then they slightly severed. A low, soft,
and, as even the startled matron was obliged to confess,
a plaintive sound issued from between them, repeating
mournfully —

" Miantonimoh!"

The word was uttered with a distinct but deeply guttural enunciation.

" The child mourneth for its parent," exclaimed the
sensitive mother. " The hand that slew that warrior may
have done an evil deed!"

" I see the evident and fore-ordering will of a wise
Providence in this," said Mark Heathcote, with solemnity.
" The youth hath been deprived of one who might have
enticed him still deeper into the bonds of the heathen, and
hither hath he been led in order to be placed upon the
straight and narrow path. He shall become a dweller
among mine, and we will strive against the evil of his
mind until instruction shall prevail. Let him be fed and
nurtured, equally with the things of life and the things of
the world, for who knoweth that which is designed in his
behalf!"

If there were more of faith than of rational conclusion
in this opinion of the old Puritan, there was no external
evidence to contradict it. While the examination of the
boy was going on in the dwelling, a keen scrutiny had
taken place in the out-buildings and in the adjacent fields.
Those engaged in this duty soon returned to say, that not
the smallest trace of an ambush was visible about the
place, and as the captive himself had no weapons of hostility, even Ruth began to hope that the mysterious conceptions of her father on the subject were not entirely
delusive. The captive was now fed, and old Mark was on
the point of making a proper beginning in the task he had
so gladly assumed, by an up-offering of thanks, when
Whittal Ring broke rudely into the room, and disturbed

the solemnity of his preparations by a sudden and boiste-rous outcry.

"Away with scythe and sickle !" shouted the witling ; "it's many a day since the fields of the Wish-Ton-Wish have been trodden down by horsemen in buff jerkins, or ambushed by creeping Wampanoags."

"There is danger at hand !" exclaimed the sensitive Ruth. "Husband, the warning was timely ; there is certainly great danger near."

"Here are truly some riding from the forest, and drawing nigh to the dwellings ; but as they are seemingly men of our kind and faith, we have need rather of rejoicing than terror. They bear the air of messengers from the R ver."

Mark Heathcote listened with surprise, and perhaps with a momentary uneasiness ; but all emotion passed away on the instant, for one so disciplined in mind rarely permitted an outward exposure of his secret thoughts. The Puritan calmly issued an order to replace the prisoner in the block-house, assigning the upper of the two prin-cipal floors for his keeping : and then he prepared himself to receive guests that were little wont to disturb the quiet of his secluded valley. He was still in the act of giving forth the necessary mandates, when the tramp of horses was heard in the court, and he was summoned to the door to greet his unknown visiters.

"We have reached Wish-Ton-Wish, and the dwelling of Captain Mark Heathcote," said one, who appeared, by his air and better attire, to be the principal of four that composed the party.

"By the favour of Providence, I call myself the un-worthy owner of this place of refuge."

"Then a subject so loyal, and a man who hath so long proved himself faithful in the wilderness, will not turn from his door the agents of his Anointed Master "

"There is one greater than any of earth, who hath taught us to leave the latch free. I pray you to alight, and to partake of that we can offer."

With this courteous but quaint explanation the horsemen dismounted, and giving their steeds into the keeping of the labourers of the farm, they entered the dwelling.

While the maidens of Ruth were preparing a repast suited to the hour and to the quality of the guests, Mark and his son had abundant opportunity to examine the appearance of the strangers. They were men who seemed to wear visages peculiarly adapted to the characters of their entertainers, being in truth so singularly demure and grave in aspect, as to excite some suspicion of their being newly converted zealots to the mortifying customs of the colony. Notwithstanding their extraordinary gravity, and contrary to the usages of those regions, too, they bore about their persons certain evidence of their being used to the fashions of the other hemisphere. The pistols attached to their saddle bows, and other accoutrements of a warlike aspect, would perhaps have attracted no observation, had they not been accompanied by a fashion in the doublet, the hat, and the boot, that denoted a greater intercourse with the mother country than was usual among the less sophisticated natives of those regions. None traversed the forests without the means of defence ; but, on the other hand, few wore the hostile implements with so much of a worldly air, or with so many minor particularities of some recent caprice in fashion. As they had however announced themselves to be officers of the king, they who of necessity must be chiefly concerned in the object of their visit, patiently awaited the pleasure of the strangers, to learn why duty had called them so far from the ordinary haunts of men : for, like the native owners of the soil, the self-restrained religionists appeared to reckon an indiscreet haste in any thing, among the more unmanly weaknesses. Nothing for the first half hour of their visit escaped the guarded lips of men evidently well skilled in their present duty, which might lead to a clue of its purport. The morning meal passed almost without discourse, and one of the party had arisen with the professed object of looking to their steeds, before he who seemed the chief led the conversation to a subject that, by its political bearing, might, in some degree, be supposed to have a remote connection with the principal object of his journey to that sequestered valley.

" Have the tidings of the gracious boon that hath lately flowed from the favour of the King reached this distant settlement?" asked the principal personage, one that wore a far less military air than a younger companion, who, by his confident mien, appeared to be the second in authority.

" To what boon hath thy words import?" demanded the Puritan, turning a glance of the eye at his son and daughter, together with the others in hearing, as if to ad_ monish them to be prudent.

" I speak of the Royal Charter, by which the people on the banks of the Connecticut, and they of the colony of New-Haven *, are henceforth permitted to unite in govern- ment; granting them liberty of conscience, and great free- dom of self-control."

" Such a gift were worthy of a king! Hath Charles truly done this?"

" That hath he, and much more that is fitting in a kind and royal mind. The realm is finally freed from the abuses of usurpers, and power now resteth in the hands of a race long set apart for its privileges."

" It is to be wished that practice shall render them ex_ pert and sage in its uses," rejoined Mark, somewhat drily.

" It is a merry prince! and one but little given to the study and exercises of his martyred father; but he hath great cunning in discourse, and few around his dread per- son have keener wit, or a more ready tongue."

Mark bowed his head in silence, seemingly little disposed to push the discussion of his earthly master's qualities to a conclusion that might prove offensive to so loyal an admirer. One inclining to suspicion would have seen, or thought he saw, certain equivocal glances from the stranger, while he was thus lauding the vivacious qualities of the restored mo- narch, which should denote a desire to detect how far the eulogiums might be grateful to his host. He acquiesced,

---

* The little state of Connecticut was originally divided into two small co- lonies; that of New-Haven and that of Connecticut. They were united about a century and a half ago under the provisions of a charter which continued to be its sole constitution until the year 1818.

however, in the wishes of the Puritan, though whether understandingly, or without design, it would have been difficult to say, and submitted to change the discourse.

" It is likely, by thy presence, that tidings have reached
the colonies from home," said Content, who understood, by
the severe and reserved expression of his father's features,
that it was a fitting time for him to interpose.

" There is one lately arrived in the Bay, by means of a
king's frigate ; but no trader hath yet passed between the
countries, except the ship which maketh the annual voyage
from Bristol to Boston."

" And he who hath arrived, doth he come with authority?" demanded Mark ; " or is he merely another servant
of the Lord, seeking to rear his tabernacle in the wilderness?"

" Thou shalt know the nature of his errand," returned
the stranger, casting a glance of malicious intelligence
obliquely towards his companions, at the same time that he
arose and placed in the hand of his host a commission which
evidently bore the seal of state.   " It is expected that all
aid will be given to one bearing this warranty, by a subject
of a loyalty so approved as that of Captain Mark Heathcote."

CHAPTER VI.

But, by your leave,
I am an officer of state, and come
To speak with ——   *Coriolanus.*

NOTWITHSTANDING the sharp look which the messenger of
the crown deliberately and now openly fastened on the
master of Wish-Ton-Wish, while the latter was reading
the instrument that was placed before his eyes, there was
no evidence of uneasiness to be detected in the unmoved
features of the latter. Mark Heathcote had too long schooled
his passions to suffer an unseemly manifestation of surprise

to escape him, and he was by nature a man of far too much nerve to betray alarm at a trifling exhibition of danger. Returning the parchment to the other, he said, with un-moved calmness, to his son,—

" We must open wide the doors of Wish-Ton-Wish. Here is one charged with authority to look into the secrets of all the dwellings of the colony." Then turning with dignity to the agent of the crown, he added, " Thou hadst better commence thy duty in season, for we are many, and occupy much space."

The face of the stranger flushed a little; it might have been with shame for the vocation in which he had come so far, or it might have been in resentment at so direct a hint that the sooner his disagreeable office should be ended the better it would please his host. Still he betrayed no inten-tion of shrinking from its performance. On the contrary, discarding somewhat of that subdued manner which he had probably thought it politic to assume while sounding the opinions of one so rigid, he broke out rather suddenly in the exhibition of a humour somewhat better suited to the tastes of him he served.

" Come, then," he cried, winking at his companions, " since doors are opened, it would speak ill of our breeding should we refuse to enter. Captain Heathcote hath been a soldier, and he knows how to excuse a traveller's freedom. Surely one who has tasted of the pleasures of the camp must weary at times of this sylvan life ! "

" The steadfast in faith weary not, though the road be long, and the wayfaring grievous."

" Hum —'t is pity that the journeying between merry England and these colonies is not more brisk. I do not presume to instruct a gentleman who is my senior, and peradventure my better, but opportunity is every thing in a man's fortunes. It were charity to let you know, worthy sir, that opinions have changed at home : it is full a twelvemonth since I have heard a line of the Psalms, or a verse of St. Paul quoted, in discourse ; at least by men who are at all esteemed for their discretion."

" This change in the fashion of speech may better suit

thy earthly than thy heavenly Master," said Mark Heathcote, sternly.

" Well, well, that peace may exist between us, we will
not bandy words about a text more or less, if we may
escape the sermon," rejoined the stranger, no longer affecting restraint, but laughing with sufficient freedom at nis
own conceit; a species of enjoyment in which his companions mingled with great good will, and without much
deference to the humour of those under whose roof they
found themselves.

A small glowing spot appeared on the pale cheek of the
Puritan, and disappeared again, like some transient deception produced by the play of light.   Even the meek eye of
Content kindled at the insult ; but, like his father, the
practice of self-denial, and a never slumbering consciousness
of his own imperfections, smothered the momentary exhibition of displeasure.

" If thou hast authority to look into the secret places of
our habitations, do thy office," he said, with a peculiarity
of tone which served to remind the other, that though he
bore the commission of the Stuart, he was in an extremity
of his empire, where even the authority of a king lost
some of its value.

Affecting to be, and possibly in reality conscious of his
indiscretion, the stranger hastily disposed himself to the
execution of his duty.

" It would be a great and a pain-saving movement," he said, " were we to assemble the household
in one apartment.   The government at home would be
glad to hear something of the quality of its lieges in this
distant quarter.   Thou hast doubtless a bell to summon
thy flock at stated periods."

" Our people are yet near the dwelling," returned Content : " if it be thy pleasure, none shall be absent from the
search."

Gathering from the eye of the other that he was
serious in this wish, the quiet colonist proceeded to the
gate, and placing a shell to his mouth, blew one of those
blasts that are so often heard in the forests summoning families to their homes, and which are alike used as the

signals of peaceful recall, or of alarm. The sound soon brought all within hearing to the court, whither the Puritan and his unpleasant guests now repaired, as the spot best suited to the purposes of the latter.

" Hallam," said the principal personage of the four visiters, addressing him who might once have been, if he were not still, some subaltern in the forces of the crown, for he was attired in a manner that bespoke him but a half-disguised dragoon, " I leave thee to entertain this goodly assemblage. Thou mayest pass the time in discoursing on the vanities of the world, of which I believe few are better qualified to speak understandingly than thyself ; or a few words of admonition to hold fast to the faith would come with fitting weight from thy lips. But look to it, that none of thy flock wander ; for here must every creature of them remain, stationary as the indiscreet partner of Lot, till I have cast an eye into all the cunning places of their abode. So set wit at work, and show thy breeding as an entertainer."

After this irreverent charge to his subordinate, the speaker signified to Content and his father that he and his remaining attendant would proceed to a more minute examination of the premises.

When Mark Heathcote saw that the man who had so rudely broken in upon the peaceful habits of his family was ready to proceed, he advanced steadily in his front, like one who boldly invited enquiry, and by a grave gesture desired him to follow. The stranger, perhaps, as much from habit as from any settled design, first cast a free glance around at the bevy of fluttered maidens, leered even upon the modest and meek-eyed Ruth herself, and then took the direction indicated by him who had so unhesitatingly assumed the office of a guide.

The object of this examination still remained a secret between those who made it and the Puritan, who had probably found its motive in the written warranty which had been submitted to his inspection. That it proceeded from fitting authority none might doubt ; and that it was in some manner connected with the events that were known to have wrought so sudden and so great a change in the govern-

ment of the mother country, all believed probable.   Notwithstanding the seeming mystery of the procedure, the
search was not the less rigid.   Few habitations, of any
size or pretension, were erected in those times, which did
not contain certain secret places, where valuables and even
persons might be concealed at need.   The strangers displayed
great familiarity with the nature and ordinary positions
of these private recesses.   Not a chest, a closet, or even a
drawer of size, escaped their vigilance, nor was there a
plank that sounded hollow, but the master of the valley
was called on to explain the cause.   In one or two
instances, boards were wrested violently from their fastenings, and the cavities beneath were explored with a wariness that increased as the investigation proceeded without
success.

The strangers appeared irritated by their failure.   An
hour passed in the keenest scrutiny, and nothing had
transpired which brought them any nearer to their object.
That they had commenced the search with more than
usually confident anticipations of a favourable result, might
have been gathered from the boldness of tone assumed by
their chief, and the pointed personal allusions in which,
from time to time, he indulged, often too freely, and always.
at some expense to the loyalty of the Heathcotes.   But
when he had completed the circuit of the buildings, having
entered all parts from their cellars to the garrets, his spleen
became so strong as, in some degree, to get the better of a
certain parade of discretion, which he had hitherto managed
to maintain in the midst of all his levity.

" Hast seen nothing, Mr. Hallam ? " he demanded of
the individual left on watch, as they crossed the court in
retiring from the last of the outbuildings ; " or have those
traces which led us to this distant settlement proved false ?
Captain Heathcote, you have seen that we come not without sufficient warranty, and it is in my power to say we
come not without sufficient —— "

Checking himself, as if about to utter more than was
prudent, he suddenly cast an eye on the block-house and
demanded its uses.

" It is, as thou seest, a building erected for the purposes

of defence," replied Mark; "one to which, in the event of an inroad of the savages, the family may fly for refuge."

"Ah! these citadels are not unknown to me. I have met with others during my journey, but none so formidable or so military as this. It hath a soldier for its governor, and should hold out for a reasonable siege. Being a place of pretension, we will look closer into its mystery."

He then signified an intention to close the search by an examination of this edifice. Content unhesitatingly threw open its door, and invited him to enter.

"On the word of one who, though now engaged in a more peaceful calling, has been a campaigner in his time, 't would be no child's play to carry this tower without artillery. Had thy spies given notice of our approach, Captain Heathcote, the entrance might have been more difficult than we now find it. We have a ladder, here! Where the means of mounting are found, there must be something to tempt one to ascend. I will taste your forest air from an upper room."

"You will find the apartments above, like this below, merely provided for the security of the unoffending dwellers of the habitations," said Content, while he quietly arranged the ladder before the trap, and then led the way himself to the floor above.

"Here have we loops for the musketoons," cried the stranger, looking about him, understandingly, "and reasonable defences against shot. Thou hast not forgotten thy art, Captain Heathcote, and I consider myself fortunate in having entered thy fortress by surprise, or, I should rather say, in amity, since the peace is not yet broken between us. But why have we so much of household gear in a place so evidently equipped for war?"

"Thou forgettest that women and children may be driven to this block for a residence," replied Content. "It would show little discretion to neglect matters that might be useful to their wants."

"Is there trouble with the savages?" demanded the stranger, a little quickly; "the gossips of the colony bade us fear nothing on that head."

"One cannot say at what hour creatures trained in their

wild natures may choose to rise. The dwellers on the borders, therefore, never neglect a fitting caution."

" Hist!" interrupted the stranger; " I hear a footstep above. Ha! the scent will prove true at last! Hilloa, Master Hallam!" he cried from one of the loops, " let thy statues of salt dissolve, and come hither to the tower. Here is work for a regiment; for well do we know the nature of that we are to deal with."

The sentinel in the court shouted to his companion in the stables, and then, openly and boisterously exulting in the prospects of a final success to a search which had hitherto given them useless employment throughout many a long day and weary ride, they rushed together to the block-house.

" Now, worthy lieges of a gracious master," said the leader, when he perceived himself backed by all his armed followers, and speaking with the air of a man flushed with success, " now quickly provide the means of mounting to the upper story. I have thrice heard the tread of man moving across that floor; though it hath been light and wary, the planks are tell-tales, and have not had their schooling."

Content heard the request, which was uttered sufficiently in the manner of an order, perfectly unmoved. Without betraying either hesitation or concern, he disposed himself to comply. Drawing the light ladder through the trap below, he placed it against the one above him, and ascending, he raised the door. He then returned to the floor beneath, making a quiet gesture to imply that they who chose might mount. But the strangers regarded each other with very visible doubts. Neither of the inferiors seemed disposed to precede his chief, and the latter evidently hesitated as to the order in which it was meet to make the necessary advance.

" Is there no other manner of mounting, but by this narrow ascent?" he asked.

" None: thou wilt find the ladder secure, and of no difficult height. It is intended for the use of women and children."

" Ay," muttered the officer, " but your women and

children are not called upon to confront the devil in a human form. Fellows, are thy weapons in serviceable condition? Here may be need of spirit ere we get our —— Hist! by the divine right of our gracious master, there is truly one stirring above. Harkee, my friend; thou knowest the road so well, we will choose to follow thy conduct."

Content, who seldom permitted ordinary events to disturb the equanimity of his temper, quietly assented, and led the way up the ladder, like one who saw no ground for apprehension in the undertaking. The agent of the crown sprang after him, taking care to keep as near as possible to the person of his leader, and calling to his inferiors to lose no time in backing him with their support. The whole mounted through the trap, with an alacrity nothing short of that with which they would have pressed through a dangerous breach; nor did either of the four take time to survey the lodgment he had made, until the whole party was standing in array, with hands grasping the handles of their pistols, or seeking, as it were instinctively, the hilts of their broadswords.

" By the dark visage of the Stuart!" exclaimed the principal personage, after satisfying himself by a long and disappointed gaze, that what he said was true, " here is nought but an unarmed savage boy!"

" Didst expect to meet else?" demanded the still unmoved Content.

" Hum—that which we expected to meet is sufficiently known to the quaint old gentleman below, and to our own good wisdom. If thou doubtest of our right to look into thy very hearts, warranty for that we do can be forthcoming. King Charles hath little cause to be tender of his mercies to the dwellers of these colonies, who lent but too willing ears to the whinings and hypocrisies of the wolves in sheep's clothing, of whom old England hath now so happily gotten rid. Thy buildings shall again be rummaged from the bricks of the chimney tops to the corner stone in thy cellars, unless thy deceit and rebellious cunning are abandoned, and the truth proclaimed with the openness and fairness of bold-speaking Englishmen."

" I know not what is called the fairness of bold-speaking Englishmen, since fairness of speech is not a quality of one people, or of one land ; but well I do know that deceit is sinful, and little of it, I humbly trust, is practised in this settlement. I am ignorant of what is sought, and therefore it cannot be that I meditate treachery."

" Thou hearest, Hallam ; he reasoneth on a matter touching the peace and safety of the King ! But why is this dark-skinned boy a prisoner ? Dost dare to constitute thyself a sovereign over the natives of this continent, and affect to have shackles and dungeons for such as meet thy displeasure ?"

" The lad is in truth a captive ; but he has been taken in defence of life, and hath little to complain of more than loss of freedom."

" I will enquire closely into this proceeding. Though commissioned on an errand of different interest, yet, as one trusted in a matter of moment, I take upon me the office of protecting every oppressed subject of the crown. There may grow discoveries out of this practice, Hallam, fit to go before the council itself."

" Thou wilt find but little here, worthy of the time and attention of those burdened with the care of a nation," returned Content. " The youthful heathen was found lurking near our habitations the past night, and he is kept where thou seest, that he may not carry the tidings of our condition to his people, who are, doubtless, outlying in the forest, waiting for the fit moment to work their evil."

" How meanest thou ?" hastily exclaimed the other, changing colour in spite of a desire to conceal his alarm ; " at hand in the forest, didst say ?"

" There can be little doubt. One young as this would scarce be found distant from the warriors of his tribe ; and that the more especially, as he was taken in the commission of an ambush."

" I hope thy people are not without good provision of arms, and other sufficient muniments of resistance. I trust the palisadoes are firm, and the posterns ingeniously defended."

" We look with a diligent eye to our safety ; for it is

well known to us dwellers on the borders, that there is
little security but in untiring watchfulness. The young
men were at the gates until the morning, and we did
intend to make a strong scouting into the woods as the
day advanced, in order to look for those signs that may
lead us to conclusions on the number and purposes of
those by whom we are environed, had not thy visit called
us to other duties."

" And why so tardy in speaking of this intent ?" demanded the agent of the King, leading the way down the
ladder with suspicious haste. " It is a commendable
prudence, and must not be delayed. I take upon me the
responsibleness of commanding that all proper care be had
in defence of the weaker subjects of the crown who are
here collected. Are our roadsters well replenished, Hallam?
Duty, as thou sayest, is an imperative master ; it recalls us
more into the heart of the colony. I would it might shortly
point the way to Europe !" he muttered as he reached the
ground. " Go, fellows ; see to our beasts, and let them
be speedily prepared for departure."

The attendants, though men of sufficient spirit in open
war, and when it was to be exercised in a fashion to which
they were accustomed, had, like other mortals, a wholesome
deference for unknown and terrific looking danger. It is
a well-known truth, and one that has been proved by the
experience of two centuries, that while the European soldier
has ever been readiest to have recourse to the assistance of
the terrible warrior of the American forest, he has, in
nearly every instance, when retaliation or accident has
made him the object instead of the spectator of the ruthless nature of his warfare, betrayed the most salutary, and
frequently the most abject and ludicrous apprehension of
the prowess of his ally. While Content, therefore, looked
so steadily, though still seriously, at the peculiar danger in
which he was placed, the four strangers seemingly saw all
of its horrors without any of the known means of avoiding
them. Their chief quickly abandoned the insolence of
office, and the tone of disappointment, for a mien of
greater courtesy ; and as policy is often seen suddenly to
change the sentiments of even more pretending personages,

when interests assume a new aspect, so did his language rapidly take a character of conciliation and courtesy.

The hand-maidens were no longer leered at ; the mistress of the dwelling was tr ated with marked deference ; and the air of deep respect, with which even the principal of the party addressed the aged Puritan, bordered on an exhibition of commendable reverence. Something was said in the way of apology for the disagreeable obligations of duty, and of a difference between a manner that was assumed to answer secret purposes, and that which nature and a sense of right would dictate`; but neither Mark nor his son appeared to have sufficient interest in the motives of their visiters, to put them to the trouble of repeating explanations, that were as awkward to those who uttered them, as they were unnecessary to those who listened.

So far from offering any further obstacle to the movements of the family, the borderers were seriously urged to pursue their previous intentions of thoroughly examining the woods. The dwelling was accordingly intrusted, under the orders of the Puritan, to the keeping of about half the labourers, assisted by the Europeans, who clung with instinctive attachment to the possession of the block-house ; their leader repeatedly and rightly enough declaring that, though ready at all times to risk life on a plain, he had an unconquerable distaste to putting it in jeopardy in a thicket. Attended by Eben Dudley, Reuben Ring, and two other stout youths, all well, though lightly armed, Content then left the palisadoes, and took his way towards the forest. They entered the woods at the nearest point, always marching with the caution and vigilance that a sense of the true nature of the risk they ran would inspire, and much practice only could properly direct.

The manner of the search was as simple as it was likely to prove effectual. The scouts commenced a circuit around the clearing, extending their line as far as might be done without cutting off support, and each man lending his senses attentively to the signs of the trail, or of the lairs, of those dangerous enemies who, they had reason to think, were outlying in their neighbourhood. But like the recent search in the buildings, the scouting was for a long time attended by no results. Many weary miles were passed slowly over, and more than half their task was ended and no sign of a being having life was met, except the very visible trail of their four guests, and the tracks of a single horse along a path leading to the settlements, from the quarter by which the visiter of the preceding night had been known to approach. No comments were made by any of the party, as each in succession struck and crossed this path, nearly at the same instant ; but a low call from Reuben Ring, which soon after met their ears, caused them to assemble in a body at the spot, whence the summons had proceeded.

" Here are signs of one passing *from* the clearing," said the quick-eyed woodsman, " and of one too that is not numbered among the family of Wish-Ton-Wish ; since his beast hath had a shodden hoof, a mark which belongeth to no animal of ours."

" We will follow," said Content, immediately striking in upon a straggling trail, that by many unequivocal signs had been left by some animal which had passed that way not many hours before. Their search, however, soon grew to a close. Ere they had gone any great distance, they came upon the half-demolished carcass of a dead horse. There was no mistaking the proprietor of this unfortunate animal. Though some beast, or rather beasts, of prey, had fed plentifully on the body, which was still fresh, and had scarcely yet done bleeding, it was plain, by the remains of the torn equipments, as well as by the colour and size of the animal, that it was no other than the hack ridden by the unknown and mysterious guest, who, after sharing in the worship and in the evening meal of the family of the Wish-Ton-Wish, had so strangely and so suddenly disappeared. The leathern sack, the weapons which had so singularly rivetted the gaze of old Mark, and indeed all but the carcass and a ruined saddle, were gone ; but what was left sufficiently served to identify the animal.

" Here has been the tooth of wolf," said Eben Dudley, stooping to examine into the nature of a ragged wound in the neck ; " and here, too, has been cut of knife ; but whether by the hand of a red-skin it exceedeth my art to say."

Each individual of the party now bent curiously over the wound ; but the results of their enquiries went no further than to prove that the carcass was undeniably that of the horse of the stranger. To the fate of its master, however, there was not the slightest clue. Abandoning the investigation, after a long and fruitless examination, they proceeded to finish the circuit of the clearing. Night had approached ere the fatiguing task was accomplished. As Ruth stood at the postern, waiting anxiously for their return, she saw, by the countenance of her husband, that, while nothing had transpired to give any grounds of additional alarm, no satisfactory testimony had been obtained to explain the nature of the painful doubts with which, as a tender and sensitive mother, she had been distressed throughout the day.

CHAPTER VII.

Is there not milking-time,
When you go to bed, or kiln-hole,
To whistle off these secrets ; but you must be
Tattling before all our guests?   *Winter's Tale.*

Long experience hath shown that the white man, when placed in situations to acquire such knowledge, readily becomes the master of most of that peculiar skill for which the North American Indian is so remarkable, and which enables him, among other things, to detect the signs of a forest trail, with a quickness and an accuracy of intelligence that amount nearly to an instinct. The fears of the family were therefore greatly quieted by the reports of the scouts, all of whom agreed in the opinion that no party of savages, that could be at all dangerous to a force like their own, was lying near the valley ; and some of whom, the loudest of which number being stout Eben Dudley, boldly offered to answer for the security of those who depended on their vigilance with their own lives. These assurances had, beyond a doubt, a soothing influence on the apprehensions of Ruth and her hand-maidens ; but they somewhat failed

of their effect with those unwelcome visiters who still continued to cumber the Wish-Ton-Wish with their presence.
Though they had evidently abandoned all ideas connected
with the original object of their visit, they spoke not of departure. On the contrary, as night approached, their chief
entered into council with old Mark Heathcote; and made
certain propositions for the security of his dwelling which
the Puritan saw no reason to oppose.

A regular watch was in consequence set, and maintained
till morning, at the palisadoes. The different members of
the family retired to their usual places of rest, tranquil in
appearance, if not in entire confidence of peace ; and the
military messengers took post in the lower of the two fighting apartments of the citadel. With this simple, and, to the
strangers, particularly satisfactory arrangement, the hours
of darkness passed away in quiet, morning returning to the
secluded valley, as it had so often done before, with its loveliness unimpaired by violence or tumult.

In the same peaceful manner did the sun set successively
three several times, and as often did it arise on the abode of
the Heathcotes without further sign of danger, or motive
of alarm. With the passage of time, the agents of the
Stuart gradually regained their confidence. Still, they never
neglected to withdraw within the protection of the block-
house with the retiring light, a post which the subordinate
named Hallam more than once gravely observed they were,
by their disciplined and military habits, singularly qualified
to maintain. Though the Puritan secretly chafed under
this protracted visit, habitual self-denial, and a manner so
long subdued, enabled him to conceal his disgust. For the
first two days after the alarm, the deportment of his guests
was unexceptionable. All their faculties appeared to be
engrossed with keen and anxious watchings of the forest,
out of which, it would seem, they expected momentarily to
see a band of ferocious and ruthless savages issue ; but
symptoms of returning levity began to be apparent, as confidence and a feeling of security increased with the quiet
passage of the hours.

It was on the evening of the third day from that on
which they had made their appearance in the settlement,

that the man called Hallam was seen strolling, for the first time, through the postern so often named, and taking a direction which led towards the outbuildings. His air was less distrustful than it had been for many a weary hour, and his step proportionably confident and assuming. Instead of wearing, as had been his wont, a pair of heavy horseman's pistols at his girdle, he had even laid aside his broad-sword, and appeared more in the guise of one who sought his personal ease, than in that cumbersome and martial attire which all of his party, until now, had deemed it prudent to maintain. He cast his glance cursorily over the fields of the Heathcotes, as they glowed under the soft light of a setting sun; nor did his eye even refuse to wander vacantly along the outline of that forest, which his imagination had so lately been peopling with beings of a fierce and ruthless nature.

The hour was one when rustic economy brings the labours of the day to a close. Among those who were more than usually active at that busy moment was a hand-maiden of Ruth, whose clear sweet voice was heard in one of the enclosures, occasionally rising on the notes of a spiritual song, and as often sinking to a nearly inaudible hum, as she extracted from a favourite animal liberal portions of its nightly tribute to the dairy of her mistress. To that enclosure the stranger, as it were by accident, suffered his sauntering footsteps to stroll, seemingly as much in admiration of the sleek herd, as of any other of its comely tenants.

" From what thrush hast taken lessons, my pretty maid, that I mistook thy notes for one of the sweetest songsters of thy woods?" he asked, trusting his person to the support of the pen, in an attitude of easy superiority. " One might fancy it a robin or a wren, trolling out his evening song, instead of human voice rising and falling in every-day psalmody."

" The birds of our forest rarely speak," returned the girl; " and the one among them which has most to say does it like those who are called gentlemen, when they set wit to work to please the ear of simple country maidens."

" And in what fashion may that be?"

" Mockery."

" Ah! I have heard of the creature's skill. It is said
to be a compound of the harmony of all other forest
songsters ; and yet I see little resemblance to the honest
language of a soldier in its manner of utterance."

" It speaketh without much meaning ; and oftener to
cheat the ear than in honest reason."

" Thou forgettest that which I told thee in the morning,
child. It would seem that they who named thee have no
great cause to exult in their judgment of character, since
Unbelief would better describe thy disposition than Faith."

" It may be that they who named me, little knew how
great must be credulity to give ear to all I have been
required to credit."

" Thou canst have no difficulty in admitting that thou
art comely, since the eye itself will support thy belief ; nor
can one of so quick speech fail to know that her wit is
sharper than common. Thus far, I admit, the name of
Faith will not surely belie thy character."

" If Eben Dudley hear thee use such vanity-stirring
discourse," returned the half-pleased girl, " he might give
thee less credit for wit than thou seemest willing to yield
to others. I hear his heavy foot among the cattle, and ere
long we shall be sure to see a face that hath little more of
lightness to boast."

" This Eben Dudley is a personage of no mean importance, I find !" muttered the other, continuing his walk,
as the borderer named made his appearance at another entrance of the pen. The glances exchanged between them
were far from friendly, though the woodsman permitted
the stranger to pass without any oral expression of displeasure.

" The skittish heifer is getting gentle at last, Faith
Ring," said the borderer, casting the butt of his musket on
the ground with a violence that left a deep impression on the
faded sward at his feet. " That brindled ox, old Logger,
is not more willing to come into his yoke, than is the four-
year-old to yield her milk."

" The creature has been getting kind, since you taught
me the manner to tame its humour," returned the dairy

G

girl, in a voice that, in spite of every effort of maiden pride, betrayed something of the flurry of her spirits, while she plied her light task with violent industry.

"Umph! I hope some other of my teachings may be as well remembered; but thou art quick at the trick of learning, Faith, as is plain by the ready manner in which thou hast so shortly got the habit of discourse with a man as nimble-tongued as yon riding reprobate from over sea."

"I hope that civil listening is no proof of unseemly discourse on the part of one who hath been trained in modesty of speech, Eben Dudley. Thou hast often said it was the bounden duty of her who was spoken to, to give ear, lest some might say she was of scornful mind, and her name for pride be better earned than that for good nature."

"I see that more of my lessons than I had hoped for are remembered. So thou listenest thus readily, Faith, because it is meet that a maiden should not be scornful!"

"Thou sayest so. Whatever ill name I may deserve, thou hast no right to count scorn among my failings."

"If I do, may I—" Eben Dudley bit his lip, and checked an expression which would have given grievous offence to one whose habits of decency were as severe as those of his companion. "Thou must have heard much that was profitable to-day, Faith Ring," he added, "considering that thy ear is so open, and that thy opportunities have been great."

"I know not what thou wouldst say by speaking of my opportunities," returned the girl, bending still lower beneath the object of her industry, in order to conceal the glow which her own quick consciousness told her was burning on her cheek.

"I would say that the tale must be long that needeth four several trials of private speech to finish."

"Four!—as I hope to be believed for a girl of truth in speech or deed, this is but the third time that the stranger hath spoken to me apart, since the sun hath risen."

"If I know the number of the fingers of my hand, it is the fourth!"

" Nay, how canst thou, Eben Dudley, who hast [been afield since the crowing of the cock, know what hath passed about the dwellings? It is plain that envy, or some other evil passion, causeth thee to speak angrily."

" How is it that I know!— perhaps thou thinkest, Faith, thy brother Reuben only hath the gift of sight."

" The labour must have gone on with great profit to the Captain, whilst his people's eyes have been roving over other matters! But perhaps they kept the strong of arm for the lookers-out, and have set them of feebler bodies to the toil."

" I have not been so careless of thy life as to forget, at passing moments, to cast an eye abroad, pert one. Whatever thou mayst think of the need, there would be fine wailings in the butteries and dairies, did the Wompanoags get into the clearing, and were there none to give the alarm in season."

" Truly, Eben, thy terror of the child in the block must be grievous for one of thy manhood, else wouldst thou not watch the buildings so narrowly," retorted Faith, laughing; for, with the dexterity of her sex, she began to feel the superiority she was gradually obtaining over her admirer. " Thou dost not remember that we have valiant troopers from old England, to keep the younker from doing harm! But here cometh the brave soldier himself: it will be well to ask vigilance at his hands, or this very night may bring us to the tomahawk in our sleep!"

" Thou speakest of the weapon of the savages!" said the messenger, who had drawn near again, with a visible willingness to share in an interview which, while he had watched its progress at a distance, appeared to be growing interesting. " I trust all fear is over from that quarter."

" As you say, for *this* quarter," said Eben, adjusting his lips to a low whistle, and coolly looking up to examine the heavenly body to which he meant allusion. " But the *next* quarter may bring us a pretty piece of Indian skirmishing."

" And what hath the moon in common with an incursion of the savages? Are there those among them, who study the secrets of the stars?"

" They study deviltries and other wickedness, more than
aught else.   It is not easy for the mind of man to fancy
horrors such as they design, when Providence has given
them success in an inroad."

" But thou didst speak of the moon.   In what manner
is the moon leagued with their bloody plots?"

" We have her now in the full, and there is little of the
night when the eye of a watcher might not see a red skin
in the clearing : but a different tale may be heard when
an hour or two of jet darkness shall again fall among these
woods.   There will be a change shortly ; it behoveth us,
therefore, to be on our guard."

" Thou thinkest then, truly, that there are outlyers
waiting for the fitting moment," said the officer, with an
interest so marked as to cause even the but half pacified
Faith to glance an arch look at her companion, though he
still had reason to distrust a wilful expression that lurked
in the corner of her eyes, which threatened at each moment
to contradict his relation of the sinister omens.

" There may be savages lying in the hills at a day's
journey in the forest : but they know the aim of a white
man's musket too well to be sleeping within reach of its
range.   It is the nature of an Indian to eat and sleep
while he has time for quiet, and to fast and murder when
the killing hour hath come."

" And what call you the distance to the nearest settlement on the Connecticut?" demanded the other, with an
air so studiously indifferent as to furnish an easy clue to
the inner workings of his mind.

" Some twenty hours would bring a nimble runner to
the outer habitations, granting small time for food and rest.
He that is wise, however, will take but little of the latter,
until his head be safely housed within some such building
as yon block, or until there shall stand between him and
the forest at least a goodly row of oaken pickets."

" There is no path ridden by which travellers may
avoid the forest during the darkness?"

" I know of none.   He who quits Wish-Ton-Wish for
the towns below, must make his pillow of the earth, or be
fain to ride as long as beast can carry."

" We have truly had experience of this necessity, journeying hither. Thou thinkest, friend, the savages are in their
resting time, and that they wait the coming quarter of the
moon ? "

" To my seeming we shall not have them sooner," returned Eben Dudley, taking care to conceal all qualification
of this opinion, if any such he entertained, by closely
locking its purport in a mental reservation.

" And what season is it usual to choose for getting
into the saddle, when business calls any to the settlements
below ? "

" We never fail to take our departure about the time
the sun touches the tall pine, which stands on yonder
height of the mountain. Much experience hath told us it
is the safest hour; hand of time-piece is not more sure
than yon tree."

" I like the night," said the other, looking about him
with the air of one suddenly struck with the promising
appearance of the weather. " The blackness no longer
hangs about the forest, and it seems a fitting moment to
push the matter on which we are sent nearer to its conclusion."

So saying, and probably believing that he had sufficiently
concealed the motive of his decision, the uneasy dragoon
walked with an air of soldierly coolness towards the dwellings, signing at the same time to one of his companions,
who was regarding him from a distance, to approach.

" Now dost thou believe, witless Dudley, that the four
fingers of thy clumsy hand have numbered the full amount
of all that thou callest my listenings !" said Faith, when
she thought no other ear but his to whom she spoke could
catch her words, and at the same time laughing merrily
beneath her heifer, though still speaking with a vexation
she could not entirely repress.

" Have I spoken aught but truth ? It is not for such
as I to give lessons in journeying, to one who follows the
honest trade of a man-hunter. I have said that which all
who dwell in these parts know to be reasonable."

" Surely not a word else ! But truth is made so powerful in thy hands, that it needs be taken, like a bitter heal-

ing draught, with closed eyes and at many swallows. One who drinketh of it too freely, may well nigh be strangled. I marvel that he who is so vigilant in providing for the cares of others, should take so little heed of those he is set to guard."

" I know not thy meaning, Faith. When was danger near the valley, and my musket wanting ?"

" The good piece is truer to its duty than its master. Thou mayest have lawful license to sleep on thy post, for we maidens know nothing of the pleasure of the Captain in these matters ; but it would be as seemly, if not as soldierly, to place the arms at the postern and thyself in the chambers, when next thou hast need of watching and sleeping in the same hour."

Dudley looked as confused as one of his mould and unbending temperament might well be, though he stubbornly refused to understand the allusion of his offended companion.

" Thou hast not discussed with the trooper from over sea in vain," he said, " since thou speakest so wisely of watches and arms."

" Truly he hath much schooled me in the matter."

" Umph ! and what may be the amount of his teaching ?"

" That he who sleepeth at a postern should neither talk too boldly of the enemy, nor expect maidens to put too much trust—"

" In what, Faith ?"

" Thou surely knowest I mean in his watchfulness. My life on it, had one happened to pass at a later hour than common near the night post of that gentle spoken soldier, he would not have been found, like a sentinel of this household in the second watch of the night that is gone, dreaming of the good things of the madam's buttery."

" Didst truly come then, girl ?" said Eben, dropping his voice, and equally manifesting his satisfaction and his shame. " But thou knowest, Faith, that the labour had fallen behind in behalf of the scouting party, and that the toil of yesterday exceeded that of our usual burthens. Nevertheless I keep the postern again to-night from eight to twelve, and——"

" Will make a goodly rest of it, I doubt not. No, he who hath been so vigilant throughout the day, must needs tire of the task as night draws on. Fare thee well, wakeful Dudley; if thine eyes should open on the morrow, be thankful that the maidens have not stitched thy garments to the palisadoes!"

Notwithstanding the efforts of the young man to retain her, the light-footed girl eluded his grasp, and bearing her burden towards the dairy, she tripped along the path with a half-averted face, in which triumph and repentance were already struggling for the possession.

In the mean time, the leader of the messengers and his military subordinate had a long and interesting conference. When it was ended, the former took his way to the apartment in which Mark Heathcote was wont to pass those portions of his time that were not occupied in his secret strivings for the faith, or in exercise without while superintending the labourers in the fields. With some little circumlocution, which was intended to mask his real motives, the agent of the King announced his intention to take his final departure that very night.

" I felt it a duty as one who has gained experience in arms by some practice in the wars of Europe," he said, " to tarry in thy dwelling while danger threatened from the lurking savage. It would ill become soldiers to speak of their intentions; but had the alarm in truth sounded, thou wilt believe me when I say that the blockhouse would not have been lightly yielded! I shall make report to them that sent me, that in Captain Mark Heathcote Charles hath a loyal subject, and the constitution a firm supporter. The rumours of a seemingly mistaken description, which have led us hither, shall be contradicted, and doubtless it will be found that some accident hath given rise to the deception. On the other hand, should there be occasion to dwell on the particulars of the late alarm, I trust the readiness of my followers to do good service to one of the King's subjects, will not be overlooked."

" It is the striving of a humble spirit to speak nought evil of its fellows, and to conceal no good," returned the

reserved Puritan. " If thou hast found thy abode in my
dwelling to thy liking, thou art welcome ; and if duty or
pleasure calleth thee to quit it, peace go with thee. It will
be useful to unite with us in asking that thy passage
through the wilderne s may be unharmed ; that He who
watcheth over the meanest of his creatures should take thee
in his especial keeping ; and that the savage heathen —"

" Dost think the savage out of his villages ? " demanded
the messenger, with an indecorous rapidity, that cut short
the enumeration of the particular blessings and dangers
that his host thought it meet to include in the leave-taking
prayer.

" Thou surely hast not tarried with us to aid in the defence, and yet feel it doubtful that thy services might be
useful ? " observed Mark Heathcote, drily.

" I would the Prince of Darkness had thee and all the
other diabolicals of these woods in his own good gripe ! "
muttered the messenger between his teeth ; and then, as if
guided by a spirit that could not long be quelled, he
assumed something more of his unbridled and natural air,
boldly declining to join in the prayer, on the plea of haste,
and the necessity of his looking in person to the movements of his followers. " But this need not prevent thee,
worthy Captain, from pouring out an asking in our behalf,
while we are in the saddle," he concluded ; " for ourselves,
there remaineth much of thy previously bestowed pious
aliment to be digested, though we doubt not that should thy
voice be raised in our behalf, while journeying along the
first few leagues of the forest, the tread of the hacks would
not be heavier, and, of a certainty, we ourselves should
be none the worse for the favour."

Then casting a glance of ill-concealed levity at one of his
followers, who had come to say that their steeds awaited,
he made the parting salutation with an air in which the
respect that one like the Puritan could scarce fail to excite,
struggled with his habitual contempt for things of a serious
character.

The family of Mark Heathcote, the lowest dependant
included, saw these strangers depart with great inward
satisfaction. Even the maidens, in whom nature, in mo-

ments weaker than common, had awakened some of the lighter vanities, were gladly rid of gallants, who could not soothe their ears with the unction of flattery without frequently giving great offence to their severe principles by light and irreverent allusions to things on which they themselves were accustomed to think with fitting awe. Eben Dudley could scarcely conceal the chuckle with which he saw the party bury themselves in the forest, though neither he, nor any of the more instructed in such matters, believed they incurred serious risk from their sudden enterprise.

The opinions of the scouts proved to be founded on accurate premises. That and many a subsequent night passed without alarm. The season continued to advance, and the labourers pursued their toil to its close, without another appeal to their courage, or any additional reasons for vigilance. Whittal Ring followed his colts with impunity among the recesses of the neighbouring forests, and the herds of the family went and came as long as the weather would permit them to range the woods, in regularity and peace. The period of the alarm, and the visit of the agents of the crown, came to be food for tradition: and during the succeeding winter, the former often furnished motive of merriment around the blazing fires that were so necessary to the country and the season.

Still there existed in the family a living memorial of the unusual incidents of that night. The captive remained, long after the events which had placed him in the power of the Heathcotes were beginning to be forgotten.

A desire to quicken the seeds of spiritual regeneration which, however dormant they might be, old Mark Heathcote believed to exist in the whole family of man, and consequently in the young heathen as well as in others, had become a sort of ruling passion in the Puritan. The fashions and mode of thinking of the times had a strong leaning towards superstition: and it was far from difficult for a man of his ascetic habits and exaggerated doctrines, to believe that a special interposition had cast the boy into his hands, for some hidden but mighty purpose, that time in the good season would not fail to reveal.

Notwithstanding the strong colouring of fanaticism which tinged the characters of the religionists of those days, they were rarely wanting in worldly discretion. The agents they saw fit to employ, in order to aid the more hidden purposes of Providence, were in common useful and rational. Thus, while Mark never forgot to summon the lad from his prison at the hour of prayer, or to include an especial asking, in behalf of the ignorant heathen in general, and of this chosen youth in particular, he hesitated to believe that a manifest miracle would be exerted in his favour. That no blame might attach to the portion of duty that was confided to human means, he had recourse to the discreet agency of kindness and unremitted care. But all attempts to lure the lad into the habits of a civilised man were completely unsuccessful. As the severity of the weather increased, the compassionate and thoughtful Ruth endeavoured to induce him to adopt the garments that were found so necessary to the comfort of men who were greatly his superiors in hardihood and in strength. Clothes, decorated in a fashion suited to the taste of an Indian, were considerately provided, and entreaties and threats were both freely used, with a view to make the captive wear them. On one occasion he was even forcibly clad by Eben Dudley, and being brought in the unwonted guise, into the presence of old Mark, the latter offered up an especial petition that the youth might be made to feel the merits of this concession to the principles of a chastened and instructed man. But within an hour, the stout woodsman, who had been made on this occasion so active an instrument of civilisation, announced to the admiring Faith that the experiment was unsuccessful ; or, as Eben somewhat irreverently described the extraordinary effort of the Puritan, " the heathen hath already resumed his skin leggings and painted waist-cloth, notwithstanding the Captain has strove to pin better garments on his back, by virtue of a prayer that might have clothed the nakedness of a whole tribe." In short the result proved, in the case of this lad, as similar experiments have since proved in so many other instances, the difficulty of tempting one trained in the freedom and ease of a savage, to consent to admit of the restraints of a state of being that

is commonly thought to be so much superior. In every
instance in which the youthful captive had liberty of choice,
he disdainfully rejected the customs of the whites, adhering,
with a singular and almost heroic pertinacity, to the usages
of his people and his condition.

The boy was not kept in his bondage without extra
ordinary care. Once, when trusted in the fields, he had
openly attempted to escape, nor was the possession of his
person recovered without putting the speed of Eben Dudley
and Reuben Ring to a more severe trial, as was confessed
by the athletic young borderers themselves, than any they
had hitherto undergone. From that moment he was never
permitted to pass the palisadoes. When duty called the
labourers afield the captive was invariably secured in his
prison, where, as some compensation for his confinement,
he was supposed to enjoy the benefit of long and familiar
communications with Mark Heathcote, who had the habit
of passing many hours of each day, and not unfrequently,
long portions of the night too, within the retirement of the
blockhouse. During the time only when the gates were
closed, or when some one of strength and activity sufficient
to control his movements was present, was the lad permitted to stroll, at will, among the buildings of the border
fortress. This liberty he never failed to exercise, and often
in a manner that overcame the affectionate Ruth with a
painful excess of sensibility.

Instead of joining in the play of the other children, the
young captive would stand aloof, and regard their sports
with a vacant eye : or, drawing near to the palisadoes, he
often passed hours in gazing wistfully at those endless forests
in which he first drew breath, and which probably contained all that was most prized in the estimation of his
simple judgment. Ruth, touched to the heart by this silent
but expressive exhibition of suffering, endeavoured in vain
to win his confidence, with a view of enticing him into
employments that might serve to relieve his care. The
resolute but still quiet boy would not be lured into a for-
getfulness of his origin. He appeared to comprehend the
kind intentions of his gentle mistress, and frequently he
even suffered himself to be led by the mother into the

centre of her own joyous and merry offspring, but it was only to look upon their amusements with his former cold air, and to return, at the first opportunity, to his beloved site at the pickets. Still there were singular and even mysterious evidences of a growing consciousness of the nature of the discourse of which he was occasionally an auditor, that would have betrayed greater familiarity with the language and opinions of the inhabitants of the valley, than his known origin and his absolute withdrawal from commmunication could give reason to expect. This important and inexplicable fact was proved by the frequent and meaning glances of his dark eye, when aught was uttered in his hearing that affected, ever so remotely, his own condition; and, once or twice, by the haughty gleamings of ferocity that escaped him, when Eben Dudley was heard to vaunt the prowess of the white men in their encounters with the original owners of the country. The Puritan did not fail to note these symptoms of a budding intelligence, as the pledges of a fruit that would more than reward his pious toil, and they served to furnish a great relief to certain occasional repugnance, which all his zeal could not entirely subdue, at being the instrument of causing so much suffering to one who, after all, had inflicted no positive wrong on himself.

At the period of which we are writing, the climate of these States differed materially from that which is now known to their inhabitants. A winter in the province of Connecticut was attended by many successive falls of snow, until the earth was entirely covered with firmly compressed masses of the frozen element. Occasional thaws and passing storms of rain, that were driven away by a return of the clear and cutting cold of the north-western gales, were wont at times to lay a covering on the ground that was congealed to the consistency of ice, until men, and not unfrequently beasts, and sometimes sleighs, were seen moving on its surface, as on the bed of a frozen lake. During the extremity of a season like this, the hardy borderers, who could not toil in their customary pursuits, were wont to range the forest in quest of game, which, driven for food to known resorting places in the woods, then fell most easily

a prey to the intelligence and skill of such men as Eben
Dudley and Reuben Ring.

The youths never left the dwellings on these hunts without exciting the most touching interest in their movements,
on the part of the Indian boy. On all such occasions he
would linger at the loops of his prison throughout the day,
listening intently to the reports of the distant muskets, as
they resounded in the forest, and the only time, during a
captivity of so many months, that he was ever seen to smile,
was when he examined the grim look and muscular claws
of a dead panther, that had fallen beneath the aim of
Dudley, in one of these excursions to the mountains. The
compassion of all the borderers was powerfully awakened
in behalf of the patient and dignified young sufferer, and
gladly would they have given their captive the pleasure of
joining in the chase, had not the task been one that was far
from easy of accomplishment. The former of the woodsmen just mentioned had even volunteered to lead him, like
a hound, in a leash ; but this was a species of degradation
against which it was certain that a young Indian, ambitious
of the character and jealous of the dignity of a warrior,
would have openly rebelled.

The quick interest of the observant Ruth had, as it
has been seen, early detected a growing intelligence in the
boy. The means by which one, who never mingled in the
employments, and who rarely seemed to listen to the
dialogues of the family, could come to comprehend the
meaning of a language that is found sufficiently difficult
for a scholar, were, however, as much of a mystery to her,
as to all around her. Still, by the aid of that instinctive
tact, which so often enlightens the mind of woman, was
she certain of the fact. Profiting by this knowledge, she
assumed the task of endeavouring to obtain an honorary
pledge from her protégé, that, if permitted to join the hunters, he would return to the valley at the end of the day.
But though the language of the woman was gentle as her
own kind nature, and her entreaties that he would give
some evidence of having comprehended her meaning were
zealous and oft repeated, not the smallest symptom of
intelligence, on this occasion, could be extracted from her

pupil. Disappointed, and not without sorrow, Ruth had abandoned the compassionate design in despair, when on a sudden, the old Puritan, who had been a silent spectator of her fruitless efforts, announced his faith in the integrity of the lad, and his intention to permit him to make one of the very next party that should leave the habitations.

The cause of this sudden change in the hitherto stern watchfulness of Mark Heathcote was, like so many other of his impulses, a secret in his own bosom. It has just been said, that during the time Ruth was engaged in her kind and fruitless experiment to extract some evidence of intelligence from the boy, the Puritan was a close and interested observer of her efforts. He appeared to sympathise in her disappointment; by the weal of those unconverted tribes who were to be led from the darkness of their ways by the instrumentality of this youth, was far too important to admit the thought of rashly losing the vantage ground he had gained, in the gradually expanding intellect of the boy, by running the hazard of an escape. To all appearance, the intention of permitting him to quit the defences had therefore been entirely abandoned, when old Mark so suddenly announced a change of resolution. The conjectures on the causes of this unlooked-for determination were exceedingly various. Some believed that the Puritan had been favoured with a mysterious intimation of the pleasure of Providence in the matter : and others thought that, beginning to despair of success in his undertaking, he was willing to seek for a more visible manifestation of its purposes, by hazarding the experiment of trusting the boy to the direction of his own impulses. All appeared to be of opinion, that if the lad returned, the circumstance might be set down to the intervention of a miracle. Still, with his resolution once taken, the purpose of Mark Heathcote remained unchanged. He announced this unexpected intention after one of his long and solitary visits to the blockhouse, where it is possible he had held a powerful spiritual strife on the occasion ; and, as the weather was exceedingly favourable for such an object, he commanded his dependants to prepare to make the sortie on the following morning.

A sudden and an uncontrollable gleam of delight flashed

on the dark features of the captive, when Ruth was about to place in his hands the bow of her own son, and, by signs and words, she gave him to understand that he was to be permitted to use it in the free air of the forest. But the exhibition of pleasure disappeared as quickly as it had been betrayed. When the lad received the weapons, it was rather with the manner of a hunter accustomed to their use, than of one to whose hands they had so long been strangers. As he left the gates of Wish-Ton-Wish, the handmaidens of Ruth clustered about him in wondering interest, for it was strange to see a youth so long guarded with jealous care, again free and unwatched. Notwithstanding their ordinary dependence on the secret lights and great wisdom of the Puritan, there was a very general impression that the lad, around whose presence there was so much that was mysterious and of interest to their own security, was now to be gazed upon for the last time. The boy himself was unmoved to the last. Still he paused, with his foot on the threshold of the dwelling, and appeared to regard Ruth and her young offspring with momentary concern. Then, assuming the calm air of an Indian warrior, he suffered his eye to grow cold and vacant, following with a nimble step the hunters who were already passing without the palisadoes.

CHAPTER VIII.

Well, I am your theme; you have the start of me; I am dejected; I am not able to answer the Welsh flannel; ignorance itself is a plummet over me: use me as you will.— *Merry Wives of Windsor.*

POETS, aided by the general longing of human nature, have given a reputation to the spring that it rarely merits. Though this imaginative class of writers have said so much of its balmy airs and odoriferous gales, we find it nearly everywhere the most reluctant, churlish, and fickle of the four seasons. It is the youth of the year, and, like that probationary period of life, most fitted to afford the promise of better things. There is a constant struggle between

reality and hope, throughout the whole of this slow-moving
and treacherous period, which has an unavoidable tendency
to deceive. All that is said of its grateful productions is
fallacious, for the earth is as little likely to yield a generous
tribute without the quickening influence of the summer
heats, as man is wont to bring forth commendable fruits,
without the agency of a higher moral power than any he
possesses in virtue of his innate propensities. On the other
hand, the fall of the year possesses a sweetness, a repose,
and a consistency, which may be justly likened to the decline
of a well-spent life. It is, in all countries, and in every
climate, the period when physical and moral causes unite
to furnish the richest sources of enjoyment. If the spring
is the time of hope, autumn is the season of fruition. There
is just enough of change to give zest to the current of
existence, while there is too little of vicissitude to be pregnant of disappointment. Succeeding to the nakedness of
winter, the spring is grateful chiefly by contrast, while the
glories of autumn are enjoyed and will sustain the comparison after the genial powers of summer have been
lavishly expended.

In obedience to this great law of the earth, let poets sing
and fancy as they may, the spring and autumn of America
partake largely of the universally distinctive characters of
the rival seasons. What nature has done on this continent
has not been done niggardly ; and while we may boast of
a decline of the year, that certainly rivals, and, with few
exceptions, eclipses the glories of most of the climates of the
old world, the opening months rarely fail of equalising the
gifts of Providence, by a very decided exhibition of all the
disagreeable qualities for which they are remarkable.

More than half a year had elapsed, between the time
when the Indian boy had been found lurking in the valley
of the Heathcotes and that day when he was first permitted to go into the forest, fettered by no other restraint than
the moral tie which the owner of the valley either knew,
or fancied, would not fail to cause him to return to a bondage he had found so irksome. It was April ; but it was
April as the month was known a century ago in Connecticut,
and as it is even now so often found to disappoint all ex-

pectations of that capricious season of the year. The weather
had returned suddenly and violently to the rigour of winter.
A thaw had been succeeded by a storm of snow and sleet,
and the interlude of the spring-time of blossoms had terminated with a biting gale from the north-west, which had
apparently placed a permanent seal on the lingering presence of a second February.

On the morning that Content led his followers into the
forest, they issued from the postern clad in coats of skin.
Their lower limbs were protected by the coarse leggings
which they had worn in so many previous hunts during
the past winter, if that might be called past which had returned, weakened but little of its keenness, and bearing all
the outward marks of January. When last seen, Eben
Dudley, the heaviest of the band, was moving firmly on
the crust of the snow, with a step as sure as if he had
trodden on the frozen earth itself. More than one of the
maidens declared, that though they had endeavoured to trace
the footsteps of the hunters from the palisadoes, it would
have exceeded even the sagacity of an Indian eye to follow
their trail along the icy path they travelled.

Hour after hour passed, without bringing tidings from
the chase. The reports of firearms had indeed been occasionally heard ringing among the arches of the woods, and
broken echoes were, for some hours, rolling from one recess
of the hills to another. But even these signs of the presence of the hunters gradually receded with the advance of
the day : and long ere the sun had gained the meridian,
and its warmth — at that advanced season, not without
power — was shed into the valley, the whole range of the
adjoining forest lay in its ordinary dull and solemn silence.

The incident of the hunt, apart from the absence of the
Indian boy, was one of too common occurrence to give
birth to any particular motives of excitement. Ruth quietly
busied herself among her women: and when the recollection
of those who were scouring the neighbouring forest came
at all to her mind, it was coupled with the care with which
she was providing to administer to their comforts, after the
fatigue of a day of extraordinary personal efforts. This
was a duty never lightly performed. Her situation was

H

one eminently fitted to foster the best affections of woman, since it admitted of few temptations to yield to other than the most natural feelings; she was, in consequence, known on all occasions to exercise them with the devotedness of her sex.

"Thy father and his companions will look on our care with pleasure," said the thoughtful matron to her youthful image, as she directed a more than usual provision of her larder to be got in readiness for the hunters; "home is ever sweetest after toil and exposure."

"I doubt if Mark be not ready to faint with so weary a march," said the child already introduced by the name of Martha; "he is young to go into the woods with scouters tall as great Dudley."

"And the heathen," added the little Ruth; "he is young too as Mark, though more used to the toil. It may be, mother, that he will never come to us more!"

"That would grieve our venerable parent; for thou knowest, Ruth, that he hath hopes of working on the mind of the boy, until his savage nature shall yield to the secret power. But the sun is falling behind the hill, and the evening is coming in cool as winter; go to the postern, and look out upon the fields. I would know if there be any signs of thy father and his party."

Though Ruth gave this mandate to her daughter, she did not the less neglect to exercise her own faculties in the same grateful office. While the children went, as they were ordered, to the outer gate, the matron herself ascended to the lower apartment of the block, and, from its different loops, she took a long and anxious survey of the limited prospect. The shadows of the trees, that lined the western side of the view, were already thrown far across the broad sheet of frozen snow, and the sudden chill, which succeeded the disappearance of the sun, announced the rapid approach of a night that promised to support the severe character of the past day. A freezing wind, which had brought with it the cold airs of the great lakes, and which had even triumphed over the more natural influence of an April sun, had however fallen, leaving a temperature not unlike that which dwells in the milder seasons of the year among the glaciers of the Upper Alps.

Ruth was too long accustomed to such forest scenes, and to such a " lingering of winter in the lap of May," to feel, on their account, any additional uneasiness. But the hour had now arrived when she had reason to look for the return of the hunters. With the expectation of seeing their forms issuing from the forest, came the anxiety which is an unavoidable attendant of disappointment. The shadows continued to deepen in the valley, until the gloom thickened to the darkness of night, without bringing any tidings from those without.

When a delay, which was unusual in the members of a family circumstanced like that of the Wish-Ton-Wish, came to be coupled with various little observations that had been made during the day, it was thought that reasons for alarm were beginning, at each instant, to grow more plausible. Reports of fire-arms had been heard, at an early hour, from opposite points in the hills, and in a manner too distinct to be mistaken for echoes — a certain proof that the different members of the hunt had separated in the forest. Under such circumstances, it was not difficult for the imagination of a wife and a mother, of a sister, or of her who secretly confessed a still more tender interest in some one of the hunters, to conjure to the imagination the numberless dangers to which those who were engaged in these expeditions were known to be exposed.

" I doubt that the chase hath drawn them further from the valley than is fitting for the hour and the season," observed Ruth to her maidens, who had gathered in a group about her, at a point that overlooked as much of the cleared land around the buildings as the darkness would allow ; " the gravest man becomes thoughtless as the unreflecting child when led by the eagerness of the pursuit. It is the duty of older heads to think for those that want experience. But into what indiscreet complaints are my fears leading ! It may be that my husband is even now striving to collect his party, in order to return. Has any heard his conch sounding the recall ? "

" The woods are still as the day the first echo of the axe was heard among the trees," returned Faith. " I did hear that which sounded like a strain of brawling Dudley's songs, but it proved to be no more than the lowing of one of his own oxen. Perchance the animal misseth some of its master's care."

" Whittal Ring hath looked to the beasts, and it may not be that he hath neglected to feed, among others, the creatures of Dudley. Thy mind is given to levity, Faith, in the matter of this young man. It is not seemly that one of thy years and sex should manifest so great displeasure at the name of a youth, who is of an honest nature, and of honest habits, too, though he may appear ungainly to the eye, and have so little favour with one of thy disposition."

" I did not fashion the man," said Faith, biting her lip and tossing her head ; " nor is it aught to me whether he be gainly or not. As to my favour, when he asks it, the man shall not wait long to know the answer. But is not yon figure the fellow himself, Madame Heathcote — here, coming in from the eastern hill, along the orchard path ? The form I mean is just here ; you may see it at this moment turning by the bend in the brook."

" There is one, of a certainty, and it should be one of our hunting party, too ; and yet he doth not seem to be of a size, or of a gait like that of Eben Dudley. Thou shouldst have a knowledge of thy kindred, girl ; to me it seemeth thy brother."

" Truly, it may be Reuben Ring ; still it hath much of the swagger of the other, though their statures be nearly equal. The manner of carrying the musket is much the same with all the borderers, too. One cannot easily tell the form of man from a stump by this light — and, yet do I think it will prove to be the loitering Dudley."

" Loiterer or not, he is the first to return from this long and weary chace," said Ruth, breathing heavily, like one who regretted that the truth were so. " Go thou to the postern, and admit him, girl. I ordered bolts to be drawn, for I like not to leave a fortress defended by a female garrison, at this hour, with open gates. I will hie to the dwelling, and see to the comforts of those who are a-hungred, since it will not be long ere we shall have more of them at hand."

Faith complied, with affected indifference and sufficient delay. By the time she had reached the place of admission, a form was seen ascending the acclivity, and taking the direction which led to the same spot. In the next minute, a rude effort to enter announced an arrival without.

" Gently, Master Dudley," said the wilful girl, who held the bolt with one hand, though she maliciously delayed to remove it. " We know thou art powerful of arm, and yet the palisadoes will scarcely fall at thy touch. Here are no Samsons to pull down the pillars on our heads. Perhaps we may not be disposed to give entrance to them who stay abroad out of all season."

" Open the postern, girl," said Eben Dudley; " after which, if thou hast aught to say, we shall be better con- venienced for discourse."

" It may be that thy conversation is most agreeable when heard from without. Render an account of thy backslidings throughout this day, penitent Dudley, that I may take pity on thy weariness. But lest hunger should have overcome thy memory, I may serve to help thee to the particulars. The first of thy offences was to consume more than thy portion of the cold meats ; the second was to suffer Reuben Ring to kill the deer, and for thee to claim it ; and a third was the trick thou hast of listening so much to thine own voice, that even the beasts fled thee, from dislike of thy noise."

" Thou triflest unseasonably, Faith ; I would speak with the Captain without delay."

" It may be that he is better employed than to desire such company. Thou art not the only strange animal by many who hath roared at the gate of Wish-Ton-Wish."

" Have any come within the day, Faith ?" demanded the borderer, with the interest such an event would be likely to create in the mind of one who habitually lived in so great retirement.

" What sayest thou to a second visit from the gentle spoken stranger, — he who favoured us with so much gay discourse, the by-gone fall of the year ? That would be a

H 3

guest fit to receive! I warrant me his knock would not be heard a second time."

"The gallant had better beware the moon!" exclaimed Dudley, striking the butt of his musket against the ice with so much force as to cause his companion to start in alarm. "What fool's errand hath again brought him to prick his nag so deep into the forest?"

"Nay, thy wit is ever like the unbroken colt, a head-strong run-away. I said not in full meaning, that the man had come; I only invited thee to give an opinion in the event that he should arrive unexpectedly, though I am far from certain that any here ever expect to see his face again."

"This is foolish prating," returned the youth, provoked at the exhibition of jealousy into which he had been incautiously betrayed. "I tell thee to withdraw the bolt, for I have great need to speak with the Captain, or with his son."

"Thou mayest open thy mind to the first, if he will listen to what thou hast to say," returned the girl, removing the impediment to his entrance; "but thou wilt sooner get the ear of the other by remaining at the gate, since he has not yet come in from the forest."

Dudley recoiled a pace and repeated her words, in the tone of one who admitted a feeling of alarm to mingle with his surprise.

"Not in from the forest!" he said; "surely there are none abroad, now that I am home!"

"Why dost say it? I have put my jibes upon thee more in payment of ancient transgressions than for any present offence. So far from being last, thou art the first of the hunters we have yet seen. Go in to the Madam without delay, and tell her of the danger, if any there be, that we take speedy measures for our safety."

"That would do little good, truly," muttered the bor-derer, like one musing. "Stay thou here, and watch the postern, Faith; I will back to the woods; for a timely word, or a signal blown from my conch, might quicken their footsteps."

"What madness hath beset thee, Dudley! Thou wouldst

not go into the forest again, at this hour, and alone, if there be reason for fear. Come farther within the gate, man, that I may draw the bolt; the Madam will wonder that we tarry here so long."

"Ha!—I hear feet moving in the meadow; I know it by the creaking of the snow; the others are not lagging."

Notwithstanding the apparent certainty of the young man, instead of going forth to meet his friends, he withdrew, a step, and with his own hand drew the bolt that Faith had just desired might be fastened; taking care, at the same time, to let fall a swinging bar of wood, which gave additional security to the fastenings of the postern. His apprehensions, if any such had induced this caution, were, however, unnecessary; for ere he had time to make, or even to reflect on, any further movement, admission was demanded, in the well-known voice of the son of him who owned the valley. The bustle of the arrival—for with Content entered a group of companions, loaded with venison —put an end to the dialogue. Faith seized the opportunity to glide away in the obscurity, in order to announce to her mistress that the hunters had returned—an office which she performed without entering at all into the particulars of her own interview with Eben Dudley.

It is needless to dwell on the satisfaction with which Ruth received her husband and son, after the uneasiness she had just suffered. Though the severe manners of the province admitted of no violent exhibition of passing emotions, secret joy was reigning in the mild eyes, and glowing about the flushed cheeks, of the discreet matron, while she personally officiated in the offices of the evening meal.

The party had returned teeming with no extraordinary incidents; nor did they appear to be disturbed with any of that seriousness of air which had so unequivocally characterised the deportment of him who had preceded them. On the contrary, each had his quiet tale to relate,— now, perhaps, at the expense of a luckless companion, and sometimes in order that no part of his own individual skill as a hunter should be unknown. The delay was accounted for, as similar delays are commonly explained, by the distance and the temptations of an unusually successful chase. As

the appetites of those who had passed the day in the exciting
toil were keen, and the viands tempting, the first half hour
passed quickly, as all such half hours are wont to pass, in
garrulous recitals of personal exploits, and of the hair-
breadth escapes of deer, which, had fortune not been fickle,
should have now been present, as trophies of the skill of the
hand by which they fell.   It was only after personal vanity
was sufficiently appeased, and when the hunger even of a
border man could achieve no more, that the hunters began
to look about them with a diminished excitement, and to
discuss the events of the day with a fitting calmness, and
with a discretion more suited to their ordinary self-command.

" We lost the sound of thy conch, wandering Dudley,
as we fell into the deep hollow of the mountain," said Content, in a pause of the discourse : " since which time
neither eye nor ear of any has had trace of thy movements,
until we met thee at the postern, stationed like a looker-out
on his watch."

The individual addressed had mingled in none of the
gaiety of the hour.   While others fed freely, or joined in
the quiet joke, which could escape the lips of even men
chastened as his companions, Eben Dudley had tasted
sparingly of the viands.   Nor had the muscles of his hard
countenance once relaxed in a smile.   A gravity and
silence so extraordinary, in one little accustomed to exhibit
either quality, did not fail to attract attention.   It was universally ascribed to the circumstance that he had returned
empty-handed from the hunt ; and now that one having
authority had seen fit to give such a direction to the discourse, the imaginary delinquent was not permitted to escape unscathed.

" The butcher had little to do with this day's killing,"
said one of the young men ; " as a punishment for his absence from the slaughter, he should be made to go on the
hill, and bring in the two bucks he will find hanging from
a maple sapling near the drinking spring.   Our meat should
pass through his hands in some fashion or other, else will
it lack savour."

" Ever since the death of the straggling wether, the trade
of Eben hath been at a stand," added another ; the down-

hearted youth seems like one ready to give up his calling
to the first stranger that shall ask it."

"Creatures which run at large prove better mutton than
the stalled wether," continued a third ; " and thereby custom was getting low before this hunt. Beyond a doubt,
he has a full supply for all who shall be likely to seek venison in his stall."

Ruth observed that the countenance of her husband grew
grave, at these allusions to an event he had always seemed
to wish forgotten ; and she interposed, with a view to lead
the minds of those who listened back to matter more fitting
to be discussed.

" How is this !" she exclaimed in haste ; " hath the
stout Dudley lost any of his craft? I have never counted
with greater certainty on the riches of the table, than when
he hath been sent among the hills for the fat deer, or the
tender turkey. It would much grieve me to learn that he
beginneth to lack the hunter's skill."

" The man is getting melancholy with over feeding,"
muttered the wilful tones of one busied among the vessels,
in a distant part of the room. " He taketh his exercise
alone, in order that none need discover the failing. I think
he be much disposed to go over sea, in order to become a
trooper."

Until now, the subject of these mirthful attacks had listened like one too confident of his established reputation to
feel concern ; but at the sound of the last speaker's voice,
he grasped the bushy covering of one entire cheek in his
hand, and, turning a reproachful and irritated glance at the
already half-repentant eye of Faith Ring, all his natural
spirit returned.

" It may be that my skill hath left me," he said, " and
that I love to be alone, rather than to be troubled with the
company of some that might readily be named, no reference
being had to such gallants as ride up and down the colony,
putting evil opinions into the thoughts of honest men's
daughters ; but why is Eben Dudley to bear all the small
shot of your humours, when there is another who, it might
seem, hath strayed even further from your trail than he ? "

Eye sought eye, and each youth, by hasty glances, endeavoured to read the countenances of all the rest in company, in order to learn who the absentee might be.   The young borderers shook their heads, as the features of every well-known face were recognised, and a general exclamation of denial was about to break from their lips, when Ruth exclaimed—

"Truly the Indian is wanting!"

So constant was the apprehension of danger from the savages, in the breasts of those who dwelt on that exposed frontier, that every man arose at the words, by a sudden and common impulse, and each individual gazed about him, in a surprise that was a little akin to dismay.

"The boy was with us when we quitted the forest," said Content, after a moment of death-like stillness.   "I spoke to him in commendation of his activity, and of the knowledge he had shown in beating up the secret places of the deer, though there is little reason to think my words were understood."

"And were it not sinful to take such solemn evidence in behalf of so light a matter, I could be qualified on the book itself, that he was at my elbow as we entered the orchard," added Reuben Ring, a man renowned in that little community for the accuracy of his vision.

"And I will make oath, or declaration of any sort, lawful or conscientious, that he came not within the postern, when it was opened by my own hand," returned Eben Dudley. "I told off the number of the party, as you passed, and right sure am I that no red-skin entered."

"Canst thou tell us aught of the lad?" demanded Ruth, quick to take the alarm on a subject that had so long exercised her care and given food to her imagination.

"Nothing.   With me he hath not been since the turn of the day.   I have not seen the face of living man from that moment, unless, in truth, one of mysterious character, whom I met in the forest, may be so called."

The manner in which the woodsman spoke was too serious and too natural, not to give birth in his auditors to some of his own gravity.   Perhaps the appearance of the Puritan, at that moment, aided in quieting the levity that had been uppermost in the minds of the young men; for it is certain, that when he entered, a deeper and a general curiosity came over the countenances of all present. Content waited a moment in respectful silence, till his father had moved slowly through the circle, and then he prepared himself to look further into an affair that began to assume the appearance of matter worthy of investigation.

CHAPTER IX.

Ber. Last night of all,
When yon same star, that 's westward from the pole,
Had made its course to illume that part of heaven
Where now it burns, Marcellus, and myself,
The bell then beating one —
Mar. Peace, break thee off; look, where it comes again !— *Hamlet.*

IT is our duty, as faithful historians of the events recorded in this homely legend, to conceal no circumstance which may throw the necessary degree of light on its incidents, nor any opinion that may serve for the better instruction of the reader in comprehending the characters of its actors. In order that this obligation may be discharged with sufficient clearness and precision, it has now become necessary to make a short digression from the immediate action of the tale.

Enough has been already shown, to prove that the Heathcotes lived at a time, and in a country, where very quaint and peculiar religious dogmas had the ascendancy. At a period when visible manifestations of the goodness of Providence, not only in spiritual but in temporal gifts, were confidently expected and openly proclaimed, it is not at all surprising that more evil agencies should be thought to exercise their power in a manner that is somewhat opposed to the experience of our own age. As we have no wish, however, to make these pages the medium of a theological or metaphysical controversy, we shall deal tenderly with certain important events, that most of the writers, who were contemporary with the facts, assert took place in the colonies of New England, at and about the period of which we are now writing. It is sufficiently known that the art of witchcraft, and one even still more diabolical and direct in its origin, were then believed to flourish in that quarter of the world, to a degree that was probably in a very just proportion to the neglect with which most of the other arts of life were treated.

There is so much grave and respectable authority to prove the existence of these evil influences, that it requires a pen hardier than any we wield, to attack them without a suitable motive. "Flashy people," says the learned and pious Cotton Mather, Doctor of Divinity, and Fellow of the Royal Society, "may burlesque these things ; but when hundreds of the most sober people, in a country where they have as much mother wit, certainly, as the rest of mankind, *know them to be true,* nothing but the absurd and froward spirit of Sadducism can question them." Against this grave and credited authority we pretend to raise no question of scepticism. We submit to the testimony of such a writer as conclusive, though, as credulity is sometimes found to be bounded by geographical limits, and to possess something of a national character, it may be prudent to refer certain readers, who dwell in the other hemisphere, to the Common Law of England on this interesting subject, as it is ingeniously expounded by Keeble, and approved by the twelve judges of that highly civilised and enlightened island. With this brief reference to so grave authorities, in support of what we have now to offer, we shall return to the matter of the narrative, fully trusting that its incidents will throw some additional light on a subject of so deep and so general concern.

Content waited respectfully until his father had taken his seat, and then perceiving that the venerable Puritan had no immediate intention of moving personally in the affair, he commenced the examination of his dependant as follows : opening the matter with a seriousness that was abundantly warranted by the gravity of the subject itself.

"Thou hast spoken of one met in the forest," he said ; "proceed with the purport of that interview, and tell us what manner of man it was."

Thus directly interrogated, Eben Dudley disposed himself to give a full and satisfactory answer. First casting a

glance around, so as to embrace every curious and eager
countenance, and letting his look rest a little longer than
common on a half-interested, half-incredulous, and a somewhat ironical dark eye, that was riveted on his own from
a distant corner of the room, he commenced his statement
as follows : —

" It is known to you all," said the borderer, " that when
we had gained the mountain top, there was a division of
our numbers, in such a fashion that each hunter should
sweep his own range of the forest, in order that neither
moose, deer, nor bear, might have reasonable chance of
escape. Being of large frame, and it may be of swifter
foot than common, the young captain saw fit to command
Reuben Ring to flank one end of the line, and a man who
is nothing short of him in speed or strength, to do the same
duty on the other. There was nothing particularly worthy
of mention that took place on the flank I held, for the first
two hours, unless, indeed, the fact that three several times
did I fall upon a maze of well beaten deer tracks, that as
often led to nothing—-"

" These are signs common to the woods, and they are
no more than so many proofs that the animal has its sports,
like any other playful creature, when not pressed by hunger
or by danger," quietly observed Content.

" I pretend not to take those deceitful tracks much into
the account," resumed Dudley ; " but shortly after losing
the sound of the conchs, I roused a noble buck from his
lair beneath a thicket of hemlocks, and having the game
in view, the chase led me wide off towards the wilderness,
it may have been the distance of two leagues."

" And in all that time had you no fitting moment to
strike the beast ? "

" None, whatever ; nor, if opportunity had been given,
am I bold to say that hand of mine would have been hardy
enough to aim at its life."

" Was there aught in the deer that a hunter should
seek to spare it ? "

" There was that in the deer that might bring a
christian man to much serious reflection."

" Deal more openly with the nature and appearance of

the animal," said Content, a little less tranquil than usual; while the youths and maidens placed themselves in attitudes still more strongly denoting attention.

Dudley pondered an instant, before he commenced a less equivocal enumeration of what he conceived to be the marvels of his tale.

" Firstly," he said, " there was no trail, neither to nor from the spot where the creature had made its lair; secondly, when roused, it took not the alarm, but leaped, sportingly, ahead, taking sufficient care to be beyond the range of musket, without ever becoming entirely hid from the eye; and, lastly, its manner of disappearance was as worthy of mention as any other of its movements."

" And in what manner didst thou lose the creature?"

" I had gotten it upon the crest of a hillock, where true eye and steady hand might make sure of a buck of much smaller size, when —— didst hear aught that might be accounted wonderful at a season of the year when the snows are still lying on the earth?"

The auditors regarded one another curiously, each endeavouring to recall some unwonted sound which might sustain a narrative that was fast obtaining the seducing interest of the marvellous.

" Wast sure, Charity, that the howl we heard from the forest was the yell of the beaten hound?" demanded a handmaiden of Ruth, of a blue-eyed companion, who seemed equally well disposed to contribute her share of evidence in support of any exciting legend.

" It might have been other," was the answer; " though the hunters do speak of their having beaten the pup for restiveness."

" There was a tumult among the echoes, that sounded like the noises which follow the uproar of a falling tree," said Ruth, thoughtfully. " I remember to have asked if it might not be that some fierce beast had caused a general discharge of the musketry; but my father was of opinion that death had undermined some heavy oak."

" At what hour did this happen?"

" It was past the turn of the day; for it was at the

moment I bethought me of the hunger of those who had toiled since night in the hills."

" That, then, was the sound I mean! It came not from a falling tree, but was uttered in the air, far above all forests. Had it been heard by one better skilled in the secrets of nature — "

" He would say it thundered," interrupted Faith Ring, who, unlike most of the other listeners, manifested little of the quality which was expressed by her name. " Truly, Eben Dudley hath done marvels in this hunt; he hath come in with a thunderbolt in his head, instead of a fat buck on his shoulders!"

" Speak reverently, girl, of that thou dost not comprehend," said Mark Heathcote, sternly. " Marvels are manifested equally to the ignorant and to the learned: and although vain-minded pretenders to philosophy affirm that the warring of the elements is no more than nature working out its own purification, yet do we know, from all ancient authorities, that other manifestations are therein exhibited. Satan may have control over the magazines of the air; and he can let off the ordnance of Heaven. That the prince of the powers of darkness hath as good a share in Chemistry as goes to the making of aurum fulminans is asserted by one of the wisest writers of our age."

From this declaration, and more particularly from the learning discovered in the Puritan's speech, there was no one so hardy as to dissent. Faith was glad to shrink back among the bevy of awe-struck maidens, while Content, after a sufficiently respectful pause, invited the woodsman, who was yet teeming with the most important part of his communication, to proceed.

" While my eye was searching for the lightning, which should in reason have attended that thunder, had it been uttered in the manner of nature, the buck vanished; and when I rushed upon the hillock, in order to keep the game in view, a man mounting its opposite side came so suddenly upon me, that our muskets were at each other's breasts before either had time for speech."

" What manner of man was he?"

" So far as human judgment might determine, he

seemed a traveller, who was endeavouring to push through the wilderness from the towns below, to the distant settle-.ments of the Bay Province ; but I account it exceeding wonderful, that the trail of a leaping buck should have brought us together in so unwonted a manner !"

" And didst thou see aught of the deer after that en-counter ? "

" In the first hurry of the surprise, it did certainly ap-pear as if, an animal were bounding along the wood into a distant thicket ; but it is known how readily one may be led by seeming probabilities into a false conclusion, and so I account that glimpse as delusion. No doubt, the animal having done that which it was commissioned to perform, did then and there disappear, in the manner I have named."

" It might have been thus. And the stranger — had you discourse with him before parting ? "

" We tarried together a short hour. He related much marvellous matter of the experiences of the people near the sea. According to his testimony, the powers of darkness have been manifested in the provinces in a hideous fashion. Numberless of the believers have been persecuted by the invisibles, and greatly have they endured suffering, both in soul and body."*

" Of all this have I witnessed surprising instances, in my day," said Mark Heathcote, breaking the awful still-ness that succeeded the annunciation of so heavy a visit-ation on the peace of the colony, with his deep-toned and imposing voice. " Did he, with whom thou conferred, enter into the particulars of the trials ? "

" He spoke also of certain other signs, that are thought to foretell the coming of trouble. When I named the weary chase that I had made, and the sound which came from the air, he said that these would be accounted trifles in the towns of the Bay†, where the thunder and its

---

* The reader who is acquainted with the history of New-England will recognise in this dialogue much of the jargon and the peculiar opinions that were so prevalent in that portion of America at the period of this tale.

† The colony of Massachusetts Bay was familiarly called " The Bay Colony, as it is even now frequently termed " The Bay State."   It obtained this appellation from the circumstance of being situated on Massachusetts Bay.

lightnings had done much evil work, the past season ;
Satan having especially shown his spite, by causing them
to do injury to the houses of the Lord."

" There has long been reason to think, that the pilgrim_
age of the righteous into these wilds will be visited by
some fierce opposition of those envious natures which, fostering evil themselves, cannot brook to look upon the toiling
of such as strive to keep the narrow path. We will now
resort to the only weapon it is permitted us to wield in
this controversy, but which, when handled with diligence
and zeal, never fails to lead to victory."

So saying, without waiting to hear more of the tale of
Eben Dudley, old Mark Heathcote arose, and assuming the
upright attitude usual among the people of his sect, he addressed himself to prayer. The grave and awe-struck, but
deeply confiding, congregation imitated his example, and
the lips of the Puritan had parted in the act of utterance,
wh.. a low, faltering note, like that produced by a wind
1 strument, rose on the outer air, and penetrated to the
place where the family was assembled. A conch was suspended at the postern, in readiness to be used by any of
the family whom accident or occupation should detain beyond the usual hour of closing the gates ; and, both by the
direction and nature of this interruption, it would now
seem that an applicant for admission stood at the portal.
The effect on the auditors was general and instantaneous.
Notwithstanding the recent dialogue, the young men involuntarily sought their arms, while the startled females hud-
dled together like a flock of trembling and timid deer.

" There is, of a certainty, a signal from without !"
Content at length observed, after waiting to suffer the
sounds to die away among the angles of the buildings.
" Some hunter, who hath strayed from his path claimeth
hospitality."

Eben Dudley shook his head like one who dissented ;
but, having with all the other youths grasped his musket, he
stood as undetermined as the rest concerning the course it
was proper to pursue. It is uncertain how long this indecision might have continued, had no further summons been
given ; but he without appeared too impatient of delay to

I

suffer much time to be lost. The conch sounded again, and with far better success than before. The blast was longer, louder, and bolder than that which had first pierced the walls of the dwelling, rising full and rich on the air, as if one well practised in the use of the instrument had placed his lips to the shell.

Content would scarcely have presumed to disobey a mandate coming from his father, had it been little in conformity with his own intentions. But second thoughts had already shown him the necessity of decision, and he was in the act of motioning to Dudley and Reuben Ring to follow, when the Puritan bade him look to the matter. Making a sign for the rest of the family to remain where they were, and arming himself with a musket which had more than once that day been proved to be of certain aim, he led the way to the postern which has already been so often mentioned.

" Who sounds at my gate ? " demanded Content, when he and his followers had gained a position, under cover of a low, earthen mound, erected expressly for the purpose of commanding the entrance ; " who summons a peaceful family, at this hour of the night, to their outer defences ? "

" One who hath need of what he asketh, or he would not disturb thy quiet," was the answer. " Open the postern, Master Heathcote, without fear ; it is a brother in the faith, and a subject of the same laws, that asketh a boon."

" Here is truly a Christian man, without," said Content, hurrying to the postern ; which, without a moment's delay he threw freely open, saying, as he did so, — " Enter, of Heaven's mercy, and be welcome to that we have to bestow."

A tall, and, by his tread, a heavy man, wrapped in a riding cloak, bowed to the greeting, and immediately passed beneath the low lintel. Every eye was keenly fastened on the stranger, who, after ascending the acclivity a short distance, paused, while the young men, under their master's orders, carefully and scrupulously renewed the fastenings of the gate. When bolts and bars had done their office, Content joined his guest, and after making another fruitless effort, by the feeble light which fell from the stars, to scan his person, he said, in his own meek and quiet manner—

" Thou must have great need of warmth and nourishment. The distance from this valley to the nearest habitation is wearisome, and one who hath journeyed it, in a season like this, may well be nigh fainting. Follow, and deal with that we have to bestow as freely as if it were thine own."

Although the stranger manifested none of that impatience, which the heir of the Wish-Ton-Wish appeared to think one so situated might in all reason feel, thus invited he did not hesitate to comply. As he followed in the footsteps of his host, his tread, however, was leisurely and dignified : and once or twice, when the other half delayed in order to make some passing observation of courtesy, he betrayed no indiscreet anxiety to enter on those personal indulgences, which might in reality prove so grateful to one who had journeyed far in an inclement season, and along a road where neither dwelling nor security invited repose.

" Here is warmth and a peaceful welcome," pursued Content, ushering his guest into the centre of a group of fearfully anxious faces ; " in a little time other matters shall be added to thy comfort."

When the stranger found himself under the glare of a powerful light, and confronted to so many curious and wondering eyes, for a single instant he hesitated. Then stepping calmly forward, he cast the short riding cloak, which had closely muffled his features, from his shoulders, and discovered the severe eye, the stern lineaments, and the athletic form of him, who had once before been known to enter the doors of Wish-Ton-Wish with little warning, and to have quitted them so mysteriously.

The Puritan had arisen, with quiet and grave courtesy, to receive his visiter ; but obvious, powerful, and extraordinary interest gleamed about his usually subdued visage, when, as the features of the other were exposed to view, he recognised the person of the man who advanced to meet him.

" Mark Heathcote," said the stranger, " my visit is to

thee. It may, or it may not, prove longer than the last, as thou shalt receive my tidings. Affairs of the last moment demand that there should be little delay in hearing that which I have to offer."

Notwithstanding the excess and the nature of the surprise which the veteran Mark had certainly betrayed, it endured just long enough to allow those wondering eyes, which were eagerly devouring all that passed, to note its existence. Then the subdued and characteristic manner, which in general marked his air, instantly returned, and with a quiet gesture, like that which friends use in moments of confidence and security, he beckoned to the other to follow to an inner room. The stranger complied, making a slight bow of recognition to Ruth, as he passed her on the way to the apartment chosen for an interview that was evidently intended to be private.

CHAPTER X.

Mar.—Shall I strike at it with my partizan?
Hor.—Do, if it will not stand.
Ber.—'Tis here!
Hor.—'Tis here!
Mar.—'Tis gone!   *Hamlet.*

THE time that this unexpected visiter stood uncloaked and exposed to recognition, before the eyes of the curious group in the outer room, did not much exceed a minute. Still it was long enough to allow men who rarely overlooked the smallest peculiarity of dress or air, to note some of the more distinguishing accompaniments of his attire. The heavy horseman's pistols, once before exhibited, were in his girdle, and young Mark got a glimpse of a silver-handled dagger which had pleased his eye before that night. But the passage of his grandfather and the stranger from the room, prevented the boy from determining whether it was entirely of the same fashion as that which, rather as a memorial of by-gone scenes than for any service that it might now be expected to perform, hung above the bed of the former.

" The man hath not yet parted with his arms !" exclaimed the quick-sighted youth, when he found that every other tongue continued silent. " I would he may now leave them with my grandfather, that I may chase the skulking Wompanoag to his hiding ———"

" Hot-headed boy ! Thy tongue is too much given to levity," said Ruth, who had not only resumed her seat, but the light employment that had been interrupted by the blast at the gate, with a calmness of mien that did not fail, in some degree, to re-assure her maidens. " Instead of cherishing the lessons of peace that are taught thee, thy unruly thoughts are ever bent on strife."

" Is there harm in wishing to be armed with a weapon suited to my years, that I may do service in beating down the power of our enemies, and perhaps aid something, too, in affording security to my own mother ?"

" Thy mother hath no fears, " returned the matron, gravely, while grateful affection prompted a kind but furtive glance towards the high-spirited though sometimes froward lad. " Reason hath already taught me the folly of alarm, because one has knocked at our gate in the night season. Lay aside thy arms, men ; ye see that my husband no longer clings to the musket. Be certain that his eye will give us warning, when there shall be danger at hand."

The unconcern of her husband was even more strikingly true than the simple language of his wife would appear to convey. Content had not only laid aside his weapon; but he had resumed his seat near the fire, with an air as calm, as assured, and, it might have seemed to one watchfully observant, as understanding as her own. Until now, the stout Dudley had remained leaning on his piece, immoveable and apparently unconscious as a statue. But following the injunctions of one he was accustomed to obey, he placed the musket against the wall, with the care of a hunter, and then running a hand through his shaggy locks, as if to quicken ideas that were never remarkably active, he bluntly exclaimed —

" An armed hand is well in these forests, but an armed
heel is not less wanting, to him who would push a roadster
from the Connecticut to the Wish-Ton-Wish, between a
rising and a setting sun ! The stranger no longer journeys
in the saddle, as is plain by the sign that his boot beareth
no spur. When he worried through the forest, by dint of
hard pricking, the miserable hack that proved food for the
wolves, he had better appointments. I saw the bones of
the animal no later than this day. They have been polished by fowls and frost, till the driven snow of the
mountains is not whiter !"

Meaning and uneasy, but hasty, glances of the eye were
exchanged between Content and Ruth, as Eben Dudley
thus uttered the thoughts which had been suggested by the
unexpected return of the stranger.

" Go you to the look-out at the western palisadoes,"
said the latter ; " and see if perchance the Indian may not
be lurking near the dwellings, ashamed of his delay, and
perchance fearful of calling us to his admission. I cannot
think that the child means to desert us with no sign of
kindness, and without even a word of leave-taking."

" I will not take upon me to say how much, or how
little, of ceremony the youngster may fancy to be due to
the master of the valley and his kin ; but if not gone already, the snow will not melt more quietly in the thaw,
than the lad will one day disappear. Reuben Ring, thou
hast an eye for light or darkness ; come forth with me,
that no sign escape us. Should thy sister, Faith, see fit
to make one of our party, it would not be easy for the red-
skin to pass the clearing without a hail."

" Go to," hurriedly answered the female ; " it is more
womanly that I tarry to see to the wants of him who hath
journeyed far and hard since the rising of the sun. If the
boy pass thy vigilance, wakeful Dudley, he will have little
cause to fear that of others !"

Though Faith so decidedly declined to make one of the
party, her brother complied without reluctance. The young
men were about to quit the place together, when the latch,
on which the hand of Dudley was already laid, rose quietly
without aid from his finger, the door opened, and the ob-

ject of their intended search glided past them, and took his
customary position in one of the more retired corners of
the room. There was so much of the ordinary noiseless
manner of the young captive in this entrance, that for a
moment they who witnessed the passage of his dark form
across the apartment, were led to think the movement no
more than the visit he was always permitted to make at
that hour. But recollection soon came, and with it not
only the suspicious circumstance of his disappearance, but
the inexplicable manner of his admission within the gates.

"The pickets must be looked to!" exclaimed Dudley,
the instant a second look assured him that his eyes in truth
beheld him who had been missing. "The place that a
stripling can scale may admit a host."

"Truly," said Content, "this needeth explanation.
Hath not the boy entered when the gate was opened for the
stranger? Here cometh one that may speak to the fact!"

"It is so," said the individual named, who re-entered
from the inner room in season to hear the nature of the remark. "I found this native child near thy gate, and took
upon me the office of a Christian man to bid him welcome.
Certain am I, that one, kind of heart and gently disposed,
like the mistress of this family, will not turn him away in
anger."

"He is no stranger at our fire, or at our board," said
Ruth; "had it been otherwise, thou wouldst have done
well."

Eben Dudley looked incredulous. His mind had been
powerfully exercised that day with visions of the marvellous, and, of a certainty, there was some reason to distrust
the manner in which the re-appearance of the youth was
effected.

"It will be well to look to the fastenings," he muttered,
"lest others, less easy to dispose of, should follow. Now
that invisible agencies are at work in the colony, one may
not sleep too soundly!"

"Then go thou to the look-out, and keep the watch till
the clock shall strike the hour of midnight," said the Puritan, who uttered the command in a manner to show that
he was in truth moved by considerations deeper than the

vague apprehensions of his dependent. " Ere sleep overcome thee, another shall be ready for the relief."

Mark Heathcote seldom spoke, but respectful silence
permitted the lowest of his syllables to be audible. On the
present occasion, when his voice was first heard, such a
stillness came over all in presence, that he finished the
sentence amid the nearly imperceptible breathings of the
listeners. In this momentary but death-like quiet, there
arose a blast from the conch at the gate, that might have
seemed an echo of that which had so lately startled the
already excited inmates of the dwelling. At the repetition
of sounds so unwonted all sprang to their feet, but no one
spoke. Content cast a hurried and enquiring glance at his
father, who in his turn anxiously sought the eye of the
stranger. The latter stood firm and unmoved. One hand
was clenched upon the back of the chair from which he
had arisen, and the other grasped, perhaps unconsciously,
the handle of one of those weapons which had attracted
the attention of young Mark, and which still continued
thrust through the broad leathern belt that girded his
doublet.

" The sound is like that which one little used to deal
with earthly instruments might raise," muttered one of
those whose mind had been prepared by the narrative of
Dudley to believe in any thing marvellous.

" Come from what quarter it may, it is a summons that
must be answered," returned Content. " Dudley, thy
musket; this visit is so unwonted, that more than one
hand should do the office of porter."

The borderer instantly complied, muttering between his
teeth, as he shook the priming deeper into the barrel of his
piece, " Your over-sea gallants are quick on the trail to-
night!" Then throwing the musket into the hollow of his
arm, he cast a look of discontent and resentment towards
Faith Ring, and was about to open the door for the passage of Content, when another blast arose on the silence
without. The second touch of the shell was firmer, longer,
louder, and more true than that by which it had just been
preceded.

" One might fancy the conch was speaking in mockery,"

observed Content, looking with meaning towards their guest. "Never did sound more resemble sound than these we have just heard, and those ye drew from the shell when asking admission."

A sudden light appeared to break in upon the intelligence of the stranger. Advancing more into the circle, rather with the freedom of long familiarity than with the diffidence of a newly arrived guest, he motioned for silence, as he said —

"Let none move, but this stout woodsman, the young captain, and myself. We will go forth, and doubt not that the safety of those within shall be regarded."

Notwithstanding the singularity of this proposal, as it appeared to excite neither surprise nor opposition in the Puritan or his son, the rest of the family offered no objection. The stranger had no sooner spoken, than he advanced near to the torch, and looked closely into the condition of his pistols. Then, turning to old Mark, he continued, in an under tone —

"Peradventure there will be more worldly strife than any which can flow from the agencies that stir up the unquiet spirit of the Colonies. In such an extremity, it may be well to observe a soldier's caution."

"I like not this mockery of sound," returned the Puritan ; "it augureth a taunting and fiend-like temper. We have of late had in this colony tragical instances of what the disappointed malice of Azazel can attempt, and it would be vain to hope that the evil agencies are not vexed with the sight of my Bethel."

Though the stranger listened to the words of his host with respect, it was plain that his thoughts dwelt on dangers of a different character. The hand that still rested on his weapon was clenched with greater firmness, and a grim, though melancholy, expression was seated about a mouth, that was compressed in a manner to denote the physical rather than the spiritual resolution of the man. He made a sign to the two companions he had chosen, and led the way to the court.

By this time, the shades of night had materially thickened, and, although the hour was still early, a darkness had come over the valley that rendered it difficult to distinguish objects at any distance from the eye. The obscurity made it necessary that they, who now issued from the door of the dwelling, should advance with caution, lest, ere pro- perly admonished of its presence, their persons should be exposed to some lurking danger. When the three, how- ever, were safely established behind the thick curtain of plank and earth that covered and commanded the entrance, and where their persons, from the shoulders downward, were completely protected, alike from shot and arrow, Content again demanded to know who applied at his gates for admission at an hour when they were habitually closed for the night? Instead of receiving, as before, a ready answer, the silence was so profound, that his own words were very distinctly heard repeated, as was not uncommon at that quiet hour, among the recesses of the neighbouring woods.

" Come it from devil, or come it from man, here is treachery!" whispered the stranger, after a fitting pause. " Artifice must be met by artifice ; but thou art much abler to advise against the wiles of the forest, than one trained, as I have been, in the less cunning deceptions of Christian warfare."

" What thinkst, Dudley ?" asked Content — " will it be well to sally, or shall we wait another signal from the conch ?"

" Much dependeth on the quality of the guests ex- pected," returned he of whom counsel was asked. " As for the braggart gallants, that are over valiant among the maidens, and heavy of heart when they think the screech of the jay an Indian whoop, I care not if ye beat the picquets to the earth, and call upon them to enter on the gallop. I know the manner to send them to the upper story of the block quicker than the cluck of the turkey can muster its young ; but ―― "

" 'Tis well to be discreet in language, in a moment of such serious uncertainty," interrupted the stranger ; " we look for no gallants of the kind."

" Then will I give you a conceit that shall know the reason of the music of yon conch. Go ye two back into the house, making much conversation by the way, in order that any without may hear. When ye have entered, it shall be my task to find such a post nigh the gate, that none shall knock again, and no porter be at hand to question them in the matter of their errand."

" This soundeth better," said Content ; " and that it may be done with all safety, some others of the young men, who are accustomed to this species of artifice, shall issue by the secret door, and lie in wait behind the dwellings, in order that support shall not be wanting in case of violence. Whatever else thou dost, Dudley, remember that thou dost not undo the fastenings of the postern."

" Look to the support," returned the woodsman ; " should it be keen-eyed Reuben Ring, I shall feel none the less certain that good aid is at my back. The whole of that family are quick of wit and ready of invention, unless it may be the wight who hath got the form without the reason of a man."

" Thou shalt have Reuben, and none other of his kin," said Content. " Be well advised of the fastenings, and so I wish thee all fitting success, in a deception that cannot be sinful, since it aims only at our safety."

With this injunction, Content and the stranger left Dudley to the practice of his own devices, the former observing the precaution to speak aloud while returning, in order that any listeners without might be led to suppose the whole party had retired from the search, satisfied of its fruitlessness.

In the mean time, the youth left nigh the postern set about the accomplishment of the task he had undertaken, in sober earnest. Instead of descending in a direct line to the palisadoes, he also ascended, and made a circuit among the out-buildings on the margin of the acclivity. Then bending so low as to blend his form with objects on the snow, he gained an angle of the palisadoes, at a point remote from the spot he intended to watch, and, as he hoped, aided by the darkness of the hour and the shadows of the hill, complete y protected from observation. When beneath the palisadoes, the sentinel crouched to the earth, creeping with extreme caution along the large piece of

timber which united their lower ends, until he found himself arrived at a species of sentry box, that was erected for
the very purpose to which he now intended it should be
applied.   Once within the cover of this little recess, the
sturdy woodsman bestowed his large frame, with as much
attention to comfort and security as the circumstances
would permit.   Here he was prepared to pass many weary
minutes before there should be further need of his services.

The reader will find no difficulty in believing that one
of opinions like those of the borderer, did not enter on his
silent watch without much distrust of the character of the
guests that he might be called upon to receive.   Enough
has been shown to prove that the suspicion uppermost in
his mind was that the unwelcome agents of the government
had returned on the heels of the stranger.   But, notwith_
standing the seeming probability of this opinion, there were
secret misgivings of the earthly origin of the two last windings of the shell.   All the legends, and all the most credited
evidence in cases of prestigious agency, as it had been
exhibited in the colonies of New England, went to show
the malignant pleasure the evil spirits found in indulging
their wicked mockeries, or in otherwise tormenting those
who placed their support on a faith that was believed to be
so repugnant to their own ungrateful and abandoned
natures.   Under the impressions naturally excited by the
communication he had held with the traveller in the
mountains, Eben Dudley found his mind equally divided
between the expectation of seeing, at each moment, one of
the men whom he had induced to quit the valley so un-
ceremoniously, returning to obtain, surreptitiously, admission within the gate, or of being made an unwilling witness
of some wicked manifestation of that power which was
temporarily committed to the invisibles.   In both of these
expectations, however, he was fated to be disappointed.
Notwithstanding the strong spiritual bias of the opinions
of the credulous sentinel, there was too much of the dross
of temporal things in his composition, to elevate him
altogether above the weakness of humanity.   A mind so
incumbered began to weary with its own contemplations,

and, as it grew feeble with its extraordinary efforts, the
dominion of matter gradually resumed its sway. Thought,
instead of being clear and active, as the emergency would
have seemed to require, began to grow misty. Once or twice
the borderer half arose, and appeared to look about him
with observation ; and then, as his large frame fell heavily
back into its former semi-recumbent attitude, he grew
tranquil and stationary. This movement was several
times repeated, at intervals of increasing length, till, at
the end of an hour, forgetting alike the hunt, the troopers,
and the mysterious agents of evil, the young man yielded
to the fatigue of the day. The tall oaks of the adjoining
forest stood not more immoveable in the quiet of the
tranquil hour, than his frame now leaned against the side
of its narrow habitation.

How much time was thus lost in inactivity, Eben Dudley could never precisely tell. He always stoutly maintained it could not have been long, since his watch was
not disturbed by the smallest of those sounds from the
woods which sometimes occur in deep night, and which
may be poetically termed the breathing of the forest in its
slumbers. His first distinct recollection was that of feeling
a hand grasped with the power of a giant. Springing to
his feet, the young man eagerly stretched forth an arm,
saying, as he did so, in words sufficiently confused :—

" If the buck hath fallen by a shot in the head, I grant
him to be thine, Reuben Ring : but if struck in limb or
body, I claim the venison for a surer hand."

" Truly a very just division of the spoil," returned one
in an under tone, who spoke as if sounds too loud might
be dangerous. " Thou givest the head of the deer for a
target to Reuben Ring, and keepest the rest of the creature
to thine own uses."

" Who hath sent thee, at this hour, to the postern ?
Dost not know that there are thought to be strangers outlying in the fields ? "

" I knew that there are some, who are not strangers, in-
lying on their watch ! " said Faith Ring. " What shame
would come upon thee, Dudley, did the Captain, and they
who have been so strongly exercised in prayer within, but

suspect how little care thou hast had of their safety, the while ! "

" Have they come to harm ? If the Captain hath held them to spiritual movements, I hope he will allow that nothing earthly hath passed this postern to disturb the exercise. As I hope to be dealt honestly by, in all matters of character, I have not once quitted the gate since the watch was set."

" Else wouldst thou be the famousest sleep-walker in the Connecticut Colony ! Why, drowsy one, conch cannot raise a louder blast, than that thou soundest, when thine eyes are fairly shut in sleep. This may be watching according to thy meaning of the word ; but the infant in its cradle is not half so ignorant of that which passeth around it, as thou hast been."

" I think, Faith Ring, that thou hast gotten to be much given to backbiting, and to indulge in evil saying against thy friends, since the visit of the gallants from over sea ———"

" Out upon the gallants from over sea, and thee too, man ! I am not a girl to be flouted with bold speech from one who doth not know whether he be sleeping or waking. I tell thee, thy good name would be lost in the family, did it come to the ears of the Captain, and more particularly to the knowledge of that soldier stranger, up in the dwelling, of whom even the Madam maketh so great ceremony, that thou hast been watching with a tuneful nose, an open mouth, and a sealed eye."

" If any but thee hadst said this slander of me, girl, it would go nigh to raise hot speech between us ! Thy brother, Reuben Ring, knows better than to stir my temper, by such falsity of accusation."

" Thou dealest so generously by him, that he is prone to forget thy misdeeds. Truly he hath the head of the buck, while thou contentest thyself with the offals and all the less worthy parts ! Go to, drowsy Dudley ; thou wast in a dream when I caused thee to awake."

" A pretty time have we fallen upon, when petticoats are used instead of beards and strong armed men, to go the rounds of the sentinels, and to say who sleepeth and who

is watchful ! What hath brought thee so far from the exercises and so nigh the gates, Mistress Faith, now that
there is no over-sea gallant to soothe thy ears with lying
speech and light declarations."

" If speech not to be credited is that I seek," returned
the girl, " truly the errand hath not been without its reward ! What brought me hither, sooth ! why, the Madam
hath need of articles from the outer buttery — and — ay —
and my ears led me to the postern. Thou knowest, musical
Dudley, that I have had occasion to harken to thy watchful notes before this night. But my time is too useful to
be wasted in idleness ; thou art now awake, and may thank
her who hath done thee a good turn with no wish to boast
of it, that one of a black beard is not the laughing stock of
all the youths in the family. If thou keepest thine own
counsel, the Captain may yet praise thee for a vigilant
sentinel; though Heaven forgive him the wrong he will do
the truth !"

" Perhaps a little anger at unjust suspicions may have
prompted me to say more than the matter needed, Faith,
when I taxed thee with the love of backbiting, and I do
now recall that word. Though I will ever deny that
aught more, than some wandering recollection concerning
the hunt of this day, hath come over my thoughts, and
perhaps made me even forgetful that it was needful to be
silent at the postern ; and therefore, on the truth of a
Christian man, I do forgive thee, the ——"

But Faith was already out of sight and out of hearing.
Dudley himself, who began to have certain prickings of
conscience concerning the ingratitude he had manifested to
one who had taken so much interest in his reputation, now
bethought him seriously of that which remained to be done.
He had much reason to suspect, that there was less of the
night before him than he had at first believed, and he became in consequence more sensible of the necessity of
making some report of the events of his watch. Accordingly he cast a scrutinizing glance around, in order to
make sure that the facts should not contradict his testimony, and then, first examining the fastenings of the postern, he mounted the hill, and presented himself before the

family. The members of the latter, having in truth passed most of the long interval of his absence in spiritual exercises, and in religious conversation, were not so sensible of his delay in reporting, as they might otherwise have been.

" What tidings dost thou bring us from without ? " said Content, so soon as the self-relieved sentinel appeared. " Hast seen any, or hast heard that which is suspicious ? "

Ere Dudley would answer, his eye did not fail to study the half-malicious expression of the countenance of her who was busy in some domestic occupation, directly opposite to the place where he stood. But reading there no more than a glance of playful though smothered irony, he was encouraged to proceed in his report.

" The watch has been quiet," was the answer ; " and there is little cause to keep the sleepers longer from their beds. Some vigilant eyes, like those of Reuben Ring and my own, had better be open until the morning ; further than that, is there no reason for being wakeful."

Perhaps the borderer would have dwelt more at large on his own readiness to pass the remainder of the hours of rest in attending to the security of those who slept, had not another wicked glance from the dark, laughing eye of her who stood so favourably placed to observe his countenance, admonished him of the prudence of being modest in his professions.

" This alarm hath then happily passed away," said the Puritan, arising. " We will now go to our pillows in thankfulness and peace. Thy service shall not be forgotten, Dudley ; for thou hast exposed thyself to seeming danger, at least, in our behalf."

" That hath he !" half-whispered Faith ; " and sure am I, that we maidens will not forget his readiness to lose the sweets of sleep, in order that the feeble may not come to harm."

" Speak not of the trifle," hurriedly returned the other. " There has been some deception in the sounds, for it is now my opinion, except to summon us to the gate, that this stranger might enter, the conch hath not been touched at all to-night."

" Then is it a deception which is repeated !" exclaimed

Content, rising from his chair as a faint and broken blast from the shell, like that which had first announced their visiter, again struggled among the buildings, until it reached every ear in the dwelling.

" Here is warning as mysterious as it may prove portentous !" said old Mark Heathcote, when the surprise, not to say consternation, of the moment, had subsided. " Hast seen nothing that might justify this ?"

Eben Dudley, like most of the auditors, was too much confounded to reply. All seemed to attend anxiously for the second and more powerful blast, which was to complete the imitation of the stranger's summons. It was not necessary to wait long, for in a time, as near as might be to that which had intervened between the two first peals of the horn, followed another, and in a note so true, again, as to give it the semblance of an echo.

END OF THE FIRST VOLUME.

VOLUME THE SECOND.

CHAPTER I.

I will watch to-night;
Perchance 't will walk again.   *Hamlet.*

" MAY not this be a warning given in mercy ?" the Puritan, at all times disposed to yield credit to supernatural manifestations of the care of Providence, demanded, with a solemnity that did not fail to produce its impression on most of his auditors. " The history of our colonies is full of the evidences of these merciful interpositions."

" We will thus consider it," returned the stranger, to whom the question seemed more particularly addressed. " The first measure shall be to seek out the danger to which it points. Let the youth they call Dudley again give me the aid of his powerful frame and manly courage; then trust the discovery of the meaning of these frequent speakings of the conch to me."

" Surely, Submission, thou wilt not again be the first to go forth !" exclaimed Mark, in a surprise that was equally manifested by Content and Ruth, the latter of whom pressed her little image to her side, as if the bare proposal presented a powerful picture of supernatural danger. " 'T will be well to think maturely on the step ere thou runnest the hazard of such an adventure."

" Better it should be I," said Content, " who am accustomed to forest signs, and all the usual testimonials of the presence of those who may wish us harm."

" No," said he, who for the first time had been called " Submission," a name that savoured of the religious enthusiasm of the times, and which might have been adopted as an open avowal of his readiness to bow beneath some

peculiar dispensation of Providence; " this service shall
be mine. Thou art both husband and father; and many
are there who look to thy safety as to their rock of earthly
support and comfort, while neither kindred, nor—but we
will not speak of things foreign to our purpose. Thou
knowest, Mark Heathcote, that peril and I are no strangers.
There is little need to bid me be prudent. Come, bold
woodsman, shoulder thy musket, and be ready to do credit
to thy manhood, should there be reason to prove it."

" And why not Reuben Ring?" said a hurried female
voice, that all knew to proceed from the lips of the sister
of the youth just named. " He is quick of eye, and ready
of hand, in trials like these; would it not be well to suc_
cour thy party with his aid ?"

" Peace, girl," meekly observed Ruth. " This matter
is already in the ordering of one used to command; there
needeth no counsel from thy short experience."

Faith shrunk back abashed, the flush which had mantled
over her brown cheek deepening to a tint like that of blood,
at the sudden conviction that she had betrayed an indiscreet interest in the safety of her suitor.

Submission (we use the appellation in the absence of all
others) fastened a searching glance for a single moment on
the countenance of the girl, and then, as if his attention
had not been devoted from the principal subject in hand,
he rejoined, coolly,—

" We go as scouters, and observers of that which may
hereafter call for the ready assistance of this youth; but
numbers would expose us to observation without adding to
our usefulness. And yet," he added, arresting his foot_
step, which was already turned towards the door, and
looking earnestly and long at the Indian boy, " perhaps
there standeth one who might much enlighten us, would
he but speak !"

This remark drew every eye on the person of the captive. The lad stood the scrutiny with the undismayed
and immovable composure of his race. But though his
eye met the looks of those around him haughtily and in
pride, it was not gleaming with any of that stern defiance
which had so often been known to glitter in his glances,

when he had reason to think that his fortunes or his person was the subject of the peculiar observation of those with whom he dwelt. On the contrary, the expression of his dark visage was rather that of amity than of hatred, and there was a moment when the look he cast upon Ruth and her offspring was visibly touched with a feeling of concern. A glance, charged with such a meaning, could not escape the quick-sighted vigilance of a mother.

" The child hath proved himself worthy to be trusted," she said ; " and in the name of Him who looketh into and knoweth all hearts, let him go forth."

Her lips became sealed, for again the conch announced the seeming impatience of those without to be admitted. The full tones of the shell thrilled on the nerves of the listeners, as if they proclaimed the coming of some great and fearful judgment.

In the midst of these often-repeated and mysterious sounds, Submission alone seemed calm and unmoved. Turning his look from the countenance of the boy, whose head had dropped upon his breast as the last notes of the conch rang among the buildings, he motioned hurriedly to Dudley to follow, and left the place.

There was, in good truth, that in the secluded situation of the valley, the darkness of the hour, and the nature of the several interruptions, which might readily awaken deep concern in the breasts of men as firm even as those who now issued into the open air, in quest of the solution of doubts that were becoming intensely painful. The stranger, or Submission, as we may in future have frequent occasion to call him, led the way in silence to a point of the eminence without the buildings, where the eye might overlook the palisadoes that hedged the sides of the acclivity and command a view beyond of all that the dusky and imperfect light would reveal.

It was a scene that required familiarity with a border life to be looked on, at any moment, with indifference. The broad, nearly interminable, and seemingly trackless forest, lay about them, bounding the view to the narrow limits of the valley, as if it were some straitened oasis amidst an ocean of wilderness. Within the boundaries of the cleared land, objects were less indistinct ; though even those nearest and most known were now seen only in the confused and gloomy outlines of night.

Across this dim prospect, Submission and his companion gazed long and cautiously.

" There is nought but motionless stumps, and fences loaded with snow," said the former, when his eye had roamed over the whole circuit of the view, which lay on the side of the valley where they stood. " We must go forth, and look nearer to the fields."

" Thither then is the postern," said Dudley, observing that the other took a direction opposite to that which led to the gate. But a gesture of authority induced him at the next instant to restrain his voice, and to follow whither his companion chose to lead the way.

The stranger made a circuit of half the hill ere he descended to the palisadoes, at a point where lay the long and massive piles of wood which had been collected for the fuel of the family. This spot was one that overlooked the steepest acclivity of the eminence, which was in itself, just there, so difficult of ascent, as to render the provision of the pickets far less necessary than in its more even faces. Still no useful precaution for the security of the family had been neglected, even at this strong point of the works. The piles of wood were laid at such a distance from the pickets as to afford no facilities for scaling them; while, on the other hand, they formed platforms and breast-works that might have greatly added to the safety of those who should be required to defend this portion of the fortress. Taking his way directly amid the parallel piles, the stranger descended rapidly through the whole of their mazes, until he had reached the open space between the outer of the rows and the palisadoes, a space that was warily left too wide to be passed by the leap of man.

" 'T is many a day since foot of mine has been in this spot," said Eben Dudley, feeling his way along a path that his companion threaded without any apparent hesitation. " My own hand laid this outer pile, some winters since, and certain am I, that from that hour to this, man hath not touched a billet of the wood ; and yet, for one who

K 3

hath come from over sea, it would appear that thou hast no great difficulty in making your way among the narrow lanes !"

" He that hath sight may well choose between air and beechen logs," returned the other, stopping at the palisadoes, and in a place that was concealed from any prying eyes within the works, by triple and quadruple barriers of wood. Feeling in his girdle, he then drew forth something which Dudley was not long in discovering to be a key. While the latter, aided by the little light that fell from the heavens, was endeavouring to make the most of his eyes, Submission applied the instrument to a lock that was artfully sunk in one of the timbers, at the height of a man's breast from the ground, and giving a couple of vigorous turns, a piece of the palisado, some half a fathom long, yielded on a powerful hinge below, and falling, made an opening sufficiently large for the passage of a human body.

" Here is a sally-port ready provided for our sortie," the stranger coolly observed, motioning for the other to precede him. When Dudley had passed, his companion followed, and the opening was then carefully closed and locked.

" Now is all fast again, and we are in the fields without raising alarm to any of mortal birth, at least," continued the guide, thrusting a hand into the folds of his doublet, as if to feel for a weapon, and preparing to descend the difficult declivity which still lay between him and the base of the hill. Eben Dudley hesitated to follow. The interview with the traveller in the mountains occurred to his heated imagination, and the visions of a prestigious agency revived with all their original force. The whole manner and the mysterious character of his companion, too, was little likely to re-assure a mind disturbed with such images.

" There is a rumour going in the colony," muttered the borderer, " that the invisibles are permitted for a time to work their evil, and it may well happen that some of their ungodly members shall journey to the Wish-Ton-Wish, in lack of better employment."

" Thou sayest truly," replied the stranger ; " but the power that allows of their wicked torments may have seen fit to provide an agent of its own, to defeat their subtleties. We will now draw nearer to the gate, in order that an eye may be kept on their malicious designs."

Submission spoke with gravity, and not without a certain manner of solemnity. Dudley yielded, though with a divided and a disturbed mind, to his suggestion. Still he followed in the footsteps of the stranger, with a caution that might well have eluded the vigilance of an agency short of that which drew its means of information from sources deeper than any of human power.

When the two watchers had found a secret and suitable place, not far from the postern, they disposed themselves in silence to await the result. The outbuildings lay in deep quiet, not a sound of any sort arising from all of the many tenants they were known to contain. The lines of ragged fences ; the blackened stumps capped with little pyramids of snow ; the taller and sometimes suspiciously looking stubs ; an insulated tree, and, finally, the broad border of forest, were alike motionless, gloomy, and clothed in the doubtful forms of night. Still the space around the well-secured and trebly-barred postern was vacant. A sheet of spotless snow served as a back ground, that would have been sure to betray the presence of any object passing over its surface. Even the conch might be seen suspended from one of the timbers, as mute and inoffensive as the hour when it had been washed by the waves on the sands of the sea-shore.

" Here will we watch for the coming of the stranger, be he commissioned by the powers of air, or be he one sent on an errand of earth," whispered Submission, preparing his arms for immediate use, and disposing of his person, at the same time, in a manner most convenient to endure the weariness of a patient watch.

" I would my mind were at ease, on the question of right-doing in dealing harm to one who disturbs the quiet of a border family," said Dudley, in a tone sufficiently repressed for caution ; " it may be found prudent to strike the first blow, should one like an over-sea gallant, after all, be inclined to trouble us at this hour."

" In that strait thou wilt do well to give little heed to

the order of the offences," gloomily returned the other. " Should another messenger of England appear——"

He paused, for a note of the conch was heard rising gradually on the air, until the whole of the wide valley was filled with its rich and melancholy sound.

" Lip of man is not at the shell!" exclaimed the stranger, who, like Dudley, had made a forward movement towards the postern, the instant the blast reached his ear, and who, like Dudley, recoiled, in an amazement that even his practised self-command could not conceal, as he undeniably perceived the truth of what he had just affirmed. " This exceedeth all former instances of marvellous visitations!"

" It is vain to pretend to raise the feeble nature of man to the level of things coming from the invisible world," returned the woodsman at his side. " In such a strait it is seemly that sinful men should withdraw to the dwellings, where we may sustain our feebleness by the spiritual strivings of the captain."

To this discreet proposal the stranger raised no objection. Without taking the time necessary to effect their retreat, with the precaution that had been observed in their advance, the two adventurers quickly found themselves at the secret entrance, through which they had so lately issued.

" Enter," said the stranger, lowering the piece of the palisado, for the passage of his companion, " enter for Heaven's sake! for it is truly meet that we assemble all our spiritual succour."

Dudley was in the act of complying, when a dark line, accompanied by a low rushing sound, cut the air between his head and that of his companion. At the next instant a flint-headed arrow quivered in the timber.

" The heathen!" shouted the borderer, recovering all his manhood as the familiar danger became apparent, and throwing back a stream of fire in the direction from which the treacherous missile had come. " To the palisadoes, men! the bloody heathen is upon us!"

" The heathen!"—echoed the stranger, in a deep, steady, commanding voice, that had often raised the warning in scenes of even greater emergency, and levelling a pistol which brought a dark form that was gliding across the snow, to one knee,—" the heathen! the bloody heathen is upon us!"

As if both assailants and assailed paused, one moment of profound stillness succeeded this fierce interruption of the quiet of the night. Then the cries of the two adventurers were answered by a burst of yells from a wide circle, that nearly environed the hill. At the same moment, every dark object in the fields appeared to give up a human form. The shouts were followed by a cloud of arrows, that rendered further delay without the cover of the palisadoes eminently hazardous. Dudley entered, but the passage of the stranger would have been cut off, by a leaping, whooping band that pressed fiercely on his rear, had not a broad sheet of flame, glancing from the hill directly in their swarthy and grim countenances, driven the assailants back upon their own footsteps. In another moment, the bolts of the lock were passed, and the two fugitives were in safety behind the ponderous piles of wood.

CHAPTER II.

There need no ghost, my lord, come from the grave,
To tell us this.   *Hamlet.*

ALTHOUGH the minds of most, if not of all, the inmates of the Wish-Ton-Wish had been so powerfully exercised that night, with a belief that the powers of the invisible world were about to be let loose upon them, the danger had now presented itself in a shape too palpable to admit of further doubt. The cry of "the heathen!" had been raised from every lip; even the daughter and élève of Ruth repeated it, as they fled wailing through the buildings, and, for a moment, terror and surprise appeared to involve the assailed in inextricable confusion. But the promptitude of the young men in rushing to the rescue, with the steadiness of Content, soon restored order. The females immediately assumed the semblance of composure ; the family having been too long trained to meet the exigencies of such an emergency to be thrown entirely off its guard, for more than the first and the most appalling moments of the alarm.

The effect of the sudden repulse was such as all experience had taught the colonists to expect in their Indian warfare. The uproar of the onset ceased as abruptly as it had commenced ; and a calmness so tranquil and a stillness so profound succeeded, that one who had for the first time witnessed such a scene might readily have fancied it the effects of some wild and fearful illusion.

During these moments of general and deep silence, the two adventurers, whose retreat had probably hastened the assault, by offering the temptation of an easy passage within the works, left the cover of the piles of wood, and ascended the hill to the place where Dudley knew Content was to be posted, in the event of a summons to the defences.

" Unless much enquiry hath deceived me in the nature of the heathen's craftiness," said the stranger, " we shall have breathing time, ere the onset be renewed. The experience of a soldier bids me say that prudence now urges us to look into the number and position of our foes, that we may order our resistance with better understanding of their force."

" In what manner may this be done ? Thou seest nought about us but the quiet and the darkness of night. Speak of the number of our enemies we cannot ; and sally forth we may not, without certain destruction to all who quit the palisadoes."

" Thou forgettest that we have a hostage in the boy ; he may be turned to some advantage, if our power over his person be used with discretion."

" I doubt that we deceive ourselves with a hope that is vain," returned Content, leading the way as he spoke, however, towards the court which communicated with the principal dwelling. " I have closely studied the eye of that lad, since his unaccountable entrance within the works, and little do I find there that should teach us to expect confidence. It will be happy if some secret understanding with those without has not aided him in passing the palisadoes, and that he prove not a dangerous spy on our force and movements."

" In regard to that he hath entered the dwelling without sound of conch or aid of postern, be not disturbed," returned the stranger, with composure. " Were it fitting, this mystery might be of easy explanation ; but it may truly need all our sagacity to discover whether he hath connection with our foes. The mind of a native does not give up its secrets like the surface of a vanity-feeding mirror."

The stranger spoke like a man who wrapped a portion of his thoughts in reserve ; and his companion listened as one who comprehended more than it might be seemly or discreet to betray. With this secret and yet equivocal understanding of each other's meaning, they entered the dwelling, and soon found themselves in the presence of those they sought.

The constant danger of their situation had compelled the family to bring themselves within the habits of a methodical and severely regulated order of defence. Duties were assigned, in the event of alarm, to the feeblest bodies and the faintest hearts ; and during the moments which preceded the visit of her husband, Ruth had been endeavouring to commit to her female subordinates the several necessary charges that usage, and more particularly the emergency of the hour, appeared so imperiously to require.

" Hasten, Charity, to the block," she said, " and look into the condition of the buckets and the ladders, that, should the heathen drive us to its shelter, provision of water and means of retreat be not wanting in our extremity ; and hie thee, Faith, into the upper apartments, to see that no lights may direct their murderous aim at any in the chambers. Thoughts come tardily when the arrow or the bullet hath already taken its flight. And now that the first assault is over, Mark, and we may hope to meet the wiles of the enemy by some prudence of our own, thou mayest go forth to thy father. It would have been tempting Providence too rashly, hadst thou rushed unbidden

and uninformed, into the first hurry of the danger. Come
hither, child, and receive the blessing and prayers of thy
mother; after which thou shalt, with better trust in Pro
vidence, place thy young person among the combatants, in
the hope of victory. Remember that thou art now of an
age to do justice to thy name and origin; and yet art thou
of years too tender to be foremost in speech, and far less in
action, on such a night as this."

A momentary flush, that only served to render the succeeding paleness more obvious, passed across the brow of
the mother. She stooped and imprinted a kiss on the forehead of the impatient boy, who scarcely waited to receive
this act of tenderness ere he hurried to place himself in the
ranks of her defenders.

" And now," said Ruth, slowly turning her eye from
the door by which the lad had disappeared, and speaking
with a sort of unnatural composure,—" and now will we
look to the safety of those who can be of but little service,
except as sentinels to sound the alarm. When thou art
certain, Faith, that no neglected light is in the rooms
above, take the children to the secret chamber; thence they
may look upon the fields without danger from any chance
direction of the savages' aim. Thou knowest, Ruth, my
frequent teaching in this matter; let no sounds of alarm
nor frightful whoopings of the people without, cause thee
to quit the spot; since thou wilt there be safer even than
in the block, against which many missiles will doubtless be
driven, on account of its seeming air of strength. Timely
notice shall be given of the change, should we seek its
security. Thou wilt descend, only, shouldst thou see
enemies scaling the palisadoes on the side which overhangs
the stream, since there have we the fewest eyes to watch
their movements. Remember that on the side of the out-
buildings and of the fields, our force is chiefly posted;
there can be less reason therefore that thou shouldst expose
thy lives by endeavouring to look too curiously into that
which passeth in the fields. Go, my children, and a
heavenly Providence prove thy guardian."

Ruth stooped to kiss the cheek that her daughter offered
to the salute. The embrace was then given to the other

child, who was in truth scarcely less near her heart, being
the orphan daughter of one who had been as a sister in her
affections. But unlike the kiss she had impressed on the
forehead of Mark, the present embraces were hasty, and
evidently awakened less intense emotion. She had committed the boy to a known and positive danger; but,
under the semblance of some usefulness, she sent the others
to a place believed to be even less exposed, so long as the
enemy could be kept without the works, than the citadel
itself. Still a feeling of deep and maternal tenderness
came over her mind as her daughter retired, and yielding
to its sudden impulse, she recalled the girl to her side.

" Thou wilt repeat the prayer for especial protection
against the dangers of the wilderness," she solemnly continued. " In thy asking, fail not to remember him to
whom thou owest being, and who now exposeth his precious
life, that we may be safe. Thou knowest the Christian's
rock; place thy faith on its foundation."

" And they who seek to kill us," demanded the well
instructed child; " are they too of the number of those
for whom he died?"

" It may not be doubted, though the manner of the
dispensation be so mysterious! Barbarians in their habits,
and ruthless in their enmities, they are creatures of our
nature, and equally objects of his care."

Flaxen locks, that half covered a forehead and face,
across which ran the most delicate tracery of veins, added
lustre to a skin as spotlessly fair as if the warm breezes of
that latitude had never fanned the countenance of the
girl. Through this maze of ringlets, the child turned her
full, clear, blue eyes, bending her looks in wonder and
in fear on the dark visage of the captive Indian youth,
who at that moment was to her a subject of secret horror.
Unconscious of the interest he excited, the lad stood calm,
haughty, and seemingly unobservant. cautious to let no
sign of weakness or of concern escape him in this scene of
womanly emotion.

" Mother," whispered the still wondering child, " may
we not let him go into the forest? I do not love to——"

" This is no time for speech. Go to thy hiding place,

my child, and remember both thy askings and the cautions I have named. Go, and heavenly care protect thy inno-cent head!"

Ruth again stooped, and bowing her face until the features were lost in the rich tresses of her daughter, a moment passed, during which there was an eloquent silence. When she arose, a tear glistened on the cheek of the child. The latter had received the embrace more in apathy than in concern; and now, when led towards the upper rooms, she moved from the presence of her mother, it was with an eye that never bent its rivetted gaze from the features of the young Indian, until the intervening walls hid him entirely from her sight.

" Thou hast been thoughtful and like thyself, my good Ruth," said Content, who at that moment entered, and who rewarded the self-command of his wife by a look of the kindest approbation. " The youths have not been more prompt in meeting the foe at the stockades than thy maidens in looking to their less hardy duties. All is again quiet without; and we come now rather for consultation than for any purposes of strife."

" Then must we summon our father from his post at the artillery in the block."

" It is not needful," interrupted the stranger. " Time presses, for this calm may be too shortly succeeded by a tempest that all our power shall not quell. Bring forth the captive."

Content signed to the boy to approach, and when he was in reach of his hand, he placed him full before the stranger.

" I know not thy name, nor yet even that of thy people," commenced the latter, after a long pause, in which he seemed to study deeply the countenance of the lad; " but certain am I, though a more wicked spirit may still be struggling for the mastery in thy wild mind, that nobleness of feeling is no stranger to thy bosom. Speak; hast thou aught to impart concerning the danger that besets this family? I have learned much this night from thy manner, but to be clearly understood, it is now time that thou shouldst speak in words."

The youth kept his eye fastened on that of the speaker, until the other had ended, and then he bent it slowly, but with searching observation, on the anxious countenance of Ruth.   It seemed as if he balanced between his pride and his sympathies.   The latter prevailed ; for, conquering the deep reluctance of an Indian, he spoke openly, and for the first time, since his captivity, in the language of the hated race.

" I hear the whoops of warriors," was his calm answer. " Have the ears of the pale men been shut ? "

" Thou hast spoken with the young men of thy tribe in the forest, and thou hadst knowledge of this onset ? "

The youth made no reply, though the keen look of his interrogator was met steadily and without fear.   Perceiving that he had demanded more than would be answered, the stranger changed his mode of investigation, masking his enquiries with a little more of artifice.

" It may not be that a great tribe is on the bloody path ! " he said ; " warriors would have walked over the timbers of the palisadoes like bending reeds !   'T is a Pequot who hath broken faith with a Christian, and who is now abroad, prowling as a wolf in the night."

A sudden and wild expression gleamed over the swarthy features of the boy.   His lips moved, and the words that issued from between them were uttered in the tones of biting scorn.   Still he rather muttered, than pronounced aloud, —

" The Pequot is a dog ! "

" It is as I had thought ; the knaves are out of their villages that the Yengeese * may feed their squaws.   But a Narragansett, or a Wompanoag is a man ; he scorns to lurk in the darkness.   When he comes, the sun will light his path.   The Pequot steals in silence, for he fears that the warriors will hear his tread."

It was not easy to detect any evidence that the captive listened, either to the commendation or the censure, with

* The Indian tribes who first became known to the colonists of New-England called the whites " Yengeese," the nearest approach they could make to the word " English," which is still pronounced by many in that region as it is spelt, instead of *Ing*lish.   The most rational explanation of the well-known *soubriquet* of " Yankees " is derived from " Yengeese."

answering sympathy, for marble is not colder than were the muscles of his unmoved countenance.

The stranger studied the expression of his features in vain, and drawing so near as to lay his hand on the naked shoulder of the lad, he added,— "Boy, thou hast heard much moving matter concerning the nature of our Christian faith, and thou hast been the subject of many a fervent asking; it may not be that so much good seed hath been altogether scattered by the way side! Speak; may I again trust thee?"

"Let my father look on the snow. The print of my moccasin goes and comes."

"It is true. Thus far hast thou proved honest; but when the war-whoop shall be thrilling through thy young blood, the temptation to join the warriors may be too strong. Hast any gage, any pledge in which we may find warranty for letting thee depart?"

The boy regarded his interrogator with a look that plainly denoted ignorance of his meaning.

"I would know what thou canst leave with me, to show that our eyes shall again look upon thy face, when we have opened the gate for thy passage into the fields."

Still the gaze of the other was wondering and confused.

"When the white man goes upon the war-path, and would put trust in his foe, he takes surety for his faith, by holding the life of one dear as a warranty of its truth. What canst offer, that I may know thou wilt return from the errand on which I would fain send thee?"

"The path is open?"

"Open, but not certain to be used. Fear may cause thee to forget the way it leads."

The captive now understood the meaning of the other's doubts; but, as if disdaining to reply, he bent his eyes aside, and stood in one of those immovable attitudes, which so often gave him the air of a piece of dark statuary.

Content and his wife had listened to this short dialogue, in a manner to prove that they possessed some secret knowledge, which lessened the wonder they might otherwise have felt, at witnessing so obvious proofs of a secret acquaintance between the speakers. Both, however, manifested unequivocal signs of astonishment, when they first heard English sounds issuing from the lips of the boy. There was, at least, the semblance of hope in the mediation of one who had received, and who had appeared to acknowledge, so much kindness from herself, and Ruth clung to the cheering expectation with the quickness of maternal care.

" Let the boy depart," she said. " I will be his hostage ; should he prove false, there can be less to fear in his absence than in his presence."

The obvious truth of the latter assertion, probably weighed more with the stranger than the unmeaning pledge of the woman.

" There is reason in this," he resumed. " Go, then, into the fields, and say to thy people that they have mistaken the path ; that they are on, hath led them to the dwelling of a friend ; here are no Pequots ; nor any of the men of the Manhattoes ; but Christian Yengeese, who have long dealt with the Indian as one just man dealeth with another. Go, and when thy signal shall be heard at the gate, it shall be open to thee for re-admission."

Thus saying, the stranger motioned to the boy to follow, taking care, as they left the room together, to instruct him in all such minor matter, as might assist in effecting the pacific object of the mission on which he was employed.

A few minutes of doubt and fearful suspense succeeded this experiment. The stranger, after seeing that egress was permitted to his messenger, had returned to the dwelling, and rejoined his companions. He passed the moments in pacing the apartment, with the strides of one in whom powerful concern was strongly at work. At times, the sound of his heavy footstep ceased, and then all listened intently in order to catch any sound that might instruct them in the nature of the scene that was passing without. In the midst of one of these pauses, a yell like that of savage delight rose in the fields. It was then succeeded by the death-like and portentous calm, which had rendered the time since the momentary attack, even more alarming

L

than when the danger had a positive and known character. But all the attention the most intense anxiety could now lend, furnished no additional clue to the movements of their foes. For many minutes, the quiet of midnight reigned, both within and without the defences. In the midst of this suspense, the latch of the door was lifted, and their messenger appeared with that noiseless tread and collected mien, which distinguish the people of his race.

" Thou hast met the warriors of thy tribe?" hastily demanded the stranger.

" The noise did not cheat the Yengeese. It was not a girl laughing in the woods."

" And thou hast said to thy people, ' we are friends ? ' "

" The words of my father were spoken."

" And heard — were they loud enough to enter the ears of the young men ?"

The boy was silent.

" Speak," continued the stranger, elevating his form proudly, like one ready to breast a shock. " Thou hast men for thy listeners. Is the pipe of the savage filled? will he smoke in peace, or holdeth he the tomahawk in a clenched hand ?"

The countenance of the boy worked with a feeling that it was not usual for an Indian to betray. He bent his look, with concern, on the mild eyes of the anxious Ruth ; then drawing a hand slowly from beneath the light robe that partly covered his body, he cast, at the feet of the stranger, a bundle of arrows, wrapped in the glossy and striped skin of the rattlesnake.

" This is warning we may not misconceive !" said Content, raising the well-known emblem of ruthless hostility to the light, and exhibiting it before the eyes of his less instructed companion. " Boy, what have the people of my race done, that thy warriors should seek their blood, to this extremity ?"

When the boy had discharged his duty he moved aside, and appeared unwilling to observe the effect which his message might produce on his companions. But thus questioned, all gentle feelings were near being forgotten, in the sudden force of passion. A hasty glance at Ruth, quelled the emotion, and he continued calm as ever, and silent.

"Boy," repeated Content, "I ask thee why thy people seek our blood?"

The passage of the electric spark is not more subtle, nor is it scarcely more brilliant, than was the gleam that shot into the dark eye of the Indian. The organ seemed to emit rays coruscant as the glance of the serpent. His form appeared to swell with the inward strivings of his spirit, and for a moment there was every appearance of a fierce and uncontrollable burst of ferocious passion. The conquest of feeling was, however, but momentary. He regained his self-command, by a surprising effort of the will, and advancing so near to him who had asked this bold question, as to lay a finger on his breast, the young savage haughtily said —

"See! this world is very wide. There is room on it, for the panther and the deer. Why have the Yengeese and the red men met?"

"We waste the precious moments in probing the stern nature of a heathen," said the stranger. "The object of his people is certain, and, with the aid of the Christian's staff, will we beat back their power. Prudence requireth at our hands, that the lad be secured; after which, we will repair to the stockades and prove ourselves men."

Against this proposal, no reasonable objection could be raised. Content was about to secure the person of his captive in a cellar, when a suggestion of his wife caused him to change his purpose. Notwithstanding the sudden and fierce mien of the youth, there had been such an intelligence created between them, by looks of kindness and interest, that the mother was reluctant to abandon all hope of his aid.

"Miantonimoh!" she said, "though others distrust thy purpose, I will have confidence. Come, then, with me; and while I give thee promise of safety in thine own person, I ask at thy hands the office of a protector for my babes."

The boy made no reply, but as he passively followed his conductress to the chambers, Ruth fancied she read assurance of his faith, in the expression of his eloquent eye. At the same moment her husband and Submission left the house, to take their stations at the palisadoes.

CHAPTER III.

Thou art my good youth, my page ;
I 'll be thy master : walk with me, speak freely.

Cymbeline.

THE apartment in which Ruth had directed the children to be placed, was in the attic, and, as already stated, on the side of the building which faced the stream that ran at the foot of the hill. It had a single projecting window, through which there was a view of the forest, and of the fields on that side of the valley. Small openings in its sides, ad_ mitted also of glimpses of the grounds which lay further in the rear. In addition to the covering of the roofs, and of the massive frame-work of the building, an interior par_ tition of timber protected the place against the entrance of most missiles then known in the warfare of the country. During the infancy of the children, this room had been their sleeping apartment ; nor was it abandoned for that purpose, until the additional outworks, which increased with time around the dwellings, had emboldened the family to trust themselves, at night, in situations more convenient, and which were believed to be no less equally secure against surprise.

" I know thee to be one who feeleth the obligations of a warrior," said Ruth, as she ushered her follower into the presence of the children. " Thou wilt not deceive me ; the lives of these tender. ones are in thy keeping. Look to them, Miantonimoh, and the Christian's God will remem_ ber thee in thine own hour of necessity !"

The boy made no reply, but in a gentle expression which was visible in his dark visage, the mother endeavoured to find the pledge she sought. Then, as the youth, with the delicacy of his race, moved aside, in order that they who were bound to each other by ties so near, might indulge their feelings without observation, Ruth again drew near her offspring, with all the tenderness of a mother beaming in her eyes.

" Once more I bid thee not to look too curiously at the fearful strife that may arise in front of our habitations," she said. " The heathen is truly upon us, with a bloody mind; young, as well as old, must now show faith in the protection of our Master, and such courage as befitteth be_lievers."

" And why is it, mother," demanded her child, " that they seek to do us harm? Have we ever done evil to them?"

" I may not say. He that hath made the earth, hath given it to us for our uses; and reason would seem to teach that if portions of its surface are vacant, he that needeth truly may occupy."

" The savage !" whispered the child, nestling still nearer to the bosom of her stooping parent; " his eye glittereth like the star which hangs above the trees."

" Peace, daughter; his fierce nature broodeth over some fancied wrong!"

" Surely, we are here rightfully. I have heard my father say, that when the Lord made me a present to his arms, our valley was a tangled forest, and that much toil only has made it as it is."

" I hope that what we enjoy, we enjoy rightfully; and yet it seemeth that the savage is ready to deny our claims."

" And where do these bloody enemies dwell? Have they, too, valleys like this, and do the Christians break into them to shed blood in the night?"

" They are of wild and fierce habits, Ruth, and little do they know of our manner of life. Woman is not che_rished as among the people of thy father's race, for force of body is more regarded than kinder ties."

The little auditor shuddered, and when she buried her face deeper in the bosom of her parent, it was with a more quickened sense of maternal affection, and with a livelier view than her infant perception had ever yet known, of the gentle charities of kindred. When she had spoken, the matron impressed the final kiss on the forehead of each of the children, and asking aloud that God might bless them, she turned to go to the performance of duties that called for the exhibition of very different qualities. Before quitting the room, however, she once more approached the boy, and, holding the light before his steady eye, she said solemnly —

" I trust my babes to the keeping of a young warrior !"

The look he returned was, like the others, cold but not discouraging. A gaze of many moments elicited no reply, and Ruth prepared to quit the place, troubled by uncertainty concerning the intentions of the protector she left with the girls, while she still hoped that the many acts of kindness she had shown him during his captivity would not go entirely without their reward. Her hand rested on the bolt of the door, in indecision. The moment was favourable to the character of the youth, for she recalled the manner of his return that night, no less than his former acts of faith, and she was about to leave the passage for his egress open, when an uproar arose on the air, which filled the valley with the hideous cries and yells of a savage onset. Drawing the bolt, the startled woman descended, without further thought, and rushed to her post, with the hurry of one who saw only the necessity of exertion in another scene.

" Stand to the timbers, Reuben Ring ! Bear back the skulking murderers on their bloody followers ! The pikes ! Here, Dudley, is an opening for thy valour. The Lord have mercy on the souls of the ignorant heathen !" mingled with the reports of musketry, the whoops of the warriors, the whizzing of bullets and arrows, with all the other accompaniments of such a contest, were the fearful sounds that saluted the senses of Ruth as she issued into the court. The valley was occasionally lighted by the explosion of fire-arms, and then, at times, the horrible din prevailed in the gloom of deep darkness. Happily, in the midst of all this confusion and violence, the young men of the household were true to their duties. An alarming attempt to scale the stockade had already been repulsed, and the true character of two or three feints having been ascertained, the principal force of the garrison was now actively employed in resisting the main attack.

" In the name of Him who is with us in every danger!" exclaimed Ruth, advancing to two figures that were so busily engaged in their own concerns, as not to heed her approach, " tell me how goes the struggle? Where are my husband and Mark? — or hath it pleased Providence that any of our people should be stricken?"

" It hath pleased the devil," returned Eben Dudley, somewhat irreverently for one of that chastened school, " to send an Indian arrow, through jerkin and skin, into this arm of mine! Softly, Faith; dost think, girl, that the covering of man is like the coat of a sheep, from which the fleece may be plucked at will? I am no moulting fowl, nor is this arrow a feather of my wing. The Lord forgive the rogue for the ill turn he hath done my flesh, say I, and amen like a Christian! He will have occasion, too, for the mercy, seeing he hath nothing further to hope for in this world. Now, Faith, I acknowledge thy kindness, and let there be no more cutting speech between us. Thy tongue often pricketh more sorely than the Indian's arrow."

" Whose fault is it if old acquaintance hath sometimes been overlooked in new conversations? Thou knowest that, wooed by proper speech, no maiden in the colony is wont to render gentler answer. Dost feel uneasiness in thine arm, Dudley?"

" 'Tis not tickling with a straw to drive a flint-headed arrow to the bone! I forgive thee the matter of too much discourse with the trooper, and all the side-cuts of thy over-ambling tongue, on condition that—"

" Out upon thee, brawler! wouldst be praying here the night-long on pretence of a broken skin, and the savage at our gates! A fine character will the Madam render of thy deeds, when the other youths have beaten back the Indian, and thou loitering among the buildings!"

The discomforted borderer was about to curse in his heart the versatile humour of his mistress, when he saw, by a side glance, that ears which had no concern in the subject had liked to have shared in the matter of their discourse. Seizing the weapon which was leaning against the foundation of the block, he hurried past the mistress of the family, and, in another minute, his voice and his musket were again ringing in the uproar.

" Does he bring tidings from the palisadoes ? " repeated Ruth, too anxious that the young man should return to his post, to arrest his retreat. " What saith he of the onset ? "

" The savage hath suffered for his boldness, and little harm hath yet come to our people. Except that yon block of a man hath managed to put an arm before the passage of an arrow, I know not that any of our people have been harmed."

" Hearken ! they retire," said Ruth. " The yells are less near, and our young men will prevail ! Go thou to thy charge among the piles of the fuel, and see that no lurker remaineth to do injury. The Lord hath remembered mercy, and it may yet arrive that this evil shall pass away from before us ! "

The ear of Ruth had not deceived her. The tumult of the assault was gradually receding from the works, and though the flashings of the muskets, and the bellowing reports that rang in the surrounding forest, were not less frequent than before, it was plain that the critical moment of the onset was already past. In place of the fierce effort to carry the place by surprise, the savages had now resorted to means that were more methodical, and which, though not so appalling in appearance, were perhaps quite as certain of final success. Ruth profited by a momentary cessation in the flight of the missiles, to seek those in whose welfare she placed her chief concern.

" Hath other than brave Dudley suffered by this assault ? " demanded the anxious wife, as she passed swiftly among a group of dusky figures that were collected in consultation, on the brow of the declivity ; " hath any need of such care as a woman's hand may bestow ? Heathcote, thy person is unharmed ? "

" Truly, One of great mercy hath watched over it, for little opportunity hath been given to look to our own safety. I fear that some of our young men have not regarded the covers with the attention that prudence requires."

" The thoughtless Mark hath not forgotten my admonitions! Boy, thou hast never lost sight of duty so far as to precede thy father?"

"One sees or thinks but little of the red skins, when the whoop is ringing among the timbers of the palisadoes, mother," returned the boy, dashing his hand across his brow, in order that the drops of blood which were trickling from a furrow left by the passage of an arrow, might not be seen. " I have kept near my father, but whether in his front or in his rear the darkness hath not permitted me to heed."

" The lad hath behaved in a bold and seemly manner," said the stranger; " and he hath shown the metal of his grandsire's stock. Ha! what is't we see gleaming among the sheds? A sortie may be needed to save the granaries and thy folds from destruction."

" To the barns! to the barns!" shouted two of the youths, from their several look-outs.

" The brand is in the buildings!" exclaimed a maiden who discharged a similar duty under cover of the dwellings. Then followed a discharge of muskets, all of which were levelled at the glancing light that was glaring in fearful proximity to the combustible materials which filled the most of the out-buildings. A savage yell, and the sudden extinguishment of the blazing knot, announced the fatal accuracy of the aim.

" This may not be neglected!" exclaimed Content, moved to extraordinary excitement by the extremity of the danger. " Father!" he called aloud, " 'tis fitting time to show our utmost strength."

A moment of suspense succeeded this summons. The whole valley was then as suddenly lighted as if a torrent of the electric fluid flashed across its gloomy bed; a sheet of flame glanced from the attic of the block, and then came the roar of the little piece of artillery which had so long dwelt there in silence. The rattling of a shot among the sheds and the rending of timber followed. Fifty dark forms were seen, by the momentary light, gliding from among the outbuildings, in an alarm natural to their ignorance, and with an agility proportioned to their alarm. The moment was propitious. Content silently motioned to Reuben Ring;

they passed the postern together, and disappeared in the direction of the barns. The period of their absence was one of intense care to Ruth, and it was not without its anxiety even to those whose nerves were better steeled. A few moments, however, served to appease these feelings, for the adventurers returned in safety, and as silently as they had quitted the defences. The trampling of feet on the crust of the snow, the neighing of horses, and the bellowing of frightened cattle, as the terrified beasts scattered about the fields, soon proclaimed the object of the risk which had just been run.

" Enter," whispered Ruth, who held the postern with her own trembling hand. " Enter, of Heaven's mercy. Hast thou given liberty to every hoof, that no living creature perish by the flames ? "

" All ; and truly not too speedily — for, see, the brand is again at work ! "

Content had much reason to felicitate himself on his expedition, for, even while he spoke, half concealed torches, made as usual of blazing knots of pine, were again seen glancing across the fields, evidently approaching the out-buildings by such indirect and covered paths as might protect those who bore them from the shot of the garrison.

A final and common effort was made to arrest the danger. The muskets of the young men were active, and more than once did the citadel of the stern old Puritan give forth its flood of flame, in order to beat back the dangerous visitants. A few shrieks of savage disappointment and of bodily anguish announced the success of these discharges ; but though most of those who approached the barns were either driven back in fear or suffered for their temerity, one among them, more wary or more practised than his companions, found means to effect his object. The firing had ceased, and the besieged were congratulating themselves on success, when a sudden light glared across the fields. A sheet of flame soon came curling over the crest of a wheat-stack, and quickly wrapped the inflammable material in its torrent. Against this destruction there remained no remedy. The barns and enclosures which so lately had been lying in darkness, were instantly

illuminated, and life would have been the penalty paid by
any of either party who should dare to trust his person
within the bright glare. The borderers were soon compelled to fall back, even within the shadows of the hill,
and to seek such covers as the stockades offered, in order to
avoid the aim of the arrow or the bullet.

" This is a mournful spectacle to one that has harvested
in charity with all men," said Content to the trembler who
convulsively grasped his arm, as the flames whirled in the
currents of the heated air, and sweeping once or twice
across the roof of a shed, left a portion of its torrent
creeping insidiously along the wooden covering. " The
in-gathering of a blessed season is about to melt into ashes
before the brand of these accur —"

" Peace, Heathcote ! What is wealth, or the fulness of
thy granaries, to that which remains ! Check these re-
pinings of thy spirit, and bless God that he leaveth us our
babes, and the safety of our inner roofs."

" Thou sayest truly," returned the husband, endeavouring to imitate the meek resignation of his companion.
" What indeed are the gifts of the world, set in the
balance against the peace of mind ! Ha ! that evil blast
of wind sealeth the destruction of our harvest ! The fierce
element is in the heart of the granaries."

Ruth made no reply ; for though less moved by worldly
cares than her husband, the frightful progress of the conflagration alarmed her with a sense of personal danger.
The flames had passed from roof to roof, and meeting
every where with fuel of the most combustible nature, the
whole of the vast range of barns, sheds, granaries, cribs,
and out-buildings was just breaking forth in the brightness
of a torrent of fire. Until this moment, suspense, with
hope on one side and apprehension on the other, had kept
both parties mute spectators of the scene. But yells of
triumph soon proclaimed the delight with which the
Indians witnessed the completion of their fell design. The
whoops followed this burst of pleasure, and a third onset
was made.

The combatants now fought under a brightness which,
though less natural, was scarcely less brilliant than that of

noon-day. Stimulated by the prospect of success which was offered by the conflagration, the savages rushed upon the stockade with more audacity than it was usual to dis_ play in their cautious warfare. A broad shadow was cast by the hill and its buildings across the fields on the side opposite to the flames, and through this belt of comparative gloom, the fiercest of the band made their way to the very palisadoes with impunity. Their presence was announced by the yell of delight, for too many curious eyes had been drinking in the fearful beauty of the conflagration, to note their approach until the attack had nealy proved success_ ful. The rushes to the defence and to the attack were alike quick and headlong. Volleys were useless, for the timbers offered equal security to both the assailants and the assailed. It was a struggle of hand to hand, in which numbers would have prevailed had it not been the 'good fortune of the weaker party to act on the defensive. Blows of the knife were past swiftly between the timbers, and occasionally there was heard the discharge of the musket or the twanging of the bow.

"Stand to the timbers, my men!" said the deep voice of the stranger, who spoke in the midst of the fierce struggle with that commanding and stirring cheerfulness, that familiarity which danger can alone inspire. "Stand to the defences, and they are impassable. Ha! 'twas well meant, friend savage," he muttered between his teeth, as he parried, at some jeopardy to one hand, a thrust aimed at his throat, while with the other he seized the warrior who had inflicted the blow, and drawing his naked breast, with the power of a giant, full against the opening between the timbers, he buried his own keen blade to its haft in the body. The eyes of the victim rolled wildly, and when the iron hand which bound him to the wood with the power of a vice loosened its grasp, he fell motionless on the earth. This death was succeeded by the usual yell of disappointment, and the assailants disappeared as swiftly as they had approached.

"God be praised that we have to rejoice in this ad_ vantage," said Content, enumerating the individuals of his force, with an anxious eye, when all were again assembled

at the stand on the hill, where, favoured by the glaring
light, they could overlook, in comparative security, the
more exposed parts of their defences   "We count our
own, though I fear many may have suffered."

The silence and the occupations of his listeners, most of
whom were staunching their blood, was a sufficient
answer.

"Hist, father!" said the quick-eyed and observant
Mark ; one remaineth on the palisado nearest the wicket.
Is it a savage ; or do I see a stump in the field beyond ?"

All eyes followed the direction of the hand of the
speaker, and there was seen, of a certainty, something
clinging to the inner side of one of the timbers, that bore a
marked resemblance to the human form.   The part of the
stockades where the seeming figure clung lay more in obscurity than the rest of the defences, and doubts as to its
character were not alone confined to the quick-sighted lad
who had first detected its presence.

"Who hangs upon our palisadoes?" called Eben Dudley.   "Speak, that we do not harm a friend!"

The wood itself was not more immovable than the dark
object, until the report of the borderer's musket was heard,
and then it came tumbling to the earth like an insensible
mass.

"Fallen like a stricken bear from his tree!   Life was
in it, or no bullet of mine could have loosened the hold!"
exclaimed Dudley, a little in exultation, as he saw the
success of his aim.

"I will go forward, and see that he is past—"

The mouth of young Mark was stopped by the hand of
the stranger, who calmly observed,—

"I will look into the fate of the heathen myself."   He
was about to proceed to the spot, when the supposed dead
or wounded man sprang to his feet, with a yell that rang
in echoes along the margin of the forest, and bounded towards the cover of the buildings, with high and active
leaps.   Two or three muskets sent their streaks of flame
across his path, but seemingly without success.   Jumping
in a manner to elude the certainty of their fire, the
unharmed savage gave forth another yell of triumph, and

disappeared among the angles of the dwellings. His cries were understood, for answering whoops were heard in the fields, and the foe without again rallied to the attack.

" This may not be neglected," said he who, more by his self-possession and air of authority, than by any known right to command, had insensibly assumed so much authority in the important business of that night: " One like this, within our walls, may quickly bring destruction on the garrison. The postern may be opened to an inroad — "

" A triple lock secures it," interrupted Content. " The key is hid where none other than such as are of our household know where to seek it."

" And happily the means of passing the private wicket are in my possession," muttered the other, in an under tone. " So far, well; but the brand! the brand! the maidens must look to the fires and lights, while the youths make good the stockade, since this assault admitteth not of further delay."

So saying, the stranger gave an example of courage by proceeding to his stand at the pickets, where, supported by his companions, he continued to defend the approaches against a discharge of arrows and bullets that was more distant, but scarcely less dangerous to the safety of those who showed themselves on the side of the acclivity, than those which had been previously showered upon the garrison.

In the mean time, Ruth summoned her assistants, and hastened to discharge the duty which had just been prescribed. Water was cast freely on all the fires, and, as the still raging conflagration continued to give far more light than was either necessary or safe, care was taken to extinguish any torch or candle that, in the hurry of alarm, might have been left to moulder in its socket throughout the extensive range of the dwellings and the offices.

CHAPTER IV.

Thou mild, sad mother —
    Quit him not so soon !
Mother, in mercy, stay !
Despair and death are with him ; and canst thou,
    With that kind, earthward look, go leave him now ? "

                                            DANA.

WHEN these precautions were taken the females returned
to their several look-outs, and Ruth, whose duty it was, in
moments of danger, to exercise a general superintendance,
was left to her meditations, and to such watchfulness as
her fears might excite. Quitting the inner rooms, she
approached the door that communicated with the court,
and for a moment lost the recollection of her immediate
cares in a view of the imposing scene by which she was
surrounded.

By this time the whole of the vast range of out-buildings, which had been constructed, as was usual in the
colonies, of the most combustible materials, and with no
regard to the expenditure of wood, was wrapt in fire. Notwithstanding the position of the intermediate edifices,
broad flashes of light were constantly crossing the court
itself, on whose surface she was able to distinguish the
smallest object, while the heavens above her were glaring
with a lurid red. Through the openings between the
buildings of the quadrangle, the eye could look out upon
the fields, where she saw every evidence of a sullen intention on the part of the savages to persevere in their object.
Dark, fierce-looking, and nearly naked human forms were
seen flitting from cover to cover, while there was not a
stump or log within arrow's flight of the defences, that did
not protect the person of a daring and indefatigable enemy.
It was plain the Indians were there in hundreds, and as
the assaults continued after the failure of a surprise, it was
too evident that they were bent on victory, at some hazard
to themselves. No usual means of adding to the horrors of
the scene were neglected.

Whoops and yells were incessantly ringing around the

place, while the loud and often repeated tones of a conch, betrayed the artifice by which the savages had so often endeavoured, in the earlier part of the night, to lure the garrison out of the palisadoes. A few scattering shot, discharged with deliberation, and from every exposed point within the works, proclaimed both the coolness and the vigilance of the defendants. The little gun in the blockhouse was silent, for the Puritan knew too well its real power to lessen its reputation by a too frequent use. The weapon was therefore reserved for those moments of pressing danger that would be sure to arrive.

On this spectacle Ruth gazed in fearful sadness. The long sustained and sylvan security of her abode was violently destroyed, and in the place of a quiet, which had approached as near as may be on earth to that holy peace for which her spirit strove, she and all she most loved were suddenly confronted with the most frightful exhibition of human horrors. In such a moment, the feelings of a mother were likely to revive, and ere time was given for reflection, aided by the light of the conflagration, the matron was moving swiftly through the intricate passages of the dwelling, in quest of those whom she had placed in the security of the chambers.

" Thou hast remembered to avoid looking on the fields, my children," said the nearly breathless woman as she entered the room. " Be thankful, babes; hitherto the efforts of the savages have been vain, and we still remain masters of our habitations."

" Why is the night so red? Come hither, mother; thou mayest look into the wood as if the sun were shining !"

" The heathens have fired our granaries, and what thou seest is the light of the flames. But happily they cannot put brand into the dwellings while thy father and the young men stand to their weapons. We must be grateful for this security, frail as it seemeth. Thou hast knelt, my Ruth, and hast remembered to think of thy father and brother in thy prayers? "

" I will do so again, mother," whispered the child, bending to her knees, and wrapping her young features in the garments of the matron.

" Why hide thy countenance? One young and innocent as thou, may lift thine eyes to heaven with confidence."

" Mother, I see the Indian, unless my face be hid. He looketh at me, I fear, with wish to do us harm."

" Thou art not just to Miantonimoh, child," answered Ruth, glancing her eye rapidly round to seek the boy, who had modestly withdrawn into a remote and shaded corner of the room. " I left him with thee for a guardian, and not as one who would wish to injure. Now think of thy God, child," imprinting a kiss on the cold, marble-like forehead of her daughter, " and have reliance in his goodness. Miantonimoh, I again leave you with a charge to be their protector," she added, quitting her daughter and advancing towards the youth.

" Mother!" shrieked the child, " come to me, or I die."

Ruth turned from the listening captive, with the quickness of instinct. A glance showed her the jeopardy of her offspring. A naked savage, dark, powerful of frame, and fierce in the frightful masquerade of his war paint, stood winding the silken hair of the girl in one hand, while he already held the glittering axe above a head that seemed inevitably devoted to destruction.

" Mercy! mercy!" exclaimed Ruth, hoarse with horror, and dropping to her knees, as much from inability to stand as with intent to petition. " Monster, strike me, but spare the child!"

The eyes of the Indian rolled over the person of the speaker, but it was with an expression that seemed rather to enumerate the number of his victims, than to announce any change of purpose. With a fiendlike coolness, that bespoke much knowledge of the ruthless practice, he again swung the quivering but speechless child in the air, and prepared to direct the weapon with a fell certainty of aim. The tomahawk had made its last circuit, and an instant would have decided the fate of the victim, when the captive boy stood in front of the frightful actor in this revolting scene. By a quick forward movement of his arm, the blow was arrested. The deep guttural ejaculation, which betrays the surprise of an Indian, broke from the chest of the savage, while his hand fell to his side, and the form of the

M

suspended girl was suffered again to touch the floor. The look and gesture with which the boy had interfered, expressed authority rather than resentment or horror. His air was calm, collected, and, as it appeared by the effect, imposing.

" Go," he said, in the language of the fierce people from whom he had sprung; " the warriors of the pale men are calling thee by name."

" The snow is red with the blood of our young men," the other fiercely answered; " and not a scalp is at the belt of my people."

" These are mine," returned the boy, with dignity, sweeping his arm, while speaking, in a manner to show that he extended protection to all present.

The warrior gazed about him grimly, and like one but half convinced. He had incurred a danger too fearful, in entering the stockade, to be easily diverted from his purpose.

" Listen!" he continued, after a short pause, during which the artillery of the Puritan had again bellowed in the uproar without. " The thunder is with the Yengeese! Our young women will look another way and call us Pequots, should there be no scalps on our pole."

For a single moment the countenance of the boy changed, and his resolution seemed to waver. The other, who watched his eyes with longing eagerness, again seized his victim by the hair, when Ruth shrieked in the accents of despair, —

" Boy! boy! if thou art not with us, God hath deserted us!"

" She is mine," burst fiercely from the lips of the lad. " Hear my words, Wompahwisset; the blood of my father is very warm within me."

The other paused, and the blow was once more suspended. The glaring eye-balls of the savage rested intently on the swelling form and stern countenance of the young hero, whose uplifted hand appeared to menace instant punishment, should he dare to disregard the mediation. The lips of the warrior severed, and the word " Miantonimoh " was uttered, as softly as if it recalled a feeling of sorrow.

Then, as a sudden burst of yells rose above the roar of the conflagration, the fierce Indian turned in his tracks, and, abandoning the trembling and nearly insensible child, he bounded away like a hound loosened on a fresh scent of blood.

" Boy ! boy !" murmured the mother ; " heathen or Christian, there is One that will bless thee !———"

A rapid gesture of the hand interrupted the fervent expression of her gratitude. Pointing after the form of the retreating savage, the lad encircled his own head with a finger, in a manner that could not be mistaken, as he uttered, steadily, but with the deep emphasis of an Indian, —

" The young pale-face has a scalp !"

Ruth heard no more. With instinctive rapidity, every feeling of her soul quickened nearly to agony, she rushed below, in order to warn Mark against the machinations of so fearful an enemy. Her step was heard but for a moment in the vacant chambers, and then the Indian boy, whose steadiness and authority had just been so signally exerted in favour of the children, resumed his attitude of meditation, as quietly as if he took no further interest in the frightful events of the night.

The situation of the garrison was now, indeed, to the last degree critical. A torrent of fire had passed from the further extremity of the out-houses to that which stood nearest to the defences, and, as building after building melted beneath its raging power, the palisadoes became heated nearly to the point of ignition. The alarm created by this imminent danger had already been given, and when Ruth issued into the court, a female was rushing past her, seemingly on some errand of the last necessity.

" Hast seen him ?" demanded the breathless mother, arresting the steps of the quick-moving girl.

" Not since the savage made his last onset ; but I warrant me he may be found near the western loops, making good the works against the enemy !"

" Surely he is not foremost in the fray ! Of whom speakest thou, Faith ? I questioned thee of Mark. There is one, even now, raging within the pickets, seeking a victim."

" Truly, I thought it had been question of ——— : the boy is with his father, and the stranger soldier, who doeth such deeds of valour in our behalf. I have seen no enemy within the palisadoes, Madam Heathcote, since the entry of the man who escaped, by favour of the powers of darkness, from the shot of Eben Dudley's musket."

" And is this evil like to pass from us ?" resumed Ruth, breathing more freely, as she learned the safety of her son ; " or does Providence veil its face in anger ?"

" We keep our own, though the savage hath pressed the young men to extremity. Oh ! it gladdened one's heart to see how brave a guard Reuben Ring, and others near him, made in our behalf. I do think me, Madam Heathcote, that, after all, there is real manhood in the brawler Dudley ! Truly, the youth hath done marvels in the way of exposure and resistance. Twenty times this night have I expected to see him slain."

" And he that lyeth there ?" half whispered the alarmed Ruth, pointing to a spot near them, where, aside from the movements of those who still acted in the bustle of the combat, one lay stretched on the earth ; " who hath fallen ? "

The cheek of Faith blanched to a whiteness that nearly equalled that of the linen, which, even in the hurry of such a scene, some friendly hand had found leisure to throw, in decent sadness, over the form.

" That !" said the faltering girl : " though hurt and bleeding, my brother Reuben surely keepeth the loop at the western angle ; nor is Whittal wanting in sufficient sense to take heed of danger. This may not be the stranger, for under the covers of the postern breastwork he holdeth council with the young captain."

" Art certain, girl ?"

" I saw them both within the minute. Would to God we could hear the shout of noisy Dudley, Madam Heath- cote : his cry cheereth the heart, in a moment awful as this !"

" Lift the cloth," said Ruth, with calm solemnity, " that we may know which of our friends hath been called to the great account."

Faith hesitated, and when, by a powerful effort, in which secret interest had as deep an influence as obedience, she did comply, it was with a sort of desperate resolution. On raising the linen, the eyes of the two women rested on the pallid countenance of one who had been transfixed by an iron-headed arrow. The girl dropped the linen, and in a voice that sounded like a burst of hysterical feeling, she exclaimed, —

" 'Tis but the youth that came lately among us ! We are spared the loss of any ancient friend."

" 'Tis one who died for our safety. I would give largely of this world's comforts that this calamity might not have been, or that greater leisure for the last fearful reckoning had been accorded. But we may not lose the moments in mourning. Hie thee, girl, and sound the alarm that a savage lurketh within our walls, and that he skulketh in quest of a secret blow. Bid all be wary. If the young Mark should cross thy path, speak to him twice of this danger ; the child hath a froward spirit, and may not hearken to words uttered in too great hurry."

With this charge Ruth quitted her maiden. While the latter proceeded to give the necessary notice, the other sought the spot where she had just learned there was reason to believe her husband might be found.

Content and the stranger were in fact met in consultation over the danger which threatened destruction to their most important means of defence. The savages themselves appeared to be conscious that the flames were working in their favour, for their efforts sensibly slackened ; and having already severely suffered in their attempts to annoy the garrison, they had fallen back to their covers, and awaited the moment when their practised cunning should tell them they might, with more flattering promises of success, again rally to the onset. A brief explanation served to make Ruth acquainted with the imminent jeopardy of their situation. Under a sense of a more appalling danger, she lost the recollection of her former

M 3

purpose, and, with a contracted and sorrowing eye, she stood, like her companions, in impotent helplessness, an entranced spectator of the progress of the destruction.

" A soldier should not waste words in useless plaints," observed the stranger, folding his arms like one who was conscious that human effort could do no more, " else should I say, 'tis pity that he who drew yon line of stock-ade hath not remembered the uses of the ditch."

" I will summon the maidens to the wells," said Ruth.

" 'T will not avail us. The arrow would be among them, nor could mortal long endure the heat of yon glow-ing furnace. Thou seest that the timbers already smoke and blacken under its fierceness."

The stranger was still speaking, when a small quivering flame played on the corners of the palisado, nearest the burning pile. The element fluttered like a waving line along the edges of the heated wood, after which it spread over the whole surface of the timber, from its larger base to the pointed summit. As if this had merely been the signal of a general destruction, the flames kindled in fifty places at the same instant, and then the whole line of the stockade, nearest the conflagration, was covered with fire. A yell of triumph arose in the fields, and a flight of arrows, sailing tauntingly into the works, announced the fierce impatience of those who watched the increase of the con-flagration.

" We shall be driven to our block," said Content. " Assemble thy maidens, Ruth, and make speedy prepar-ation for the last retreat."

" I go ; but hazard not thy life in any vain endeavour to retard the flames. There will yet be time for all that is needful to our security."

" I know not," hurriedly observed the stranger; " here cometh the assault in a new aspect !"

The feet of Ruth were arrested. On looking upward she saw the object which had drawn this remark from the last speaker. A small bright ball of fire had arisen out of the fields, and describing an arc in the air, it sailed above their heads and fell on the shingles of a building which formed part of the quadrangle of the inner court. The movement was that of an arrow thrown from a distant bow, and its way was to be traced by a long trail of light, that followed its course like a blazing meteor. This burning arrow had been sent with a cool and practised judgment. It lighted upon a portion of the combustibles that were nearly as inflammable as gunpowder, and the eye had scarcely succeeded in tracing it to its fall, ere the bright flames were seen stealing over the heated roof.

" One struggle for our habitations !" cried Content; but the hand of the stranger was placed firmly on his shoulder. At that instant a dozen similar meteor-looking balls shot into the air, and fell in as many different places on the already half-kindled pile. Further efforts would have been useless. Relinquishing the hope of saving his property, every thought was now given to personal safety.

Ruth recovered from her short trance, and hastened with hurried steps to perform her well-known office. Then came a few minutes of exertion, during which the females transferred all that was necessary to their subsistence, and which had not been already provided in the block, to the little citadel. The glowing light which penetrated the darkest passages among the buildings, prevented this movement from being made without discovery. The whoop summoned their enemies to another attack. The arrows thickened in the air, and the important duty was not performed without risk, as all were obliged, in some degree, to expose their persons while passing to and fro loaded with necessaries. The gathering smoke, however, served in some measure for a screen, and it was not long before Content received the welcome tidings that he might command the retreat of his young men from the palisadoes. The conch sounded the necessary signal, and ere the foe had time to understand its meaning, or profit by the defenceless state of the works, every individual within them had reached the door of the block in safety. Still there was more of hurry and confusion than altogether comported with their safety. They who were assigned to that duty, however, mounted eagerly to the loops, and stood in readiness to pour out their fire on whoever might dare to come within its reach, while a few still lingered in the court, to see that no necessary provision for resistance, or of safety, was forgotten. Ruth had been foremost in exertion, and she now stood pressing her hands to her temples, like one whose mind was bewildered by her efforts.

" Our fallen friend!" she said. " Shall we leave his remains to be mangled by the savage?"

ʌ " Surely not; Dudley, thy hand. We will bear the body within the lower —— Ha! death hath struck another of our family."

The alarm with which Content made this discovery passed quickly to all in hearing. It was but too apparent, by the shape of the linen, that two bodies lay beneath its folds. Anxious and rapid looks were cast, from face to face, in order to learn who was missing; and then, conscious of the hazard of further delay, Content raised the cloth, in order to remove all doubts by certainty. The form of the young borderer, who was known to have fallen, was first slowly and reverently uncovered; but even the most self-restrained among the spectators started back in horror, as his robbed and reeking head showed that a savage hand had worked its ruthless will on the unresisting corpse.

" The other!" Ruth struggled to say, and it was only as her husband had half removed the linen that she could succeed in uttering the words — " Beware the other!"

The warning was not useless, for the linen waved violently as it rose under the hand of Content, and a grim Indian sprang into the very centre of the startled group. Sweeping his armed hand widely about him, the savage broke through the receding circle, and, giving forth the appalling whoop of his tribe, he bounded into the open door of the principal dwelling, so swiftly as utterly to defeat any design of pursuit. The arms of Ruth were frantically extended towards the place where he had disappeared, and she was about to rush madly on his footsteps, when the hand of her husband stopped the movement.

" Wouldst hazard life to save some worthless trifle?"

" Husband, release me!" returned the woman, nearly choked with her agony — "nature hath slept within me!"

" Fear blindeth thy reason ! "

The form of Ruth ceased to struggle. All the madness, which had been glaring wildly about her eyes, disappeared in the settled look of an almost preternatural calm. Collecting the whole of her mental energy in one desperate effort of self-command, she turned to her husband, and as her bosom swelled with the terror that seemed to stop her breath, she said, in a voice that was frightful by its composure,—

" If thou hast a father's heart release me ! — Our babes have been forgotten ! "

The hand of Content relaxed its hold ; and, in another instant, the form of his wife was lost to view on the track that had just been taken by the successful savage. This was the luckless moment chosen by the foe to push his advantage. A fierce burst of yells proclaimed the activity of the assailants; and a general discharge from the loops of the blockhouse sufficiently apprised those in the court that the onset of the enemy was now pushed into the very heart of the defences. All had mounted but the few who lingered to discharge the melancholy duty to the dead. They were too few to render resistance prudent, and yet too many to think of deserting the distracted mother and her offspring, without an effort.

" Enter," said Content, pointing to the door of the block : " it is my duty to share the fate of those nearest my blood."

The stranger made no answer. Placing his powerful hands on the nearly stupified husband, he thrust his person, by an irresistible effort, within the basement of the building, and then he signed, by a quick gesture, for all around him to follow. After the last form had entered, he commanded that the fastenings of the door should be secured, remaining himself, as he believed, alone without. But when, by a rapid glance, he saw there was another gazing in dull awe on the features of the fallen man, it was too late to rectify the mistake. Yells were now rising out of the black smoke that was rolling in volumes from the heated buildings, and it was plain that only a few feet divided them from their pursuers. Beckoning the man who had been excluded from the block to follow, the stern soldier rushed into the principal dwelling, which was still but little injured by the fire. Guided rather by chance than by any knowledge of the windings of the building, he soon found himself in the chambers. He was now at a loss whither to proceed. At that moment, his companion, who was no other than the idiot Whittal Ring, took the lead, and in another instant they were at the door of the secret apartment.

"Hist!" said the stranger, raising a hand to command silence as he entered the room. "Our hope is in secrecy."

"And how may we escape without detection?" demanded the mother, pointing about her at objects illuminated by a light so powerful as to penetrate every cranny of the ill-constructed building. "The noonday sun is scarce brighter than this dreadful fire!"

"God is in the elements! His guiding hand shall point the way. But here we may not tarry, for the flames are already on the shingles. Follow, and speak not."

Ruth pressed the children to her side, and the whole party left the apartment of the attic in a body. Their descent to a lower room was made quickly and without discovery. But here their leader paused, for the state of things without was one to demand the utmost steadiness of nerve and great reflection.

The Indians had by this time gained command of the whole of Mark Heathcote's possessions, with the exception of the block-house; and as their first act had been to apply the brand wherever it might be wanting, the roar of the conflagration was now heard in every direction. The discharge of muskets and the whoops of the combatants, however, while they added to the horrible din of such a scene, proclaimed the unconquered resolution of those who held the citadel. A window of the room they occupied enabled the stranger to take a cautious survey of what was passing without. The court, lighted to the brilliancy of day, was empty, for the increasing heat of the fires, no less than the discharges from the loops, still kept the cautious savages to their covers. There was barely hope, that the space between the dwelling and the block-house might yet be passed in safety.

" I would I had asked that the door of the block should be held in hand," muttered Submission : " it would be death to linger an instant in that fierce light ; nor have we any manner of ——— "

A touch was laid upon his arm, and turning, the speaker saw the dark eye of the captive boy looking steadily in his face.

" Wilt do it ? " demanded the other, in a manner to show that he doubted while he hoped.

A speaking gesture of assent was the answer, and then the form of the lad was seen gliding quietly from the room.

Another instant and Miantonimoh appeared in the court. He walked with the deliberation that one would have shown in moments of the most entire security. A hand was raised towards the loops, as if to betoken amity, and then dropping the limb, he moved with the same slow step into the very centre of the area. Here the boy stood in the fullest glare of the conflagration, and turned his face deliberately on every side of him. The action showed that he wished to invite all eyes to examine his person. At this moment the yells ceased in the surrounding covers, proclaiming alike the common feeling that was awakened by his appearance, and the hazard that any other would have incurred by exposing himself in that fearful scene. When this act of exceeding confidence had been performed, the boy drew a pace nearer to the entrance of the block.

" Comest thou in peace, or is this another device of Indian treachery ? " demanded a voice, through an opening in the door, left expressly for the purposes of parley.

The boy raised the palm of one hand towards the speaker, while he laid the other with a gesture of confidence on his naked breast.

" Hast aught to offer in behalf of my wife and babes ? If gold will buy their ransom, name thy price."

Miantonimoh was at no loss to comprehend the other's meaning. With the readiness of one whose faculties had been early schooled in the inventions of emergencies, he made a gesture that said even more than his figurative words, as he answered, —

" Can a woman of the pale-faces pass through wood? An Indian arrow is swifter than the foot of my mother."

" Boy, I trust thee," returned the voice from within the loop. " If thou deceivest beings so feeble and so innocent, Heaven will remember the wrong."

Miantonimoh again made a sign to show that caution must be used, and then he retired, with a step calm and measured as that used in his advance. Another pause to the shouts betrayed the interest of those whose fierce eyes watched his movements in the distance.

When the young Indian had rejoined the party in the dwelling, he led them, without being observed, by the lurking band that still hovered in the smoke of the surrounding buildings, to a spot that commanded a full view of their short but perilous route. At this moment the door of the block-house half opened, and was closed again. Still the stranger hesitated, for he saw how little was the chance that all should cross the court unharmed, and to pass it by repeated trials he knew to be impossible.

" Boy," he said, " thou, who hast done thus much, may still do more. Ask mercy for these children, in some manner that may touch the hearts of thy people."

Miantonimoh shook his head, and pointing to the ghastly corpse that lay in the court, he answered coldly, —

" The red man has tasted blood."

" Then must the desperate trial be done ! Think not of thy children, devoted and daring mother, but look only to thine own safety. This witless youth and I will charge ourselves with the care of the innocents."

Ruth waved him away with her hand, pressing her mute and trembling daughter to her bosom, in a manner to show that her resolution was taken. The stranger yielded ; and turning to Whittal, who stood near him, seemingly as much occupied in vacant admiration of the blazing piles, as in any apprehension of his own personal danger, he bade him look to the safety of the remaining child. Moving in front himself, he was about to offer Ruth such protection as the case afforded, when a window in the rear of the house was dashed inward, announcing the entrance of the enemy, and the imminent danger that their flight would be intercepted. There was no time to lose, for it was now certain that only a single room separated them from their foes. The generous nature of Ruth was roused; and catching Martha from the arms of Whittal Ring, she endeavoured, by a desperate effort, in which feeling, rather than any reasonable motive, predominated, to envelope both the children in her robe.

" I am with ye!" whispered the agitated woman; " hush ye, hush ye, babes! thy mother is nigh!"

The stranger was very differently employed. The instant the crash of glass was heard, he rushed to the rear, and he had already grappled with the savage so often named, and who acted as guide to a dozen fierce and yelling followers.

" To the block !" shouted the steady soldier, while with a powerful arm he held his enemy in the throat of the narrow passage, stopping the approach of those in the rear by the body of his foe. " For the love of life and children, woman, to the block !"

The summons rang frightfully in the ears of Ruth, but, in that moment of extreme jeopardy, her presence of mind was lost. The cry was repeated, and not till then did the bewildered mother catch her daughter from the floor. With eyes still bent on the fierce struggle in her rear, she clasped the child to her heart and fled, calling on Whittal Ring to follow. The lad obeyed, and ere she had half crossed the court, the stranger, still holding his savage shield between him and his enemies, was seen endeavouring to take the same direction. The whoops, the flight of arrows, and the discharges of musketry that succeeded, proclaimed the whole extent of the danger. But fear had lent unnatural vigour to the limbs of Ruth, and the gliding arrows themselves scarce sailed more swiftly through the heated air, than she darted into the open door of the block. Whittal Ring was less successful. As he crossed the court, bearing the child intrusted to his care, an arrow pierced his flesh. Stung by the pain, the witless lad turned to chide the hand that had inflicted the injury.

" On, foolish boy !" cried the stranger, as he passed him, still making a target of the body of the savage that was writhing in his grasp ; " on, for thy life, and that of the babe !"

The mandate came too late. The hand of an Indian was already on the innocent victim, and in the next instant the child was sweeping the air, while with a short yell the keen axe flourished above his head. A shot from the loops laid the monster dead in his tracks. The girl was instantly seized by another hand, and as the captor with his prize darted unharmed into the dwelling, there arose in the block a common exclamation of the name of " Miantonimoh !" Two more of the savages profited by the pause of horror that followed, to lay hands on the wounded Whittal, and to drag him within the blazing building. At the same moment, the stranger cast the unresisting savage back upon the weapons of his companions. The bleeding and half-strangled Indian met the blows which had been aimed at the life of the soldier, and as he staggered and fell, his vigorous conqueror disappeared in the block. The door of the little citadel was instantly closed, and the savages, who rushed headlong against the entrance, heard the fitting of the bars which secured it against their attacks. The yell of retreat was raised, and in the next instant the court was left to the possession of the dead.

CHAPTER V.

—— Did Heaven look on,
And would not take their part ?
—— Heaven rest them now !   *Macbeth.*

" WE will be thankful for this blessing," said Content, as he aided the half unconscious Ruth to mount the ladder, yielding himself to a feeling of nature that said little against his manhood. " If we have lost one that we loved, God hath spared our own child."

His breathless wife threw herself into a seat, and folding the treasure to her bosom, she whispered rather than said aloud,—" From my soul, Heathcote, am I grateful!"

" Thou shieldest the babe from my sight," returned the father, stooping to conceal a tear that was stealing down his brown cheek, under a pretence of embracing the child —but suddenly recoiling, he added, in alarm,—" Ruth!" Startled by the tone in which her husband uttered her name, the mother threw aside the folds of her dress, which still concealed the girl, and stretching her out to the length of an arm, she saw that, in the hurry of the appalling scene, the children had been exchanged, and that she had saved the life of Martha.

Notwithstanding the generous disposition of Ruth, it was impossible to repress the feeling of disappointment which came over her with the consciousness of the mistake. Nature at first had sway, and to a degree that was fearfully powerful.

" It is not our babe!" shrieked the mother, still holding the child at the length of her arm, and gazing at its innocent and terrified countenance, with an expression that Martha had never yet seen gleaming from eyes that were, in common, so soft and so indulgent.

" I am thine! I am thine!" murmured the little trembler, struggling in vain to reach the bosom that had so long cherished her infancy. " If not thine, whose am I?"

The gaze of Ruth was still wild, the workings of her features hysterical.

" Madam — Mrs. Heathcote — mother!" came, timidly, and at intervals, from the lips of the orphan. Then the heart of Ruth relented. She clasped the daughter of her friend to her breast, and nature found a temporary relief in one of those frightful exhibitions of anguish, which appear to threaten the dissolution of the link which connects the soul with the body.

" Come, daughter of John Harding," said Content, looking around him with the assumed composure of a chastened man, while natural regret struggled hard at his heart; " this has been God's pleasure: it is meet that we kiss his parental hand. Let us be thankful," he added, with a quivering lip, but steady eye, " that even this mercy hath been shown. Our babe is with the Indian, but our hopes are far beyond the reach of savage malignity. We have not laid up treasure where moth and rust can corrupt, or where thieves may break in and steal. It may be that the morning shall bring means of parley, and, haply, opportunity of ransom."

There was the glimmering of hope in this suggestion. The idea seemed to give a new direction to the thoughts of Ruth, and the change enabled the long habits of self-restraint to regain something of their former ascendency. The fountains of her tears became dry, and, after one short and terrible struggle, she was again enabled to appear composed. But at no time, during the continuance of that fearful struggle, was Ruth Heathcote again the ready and useful agent of activity and order she had been in the earlier events of the night.

It is scarcely necessary to remind the reader that the brief burst of parental agony which has just been related, escaped Content and his wife, amid a scene in which the other actors were too much occupied by their exertions to note its exhibition. The fate of those in the block was too evidently approaching its close, to allow of any interest in such an episode to the great tragedy of the moment.

The character of the contest had in some measure changed. There was no longer any immediate apprehension from the missiles of the assailants, though danger pressed upon the besieged in a new, and even in a more horrible aspect. Now and then, indeed, an arrow quivered in the openings of the loops, and the blunt Dudley had once a narrow escape from the passage of a bullet, which, guided by chance, or aimed by a hand surer than common, glanced through one of the narrow slits, and would have terminated the history of the borderer, had not the head it obliquely encountered been too solid to yield even to such an assault. The attention of the garrison was chiefly called to the imminent danger of the surrounding fire. Though the probability of such an emergency as that in which the family was now placed had certainly been fore-seen, and in some degree guarded against in the size of the area and in the construction of the block, yet it was found that the danger exceeded all former calculations.

For the basement there was no reason to feel alarm. It was of stone, and of a thickness and a material to put at defiance any artifices that their enemy night find time to practise. Even the two upper stories were comparatively safe, for they were composed of blocks so solid as to require time to heat them, and they were consequently as little liable to combustion as wood well could be. But the roof, like all of that, and indeed like most of the present, day in America, was composed of short inflammable shingles of pine. The superior height of the tower was some little protection ; but as the flames rose roaring above the build_ ings of the court, and waved in wide circuits around the heated area, the whole of the fragile covering of the block was often wrapped in folds of fire. The result may be anticipated. Content was first recalled from the bitterness of his parental regret, by a cry, which passed among the family, that the roof of their little citadel was in flames. One of the ordinary wells of the habitation was in the basement of the edifice, and it was fortunate that no pre-caution necessary to render it serviceable, in an emergency like that which was now arrived, had been neglected. It has been already stated that a well-secured shaft of stone rose through the lower apartment into the upper floor. Profiting by this happy precaution, the handmaidens of Ruth plied the buckets with diligence, while the young men cast water freely on the roof from the windows of the attic. The latter duty, it may readily be supposed, was not performed without hazard. Flights of arrows were constantly directed against the labourers, and more than one of the youths received greater or less injuries while exposed to their annoyance. There were, indeed, a few minutes during which it remained a question of grave interest how far the risk they ran was likely to be crowned with success. The excessive heat of so many fires, and the occasional contact with the flames, as they swept in eddies over the place, began to render it doubtful whether any human efforts could long arrest the evil. Even the massive and moistened logs of the body of the work began

N

to smoke, and it was found, by experiment, that the hand could rest but a moment on their surface.

During this interval of deep suspense, all the men posted at the loops were called to aid in extinguishing the fire. Resistance was forgotten in the discharge of a duty that had become still more pressing. Ruth herself was aroused by the nature of the alarm; and all hands and all minds were arduously occupied in a toil that diverted attention from incidents which had less interest, because they were teeming less with instant destruction. Danger is known to lose its terrors by familiarity. The young borderers became reckless of their persons in the ardour of exertion; and as success began to crown their efforts, something like the levity of happier moments got the better of their concern. Stolen and curious glances were thrown around a place that had so long been kept sacred to the secret uses of the Puritan, when it was found that the flames were subdued, and that the present danger was averted. The light glared powerfully through several openings in the shingles, no less than through the windows; and every eye was enabled to scan the contents of an apartment which all had longed, though none had ever before presumed, to enter.

" The captain looketh well to the body," whispered Reuben Ring to one of his comrades, as he wiped the effects of the toil from a sun-burnt brow. " Thou seest, Hiram, that there is good store of cheer."

" The buttery is not better furnished!" returned the other, with the shrewdness and ready observation of a border man.

" It is known that he never toucheth that which the cow yields, except as it comes from the creature, and here we find the best that the madam's dairy can yield!"

" Surely yon buff jerkin is like to those worn by the idle cavaliers at home! I think it be long since the captain hath ridden forth in such a guise."

" That may be matter of ancient usage, for thou seest he hath relics of the fashion of the English troopers in this bit of steel; it is like he holdeth deep exercise over the vanities of his youth, while recalling the times in which they were worn."

This conjecture appeared to satisfy the other, though it is probable that a sight of a fresh store of bodily aliment, which was soon after exposed, in order to gain access to the roof, might have led to some further inferences, had more time been given to conjectures. But at this moment a new wail proceeded from the maidens who plied the buckets beneath.

" To the loops! to the loops, or we are lost!" was a summons that admitted of no delay. Led by the stranger, the young men rushed below; where, in truth, they found a serious demand on all their activity and courage.

The Indians were wanting in none of the sagacity which so remarkably distinguishes the warfare of this cunning race. The time spent by the family in arresting the flames had not been thrown away by the assailants. Profiting by the attention of those within being given to efforts that were literally of the last importance, they had found means to convey burning brands to the door of the block, against which they piled a mass of blazing combustibles, that threatened shortly to open the way into the basement of the citadel itself. In order to mask this design, and to protect their approaches, the savages had succeeded in dragging bundles of straw, and other similar materials, to the foot of the work, to which the fire soon communicated, and which, consequently, served both to increase the actual danger of the building, and to distract the attention of those by whom it was defended. Although the water that fell from the roof served to retard the progress of these flames, it contributed to produce the effect, of all others, that was most desired by the savages. The dense volumes of smoke that arose from the half-smothered fire first apprised the females of the new danger which assailed them. When Content and the stranger reached the principal floor of the citadel, it required some little time, and no small degree of coolness, to comprehend the situation in which they were now placed. The vapour that rolled upward from the wet straw and hay had already penetrated into the apartment, and it was with no slight difficulty that they who occupied it were enabled to distinguish objects, or even to breathe.

" Here is matter to exercise our utmost fortitude," said the stranger to his constant companion. " We must look to this new device, or we come to the fate of death by fire. Summon the stoutest-hearted of thy youths, and I will lead them to a sortie, ere the evil get to be past a remedy."

" That were certain victory to the heathen. Thou hearest by their yells that 'tis no small band of scouters who beleaguer us ; a tribe hath sent forth its chosen warriors to do their wickedness. Better is it that we bestir ourselves to drive them from our door, and to prevent the further annoyance of this cloud ; since, to issue from the block at this moment would be to offer our heads to the tomahawk, and to ask mercy is as vain as to hope to move the rock with tears."

" And in what manner may we do this ? "

" Our muskets will still command the entrance, by means of these downward loops ; and water may be yet applied through the same openings. Thought hath been had of this danger, in the disposition of the place."

" Then, of Heaven's mercy ! delay not the effort."

The necessary measures were taken instantly. Eben Dudley applied the muzzle of his piece to a loop, and discharged it downward, in the direction of the endangered door. But aim was impossible in the obscurity, and his want of success was proclaimed by a shout of triumph. Then followed a flood of water, which, however, was scarcely of more service, since the savages had foreseen its use, and had made a provision against its effects, by placing boards, and such vessels as they found scattered among the buildings, above the fire, in a manner to prevent most of the fluid from reaching its aim.

" Come hither with thy musket, Reuben Ring," said Content, hurriedly ; " the wind stirreth the smoke here ; the savages still heap fuel against the wall."

The borderer complied. There were in fact moments when dark human forms were to be seen gliding in silence around the building, though the density of the vapour rendered the forms indistinct and their movements doubt ful. With a cool and practised eye, the youth sought a victim; but as he discharged his musket an object glanced near his own visage, as though the bullet had recoiled on him who had given it a very different mission. Stepping backward a little hurriedly, he saw the stranger pointing through the smoke at an arrow which still quivered in the floor above them.

" We cannot long abide these assaults," the soldier muttered; " something must be speedily devised, or we fall."

His words ceased, for a yell that appeared to lift the floor on which he stood, announced the destruction of the door and the presence of the savages in the basement of the tower. Both parties appeared momentarily confounded at this unexpected success, for while the one stood mute with astonishment and dread, the other did little more than triumph. But this inaction was soon over. The conflict was resumed, though the efforts of the assailants began to assume the confidence of victory, while on the part of the besieged they partook fearfully of the aspect of despair.

A few muskets were discharged, both from below and above, at the intermediate floor, but the thickness of the planks prevented the bullets from doing injury. Then commenced a struggle in which the respective qualities of the combatants were exhibited in a singularly characteristic manner. While the Indians improved their advantages beneath with all the arts known to savage warfare, the young men resisted with that wonderful aptitude of expedient, and readiness of execution, which distinguish the American borderer.

The first attempt of the assailants was to burn the floor of the lower apartment. In order to effect this, they threw vast piles of straw into the basement. But ere the brand was applied, water had reduced the inflammable material to a black and murky pile. Still the smoke nearly effected a conquest which the fire itself failed to achieve. So suffocating indeed were the clouds of vapour which ascended through the crevices, that the females were compelled to seek a refuge in the attic. Here the

N 3

openings in the roof, and a swift current of air, relieved them in some degree from its annoyance.

When it was found that the command of the well afforded the besieged the means of protecting the wood-work of the interior, an effort was made to cut off the communication with the water, by forcing a passage into the circular stone shaft, through which it was drawn into the room above. This attempt was defeated by the readi-ness of the youths, who soon cut holes in the floor whence they sent down certain death on all beneath. Perhaps no part of the assault was more obstinate than that which ac-companied this effort, nor did either assailants or assailed, at any time during its continuance, suffer greater personal injury. After a long and fierce struggle the resistance was effectual, and the savages had recourse to new schemes in order to effect their object.

During the first moments of their entrance, and with a view to reap the fruits of the victory when the garrison should be more effectually subdued, most of the furniture of the dwelling had been scattered by the conquerors on the side of the hill. Among other articles, some six or seven beds had been dragged from the dormitories. These were now brought into play, as powerful instruments in the assault. They were cast, one by one, on the still burning though smothered flames, in the basement of the block, whence they sent up a cloud of their intolerable effluvia. At this trying moment the appalling cry was heard in the block, that the well had failed! The buckets ascended as empty as they went down, and they were thrown aside as no longer useful. The savages seemed to comprehend their advantage, for they profited by the confusion that succeeded among the assailed, to feed the slumbering fires. The flames kindled fiercely, and in less than a minute they became too violent to be subdued. They were soon seen playing on the planks of the floor above. The subtle element flashed from point to point, and it was not long, ere it was stealing up the outer side of the heated block itself.

The savages now knew that conquest was sure. Yells and whoopings proclaimed the fierce delight with which they witnessed the certainty of their victory. Still there was something portentous in the death-like silence with which the victims within the block awaited their fate. The whole exterior of the building was already wrapped in flames, and yet no show of further resistance, no petition for mercy, issued from its bosom. The unnatural and frightful stillness that reigned within was gradually communicated to those without. The cries and shouts of triumph ceased, and the crackling of the flames, or the falling of timber in the adjoining buildings, alone disturbed the awful calm. At length a solitary voice was heard in the block. Its tones were deep, solemn, and imploring. The fierce beings who surrounded the glowing pile bent forward to listen, for their quick faculties caught the first sounds that were audible. It was Mark Heathcote, pouring out his spirit in prayer. The petition was fervent, but steady; and though uttered in words that were unintelligible to those without, they knew enough of the practices of the colonists to be aware that it was the chief of the pale-faces holding communion with his God. Partly in awe, and partly in doubt of what might be the consequences of so mysterious an asking, the dark crowd withdrew to a little distance, and silently watched the progress of the destruction. They had heard strange sayings of the power of the Deity of their invaders, and as their victims appeared suddenly to cease using any of the known means of safety, they appeared to expect, perhaps they did expect some unequivocal manifestation of the power of the Great Spirit of the stranger.

Still no sign of pity, no relenting from the ruthless barbarity of their warfare, escaped any of the assailants. If they thought at all of the temporal fate of those who might still exist within the fiery pile, it was only to indulge in some passing regret that the obstinacy of the defence had deprived them of the glory of bearing the usual bloody tokens of victory in triumph to their villages. But even these peculiar and deeply-rooted feelings were forgotten, as the progress of the flames placed the hope of its indulgence beyond all possibility.

The roof of the block rekindled, and, by the light that

shone through the loops, it was but too evident the interior was in a blaze. Once or twice, smothered sounds came out of the place, as if suppressed shrieks were escaping the females; but they ceased so suddenly as to leave doubts among the auditors whether it were more than the deception of their own excited fancies. The savages had witnessed many a similar scene of human suffering, but never one before in which death was met by so unmoved a calmness. The serenity that reigned in the blazing block communicated to them a feeling of awe, and when the pile came a tumbling and blackened mass of ruins to the earth, they avoided the place, like men that dreaded the vengeance of a Deity who knew how to infuse so deep a sentiment of resignation in the breasts of his worshippers.

Though the yells of victory were again heard in the valley that night, and though the sun had arisen before the conquerors deserted the hill, but few of the band found resolution to approach the smouldering pile, where they had witnessed so impressive an exhibition of Christian fortitude. The few that did draw near stood around the spot, rather in the reverence with which an Indian visits the graves of the just, than in the fierce rejoicings with which he is known to glut his revenge over a fallen enemy.

CHAPTER VI.

> What are these,
> So withered, and so wild in their attire;
> That look not like the inhabitants of earth,
> And yet are on't ?   *Macbeth.*

THAT sternness of the season which has already been mentioned in these pages, is never of long continuance in the month of April. A change in the wind had been noted by the hunters, even before they retired from their range among the hills; and though too seriously occupied to pay close attention to the progress of the thaw, more

than one of the young men had found occasion to remark
that the final breaking up of the winter had arrived. Long
ere the scene of the preceding chapter reached its height,
the southern winds had mingled with the heat of the
conflagration. Warm airs, that had been following the
course of the Gulf Stream, were driven to the land, and
sweeping over the narrow island, that at this point forms
the advanced work of the continent, but a few short hours
were passed before they had destroyed every chilling
remnant of the dominion of winter. Warm, bland, and
rushing in torrents, the subtle currents penetrated the
forests, melted the snows from the fields, and as all alike
felt the genial influence, it appeared to bestow a renovated
existence on man and beast. With morning, therefore, a
landscape very different from that last placed before the
mind of the reader, presented itself in the valley of the
Wish-Ton-Wish.

The winter had entirely disappeared, and as the buds
had begun to swell under the occasional warmth of the
spring, one ignorant of the past would not have supposed
that the advance of the season had been subject to so stern
an interruption. But the principal and most melancholy
change was in the more artificial parts of the view. Instead
of those simple and happy habitations which had crowned
the little eminence, there remained only a mass of blackened
and charred ruins. A few abused and half-destroyed
articles of household furniture lay scattered on the sides of
the hill, and, here and there, a dozen palisadoes, favoured
by some accidental cause, had partially escaped the flames.
Eight or ten massive and dreary-looking stacks of chimneys
rose out of the smoking piles. In the centre of the desolation was the stone basement of the block-house, on which
still stood a few gloomy masses of the timber resembling
coal. The naked and unsupported shaft of the well raised
its circular pillar from the centre, looking like a dark
monument of the past. The wide ruin of the out-buildings blackened one side of the clearing, and, in different
places, the fences, like radii diverging from the common
centre of destruction, had led off the flames into the fields.
A few domestic animals ruminated in the back-ground, and

even the feathered inhabitants of the barns still kept aloof, as if warned by their instinct that danger lurked around the site of their ancient abodes. In all other respects the view was calm and lovely as ever. ... The sun shone from a sky in which no cloud was visible. The blandness of the winds, and the brightness of the heavens, lent an air of animation to even the leafless forest: and the white vapour, that continued to rise from the smouldering piles, floated high over the hills, like the peaceful smoke of the cottage curling above the roof.

The ruthless band which had occasioned this sudden change was already far on the way to its villages, or haply, it sought some other scene of blood. A skilful eye might have traced the route these fierce creatures of the woods had taken, by fences hurled from their places, or by the carcass of some animal that had fallen, in the wantonness of victory, beneath a parting blow. Of all these wild beings one only remained; and he appeared to linger at the spot in the indulgence of feelings that were foreign to those passions that had so recently stirred the bosoms of his comrades.

It was with a slow, noiseless step that the solitary loiterer moved about the scene of destruction. He was first seen treading, with a thoughtful air, among the ruins of the buildings that had formed the quadrangle, and then, seemingly led by an interest in the fate of those who had so miserably perished, he drew nearer to the pile in its centre. The nicest and most attentive ear could not have detected the fall of his foot, as the Indian placed it within the gloomy circle of the ruined wall, nor is the breathing of the infant less audible, than the manner in which he drew breath while standing in a place so lately consecrated by the agony and martyrdom of a Christian family. It was the boy called Miantonimoh, seeking some melancholy memorial of those with whom he had so long dwelt in amity if not in confidence.

One skilled in the history of savage passions might have found a clue to the workings of the mind of the youth in the play of his speaking features. As his dark glittering eye rolled over the smouldering fragments, it seemed to search keenly for some vestige of the human form. The element, however, had done its work too greedily to have left many visible memorials of its fury. An object resembling that he sought, however, caught his glance, and stepping lightly to the spot where it lay, he raised the bone of a powerful arm from the brands. The flashing of his eye as it lighted on this sad object, was wild and exulting, like that of the savage when he first feels the fierce joy of glutted vengeance; but gentler recollections came with the gaze, and kinder feelings evidently usurped the place of the hatred he had been taught to bear a race who were so fast sweeping his people from the earth. The relic fell from his hand, and had the gentle Ruth been there to witness the melancholy and relenting shade that clouded his swarthy features, she might have found pleasure in the certainty that all her kindness had not been wasted.

Regret soon gave place to awe. To the imagination of the Indian, it seemed as if a still voice, like that which is believed to issue from the grave, was heard in the place. Bending his body forward, he listened with the intensity and acuteness of a savage. He thought the smothered tones of Mark Heathcote were again audible, holding communion with his God. The chisel of the Grecian would have loved to delineate the attitudes and movements of the wondering boy as he slowly and reverently withdrew from the spot. His look was rivetted on the vacancy, where the upper apartments of the block had stood, and where he had last seen the family, calling in their extremity on their Deity for aid. Imagination still painted the victims in their burning pile. For a minute longer, during which brief space the young Indian probably expected to see some vision of the pale-faces, did he linger near; and then, with a musing air and softened mind, he trod lightly along the path which led on the trail of his people. When his active form reached the boundary of the forest, he again paused, and taking a final gaze at the place, where fortune had made him a witness of so much domestic peace, and of so much sudden misery, his form was quickly swallowed in the gloom of his native woods.

The work of the savages now seemed complete. An effectual check appeared to be placed to the further progress of civilisation in the ill-fated valley of the Wish-Ton-Wish. Had nature been left to its own work, a few years would have covered the deserted clearing with its ancient vegetation; and half a century would have again buried the whole of its quiet glades in the shadows of the forest. But it was otherwise decreed.

The sun had reached the meridian, and the hostile band had been gone some hours, before aught occurred likely to effect this seeming decision of Providence. To one acquainted with the recent horrors, the breathing of the airs over the ruins might have passed for the whisperings of departed spirits. In short, it appeared as if the silence of the wilderness had once more resumed its reign, when it was suddenly though slightly interrupted. A movement was made within the ruins of the block. It sounded as if billets of wood were gradually and cautiously displaced, and then a human head was reared slowly, and with marked suspicion, above the shaft of the well. The wild and unearthly air of this seeming spectre, was in keeping with the rest of the scene. A face begrimed with smoke and stained with blood, a head bound in some fragment of a soiled dress, and eyes that were glaring in a species of dull horror, were objects in unison with all the other frightful accessories of the place.

" What seest thou ? " demanded a deep voice from within the walls of the shaft. " Shall we again come to our weapons, or have the agents of Moloch departed ? Speak, entranced youth, what dost behold ? "

" A sight to make a wolf weep !" returned Eben Dudley, raising his large frame so as to stand erect on the shaft, where he commanded a bird's-eye view of most of the desolation of the valley. " Evil though it be, we may not say that forewarning signs have been withheld. But what is the cunningest man when mortal wisdom is weighed in the scale against the craft of devils ! Come forth ; Belial hath done his worst, and we have a breathing time."

The sounds, which issued still deeper from the well, denoted the satisfaction with which this intelligence was

received, no less than the alacrity with which the summons
of the borderer was obeyed. Sundry blocks of wood and
short pieces of plank were first passed, with care, up to the
hands of Dudley, who cast them, like useless lumber, among
the other ruins of the building. He then descended from
his perch, and made room for others to follow.

The stranger next arose; after him came Content, the
Puritan, Reuben Ring, and, in short, all the youths, with
the exception of those who had fallen in the contest.
After these had mounted, and each in turn had leaped to
the ground, a very brief preparation served for the libe-
ration of the more feeble of body. The readiness of
border skill soon sufficed to arrange the necessary means.
By the aid of chains and buckets, Ruth and the little
Martha, Faith, and all the handmaidens, without even
one exception, were successively drawn from the bowels of
the earth, and restored to the light of day. It is scarcely
necessary to say, to those whom experience has best fitted
to judge of such an achievement, that no great time or
labour was necessary for its accomplishment.

It is not our intention to harass the feelings of the
reader, further than is required, by a simple narrative of the
incidents of the legend. We shall, therefore, say nothing
of the bodily pain, or of the mental alarm, by which this
ingenious retreat from the flames and the tomahawk had
been effected. The suffering was chiefly confined to apprehension, for as the descent was easy, so had the readiness and ingenuity of the young men found means, by the
aid of articles of furniture first cast into the shaft, and by
well-secured fragments of the doors properly placed across,
both to render the situation of the females and children less
painful than might at first be supposed, and effectually to
protect them from the tumbling block. But little of the
latter, however, was likely to affect their safety, as the form
of the building was, in itself, a sufficient security against
the fall of its heavier parts.

The meeting of the family, amid the desolation of the
valley, though relieved by the consciousness of having escaped
a more shocking fate, may easily be imagined. The first
act was to render brief but solemn thanks for their deliver-

ance, and then, with the promptitude of people trained in
hardship, their attention was given to those measures which
prudence told them were yet necessary.

A few of the more active and experienced of the youths
were despatched, in order to ascertain the direction taken
by the Indians, and to gain what intelligence they might
concerning their future movements. The maidens hastened to collect the kine, while others searched, with heavy
hearts, among the ruins, in quest of such articles of food
and comfort as could be found, in order to administer to
the first wants of nature.

Two hours had effected most of that which could immediately be done in these several pursuits. The young
men returned with the assurance that the trails announced
the certain and final retreat of the savages. The cows had
yielded their tribute, and such provision had been made
against hunger, as circumstances would allow. The arms
had been examined, and put, as far as the injuries they
had received would admit, in readiness for instant service.
A few hasty preparations had been made, in order to protect the females against the cool airs of the coming night ;
and, in short, all was done that the intelligence of a border-
man could suggest, or his exceeding readiness in expedients
could, in so brief a space, supply.

The sun began to fall towards the tops of the beeches
that crowned the western outline of the view, before all
these necessary arrangements were ended. It was not till
then, however, that Reuben Ring, accompanied by another
youth of equal activity and courage, appeared before the
Puritan, equipped, as well as men in their situation might
be, for a journey through the forest.

" Go," said the old religionist, when the youths presented themselves before him ; " go ; carry forth the
tidings of this visitation, that men come to our succour. I
ask not vengeance on the deluded and heathenish imitators
of the worshippers of Moloch. They have ignorantly
done this evil. Let no man arm in behalf of the wrongs
of one sinful and erring. Rather let them look into the
secret abominations of their own hearts, in order that they
crush the living worm, which, by gnawing on the seeds of

a healthful hope, may yet destroy the fruits of the promise in their own souls. I would that there be profit in this example of divine displeasure. Go ; make the circuit of the settlements for some fifty miles, and bid such of the neighbours as may be spared come to our aid. They shall be welcome, and may it be long ere any of them send invitation to me or mine to enter their clearings on the like melancholy duty. Depart ; and bear in mind that ye are messengers of peace ; that your errand toucheth not the feelings of vengeance ; but that it is succour, in all fitting reason, and no arming of the hand to chase the savage to his retreats, that I ask of the brethren." *

With this final admonition, the young men took their leaves. Still it was evident, by their frowning brows and compressed lips, that some part of its forgiving principle might be forgotten, should chance, in their journey, bring them on the trail of any wandering inhabitant of the forest. In a few minutes they were seen passing, with swift steps, from the fields, into the depths of the forest, along that path which led to the towns that lay lower on the Connecticut.

Another task still remained to be performed. In making the temporary arrangements for the shelter of the family, attention had been first paid to the block-house. The walls of the basement of this building were still standing, and it was found easy, by means of half-burnt timbers, with an occasional board that had escaped the conflagration, to cover it in a manner that offered a temporary protection against the weather. This simple and hasty construction, with an extremely inartificial office erected around the stack of a chimney, embraced nearly all that could be done, until time and assistance should enable them to commence other dwellings. In clearing the ruins of the little tower of its rubbish, the remains of those who had perished in the fray were piously collected. The body of the youth who had

---

* The necessity of rendering mutual aid in a thinly peopled country has given rise to customs of exceeding liberality and friendliness among the borderers. A summons like this of old Mark Heathcote would bring men leagues to offer their assistance. It is the common practice, at this time, to summon a whole neighbourhood to help erect a building, or to do any other kind of work which requires a strong collective force. No reward is asked or would be received.

died in the earlier hours of the attack was found, but half
consumed, in the court; and the bones of two more who
fell within the block were collected from among the ruins.
It had now become a melancholy duty to consign them all
to the earth, with decent solemnity.

The time selected for this sad office was just as the
western horizon began to glow with those tints which one
of our own poets has so beautifully termed, " the pomp
that brings and shuts the day." The sun was in the tree-
tops, and a softer or sweeter light could not have been
chosen for such a ceremony. Most of the fields still lay in
a soft brightness, though the forest was rapidly getting the
obscure look of night. A broad and gloomy margin was
spreading from the boundary of the woods, and, here and
there, a solitary tree cast its shadow on the meadows without its limits, throwing a dark ragged line, in bold relief,
on the glow of the sun's rays. One—it was the dusky
image of a high and waving pine, that reared its dark green
pyramid of never-fading foliage nearly a hundred feet
above the humbler growth of beeches—cast its shade to the
side of the eminence of the block. Here the pointed extremity of the shadow was seen stealing slowly towards the
open grave, an emblem of that oblivion in which its humble
tenants were so shortly to be wrapped.

At this spot Mark Heathcote and his remaining companions had assembled. An oaken chair, saved from the
flames, was the seat of the father, and two parallel benches,
formed of planks placed on stones, held the other members
of the family. The grave lay between. The patriarch
had taken his station at one of its ends, while the stranger
so often named in these pages stood, with folded arms and
a thoughtful brow, at the other. The bridle of a horse,
that was caparisoned in the imperfect manner which the
straitened means of the borderers now rendered necessary,
was hanging from one of the half-burnt palisadoes in the
back ground.

" A just but a merciful hand hath been laid heavily on
my household," commenced the old Puritan, with the calmness of one who had long been accustomed to chasten his
regrets by humility: " He that hath given freely, hath

taken away; and One that hath long smiled upon my weakness, hath now veiled his face in anger. I have known him in his power to bless; it was meet that I should see him in his displeasure. A heart that was waxing confident would have hardened in its pride. At that which hath befallen let no man murmur. Let none imitate the speech of her who spoke foolishly. ' What! shall we receive good at the hand of God; and shall we not receive evil?' I would that the feeble-minded of the world, they that jeopard the soul on vanities, they that look with scorn on the neediness of the flesh, might behold the riches of one stedfast. I would that they might know the consolation of the righteous! Let the voice of thanksgiving be heard in the wilderness. Open thy mouths in praise, that the gratitude of a penitent be not hid!"

As the speaker ceased, his stern eye fell upon the features of the nearest youth, and it seemed to demand an audible response to his own lofty expression of resignation. But the sacrifice exceeded the power of the individual to whom had been made this silent, but intelligible appeal. After regarding the relics that lay at his feet, casting a wandering glance at the desolation which had swept over a place his own hand had helped to decorate, and receiving a renewed consciousness of his own bodily suffering in the shooting pain of his wounds, the young borderer averted his look, and seemed to recoil from so officious a display of submission. Observing his inability to reply, Mark continued: —

" Hath no one a voice to praise the Lord? The bands of the heathen have fallen upon my herds; the brand hath been kindled within my dwellings; my people have died by the violence of the unenlightened, and none are here to say that the Lord is just! I would that the shouts of thanksgiving should arise in my fields! I would that the song of praise should grow louder than the whoop of the savage, and that all the land might speak joyfulness!"

A long and expecting pause succeeded. Then Content rejoined, in his quiet tones, speaking firmly, but with the modest utterance he never failed to use: —

" The hand that hath held the balance is just," he said,

o

" and we have been found wanting. He that made the
wilderness blossom hath caused the ignorant and the barbarous to be the instruments of his will. He hath arrested
the season of our prosperity, that we may know he is the
Lord. He hath spoken in the whirlwind, but his mercy
granteth that our ears shall know his voice."

As his son ceased, a glow of holy satisfaction gleamed
in the countenance of the Puritan. His eye turned inquir-
ingly towards Ruth, who sat among her maidens, the
image of womanly sorrow. Common interest seemed to
still the breathing of the little assembly ; and sympathy
was quite as active as curiosity, when each one present
suffered a glance to steal towards her benignant but pallid
face. The eye of the mother was gazing earnestly, but
without a tear, on the melancholy spectacle before her. It
unconsciously sought, among the dried and shrivelled
remnants of mortality that lay at her feet, some relic of
the cherub she had lost. A shudder and struggle followed ; after which her gentle voice breathed so low that
those nearest her person could scarce distinguish the
words —

" The Lord gave, and the Lord hath taken away ;
blessed be his holy name !"

" Now know I that he who hath smote me is merciful,
for he chasteneth them he loveth," said Mark Heathcote,
rising with dignity to address his household. " Our life is
a life of pride. The young are wont to wax insolent,
while he of many years saith to his own heart, ' It is good
to be here.' There is a fearful mystery in One who
sitteth on high. The heavens are his throne, and he hath
created the earth for his footstool. Let not the vanity of
the weak of mind presume to understand it, for ' who that
hath the breath of life lived before the hills ? The bonds
of the evil one, of Satan, and of the sons of Belial, have
been loosened, that the faith of the elect may be purified—
that the names of those written since the foundations of
the earth were laid, may be read in letters of pure gold.
The time of man is but a moment in the reckoning of
Him whose life is eternity, — earth, the habitation of a
season. The bones of the bold, of the youthful, and of

the strong of yesterday, lie at our feet. None know what an hour may bring forth. In a single night, my children, hath this been done. They whose voices were heard in my halls are now speechless ; and they who so lately rejoiced are sorrowing. Yet hath this seeming evil been ordered that good may come of it. We are dwellers in a wild and distant land," he continued, insensibly permitting his thoughts to incline towards the more mournful details of their affliction ; " our earthly home is afar off. Hither have we been led by the flaming pillar of truth, and yet the malice of the persecutors hath not forgotten to follow. One, houseless, and sought like the hunted deer, is again driven to flee. We have nought but the canopy of the stars for a roof ; none may tarry longer to worship secretly within our walls. But the path of the faithful, though full of thorns, leadeth to quiet ; and the final rest of the just man can never know alarm. He that hath borne hunger and thirst, and the pains of the flesh, for the sake of truth, knoweth how to be satisfied ; nor will the hours of bodily suffering be accounted weary, to him whose goal is the peace of the righteous." The strong lineaments of the stranger grew more than usually austere ; and as the Puritan continued, the hand, which rested on the handle of a pistol, grasped the weapon, until the fingers seemed imbedded in the wood. He bowed, however, as if to acknowledge the personal allusion, and remained silent. " If any mourn the early death of those who have rendered up their being, struggling, as it may be permitted, in behalf of life and dwelling," continued Mark Heathcote, regarding a female near him, " let her remember that from the beginning of the world were his days numbered, and that not a sparrow falleth without answering the ends of wisdom. Rather let the fulfilment of things remind us of the vanity of life, that we may learn how easy it is to become immortal. If the youth hath been cut down, seemingly like unripened grass, he hath fallen by the sickle of the reaper who knoweth best when to begin the in-gathering of the harvest to his eternal garners. Though a spirit bound unto his as one feeble is wont to lean on the strength of man, mourn over his fall, let her sorrow be mingled with rejoicing." A convulsive sob broke out of the bosom of the hand-maiden who was known to have been affianced to one of the dead, and for a moment the address of Mark was interrupted. But when silence again ensued, he continued, the subject leading him, by a transition that was natural, to allude to his own sorrows. " Death hath been no stranger in my habitation," he said ; " his shaft fell heaviest when it struck her who, like those that have here fallen, was in the pride of her youth, and when her soul was glad with the first joy of the birth of a man-child. Thou who sittest on high !" he added, turning a glazed and tearless eye to heaven, " thou knowest how heavy was that blow ; and thou hast written down the strivings of an oppressed soul. The burthen was not found too heavy for endurance. The sacrifice hath not sufficed ; the world was again getting uppermost in my heart. Thou didst bestow an image of that innocence and loveliness that dwelleth in the skies ; and this hast thou taken away, that we might know thy power. To this judgment we bow : if thou hast called our child to the mansions of bliss, she is wholly thine, and we presume not to complain ; but if thou hast still left her to wander further in the pilgrimage of life, we confide in thy goodness. She is of a long-suffering race, and thou wilt not desert her to the blindness of the heathen. She is thine, she is wholly thine, King of Heaven ! and yet hast thou permitted our hearts to yearn towards her, with the fondness of earthly love. We await some further manifestation of thy will, that we may know whether the fountains of our affection shall be dried, in the certainty of her blessedness — " (scalding tears were rolling down the cheeks of the pallid and immovable mother) " or whether hope, nay, whether duty to thee calleth for the interference of those bound to her in the tenderness of the flesh. When the blow was heaviest on the bruised spirit of a lone and solitary wanderer in a strange and savage land, he held not back the offspring it was thy will to grant him in the place of her called to thyself ; and now that child hath become a man, he too layeth, like Abraham of old, the infant of his love, an offering at thy feet. Do with it as to thy never-

failing wisdom seemeth best — " The words were interrupted by a heavy groan that burst from the chest of
Content. A deep silence ensued at this awful indication
of nature, but when the assembly ventured to throw looks
of sympathy and condolence at the bereaved father, they
saw that he had arisen, and stood gazing steadily at the
speaker, as if he wondered, equally with the others, whence
such a sound of suffering could have come. The Puritan
renewed the subject, but his voice faltered, and for an
instant as he proceeded, his hearers were oppressed with
the spectacle of an aged and dignified man shaken with
grief. Conscious of his weakness, the old man ceased
speaking in exhortation, and addressed himself to prayer.
While thus engaged, his tones became clear, firm, and
distinct, and the petition was ended in the midst of a deep
and holy calm.

With the performance of this preliminary office, the
simple ceremony was brought to its close. The remains
were lowered, in solemn silence, into the grave, and the
earth was soon replaced by the young men. Mark Heathcote then invoked aloud the blessing of God on his household, and bowing in person, as he had before done in
spirit, to the will of Heaven, he motioned to the family
to withdraw.

The interview that succeeded was over the resting place
of the dead. The hand of the stranger was firmly clenched
in that of the Puritan, and the stern self-command of both
appeared to give way before the regrets of a friendship that
had endured through so many trying scenes.

" Thou knowest that I may not tarry," said the former,
as if he replied to some expressed wish of his companion.
" They would make me a sacrifice to the Moloch of their
vanities, and yet would I fain abide, until the weight of
this heavy blow may be forgotten. I found thee in peace,
and I quit thee in the depths of suffering ! "

" Thou distrustest me, or thou dost injustice to thine
own belief," interrupted the Puritan, with a smile that
shone on his haggard and austere visage, as the rays of
the setting sun light a wintry cloud. " Seemed I happier
when this hand placed that of a loved bride into mine own,

than thou now seest me in this wilderness, houseless,
stripped of my wealth, and, God forgive the ingratitude !
but I had almost said, childless ? No, indeed, thou
mayest not tarry, for the blood-hounds of tyranny will be
on their scent ; here is a shelter for thee no longer."

The eyes of both turned, by a common and melancholy
feeling, towards the ruin of the block. The stranger then
pressed the hand of his friend in both his own, and said,
in a struggling voice —

" Mark Heathcote, adieu ; he that had a roof for the
persecuted wanderer shall not long be houseless ; neither
shall the resigned for ever know sorrow."

His words sounded in the ears of his companion like the
revelation of a prophecy. They again pressed their hands
together, and, regarding each other with looks in which
kindness could not be altogether smothered by the repul-
sive character of an acquired air, they parted. The Puritan slowly took his way to the dreary shelter which covered
his family, while the stranger was shortly after seen urging
the beast he had mounted across the pastures of the valley,
towards one of the most retired paths of the wilderness.

CHAPTER VII.

Together towards the village then we walked,
And of old friends and places much we talked ;
And who had died, who left them would he tell,
And who still in their father's mansion dwell.   DANA.

WE leave the imagination of the reader to supply an interval of several years. Before the thread of the narrative
is resumed, it will be necessary to take another hasty view
of the condition of the country in which the scene of our
legend had place.

The exertions of the provincials were no longer limited
to the first efforts of a colonial existence. The establishments of New England had passed the ordeal of experiment, and were become permanent. Massachusetts was

already populous; and Connecticut, the colony with which we have more immediate connection, was sufficiently peopled to manifest a portion of that enterprise which has since made her active little community so remarkable. The effects of these increased exertions were becoming extensively visible, and we shall endeavour to set one of these changes, as distinctly as our feeble powers will allow, before the eyes of those who read these pages.

When compared with the progress of society in the other hemisphere, the condition of what is called in America a new settlement becomes anomalous. There the arts of life have been the fruits of an intelligence that has progressively accumulated with the advancement of civilisation; while here, improvement is, in a great degree, the consequence of experience elsewhere acquired. Necessity, prompted by an understanding of its wants, incited by a commendable spirit of emulation, and encouraged by liberty, early gave birth to those improvements which have converted a wilderness into the abodes of abundance and security, with a rapidity that wears the appearance of magic. Industry has wrought with the confidence of knowledge, and the result has been commensurate with its means.

It is scarcely necessary to say, that in a country where the laws favour all commendable enterprise, where unnecessary artificial restrictions are unknown, and where the hand of man has not yet exhausted its efforts, the adventurer is allowed the greatest freedom of choice in selecting the field of his enterprise. The agriculturist passes the heath and the barren to seat himself on the river bottom; the trader looks for the site best suited for demand and supply, and the artisan quits his native village to seek employment in situations where labour will meet a richer reward. It is a consequence of this extraordinary freedom of election, that, while the great picture of American society has been sketched with so much boldness, a large portion of the filling up still remains to be done. The emigrant has consulted his immediate interests, and while no very extensive and profitable territory throughout the whole of our imm. use possessions, has been wholly neglected, neither has any particular district yet attained the finish of improvement. The city is, even now, seen in the wilderness, and the wilderness often continues near the city while the latter is sending forth its swarms to distant scenes of industry. After thirty years of fostering care on the part of the government, the capital itself presents its disjointed and sickly villages, in the centre of the deserted ' old fields' * of Maryland, while numberless youthful rivals are flourishing, on the waters of the west, in spots where the bear has ranged and the wolf howled, long since the former has been termed a city.

Thus it is that high civilization, a state of infant existence, and positive barbarity, are often brought so near each other, within the borders of this republic. The traveller who has passed the night in an inn that would not disgrace the oldest country in Europe, may be compelled to dine in the shantee † of a hunter; the smooth and gravelled road sometimes ends in an impassable swamp; the spires of the town are often hid by the branches of a tangled forest, and the canal leads to a seemingly barren and unprofitable mountain. He that does not return to see what another year may bring forth, commonly bears away from these scenes recollections that conduce to error. To see America with the eyes of truth, it is necessary to look often; and in order to understand the actual condition of these states, it should be remembered that it is equally unjust to believe that all the intermediate points partake of the improvements of particular places, as to infer the want of civilization at more remote establishments, from a few unfavourable facts gleaned near the centre. By an accidental concurrence of moral and physical causes, much of that equality which distinguishes the institutions of the country

---

* The cultivation of the tobacco-plant exhausts the land in a few years, and as no good system of cropping and manuring has yet been adopted to restore it, a large portion of the old tobacco plantations in Virginia and Maryland lie waste in consequence. The city of Washington is situated in the centre of one of these half sterile and deserted districts.

† Shanty, or Shantee, is a word much used in the newer settlements. It strictly means a rude cabin of bark and brush, such as are often erected in the forest for temporary purposes. But the borderers often quaintly apply it to their own habitations. The only derivation which the writer has heard for this American word, is one that supposes it to be a corruption of Chienté, a term said to be used among the Canadians to express a dog-kennel.

is extended to the progress of society over its whole surface.

Although the impetus of improvement was not as great in the time of Mark Heathcote as in our own days, the principle of its power was actively in existence. Of this fact we shall furnish a sufficient evidence, by pursuing our intention of describing one of those changes to which allusion has already been made.

The reader will remember that the age of which we write had advanced into the last quarter of the seventeenth century. The precise moment at which the action of the tale must recommence, was that period of the day when the grey of twilight was redeeming objects from the deep darkness with which the night draws to its close. The month was June, and the scene such as it may be necessary to describe with some particularity.

Had there been light, and had one been favourably placed to enjoy a bird's eye view of the spot, he would have seen a broad and undulating field of leafy forest, in which the various deciduous trees of New England were relieved by the deeper verdure of occasional masses of evergreens. In the centre of this swelling and still nearly interminable outline of woods, was a valley that spread between three low mountains. Over the bottom-land, for the distance of several miles, all the signs of a settlement in a state of rapid and prosperous improvement were visible. The devious course of a deep and swift brook, that in the other hemisphere would have been termed a river*, was to be traced through the meadows by its borders of willow and sumach. At a point near the centre of the valley, the waters had been arrested by a small dam; and a mill, whose wheel at that early hour was without motion, stood on the artificial mound. Near it was the site of a New England hamlet.

* Great inaccuracy and great irregularity exist in the nomenclature of the American streams. The term river is generally given to all very large waters, though many that would be considered large in Europe are called creeks, though they are perfectly inland, and have no communication with any sea or lake. Thus Canada creek, and Schoharie creek are each larger than the Thames at Kew, and are merely tributaries of the Mowhawk. In some of the States streams of this kind are called " Branches."

The number of dwellings in the village might have been
forty.   They were constructed, as usual, of a firm frame-
work neatly covered with sidings of boards.   There was a
surprising air of equality in the general aspect of the
houses ; and, if there were question of any country but our
own, it might be added there was an unusual appearance
of comfort and abundance in even the humblest of them
all.   They were mostly of two low stories, the superior
overhanging the inferior by a foot or two ; a mode of construction much in use in the earlier days of the Eastern
Colonies.   As paint was but little used at that time, none
of the buildings exhibited a colour different from that the
wood would naturally assume after the exposure of a few
years to the weather.   Each had its single chimney in the
centre of the roof, and but two or three showed more than
a solitary window on each side of the principal or outer
door.   In front of every dwelling was a small neat court,
in greensward, separated from the public road by a light
fence of deal.   Double rows of young and vigorous elms
lined each side of the wide street, while an enormous
sycamore still kept possession of the spot in its centre,
which it had occupied when the white man entered the
forest.   Beneath the shade of this tree, the inhabitants
often collected to gather tidings of each other's welfare, or
to listen to some matter of interest that rumour had borne
from the towns nearer the sea.   A narrow and little used
wheel track ran, with a graceful and sinuous route, through
the centre of the wide and grassy street.   Reduced in
appearance to little more than a bridle-path, it was to be
traced without the hamlet between high fences of wood for
a mile or two, to the points where it entered the forest.
Here and there roses were pressing through the openings
of the fences before the doors of the different habitations,
and bushes of fragrant lilacs stood in the angles of most of
the courts.

The dwellings were detached.   Each occupied its own
insulated plot of ground, with a garden in the rear.   The
out-buildings were thrown to that distance which the
cheapness of land and security from fire rendered both
easy and expedient.

The church stood in the centre of the highway, and near one end of the hamlet. In the exterior and the ornaments of the important temple, the taste of the times had been fastidiously consul.ed, its form and simplicity furnishing no slight resemblance to the self-denying doctrines and quaint humours of the religionists who worshipped beneath its roof. This building, like all the rest, was of wood, and externally of two stories. It possessed a tower, without a spire; the former alone serving to betray its sacred character. In the construction of the edifice, especial care had been taken to eschew all deviations from direct lines and right angles. Those narrow arched passages for the admission of light, that are elsewhere so common, were then thought, by the stern moralists of New England, to have some mysterious connection with her of the scarlet mantle. The priest would as soon have thought of appearing before his flock in the vanities of stole and cassock, as the congregation of admitting the repudiated ornaments into the outline of their severe architecture. Had the Genius of the Lamp suddenly exchanged the windows of the sacred edifice with those of the inn that stood nearly opposite, the closest critic of the settlement could never have detected the liberty, since in the form, dimensions, and style of the two, there was no visible difference.

A little inclosure, at no great distance from the church, and on one side of the street, had been set apart for the final resting-place of those who had finished their race on earth. It contained but a solitary grave.

The inn was to be distinguished from the surrounding buildings by its superior size, an open horse-shed, and a sort of protruding air, with which it thrust itself on the line of the street, as if to invite the traveller to take his rest. A sign swung on a gallows-looking post, that, in consequence of frosty nights and warm days, had already deviated from the perpendicular. It bore a conceit, which, at the first glance, might have gladdened the heart of a naturalist with the belief that he had made the discovery of some unknown bird. The artist, however, had sufficiently provided against the consequences of so em-

barrassing a blunder, by considerately writing beneath the
offspring of his pencil, " This is the sign of the Whip-
Poor-Will ;" a name that the most unlettered traveller in
those regions would be likely to know was vulgarly given
to the Wish-Ton-Wish, or the American night-hawk.

But few relics of the forest remained immediately
around the hamlet. The trees had long been felled, and
sufficient time had elapsed to remove most of the vestiges
of their former existence. But as the eye receded from
the cluster of buildings, the signs of more recent inroads
on the wilderness became apparent, until the view terminated with openings, in which piled logs and felled trees
that lay piled on each other like jack-straws, announced the
recent use of the axe.

At that early day, the American husbandman, like the
agriculturists of most of Europe, dwelt in his village.
The dread of violence from the savages had given rise
to a custom similar to that which, centuries before, had
been produced in the other hemisphere by the inroads of
more pretending barbarians, and which, with few and distant exceptions, has deprived rural scenery of a charm
that, it would seem, time and a better condition of society
are never effectually to repair. Some remains of this
ancient practice are still to be traced in the portion of the
Union of which we write, where, even at this day, the
farmer often quits the village to seek his scattered fields
in its neighbourhood. Still, as man has never been the
subject of a system here, and as each individual has always
had the liberty of consulting his own temper, bolder
spirits early began to break through a practice, by which
quite as much was lost in convenience as was gained
in security. Even in the scene we have been describing,
ten or twelve humble habitations were distributed among
the recent clearings on the sides of the mountains, and in
situations too remote to promise much security against any
sudden inroad of the common enemy.

For general protection in cases of the last extremity,
however, a stockaded dwelling, not unlike that which we
have had occasion to describe in our earlier pages, stood
in a convenient spot near the hamlet. Its defences were

stronger and more elaborate than usual, the pickets being furnished with flanking block-houses ; and, in other respects, the building bore the aspect of a work equal to any resistance that might be required in the warfare of those regions. The ordinary habitation of the priest was within its gates, and hither most of the sick were timely conveyed, in order to anticipate the necessity of removals at more inconvenient moments.

It is scarcely necessary to tell the American, that heavy wooden fences subdivided the whole of this little landscape, into enclosures of some eight or ten acres in extent ; that, here and there, cattle and flocks were grazing without herdsmen or shepherds, and that, while the fields nearest to the dwellings were beginning to assume the appearance of a careful and improved husbandry, those more remote became gradually wilder and less cultivated, until the half reclaimed openings, with their blackened stubs and barked trees, were blended with the gloom of the living forest. These are more or less the accompaniments of every rural scene, in those districts of the country where time has not yet effected more than the first two stages of improvement.

At the distance of a short half mile from the fortified house, or garrison, as, by a singular corruption of terms, the stockaded building was called, stood a dwelling of pretensions altogether superior to any in the hamlet. The buildings in question, though simple, were extensive, and though scarcely other than such as might belong to an agriculturist in easy circumstances, still they were remarkable in that settlement, by the comforts which time alone could accumulate, and some of which denoted an advanced condition for a frontier family. In short, there was an air about the establishment, as in the disposition of its out-buildings, in the superior workmanship, in the materials, and in numberless other well known circumstances, which went to show that the whole of the edifices were reconstructions. The fields near this habitation exhibited smoother surfaces than those in the distance ; the fences were lighter and less rude ; the stumps had absolutely disappeared, and the gardens and homestead were well planted with flourishing fruit trees. A conical eminence

arose, at a short distance, in the rear of the principal
dwelling.   It was covered with that beautiful and peculiar
ornament of an American farm, a regular thrifty and
luxuriant apple orchard.   Still age had not given its full
beauty to the plantation, which might have had a growth
of some eight or ten years.   A blackened tower of stone,
which sustained the charred ruins of a superstructure of
wood, though of no great height in itself, rose above the
tallest of the trees, and stood a sufficient memorial of some
scene of violence in the brief history of the valley.   There
was also a small block-house near the habitation, but, by
the air of neglect that reigned around, it was quite apparent the little work had been of a hurried construction,
and of but temporary use.   A few young plantations
of fruit trees were also to be seen, in different parts of
the valley, which was beginning to exhibit many other of
the usual evidences of an improved agriculture.

So far as all these artificial changes went, they were of
an English character ; but it was England devoid alike of
its luxury and its poverty, and with a superfluity of space
that gave to the meanest habitation in the view, an air of
abundance and comfort, that is so often wanting about the
dwellings of the comparatively rich, in countries where
man is found bearing a far greater numerical proportion
to the soil than was then, or is even now, the case in the
regions of which we write.

CHAPTER VIII.

" Come hither, neighbour Sea-coal—God hath blessed you with a good name :
to be a well-favoured man is the gift of Fortune ; but to write and read comes
by Nature."—*Much Ado about Nothing.*

IT has already been said that the hour at which the action
of the tale must recommence was early morning.   The
coolness of night, so usual in a country extensively
covered with wood, had passed, and the warmth of a
summer morning of that low latitude, was causing the

streaks of light vapour, that floated about the meadows, to rise above the trees. The feathery patches united to form a cloud that sailed away towards the summit of a distant mountain, which appeared to be a common ren_dezvous for all the mists that had been generated during the past hours of darkness.

Though the burnished sky announced his near ap_proach, the sun was not yet visible. Notwithstanding the earliness of the hour a man was already mounting a little ascent in the road, at no great distance from the southern entrance of the hamlet, and at a point where he could command a view of all the objects described in the preceding chapter. A musket thrown across his left shoulder with the horn and pouch at his sides, together with the little wallet at his back, proclaimed him one who had either been engaged in a hunt, or in some short ex_pedition of even a less peaceable character. His dress was of the usual material and fashion of a countryman of the age and colony, though a short broadsword, that was thrust through a wampum belt which girded his body, might have attracted observation. In all other respects, he had the air of an inhabitant of the hamlet, who had found occa_sion to quit his abode on some affair of pleasure, or of duty, that had made no very serious demand on his time.

Whether native or stranger, few ever passed the hillock named without pausing to gaze at the quiet loveliness of the cluster of houses that lay in full view from its summit. The individual mentioned loitered as usual, but, instead of following the line of the path, his eye rather sought some object in the direction of the fields. Moving leisurely to the nearest fence, he threw down the upper rails of a pair of bars, and beckoned to a horseman, who was picking his way across a broken bit of pasture land, to enter the highway by the passage he had opened.

" Put the spur smartly into the pacer's flank," said he, who had done this act of civility, observing that the other hesitated to urge his beast across the irregular and some_what scattered pile ; " my word for it, the jade goes over them all, without touching with more than three of her four feet.   Fie, doctor, there is never a cow in the Wish-Ton-Wish but it would take the leap to be in the first at the milking."

"Softly, Ensign," returned the timid equestrian, laying the emphasis on the final syllable of his companion's title, and pronouncing the first as if it were spelt with the third instead of the second vowel; "thy courage is meet for one set apart for deeds of valour, but it would be a sorrowful day when the ailing of the valley should knock at my door, and a broken limb be made the apology for want of succour.   Thy efforts will not avail thee, man; for the mare hath had her schooling as well as her master. I have trained the beast to methodical habits, and she hath come to have a rooted dislike to all irregularities of movement.   Cease tugging at the rein, I pray thee, as if thou wouldst compel her to pass the pile in spite of her teeth, and throw down the upper bar altogether."

"A doctor in these rugged parts should be mounted on one of those ambling birds of which we read," said the other, removing the obstacles to the secure passage of his friend; "for truly a journey at night, in the paths of these clearings, is not always as safe moving as that which is said to be enjoyed by the settlers nearer the sea."

"And where hast thou found mention of a bird of a size and velocity fit to be the bearer of the weight of a man?" demanded he who was mounted, with a vivacity that betrayed some jealousy on the subject of a monopoly of learning.   "I had thought there was never a book in the valley, out of my own closet, that dealt in these abstrusities!"

"Dost think the scriptures are strangers to us? There; thou art now in the public path, and thy journey is without danger.   It is matter of marvel to many in this settlement, how thou movest about at midnight, amongst up-turned roots of trees, holes, logs, and stumps, without falling —"

"I have told thee, Ensign, it is by virtue of much training given to the beast.   Certain am I, that neither whip nor spur would compel the animal to pass the bounds of discretion.   Often have I travelled this bridle-path, when sight was a sense of as little use as that of smelling, without fear, as in truth without danger."

" I was about to say, of falling into thy own hands, which would be a tumble of little less jeopardy that even that of the wicked spirits."

The medical man affected to laugh at his companion's joke; but, remembering the dignity suited to one of his calling, he immediately resumed the discourse with gravity—

" These may be matters of levity with those who know little of the hardships that are endured in the practice of the settlements. Here have I been on yonder mountain, guided by the instinct of my horse ———"

" Ha! hath there been a call at the dwelling of my brother Ring?" demanded the pedestrian, observing, by the direction of the other's eye, the road he had been travelling.

" Truly there hath; and at the unseasonable hour that is wont, in a very unreasonable proportion of the cases of my practice."

" And Reuben numbereth another boy to the four that he could count yesterday?"

The medical man held up three of his fingers in a significant manner, and nodded.

" This putteth Faith something in arrears," returned he who has been called Ensign, and who was no other than the reader's old acquaintance, Eben Dudley, preferred to that station in the train-band of the valley. " The heart of my brother Reuben will be gladdened by these tidings, when he shall return from the scout."

" There will be occasion for thankfulness, since he will find seven beneath a roof where he left but four!"

" I will close the bargain with the young captain for the mountain lot this very day!" muttered Dudley, like one suddenly convinced of the prudence of a long debated measure. " Seven pounds of the colony money is no great price, after all, for a hundred acres of heavily timbered land; and they, too, in full view of a settlement where boys come three at a time!" *

* In the interior of America, where labourers are scarce, and where food is abundant, a poor man can have no more certain means of comfort than a large family, especially if there be many boys among them.

P

The equestrian stopped his horse, and regarding his companion with a significant air, he answered —

" Thou hast now fallen on the clue of an important mystery, Ensign Dudley. This continent was created with a design. The fact is apparent by its riches, its climate, its magnitude, its facilities of navigation, and chiefly in that it hath been left undiscovered until the advanced condition of society hath given opportunity and encouragement to men of a certain degree of merit, to adventure in its behalf. Consider, neighbour, the wonderful progress it hath already made in the arts, and in learning, in reputation and in resources, and thou wilt agree with me in the conclusion that all this hath been done with a design."

" 'Twould be presuming to doubt it; for he hath indeed a short memory to whom it shall be necessary to recall the time when this very valley was little other than a den for beasts of prey, and this beaten highway a deer-track. Dost think that Reuben will be like to raise the whole of the recent gift?"

" With judgment and by the blessing of Providence. The mind is active, Ensign Dudley, when the body is journeying among the forests; and much have my thoughts been exercised in this matter, whilst thou and others have been in your slumbers. Here have we the colonies in their first century, and yet thou knowest to what a pass of improvement they have arrived. They tell me the Hartford settlement is getting to be apportioned like the towns of mother England, — that there is reason to think the day may come when the provinces shall have a power, and a convenience of culture and communication, equalling that which belongeth to some parts of the venerable island itself!"

" Nay, nay, Doctor Ergot," returned the other, with an incredulous smile, " that is exceeding the bounds of a discretionable expectation."

" Thou wilt remember that I said equalling to *certain* parts. The heaths and commons of which we read, for instance. I think we may justly imagine, that ere many centuries shall elapse, there may be millions counted in these regions; and truly that, too, where one seeth nought at present but the savage and the beast."

" I will go with any man, in this question, as far as reason will justify; but doubtless thou hast read in the books uttered by writers over sea, the matters concerning the condition of those countries, wherein it is plain that we may never hope to reach the exalted excellence they enjoy."

" Neighbour Dudley, thou seemest disposed to push an unguarded expression to extremity. I said equalling *certain* parts, meaning always, too, in *certain* things. Now it is known in philosophy, that the stature of man hath degenerated, and must degenerate in these regions, in obedience to established laws of nature; therefore it is meet that allowance should be made for some deficiency in less material qualities."

" It is like, then, that the better sort of the men over sea are ill disposed to quit their country," returned the Ensign, glancing an eye of some unbelief along the muscular proportions of his own vigorous frame. " We have no less than three from the old countries in our village, here, and yet I do not find them men like to have been sought for at the building of Babel."

" This is settling a knotty and learned point by the evidence of a few shallow exceptions. I presume to tell you, Ensign Dudley, that the science, and wisdom, and philosophy of Europe have been exceeding active in this matter; and they have proved, to their own perfect satisfaction, which is the same thing as disposing of the question without appeal, that man and beast, plant and tree, hill and dale, lake and pond, sun, air, fire, and water, are all wanting in some of the perfectness of the older regions. I respect a patriotic sentiment, and can carry the disposition to applaud the bounties received from the hands of a beneficent Creator as far as any man; but that which hath been demonstrated by science, or collected by learning, is placed too far beyond the objections of lightly minded cavillers, to be doubted by graver faculties."

" I shall not contend against things that are proven," returned Dudley, who was quite as meek in discussion as he was powerful and active in more physical contests;

" since it needs be that the learning of men in the old
countries must have an exceeding excellence, in virtue of
its great age.   It would be a visit to remember, should
some of its rare advantages be dispersed in these our own
youthful regions ! "

" And can it be said that our mental wants have been
forgotten — that the nakedness of the mind hath been suffered to go without its comely vestment, neighbour Dudley?
To me, it seemeth, that therein we have unwonted reason
to rejoice, and that the equilibrium of nature is in a manner
restored by the healing exercises of art.   It is unseemly
in an enlightened province, to insist on qualities that have
been discreetly disproven ; but learning is a transferable
and communicable gift, and it is meet to affirm that it is
to be found here, in quantities adapted to the wants of the
colony."

" I'll not gainsay it, for having been more of an adventurer in the forest, than one who hath travelled in quest
of sights among the settlements along the sea-shore, it may
happen that many things are to be seen there, of which
my poor abilities have formed no opinion."

" And are we utterly unenlightened, even in this distant
valley, Ensign?" returned the leech, leaning over the neck
of his horse, and addressing his companion in a mild and
persuasive tone, that he had probably acquired in his extensive practice among the females of the settlement. " Are
we to be classed with the heathen in knowledge, or to be
accounted as the unnurtured men, who are known once to
have roamed through these forests in quest of their game?
Without assuming any infallibility of judgment, or aspiring to any peculiarity of information, it doth not appear
to my defective understanding, Master Dudley, that the
progress of the settlement hath ever been checked for want
of necessary foresight, nor that the growth of reason among
us hath ever been stunted from any lack of mental aliment.
Our councils are not barren of wisdom, Ensign, nor hath
it often arrived that abstrusities have been propounded,
that some one intellect, to say no more in our own favour,
hath not been known to grapple with them successfully."

" That there are men, or perhaps I ought to say that

there *is a man*, in the valley, who is equal to any marvels in the way of enlightened gifts ———"

" I knew we should come to peaceable conclusions, Ensign Dudley," interrupted the other, rising erect in his saddle, with an air of appeased dignity : " I have ever found you a discreet and consequent reasoner, and one who is never known to resist conviction, when truth is pressed with understanding. That the men from over sea are not often so well gifted is some — we will say, for the sake of a convenient illustration, as thyself, Ensign — is placed beyond the reach of debate, since sight teacheth us that numberless exceptions may be found to all the more general and distinctive laws of nature. I think we are not likely to carry our disagreement further ? "

" It is impossible to make head against one so ready with his knowledge," returned the other, well content to exist in his own person a striking exception to the inferiority of his fellows ; " though it appeareth to me that my brother Ring might be chosen, as another instance of a reasonable stature ; a fact that thou mayst see, Doctor, by regarding him as he approaches through yon meadow. He hath been, like myself, on the scout among the mountains."

" There are many instances of physical merit among thy connections, Master Dudley," returned the complaisant physician. " Though it would seem that thy brother hath not found his companion among them. He is attended by an ill grown, and, it may be added, an ill favoured comrade that I know not."

" Ha ! it would seem that Reuben hath indeed fallen on the trail of savages ! The man in company is certainly in paint and blanket. It may be well to pause at yonder opening, and await their coming."

As this proposition imposed no particular inconvenience, the Doctor readily assented. The two drew nigh to the place where the men, whom they saw crossing the fields in the distance, were expected to enter the highway.

But little time was lost in attendance. Reuben Ring, accoutred and armed like the borderer already introduced in this chapter, soon arrived at the opening, followed by the stranger whose appearance had caused so much surprise to those who watched their approach.

"What now, Sergeant!" exclaimed Dudley, when the other was within ear-shot, speaking a little in the manner of one who had a legal right to propound his questions; "hast fallen on a trail of the savage, and made a captive? or hath some owl permitted one of its brood to fall from the nest, across thy foot-path?"

"I believe the creature may be accounted a human," returned Reuben, throwing the breech of his gun to the earth, and leaning on its long barrel while he intently regarded the half-painted, vacant, and extremely equivocal countenance of his captive. "He hath the colours of a Narragansett about the brow and eyes, and yet he faileth greatly in the form and movements."

"There are anomalies in the physicals of an Indian, as in those of other men," interrupted Doctor Ergot, with a meaning glance at Dudley. "The conclusion of our neighbour Ring may be too hasty, since paint is the fruit of art, and may be applied to any of our faces, after an established usage. But the evidences of nature are far less to be distrusted. It hath come within the province of my studies to note the differences in formation which occur in the different families of man, and nothing, for instance, is more readily to be known, to an eye skilled in these abstrusities, than the aboriginal of the tribe Narragansett. Set the man more in a position of examination, neighbours, and it shall shortly be seen to which race he belongs. Thou wilt note in this little facility of investigation, Ensign, a clear evidence of most of the matters that have this morning been agitated between us. Doth the patient speak English?"

"Therein have I found some difficulty of enquiry," returned Reuben, or, as he should now be, and as he was usually called, Sergeant Ring. "He hath been spoken to in the language of a Christian, no less than in that of a heathen, and as yet no reply hath been made, while he obeys commands uttered in both forms of speech."

"It mattereth not," said Ergot, dismounting and drawing nearer to his subject, with a look towards Dudley that seemed to court his admiration ; " happily the examination before me leaneth but little on any subtleties of speech. Let the man be placed in an attitude of ease ; one in which nature may not be fettered. The conformation of the whole head is remarkably aboriginal, but the distinction of tribes is not to be sought in these general delineations. The forehead, as you see, neighbours, is retreating and narrow ; the cheek-bones, as usual, high ; and the olfactory member, as in all of the natives, inclining to Roman."

" Now to me it would seem that the nose of the man hath a marked upturning at the end," Dudley ventured to remark, as the other ran voluoly over the general and well known distinctive points of physical construction in an Indian.

" As an exception ! Thou seest, Ensign, by this elevation of the bone, and the protuberance of the more fleshy parts, that the peculiarity is an exception. I should rather have said that the nose originally inclined to the Roman. The departure from regularity has been produced by some casualty of their warfare, such as a blow from a tomahawk, or the gash of a knife — ay ! here thou seest the scar left by the weapon ! It is concealed by the paint, but remove that and you will find it hath all the form of a cicatrice of a corresponding shape. These departures from generalities have a tendency to confound pretenders ; a happy circum-stance in itself, for the progress of knowledge on fixed principles. Place the subject more erect, that we may see the natural movement of the muscles. Here is an evidence of great aquatic habits in the dimensions of the foot, which go to confirm original conceptions. It is a happy proof, through which reasonable and prudent conclusions confirm the quick-sighted glances of practice. I pronounce the fellow to be a Narragansett."

" It is then a Narragansett that hath a foot to confound a trail !" returned Eben Dudley, who had been studying the movements and attitudes of the captive with quite as much keenness, and with something more of understanding, than the leech. " Brother Ring, hast ever known an Indian leave such an out-turning foot-print on the leaves?"

" Ensign, I marvel that a man of thy discretion should

dwell on a slight variety of movement, when a case exists
in which the laws of nature may be traced to their sources.
This training for the Indian troubles, hath made thee
critical in the position of a foot. I have said that the
fellow is a Narragansett, and what I have uttered hath not
been lightly ventured. Here is the peculiar formation of
the foot which hath been obtained in infancy, a fulness in
the muscles of the breast and shoulders from unusual
exercise in an element denser than the air, and a nicer construction in——"

The physician paused, for Dudley had coolly advanced
to the captive, and, raising the thin robe of deer-skin
which was thrown over the whole of his superior members,
he exposed the unequivocal skin of a white man. This
would have proved an embarrassing refutation to one
accustomed to the conflict of wits; but monopoly, in
certain branches of knowledge, had produced in favour of
Doctor Ergot an acknowledged superiority, that, in its
effects, might be likened to the predominating influence of
any other aristocracy on those faculties that have been
benumbed by its operation. His opinions changed, which
is more than can be said of his countenance; for, with the
readiness of invention which is so often practised in the
felicitous institutions we have named, and by which the
reasoning, instead of regulating, is adapted to the practice,
he exclaimed, with uplifted hands and eyes that bespoke
the fullness of his admiration—

" Here have we another proof of the wonderful agency
by which the changes in nature are gradually wrought!
Now do we see in this Narragansett——"

" The man is white!" interrupted Dudley, tapping the
naked shoulder which he still held exposed to view.

" White, but not a tittle the less a Narragansett.
Your captive, beyond a doubt, oweth his existence to
Christian parentage, but accident hath thrown him early
mong the aboriginals, and all those parts which were
liable to change were fast getting to assume the peculiarities of the tribe. He is one of those beautiful and
connecting links in the chain of knowledge, by which
science followeth up its deductions to demonstration."

" I should ill brook coming to harm for doing violence to a subject of the King," said Reuben Ring, a steady, open-faced yeoman, who thought far less of the subtleties of his companion, than of discharging his social duties in a manner fitting the character of a quiet and well-conditioned citizen. " We have had so much of stirring tidings, latterly, concerning the manner the savages conduct their warfare, that it behoveth men in places of trust to be vigilant; for," glancing his eyes towards the ruin of the distant block-house, " thou knowest by past experience, brother Dudley, that we have occasion to be watchful, in a settlement as deep in the forest as this."

" I will answer for the indemnity, Sergeant Ring," said Dudley, with an air of dignity. " I take upon myself the keeping of this stranger, and will see that he be borne, properly and in fitting season, before the authorities. In the mean time, duty hath caused us to overlook matters of moment in thy household, which it may now be seemly to communicate. Abundance hath not been neglectful of thy interests, during the scout."

" What!" demanded the husband, with rather more of earnestness than was generally exhibited by one of habits as restrained as his own ; " hath the woman called upon the neighbours during my absence ? "

Dudley nodded an assent.

" And I shall find another boy beneath my roof ? "

Doctor Ergot nodded three times, with a gravity that might have suited a communication even more weighty than the one he made.

" Thy woman rarely doth a good turn by halves, Reuben. Thou wilt find that she hath made provision for a successor to our good neighbour Ergot, since a seventh son is born in thy house."

The broad, honest face of the father flushed with joy, and then a feeling less selfish came over him. He asked, with a slight tremor in the voice, that was none the less touching for coming from the lips of one so stout of frame and firm of movement—

" And the woman—in what manner doth Abundance bear up under the blessing ? "

"Bravely," returned the leech; "go to thy dwelling, Sergeant Ring, and praise God that there is one to look to its concerns in thy absence. He who hath received the gift of seven sons, in five years, need never be a poor nor a dependent man, in a country like this. Seven farms, added to that pretty homestead of mountain-land which thou now tillest, will render thee a patriarch in thine age, and sustain the name of Ring, hundreds of years hence, when these colonies shall become peopled and powerful, and, I say it boldly, caring not who may call me one that vaunteth out of reason, equal to some of your lofty and self-extolled kingdoms of Europe — ay, even peradventure to the mighty sovereignty of Portugal itself! I have enumerated thy future farms at seven, for the allusion of the Ensign to the virtues of men born with natural propensities to the healing art, must be taken as pleasant speech, since it is a mere delusion of old wives' fancy, and it would be particularly unnecessary here, where every reasonable situation of this nature is already occupied. Go to thy wife, Sergeant, and bid her be of good cheer; for she hath done herself, thee, and thy country a service, and that without dabbling in pursuits foreign to her comprehension."

The sturdy yeoman, on whom this rich gift of Providence had been dispensed, raised his hat, and placing it decently before his face, he offered up a silent thanksgiving for the favour. Then transferring his captive to the keeping of his superior officer and kinsman, he was soon seen striding over the fields, towards his upland dwelling, with a heavy foot though with a light heart.

In the mean time, Dudley and his companion bestowed a more particular attention on the silent and nearly motionless object of their curiosity. Though the captive appeared to be of middle age, his eye was unmeaning, his air timid and uncertain, and his form cringing and ungainly. In all these particulars he was seen to differ from the known peculiarities of a native warrior.

Previously to departing, Reuben Ring explained that while traversing the woods, on that duty of watchfulness to which the state of the colony and some recent signs had given rise, this wandering person had been encountered

and secured, as seemed necessary to the safety of the settlement. He had neither sought, nor avoided his captor ;
but when questioned concerning his tribe, his motive for
traversing those hills, and his future intentions, no satisfactory reply could be extracted. He had scarcely spoken,
and the little that he said was uttered in a jargon between
the language of his interrogator and the dialect of some
barbarous nation. Though there was much in the actual
state of the colonies, and in the circumstances in which
this wanderer had been found, to justify his detention,
little had in truth been discovered to supply a clue either to
any material facts in his history, or to any of his views in
being in the immediate vicinity of the valley.

Guided only by this barren information, Dudley and
his companion endeavoured, as they moved towards the
hamlet, to entrap their prisoner into some confession of his
object, by putting their questions with a sagacity not unusual to men in remote and difficult situations, where
necessity and danger are apt to keep alive all the native
energies of the human mind. The answers were little
connected and unintelligible, sometimes seeming to exhibit
the finest subtlety of savage cunning, and at others appearing to possess the mental helplessness of the most abject
fatuity.

CHAPTER IX.

" I am not prone to weeping, as our sex
Commonly are :—
            But I have
That honourable grief lodged here, which burns
Worse than tears drown."   *Winter's Tale.*

If the pen of a compiler, like that we wield, possessed the
mechanical power of the stage, it would be easy to shift the
scenes of this legend, as rapidly and effectively as is
required for its right understanding, and for the proper
maintenance of its interest. That which cannot be done

with the magical aid of machinery, must be attempted by less ambitious and, we fear, by far less efficacious means.

At the same early hour of the day, and at no great distance from the spot where Dudley announced his good fortune to his brother Ring, another morning meeting had place between persons of the same blood and connections. From the instant when the pale light that precedes the day was first seen in the heavens, the windows and doors of the considerable dwelling on the opposite side of the valley had been unbarred. Ere the glow of the sun had gilded the sky over the outline of the eastern woods, this example of industry and providence was followed by the inmates of every house in the village, or on the surrounding hills; and by the time the golden globe itself was visible above the trees, there was not a human being in all that settlement, of proper age and health, who was not actively afoot.

It is scarcely necessary to say that the dwelling we have particularly named was the present habitation of Mark Heathcote. Though age had sapped the foundations of his strength, and had nearly dried the channels of his existence, the venerable religionist still lived. While his physical perfection had been gradually giving way before the ordinary decay of nature, the moral man was but little altered. It is even probable that his visions of futurity were less dimmed by the mists of carnal interests than when last seen, and that the spirit had gained some portion of that energy which had certainly been abstracted from the more corporeal parts of his existence. At the hour already named, the Puritan was seated in the piazza, which stretched along the whole front of a dwelling that, however it might be deficient in architectural proportions, was not wanting in the more substantial comforts of a spacious and commodious frontier residence. In order to obtain a faithful portrait of a man so intimately connected with our tale, the reader will fancy him one who had numbered fourscore and ten years, with a visage on which deep and constant mental striving had wrought many and meaning furrows, a form that trembled while it yet exhibited the ruins of powerful limbs and flexible muscles, and a countenance in which ascetic reflections had engraved a severity that was but faintly relieved by the gleamings of a natural kindness, which no acquired habits, nor any traces of metaphysical thought, could ever entirely erase. Across this picture of venerable and self-mortifying age, the first rays of the sun were now softly cast, lighting a dimmed eye and a furrowed face with a look of brightness and peace. Perhaps the blandness of the expression belonged as much to the season and hour, as to the habitual character of the man. This benignancy of feature, unusual rather in its strength than in its existence, might have been heightened by the fact that his spirit had just wrought in prayer, in the circle of his children and dependents, ere they left those retired parts of the building where they had found rest and security during the night. Of the former, none known and cherished in the domestic circle had been absent; and the ample provision that was making for the morning meal sufficiently showed that the number of the latter had in no degree diminished since the reader was familiar with the domestic economy of his household.

Time had produced no very striking alteration in the appearance of Content. It is true that the brown hue of his features had deepened, and that his frame was be-ginning to lose some of its elasticity and ease of action, in the more measured movements of middle age. But the governed temperament of the individual had always kept the animal in perfect subjection. Even his earlier days had rather exhibited the promise than the performance of the ordinary youthful qualities. Mental gravity had long before produced a corresponding physical effect. In refer-ence to his exterior, it might be said, in the language of the painter, that, without having wrought any change in form and proportions, the colours had been mellowed by time. A few hairs of grey were sprinkled, here and there, around his brow, but it was as moss gathers on the stones of the edifice, rather furnishing evidence of its increased adhesion and stability, than denoting any symptoms of decay.

Not so with his gentle and devoted partner. That softness and sweetness of air which had first touched the heart of Content, was still to be seen, though it existed amid the traces of a constant and a corroding grief. The freshness of youth had departed, and in its place was visible the more lasting, and, in her case, the more effecting beauty of expression. The eye of Ruth had lost none of its gentleness, and her smile still continued kind and attractive: but the former was often painfully vacant, seeming to look inward upon those secret and withering sources of sorrow that were deeply and almost mysteriously seated in her heart; while the latter resembled the cold brightness of that planet, which illumines objects by repelling the borrowed lustre from its own bosom. The matronly form, the feminine beaming of the countenance, and the melodious voice remained : but the first had been shaken till it stood on the very verge of a premature decay; the second had a mingling of anxious care in its blandest expression; and the last was seldom without that fearful thrill which so deeply affects the senses, by conveying to the understanding a meaning so foreign from the words. And yet an uninterested and ordinary observer might not have seen, in the faded comeliness and blighted maturity of the matron, more than the every day signs that betray the turn in the tide of human life. As befitted such a subject, the colouring of sorrow had been traced by a hand too delicate to leave the lines visible to every vulgar eye. Like the master touches of art, her grief, as it was beyond the sympathies, so it lay beyond the ken of those, whom excellence may fail to excite, or in whom absence can deaden affections. Still her feelings were true to all who had any claims on her love. The predominance of wasting grief over the more genial springs of her enjoyments, only went to prove how much greater is the influence of the generous than the selfish qualities of our nature in a heart that is truly endowed with tenderness. It is scarcely necessary to say that this gentle and constant woman sorrowed for her offspring.

Had Ruth Heathcote known that the child ceased to live, it would not have been difficult for one of her faith to have deposited her regrets, by the side of hopes that were so justifiable, in the grave of the innocent. But the living death to which her offspring might be condemned was rarely absent from her thoughts. She listened to the maxims of resignation, which were heard flowing from lips she loved, with the fondness of a woman and the meekness of a Christian ; and then, even while the ho`y lessons were still sounding in her ears, the workings of an unconquerable nature led her insidiously back to the sorrow of a mother.

The imagination of this devoted and feminine being had never possessed an undue control over her reason. Her visions of happiness, with the man whom her judgment not less than her inclination approved, had been such as experience and religion might justify. But she was now fated to learn there is a fearful poetry in sorrow which can sketch with a grace and an imaginative power that no feebler efforts of a heated fancy can equal. She heard the sweet breathing of her slumbering infant in the whispering of the summer airs ; its plaints came to her ears amid the howlings of the gale; while the eager question and fond reply were mixed up with the most ordinary intercourse of her own household. To her the laugh of childish happiness, that often came on the still air of evening from the hamlet, sounded like the voice of mourning, and scarce an infantile sport met her eye that did not bring with it a pang of anguish. Twice, since the events of the inroad, had she been a mother, and, as if an eternal blight rested on her hopes, the little creatures to whom she had given birth slept side by side near the base of the ruined block. Thither she often went, but it was rather to be the victim of those cruel images of her fancy than as a mourner. Her visions of the dead were calm and even consolatory ; but if ever her thoughts mounted to the abodes of eternal peace, and her fancy essayed to embody the forms of the blessed, her mental eye sought her who was not, rather than those who were believed to be secure in their felicity. Wasting and delusory as were these glimpses of the mind, there were others far more harrowing because they presented themselves with more of the coarse and certain features of the world. It was the common, and perhaps it was the better opinion of the inhabitants of the valley, that death had early sealed the fate of those who had fallen into the hands of the savages on the occasion of the inroad. Such a result was in conformity with the known practices and ruthless passions of the conquerors, who seldom spared life, unless to render revenge more cruelly refined, or to bring consolation to some bereaved mother of the tribe by offering a substitute for the dead in the person of a captive. It was a relief to picture the face of the laughing cherub in the clouds ; or to listen to its light footstep in the empty halls of the dwelling, for, in these illusive images of the brain, suffering was confined to her own bosom. But when stern reality usurped the place of fancy, and she saw her living daughter, shivering in the wintry blasts, or sinking beneath the fierce heats of the climate, cheerless in the desolation of female servitude, and suffering meekly the lot of physical weakness beneath a savage master, she endured an anguish that was gradually exhausting the springs of life.

Though the father was not altogether exempt from similar sorrow, it beset him less ceaselessly. He knew how to struggle with the workings of his mind as became a man. Though strongly impressed with the belief that the captives had early been put beyond the reach of suffering, he had neglected no duty which tenderness to his sorrowing partner, parental love, or Christian duty, could require at his hands.

The Indians had retired on the crust of the snow ; and with the thaw every foot-print or sign by which such wary foes might be traced had vanished. It remained matter of doubt to what tribe, or even to what nation, the marauders belonged. The peace of the colony had not yet been openly broken, and the inroad had been rather a violent and fierce symptom of the evils that were contemplated, than the actual commencement of the ruthless hostilities which had since ravaged the frontier. But, while policy had kept the colonists quiet, private affection omitted no rational means of effecting the restoration of the sufferers, in the event of their having been spared.

Scouts had passed among the conspiring and but half peaceable tribes nearest to the settlement, and rewards and menaces had both been liberally used, in order to ascertain the character of the savages who had laid waste the valley, as well as the more interesting fortunes of their hapless victims. Every expedient to detect the truth had failed. The Narragansetts affirmed that their constant enemies the Mohicans, acting with their customary treachery, had plundered their English friends; while the Mohicans vehemently threw back the imputation on the Narragansetts. At other times, some Indians affected to make dark allusions to the hostile feelings of fierce warriors, who, under the name of the Five Nations, were known to reside within the limits of the Dutch colony of New Netherlands, and to dwell upon the jealousy of the pale-faces who spoke a language different from that of the Yengeese.* In short, enquiry had produced no result; and Content, when he did permit his fancy to represent his daughter as still living, was forced to admit the probability that she might be buried far in the ocean of wilderness, which then covered most of the surface of this continent.

Once, indeed, a rumour of an exciting nature reached the family. An itinerant trader, bound from the wilds of the interior to a mart on the sea-shore, had entered the valley. He brought with him a report that a child, answering in some respects to the appearance which might now be supposed to belong to her who was lost, was living among the savages on the banks of the smaller lakes of the adjoining colony. The distance to this spot was great, the path led through a thousand dangers, and the result was far from certain. Yet it quickened hopes which had long been dormant. Ruth never urged any request that might involve serious hazard on her husband, and for many months the latter had even ceased to speak on the subject. Still nature was working powerfully within him. His eyes, at all times reflecting and calm, grew more

---

* The colony of New York was originally a Dutch settlement. Great jealousy existed between the Hollanders and English, and there were constant disputes on the subject of boundaries. The former claimed the country between the Connecticut river and Chesapeake Bay, which included the present states of Delaware, Pennsylvania, New Jersey, New York, and part of Connecticut. As this wide belt of territory separated the English settlements of the North from those of the South, the first got the appellation of New England to distinguish it from that of its Dutch neighbours, a name that it still retains.

thoughtful — deeper lines of care gathered about his brow — and at length melancholy took possession of a countenance that was usually so placid.

It was at this precise period that Eben Dudley chose to urge the suit he had always pressed, after his own desultory fashion, on the decision of Faith. One of those well-ordered accidents which, from time to time, had brought the girl and the young borderer in private conversation, enabled him to effect his design with sufficient clearness. Faith heard him without betraying any of her ordinary waywardness, and answered with as little prevarication as the subject seemed to demand.

" This is well, Eben Dudley," she said, " and it is no more than an honest girl hath a right to hear, from one who hath taken as many means as thou to get into her favour. But he who would have his life tormented by me hath a solemn duty to do ere I listen to his wishes."

" I have been in the lower towns and studied their manner of life, and I have been upon the scouts of the colony, to keep the Indians in their wigwams," returned her suitor, endeavouring to recount the feats of manliness that might reasonably be expected of one inclined to venture on so hazardous an experiment as matrimony. " The bargain with the young Captain for the hill-lot, and for a village homestead, is drawing near a close ; and as the neighbours will not be backward at the stone-bee, or the raising, I see nothing to ——"

" Thou deceivest thyself, observant Dudley," interrupted the girl, " if thou believest eye of thine can see that which is to be sought, ere one and the same fortune shall be the property of thee and me. Hast noted, Eben, the manner in which the cheek of the Madam hath paled, and how her eye is getting sunken, since the time when the fur trader tarried with us, the week of the storm ?"

"¡I cannot say that there is much change in the wearing of the Madam, within the bearing of my memory," answered Dudley, who was never remarkable for minute observations of this nature, however keen he might prove in subjects more intimately connected with his daily pursuits. " She is not young and blooming as thou, Faith; nor is it often that we see——"

" I tell thee, man, that sorrow preyeth upon her form, and that she liveth but in the memory of the lost infant !"

" This is carrying mourning beyond the bounds of reason. The child is at peace; as is thy brother, Whittal, beyond all manner of question. That we have not discovered their bones is owing to the fire, which left but little to tell of ——"

" Thy head is a charnel-house, dull Dudley, but this picture of its furniture shall not suffice for me. The man who is to be my husband must have a feeling for a mother's sorrows !"

" What is now getting uppermost in thy mind, Faith? Is it for me to bring back the dead to life, or to place a child that hath been lost so many years, once more in the arms of its parents ?"

" It is. — Nay, open not thine eyes, as if light were first breaking into the darkness of a clouded brain ! I repeat, it is !"

" I am glad that we have got to these open declarations, for too much of my life hath been already wasted in unsettled gallanting, when sound wisdom, and the example of all around me, have shown that in order to become the father of a family, and to be esteemed for a substantial settler, I should have both cleared and wived some years ago. I wish to deal justly by all, and having given thee reason to think that the day might come when we should live together, as is fitting in people of our condition, I felt it a duty to ask thee to share my chances; but now that thou dealest in impossibilities, it is needful to seek elsewhere."

" This hath ever been thy way, when a good understanding hath been established between us. Thy mind is ever getting into some discontent, and then blame is heaped on one who rarely doth any thing that should in reason offend thee. What madness maketh thee dream that I ask impossibilities ! Surely, Dudley, thou canst not have noted the manner in which the nature of the Madam is giving way before the consuming heat of her grief; thou canst not look into the sorrow of woman, or thou wouldst have listened with more kindness to a plan of travelling the woods for a short season, in order that it might be known, whether she of whom the trader spoke is the lost one of our family, or the child of some stranger !"

Though Faith spoke with vexation, she also spoke with feeling. Her dark eye swam in tears, and the colour of her brown cheek deepened, until her companion saw new reasons to forget his discontent in sympathies, which, however obtuse they might be, were never entirely dormant.

" If a journey of a few hundred miles be all thou askest, girl, why speak in parables ?" he good-naturedly replied. " The kind word was not wanting to put me on such a trail. We will be married on the Sabbath, and, please Heaven, the Wednesday — or the Saturday at most, —shall see me on the path of the western trader."

" No delay. Thou must depart with the sun. The more active thou provest on the journey, the sooner wilt thou have the power to make me repent a foolish deed."

But Faith had been persuaded to relax a little from this severity. They were married on the Sabbath, and the following day Content and Dudley left the valley, in quest of the distant tribe on which the scion of another stock was said to have been so violently engrafted.

It is needless to dwell on the dangers and privations of such an expedition. The Hudson, the Delaware and the Susquehannah, rivers that were then better known in tales than to the inhabitants of New England, were all crossed ; and after a painful and hazardous journey, the adventurers reached the first of that collection of small interior lakes, whose banks are now so beautifully decorated with villages and farms. Here, in the bosom of savage tribes, and exposed to every danger of field and flood, supported only by his hopes, and by the presence of a stout companion that hardships or danger could not easily subdue, the father diligently sought his child.

At length a people were found, who held a captive that answered the description of the trader. We shall not dwell on the feelings with which Content approached the village that contained this little descendant of a white race. He had not concealed his errand, and the sacred character in which he came, found pity and respect even among those barbarous tenants of the wilderness. A deputation of the chiefs received him in the skirts of their clearing. He was conducted to a wigwam, where a council-fire was lighted, and an interpreter opened the subject, by placing the amount of the ransom offered, and the professions of peace with which the strangers came, in the fairest light before his auditors. It is not usual for the American savage easily to loosen his hold on one naturalised in his tribe. But the meek air and noble confidence of Content touched the latent qualities of those generous though fierce children of the woods. The girl was sent for, that she might stand in the presence of the elders of the nation.

No language can paint the sensation with which Content first looked upon this adopted daughter of the savages. The years and sex were in accordance with his wishes, but, in place of the golden hair and azure eyes of the cherub he had lost, there appeared a girl in whose jet black tresses and equally dark organs of sight, he might better trace a descendant of the French of the Canadas, than one sprung from his own Saxon lineage. The father was not quick of mind in the ordinary occupations of life, but nature was now big within him. There needed no second glance to say how cruelly his hopes had been deceived. A smothered groan struggled from his chest, and then his self-command returned with the imposing grandeur of Christian resignation. He arose, and thanking the chiefs for their indulgence, he made no secret of the mistake by which he had been led so far on a fruitless errand. While speaking, the signs and gestures of Dudley gave him reason to believe that his companion had something of importance to communicate. In a private interview, the latter suggested the expediency of concealing the truth, and of rescuing the child they had in fact discovered, from the hands of her barbarous masters. It was now too late to practise a deception that might have availed for this object, had the stern principles of Content permitted the artifice. But transferring some portion of the interest which he felt for the fortunes of his own offspring, to that of the unknown parent, who, like himself, most probably mourned the uncertain fate of the girl before him, he tendered the ransom intended for Ruth in behalf of the captive. It was rejected. Disappointed in both their objects, the adventurers were obliged to quit the village with weary feet and still heavier hearts.

If any who read these pages have ever felt the agony of suspense, in a matter involving the best of human affections, they will know how to appreciate the sufferings of the mother, during the month that her husband was absent on this holy errand. At times hope brightened around her heart, until the glow of pleasure was again mantling on her cheek, and playing in her mild blue eye. The first week of the adventure was one almost of happiness. The hazards of the journey were nearly forgotten in its anticipated results; and, though occasional apprehensions quickened the pulses of one whose system answered so fearfully to the movements of the spirit, there was a predominance of hope in all her anticipations. She again passed among her maidens, with a mien in which joy was struggling with the meekness of subdued habits, and her smiles once more began to beam with renovated happiness. To his dying day, old Mark Heathcote never forgot the sudden sensation that was created by the soft laugh, that on some unexpected occasion came to his ear from the lips of his son's wife. Though years had elapsed between the moment when that unwonted sound was heard, and the time at which the action of the tale now stands, he had never heard it repeated. To heighten the feelings which were now uppermost in the mind of Ruth, when within a day's march of the village to which he was going, Content had found means to send the tidings of his prospects of success. It was over all these renewed wishes that disappointment was to throw its chill, and it was affections thus revived that were to be again blighted by the cruellest of all withering influences, that of disappointed hope.

Content and Dudley reached the deserted clearing, on their return to the valley, near the hour of the setting sun. Their path led through this opening on the mountain side, and there was one point among the bushes, from which the buildings that had already arisen from the ashes of the burning might be distinctly seen. Until now the husband and father had believed himself equal to any effort that duty might require in the progress of this mournful service. But here he paused, and communicated a wish to his companion that he would go ahead and break the nature of the deception that had led them so far on a fruitless mission. Perhaps Content was himself ignorant of all he wished, or to what unskilful hands he had confided a commission of so extraordinary delicacy. He merely felt his own inability, and, with a weakness that may find some apology in his feelings, he saw his companion depart without instructions, or indeed without any other guide than Nature.

Though Faith had betrayed no marked uneasiness during the absence of the travellers, her quick eye was the first to discover the form of her husband, as he came with a tired step across the fields, in the direction of the dwellings. Long ere Dudley reached the house, every one of its inmates were assembled in the piazza. This was no meeting of turbulent delight, or of clamorous greetings. The adventurer drew near amid a silence so oppressive, that it utterly disconcerted a studied project by which he had hoped to announce his tidings in a manner suited to the occasion. His hand was on the gate of the little court, and still none spoke; his foot was on the low step, and no voice bade him welcome. The looks of the little group were rather fixed on the features of Ruth, than on the person of him who approached. Her face was pallid as death, her eye contracted, but filled with the mental effort that sustained her, and her lip scarce trembled, as, in obedience to a feeling still stronger than the one which had so long oppressed her, she exclaimed —

" Eben Dudley, where hast thou left my husband ? "

" The young Captain was a-foot weary, and he tarried in the second growth on the hill; but so brave a walker cannot be far behind. We shall see him soon, at the opening by the dead beech; and it is there that I recommend the Madam —— "

" It was thoughtful in Heathcote, and like his usual

kindness, to devise this well-meant caution!" said Ruth, across whose countenance a smile so radiant passed, that it imparted the expression which is believed to characterise the peculiar benignancy of angels. " Still it was unnecessary ; he should have known that we place our strength on the Rock of Ages. Tell me, in what manner hath my precious one borne the exceeding weariness of thy tangled route ? "

The wandering glance of the messenger had gone from face to face, until it became fastened on the countenance of his own wife, in a settled unmeaning gaze.

" Nay, Faith hath demeaned well, both as my assistant and as thy partner, and thou mayest see that her comeliness is in no degree changed. And did the precious babe falter in this weary passage, or did she retard thy movements by her fretfulness ? But I know thy nature, man; she hath been borne over many long miles of mountain-side and treacherous swamp, in thine own vigorous arms. Thou answerest not, Dudley !" exclaimed Ruth, taking the alarm, and laying a hand firmly on the shoulder of him she questioned, as, forcing his half-averted face to meet her eye, she seemed to read his soul.

The muscles of the sun-burnt and strong features of the borderer worked involuntarily ; his broad chest swelled to its utmost expansion ; big burning drops rolled out upon his brown cheeks, and then, taking the arm of Ruth in one of his own powerful hands, he compelled her to release her hold, with a firm but respectful exercise of his strength, and thrusting the form of his own wife aside without ceremony, he passed through the circle and entered the dwelling with the tread of a giant.

The head of Ruth dropped upon her bosom, the paleness again came over her cheeks, and it was then that the inward look of the eye might first be seen, which afterwards became so constant and so painful an expression in her countenance. From that hour, to the time in which the family of the Wish-Ton-Wish is again brought immediately before the reader, no further rumours were ever heard to lessen or to increase the wasting regrets of her bosom.

CHAPTER X.

Sir, he hath never fed of the dainties that are bred in a book; he hath
not eaten paper, as it were; he hath not drunk ink; his intellect is not replenished; he is only an animal, only sensible in the duller parts.
Love's Labour's Lost.

" HERE cometh Faith, to bring us tidings of the hamlet,"
said the husband of the woman whose character we have
so feebly sketched, as he took his seat in the piazza, at the
early hour and in the group already mentioned. " The
Ensign hath been abroad in the hills, throughout the night,
with a chosen party of our people, and perchance she hath
been sent with the substance of the tidings they have
gathered concerning the unknown trail."

" The heavy-footed Dudley hath scarce mounted to the
dividing ridge, where, report goeth, the prints of moccasins
were seen," observed a young man, who in his person bore
all the evidences of an active and healthful manhood.
" Of what service is the scouting that faileth of the necessary distance by the weariness of its leader ? "

" If thou believest, boy, that thy young foot is equal to
contend with the sinews of Eben Dudley, there may be
occasion to show the magnitude of thy error, ere the danger
of this Indian outbreaking shall pass away. Thou art too
stubborn of will, Mark, to be yet trusted with the leading
of parties that may hold the safety of all who dwell in the
Wish-Ton-Wish within their keeping."

The young man looked displeased ; but, fearful that his
father might observe and misinterpret his humour into a
personal disrespect, he turned away, permitting his frowning
eye to rest, for an instant, on the timid and stolen glance
of a maiden, whose cheek was glowing like the eastern sky,
as she busied herself with the preparations of the breakfast-
table.

" What welcome news dost bring from the sign of the
Whip-Poor-Will ? " Content asked of the woman, who had
now come within the little gate of his court. " Hast seen

the Ensign, since the party took the hill paths? — or is it some traveller who hath charged thee with matter for our ears?"

"Eye of mine hath not seen the man since he girded himself with the sword of office," returned Faith, entering the piazza, and nodding salutation to those around her; "and as for strangers, when the clock shall strike noon, it will be one month to the day that the last of them was housed within my doors. But I complain not of the want of custom, as the Ensign would never quit the bar and his gossip to go into the mountain-lots so long as there was one to fill his years with the marvels of the old countries, or even to discourse of the home-stirrings of the colonies themselves."

"Thou speakest lightly, Faith, of one who merits thy respect and thy duty."

The eye of the former studied the meek countenance of her from whom this reproof came, with an intenseness and a melancholy that showed her thoughts were on other matters, and then, as if suddenly recalled to what had passed, she resumed —

"Truly, what with duty to the man as a husband, and respect to him as an officer of the colony, Madam Heathcote, the task is not of easy bearing. If the King's representative had given the colours to my brother Reuben, and left the Dudley with the halberd in his hand, the preferment would have been ample for one of his qualities, and all the better for the credit of the settlement."

"The Governor distributed his favour according to the advice of men competent to distinguish merit," said Content. "Eben was foremost in the bloody affair among the people of the Plantations, where his manhood was of good example to all in company. Should he continue as faithful and as valiant, thou mayst yet live to see thyself the consort of a captain!"

"Not for glory gained in this night's marching, for yonder cometh the man, with a sound body, and seemingly with the stomach of a Cæsar — ay, and I'll answer for it, of a regiment too! It is no trifle that will satisfy his appetite after one of these — ha! pray Heaven the fellow be not harmed; truly, he hath our neighbour Ergot in attendance."

"There is other than he, too, for one cometh in the rear, whose gait and air is unknown to me — the trail hath been struck, and Dudley leadeth a captive! A savage, in his paint and cloak of skin, is taken."

This assertion caused all to rise, for the excitement of an apprehended inroad was still strong in the minds of those secluded people. Not a syllable more was uttered until the scout and his companion were before them.

The quick glance of Faith had scanned the person of her husband, and, resuming her spirits with the certainty that he was unharmed, she was the first to greet him with words.

"How now, Ensign Dudley?" said the woman, quite vexed that she had unguardedly betrayed a greater interest in his welfare than she might always deem prudent — "how now, Ensign; hath the campaign ended with no better trophy than this?"

"The fellow is not a chief, nor, by his step and dull look, even a warrior; but he was, nevertheless, a lurker nigh the settlements, and it was thought prudent to bring him in," returned the husband, addressing himself to Content, while he answered the salutation of his wife with a sufficiently brief nod. "My own scouting hath brought nothing to light, but my brother Ring hath fallen on the trail of this effigy of a man, and it is not a little that we are puzzled in probing, as the good Doctor Ergot calleth it, into the meaning of his errand."

"Of what tribe may the savage be?"

"There hath been discussion among us on that matter," returned Dudley, with an oblique glance of the eye towards the physician. "Some have said he is a Narragansett, while others think he cometh of a stock still further east."

"In giving that opinion, I spoke merely of his secondary or acquired habits," interrupted Ergot; "for, having reference to his original, the man is assuredly a white."

"A white!" repeated all around him.

"Beyond a cavil, as may be seen by divers particulars in his outward conformation, viz. in the shape of the head, the muscles of the arms and of the legs, the air and gait, besides sundry other signs that are familiar to men who have made the physical peculiarities of the two races their study."

"One of which is this!" continued Dudley, throwing up the robe of the captive, and giving his companions the ocular evidence which had so satisfactorily removed all his own doubts. "Though the colour of the skin may not be proof positive, like that named by our neighbour Ergot, it is still something towards helping a man of little learning to make up an opinion in such a matter."

"Madam!" exclaimed Faith, so suddenly as to cause her she addressed to start, "for the sake of Heaven's mercy, let the maidens bring soap and water, that the face of this man be cleansed of its paint."

"What foolishness is thy brain set upon?" rejoined the Ensign, who had latterly affected some of that superior gravity which might be supposed to belong to his official station. "We are not now under the roof of the Whip-Poor-Will, wife of mine, but in the presence of those who need none of thy suggestions to give proper forms to an examination of office."

Faith heeded no reproof. Instead of waiting for others to perform that which she had desired, she applied herself to the task with a dexterity that had been acquired by long practice, and a zeal that seemed awakened by some extraordinary emotion. In a minute the colours had disappeared from the features of the captive; and though deeply tanned by exposure to an American sun and to sultry winds, his face was unequivocally that of one who owed his origin to an European ancestry. The movements of the eager woman were watched with curious interest by all present, and when the short task was ended, a murmur of surprise broke simultaneously from every lip.

"There is meaning in this masquerade," observed Content, who had long and intently studied the dull and ungainly countenance that was exposed to his scrutiny by the operation. "I have heard of Christian men who have sold themselves to gain, and who, forgetting religion and the love of their race, have been known to league with the

savage, in order to pursue rapine in the settlements. This
wretch hath the subtlety of one of the French of the Canadas in his eye."

" Away ! away ! " cried Faith, forcing herself in front
of the speaker, and by placing her two hands on the shaven
crown of the prisoner, forming a sort of shade to his features, — " away with all folly about the Frenchers and
wicked leagues ! This is no plotting miscreant, but a
stricken innocent ! Whittal, my brother Whittal, dost
know me ? "

The tears rolled down the cheeks of the wayward woman, as she gazed into the face of her witless relative,
whose eye lighted with one of its occasional gleamings
of intelligence, and who indulged in a low vacant laugh,
ere he answered her earnest interrogatory.

" Some speak like men from over sea," he said, " and
some speak like men of the woods. Is there such a thing
as bear's meat, or a mouthful of hominy, in the wigwam ? "

Had the voice of one long known to be in the grave
broken on the ears of the family, it would scarcely have
produced a deeper sensation, or have quickened the blood
more violently about their hearts, than this sudden and utterly unexpected discovery of the character of their captive.
Wonder and awe held them mute for a time, and then
Ruth was seen standing before the restored wanderer, her
hands clasped in the attitude of petition, her eye contracted
and imploring, and her whole person expressive of the suspense and excitement which had roused her long latent
emotions to agony.

" Tell me," said a thrilling voice, that might have
quickened the intellect of one even duller than the man
addressed, " as thou hast pity in thy heart, tell me, if my
babe yet live ? "

" 'Tis a good babe," returned the other ; and then
laughing again, in his own vacant and unmeaning manner, he bent his eyes with a species of stupid wonder on
Faith, in whose appearance there was far less change than
in the speaking but wasted countenance of her who stood
immediately before him.

" Give leave, dearest Madam," interposed the sister ;
" I know the nature of the boy, and could ever do more
with him than any other."

But this request was useless.   The frame of the mother,
in its present state of excitement, was unequal to further
effort.   Sinking into the watchful arms of Content, she
was borne away, and for a minute the anxious interest of
the handmaidens left none but the men on the piazza.

" Whittal, my old playfellow, Whittal Ring ! " said the
son of Content, advancing with a humid eye to take the hand
of the prisoner ; " hast forgotten, man, the companion of
thy early days ?   It is young Mark Heathcote that speaks."

The other looked up into his countenance, for a moment,
with a reviving recollection ; but, shaking his head, he
drew back in marked displeasure, muttering, loud enough
to be heard, —

" What a false liar is a pale-face !   Here is one of the
tall rogues wishing to pass for a loping boy ! "

What more he uttered his auditors never knew, for he
changed his language to some dialect of an Indian tribe.

" The mind of the unhappy youth hath even been more
blunted by exposure and the usages of a savage life, than
by Nature," said Content, who, with most of the others,
had been recalled by his interest in the examination to the
scene they had momentarily quitted.   " Let his sister deal
tenderly with the lad, and in Heaven's good time shall we
learn the truth."

The feeling of the father clothed his words with authority.   The eager group gave place, and something like the
solemnity of an official examination succeeded to the irregular and hurried interrogatories which had first broken on
the dull intellect of the recovered wanderer.

The dependants took their stations in a circle, around the
chair of the Puritan, by whose side was placed Content,
while Faith induced her brother to be seated on the step
of the piazza, in a manner that all might hear.   The attention of the half-wit himself was drawn from the form-
ality of the arrangement, by placing food in his hands.

" And now, Whittal, I would know," commenced the
ready woman, when a deep silence denoted the interest of

the auditors, " I would know, if thou rememberest the day I clad thee in garments of boughten cloth from over sea, and how fond thou wast of being seen among the kine in colours so gay."

The young man looked up in her face, as if the tones of her voice gave him pleasure ; but instead of making any reply he preferred to munch the bread, with which she had endeavoured to lure him back to their ancient confidence.

" Surely, boy, thou canst not so soon have forgotten the gift I bought with the hard earnings of a wheel that turned at night. The tail of yon peacock is not finer than thou then wast. But I will make thee such another garment, that thou mayst go with the trainers to their weekly muster."

The youth dropped the robe of skin that covered the upper part of his body, and making a forward gesture with the gravity of an Indian, he answered —

" Whittal is a warrior on his path ; he has no time for the talk of the women."

" Now, brother, thou forgettest the manner in which I was wont to feed thy hunger, when the frost pinched thee in the cold mornings, and at the hour when the kine needed thy care, else thou wouldst not call me woman."

" Hast ever been on the trail of a Pequot? Knowest how to whoop among the men ? "

" What is an Indian whoop to the bleating of thy flocks, or the bellowing of cattle in the bushes ! Thou rememberest the sound of the bells, as they tingled among the second growth of an evening ? "

The ancient herdsman turned his head, and seemed to lend his attention, as a dog listens to an approaching footstep. But the gleam of recollection was quickly lost. In the next moment, he yielded to the more positive, and, possibly, more urgent demands of his appetite.

" Then hast thou lost the use of ears ; else thou wouldst not say that thou forgettest the sound of the bells."

" Didst ever hear a wolf howl ? " exclaimed the other. " That's a sound for a hunter ! I saw the Great Chief strike the striped panther, when the boldest warrior of the tribe grew white as a craving pale-face at his leaps ! "

" Talk not to me of your ravenous beasts and great
chiefs, but rather let us think of the days when we were
young, and when thou hadst delight in the sports of a
Christian childhood. Hast forgotten, Whittal, how our
mother used to give us leave to pass the idle time in games
among the snow ? "

" Nipset hath a mother in her wigwam, but he asketh
no leave to go on the hunt. He is a man ; — the next
snow he will be a warrior."

" Silly boy ! This is some treachery of the savage, by
which he has bound thy weakness with the fetters of his
craftiness. Thy mother, Whittal, was a woman of Christian belief, and one of a white race ; and a kind and
mourning mother was she over thy feeble-mindedness !
Dost not remember, unthankful of heart, how she nursed
thy sickly hours in boyhood, and how she administered to
all thy bodily wants ? Who was it that fed thee when
a-hungered, or who had compassion on thy waywardness,
when others tired of thy idle deeds, or grew impatient of
thy weakness ? "

The brother looked for an instant at the flushed features
of the speaker, as if glimmerings of some faintly distinguished scenes crossed the visions of his mind ; but the
animal still predominated, and he continued to feed.

" This exceedeth human endurance ! " exclaimed the
excited Faith. " Look into this eye, weak one, and say if
thou knowest her who supplied the place of that mother
whom thou refusest to remember ; she who hath toiled for
thy comfort, and who hath never refused to listen to all thy
plaints, and to soften all thy sufferings ? Look at this
eye, and speak ; dost know me ? "

" Certain ! " returned the other, laughing with a half
intelligent expression of recognition ; " 'tis a woman of
the pale-faces, and, I warrant me, one that will never be
satisfied till she hath all the furs of the Americas on her
back, and all the venison of the woods in her kitchen.
Didst ever hear the tradition, how that wicked race got
into the hunting grounds, and robbed the warriors of the
country ? "

The disappointment of Faith made her too impatient

to lend a pleased attention to this tale; but at that moment a form appeared at her side, and by a gesture directed her to humour the temper of the wanderer.

It was Ruth, in whose pale cheek and anxious eye all the intenseness of a mother's longings might be traced. Though so lately helpless, and sinking beneath her emotions, the sacred feelings which now sustained her seemed to supply the place of all other aid, and, as she glided past the listening circle, even Content himself had not believed it necessary to offer succour, or to interpose with remonstrance. Her quiet gesture seemed to say, " Proceed, and show indulgence to the weakness of the young man." The rising discontent of Faith was checked by habitual respect, and she prepared to obey.

" And what says the silly tradition of which you speak?" she added, ere the current of his dull ideas had time to change its direction.

" 'Tis spoken by the old men in the villages, and what is there said is true. You see all around you, land that is covered with hill and valley, and which once bore wood, without the fear of the axe, and over which game was spread with a bountiful hand There are runners and hunters in our tribe, who have been on a straight path towards the setting sun, until their legs were weary, and their eyes could not see the clouds that hang over the salt lake; and yet they say 'tis every where beautiful as yonder green mountain. Tall trees and shady woods, rivers and lakes filled with fish, and deer and beaver plentiful as the sands on the sea shore. All this land and water the Great Spirit gave to men of red skins, for them he loved, since they spoke truth in their tribes, were true to their friends, hated their enemies, and knew how to take scalps. Now a thousand snows had come and melted since this gift was made," continued Whittal, who spoke with the air of one charged with the narration of a grave tradition, though he probably did no more than relate what many repetitions had rendered familiar to his inactive mind; "and yet none but red-skins were seen to hunt the moose, or to go on the war-path. Then the Great Spirit grew angry; he hid his face from his children, because they quarrelled among

R

themselves. Big canoes came out of the rising sun, and brought a hungry and wicked people into the land. At first the strangers spoke soft and complaining, like women. They begged room for a few wigwams, and said if the warriors would give them ground to plant, they would ask their God to look upon the red men. But when they grew strong, they forgot their words, and made liars of themselves. Oh, they are wicked knaves! A pale-face is a panther. When a-hungered you can hear him whining in the bushes like a strayed infant; but when you come within his leap, beware of tooth and claw!"

" This evil-minded race, then, robbed the red warriors of their land?"

" Certain! They spoke like sick women till they grew strong, and then they out-devilled the Pequots themselves in wickedness, feeding the warriors with their burning milk, and slaying with blazing inventions that they made out of the yellow meal."

" And the Pequots! was their great warrior dead, before the coming of the men from over sea?"

" You are a woman that has never heard a tradition or you would know better! A Pequot is a weak and crawling cub."

" And thou — thou art then a Narragansett?"

" Don't I look like a man?"

" I had mistaken thee for one of our nearer neighbours, the Mohican Pequots."

" The Mohicans are basket-makers for the Yengeese! but the Narragansett goes leaping through the woods, like a wolf on the trail of the deer!"

" All this is quite in reason, and, now thou pointest to its justice, I cannot fail but see it. But we have curiosity to know more of the great tribe. Hast ever heard of one of thy people, Whittal, known as Miantonimoh? — 'tis a chief of some renown."

The witless youth had continued to eat, at intervals, but, on hearing this question, he seemed suddenly to forget his appetite. For a moment he looked down, and then he said slowly and not without solemnity, —

" A man cannot live for ever."

" What!" said Faith, motioning to her deeply interested auditors to restrain their impatience, " has he quitted
his people ? And thou livedest with him, Whittal, ere he
came to his end ?"

" He never looked on Nipset, nor Nipset on him."

" I know nought of this Nipset : tell me of the great
Miantonimoh."

" Dost need to hear twice ? The Sachem is gone to the
far land, and Nipset will be a warrior when the next snow
comes !"

Disappointment threw a cloud on every countenance, and
the beam of hope which had been kindling in the eye of
Ruth, changed to the former painful expression of inward
suffering. But Faith still managed to repress all speech
among the listeners, continuing the examination, after a
short delay that her vexation rendered unavoidable.

" I had thought that Miantonimoh was still a warrior
in his tribe," she said. " In what battle did he fall ?"

" Mohican Uncas did that wicked deed. The pale-men
gave him great riches to murder the Sachem."

" Thou speakest of the father ; but there was another
Miantonimoh : he who in boyhood dwelt among the people
of white blood."

Whittal listened attentively ; and after seeming to rally
his thoughts, he shook his head, saying before he again
began to eat, —

" There never was but one of the name, and there never
will be another. Two eagles do not build their nests in
the same tree."

" Thou sayest truly," continued Faith, well knowing
that to dispute the information of her brother was, in effect,
to close his mouth. " Now tell me of Conanchet, the
present Narragansett Sachem ; he who hath leagued with
Metacom, and hath of late been driven from his fastness
near the sea : doth he yet live ?"

The expression of the brother's countenance underwent
another change. In place of the childish importance with
which he had hitherto replied to the questions of his sister,
a look of overreaching cunning gathered about his dull eye.
The organ glanced slowly and cautiously around him, as if

its owner expected to detect some visible sign of those covert intentions he so evidently distrusted. Instead of answering, the wanderer continued his meal, though less like one who had need of sustenance, than one resolved to make no communications which might prove dangerous. This change was not unobserved by Faith, or by any of those who so intently watched the means by which she had been endeavouring to thread the confused ideas of one so dull, and yet who at need seemed so practised in savage artifice. She prudently altered her manner of interrogating, by endeavouring to lead his thoughts to other matters.

" I warrant me," continued the sister, " that thou now beginnest to call to mind the times when thou ledst the cattle among the bushes, and how thou wert wont to call on Faith to give thee food, when a-weary with threading the woods in search of the kine. Hast ever been assailed by the Narragansetts thyself, Whittal, when dwelling in the house of a pale-face ? "

The brother ceased eating. Again he appeared to muse as intently as was possible for one of his circumscribed intellects. But shaking his head in the negative, he silently resumed the grateful office of mastication.

" What ! hast come to be a warrior, and never known a scalp taken, or seen a fire lighted in the roof of a wigwam ?"

Whittal laid down the food, and turned to his sister. His face was teeming with a wild and fierce meaning, and he even indulged in a low but triumphant laugh. When this exhibition of satisfaction was over he consented to reply.

" Certain," he said. " We went on a path, in the night against the lying Yengeese, and no burning of the woods ever scorched the 'arth as we blackened their fields ! All their proud housen were turned into piles of coals."

" And where and when did you this act of brave vengeance ? "

" They called the place after the bird of night ; as if an Indian name could save them from an Indian massacre !"

" Ha ! 'T is of the Wish-Ton-Wish thou speakest ! But thou wast a sufferer, and not an actor, brother, in that heartless burning."

" Thou liest, like a wicked woman of the pale-faces as

thou art! Nipset was only a boy on that path, but he went with his people. I tell thee we singed the very 'arth with our brands, and no a head of them all ever rose again from the ashes."

Notwithstanding her great self-command, and the object that was constantly before the mind of Faith, she shuddered at the fierce pleasure with which her brother pronounced the extent of the vengeance that, in his imaginary character, he believed he had taken on his enemies. Still cautious not to destroy an illusion which might aid her in the so long defeated and so anxiously desired discovery, the woman repressed her horror and continued : —

" True — yet some were spared — surely the warriors carried prisoners back to their village. Thou didst not slay all ? "

" All."

" Nay — thou speakest now of the miserable beings who were wrapt in the blazing block ; but — but some without might have fallen into thy hands, ere the assailed sought shelter in the tower. Surely — surely — thou didst not kill all ? "

The hard breathing of Ruth caught the ear of Whittal, and for a moment he turned to regard her countenance in wonder. But again shaking his head, he answered, in a low positive tone —

" All ; — ay, to the screeching women and crying babes ! "

" Surely there is a child — I would say there is a woman in thy tribe, of fairer skin and of a form different from most of thy people. Was not such an one led a captive from the burning of the Wish-Ton-Wish ? "

" Dost think the deer will live with the wolf ? or hast ever found the cowardly pigeon in the nest of the hawk ? "

" Nay, thou art of different colour thyself, Whittal, and it well may be thou art not alone."

The youth regarded his sister a moment with displeasure, and then, on turning to eat, he muttered —

" There is as much fire in snow, as truth in a Yengeese ! "

" This examination must close," said Content, with a

heavy sigh ; " at another hour we may hope to push the
matter to some more fortunate result ; but yonder cometh
one charged with especial service from the towns below,
as would seem by the fact that he disregardeth the holiness
of the day, no less than by the earnest manner in which he
is journeying."

As the individual named was visible to all who chose to
look in the direction of the hamlet, his sudden appearance
caused a general interruption to the interest which had been
so strongly awakened on a subject that was familiar to
every resident in the valley.

The early hour, the gait at which the stranger urged his
horse, the manner in which he passed the open and inviting
door of the Whip-Poor-Will, proclaimed him a messenger,
that probably bore some communication of importance
from the Government of the Colony to the younger Heathcote, who filled the highest station of official authority in
that distant settlement.   Observations to this purport had
passed from mouth to mouth, and curiosity was actively
alive by the time the horseman rode into the court.   There
he dismounted, and, covered with the dust of the road, he
presented himself with the air of one who had passed
the night in the saddle before the man he sought.

" I have orders for Captain Content Heathcote," said the
messenger, saluting all around him with the usual grave
but studied courtesy of the people to whom he belonged.

" He is here to receive and to obey," was the answer.

The traveller wore a little of that mysteriousness that is
so grateful to certain minds, which, from inability to command respect in any other manner, are fond of making
secrets of matters that might as well be revealed.   In
obedience to this feeling, he expressed a desire that his
communications might be made apart.   Content quietly
motioned for him to follow, leading the way into an inner
apartment of the house.   As a new direction was given by
this interruption to the thoughts of the spectators of the
preceding scene, we shall also take the opportunity to
digress, in order to lay before the reader some general facts,
that may be necessary to the connection of the subsequent
parts of the legend.

CHAPTER XI.

" Be certain what you do, Sir ; lest your justice
Prove violence." *Winter's Tale.*

THE designs of the celebrated Metacom had been betrayed
to the colonists by the treachery of a subordinate warrior,
named Sausaman. The punishment of this treason led to
enquiries, which terminated in accusations against the great
Sachem of the Wompanoags. Scorning to vindicate himself before enemies that he hated, and perhaps distrusting
their clemency, Metacom no longer endeavoured to cloak
his proceedings, but, throwing aside the emblems of peace,
he openly appeared with an armed hand.

The tragedy had commenced about a year before the
period at which the tale has now arrived. A scene not
unlike that detailed in the foregoing pages took place ; the
brand, the knife, and the tomahawk doing their work of
destruction, without pity, and without remorse. But, unlike the inroad of the Wish-Ton-Wish, this expedition was
immediately followed by others, until the whole of New
England was engaged in the celebrated war to which we
have before referred.

The entire white population of the Colonies of New
England had, shortly before, been estimated at one hundred and twenty thousand souls. Of this number, it was
thought that sixteen thousand men were capable of bearing
arms. Had time been given for the maturity of the plans
of Metacom, he might have readily assembled bands of
warriors who, aided by their familiarity with the woods,
and accustomed to the privations of such a warfare, would
have threatened serious danger to the growing strength of
the whites. But the ordinary and selfish feelings of man
were as active among these wild tribes as they are known
to be in more artificial communities. The indefatigable
Metacom, like that Indian hero of our own times Tecumthè,
had passed years in endeavouring to appease ancient enmities and to lull jealousies, in order that all of red blood

R 4

might unite in crushing a foe, that promised, should he be longer undisturbed in his march to power, soon to be too formidable for their united efforts to subdue. The premature explosion in some manner averted the danger. It gave the English time to strike several severe blows against the tribe of their great enemy before his allies had determined to make common cause in his design. The summer and autumn of 1675 had been passed in active hostilities between the English and the Wompanoags, without openly drawing any other nation into the contest. Some of the Pequots, with their dependent tribes, even took sides with the whites, and we read of the Mohicans being actively employed in harassing the Sachem, on his well known retreat from that neck of land where he had been hemmed in by the English with the expectation that he might be starved into submission.

The warfare of the first summer was attended by various degrees of success, fortune quite as often favouring the red men, in their desultory attempts at annoyance, as their more disciplined enemies. Instead of confining his operations to his own circumscribed and easily environed districts, Metacom led his warriors to the distant settlements on the Connecticut, and it was during the operations of this season that several of the towns on that river were first assailed and laid in ashes. Active hostilities had in some measure ceased between the Wompanoags and the English with the cold weather, most of the troops retiring to their homes, while the Indians apparently paused to take breath for their final effort.

It was, however, previously to this cessation of activity, that the Commissioners of the United Colonies, as they were called, met to devise the means of a concerted resistance. Unlike their former dangers from the same quarter, it was manifest, by the manner in which a hostile feeling was spreading around their whole frontier, that a leading spirit had given as much of unity and design to the movements of the foe, as could probably ever be created among a people so separated by distance, and so divided in communities. Right or wrong, the colonists gravely decided that the war, on their part, was just. Great-preparations were therefore made to carry it on the ensuing summer, in a manner more suited to their means, and to the absolute necessities of their situation. It was in consequence of the arrangements made for bringing a portion of the inhabitants of the colony of Connecticut into the field, that we find the principal characters of our legend in the warlike guise in which they have just been presented to the reader.

Although the Narragansetts had not, at first, been openly implicated in the attacks on the colonists, facts soon came to the knowledge of the latter, which left no doubt of the state of feeling in that nation. Many of their young men were discovered among the followers of Metacom, and arms taken from whites who had been slain in the different encounters were also seen in their villages. One of the first measures of the commissioners, therefore, was to anticipate more serious opposition, by directing an overwhelming force against this people. The party collected on that occasion was probably the largest military body which the English, at that early day, had ever assembled in their colonies. It consisted of a thousand men, of whom no inconsiderable number was cavalry,—a species of troops that, as all subsequent experience has shown, is admirably adapted to operations against so active and so subtle a foe.

The attack was made in the depth of winter, and it proved fearfully destructive to the assailed. The defence of Conanchet, the young Sachem of the Narragansetts, was every way worthy of his high character for courage and mental resources, nor was the victory gained without serious loss to the colonists. The native chief had collected his warriors and taken post on a small area of firm land, that was situated in the centre of a densely wooded swamp, and the preparations for resistance betrayed a singular familiarity with the military expedients of a white man. There had been a palisadoed breast-work, a species of redoubt, and a regular block-house to overcome, ere the colonists could penetrate into the fortified village itself. The first attempts were unsuccessful, the Indians having repulsed their enemies with loss. But better arms and greater concert finally prevailed, though not without a struggle that lasted for many hours, and not until the defendants were, in truth, nearly surrounded.

The events of that memorable day made a deep impression on the minds of men who were rarely excited by any incidents of a great and moving character. It was still the subject of earnest and not unfrequently of melancholy discourse around the fire-sides of the colonists ; nor was the victory achieved without accompaniments which, however unavoidable they might have been, had a tendency to raise doubts in the minds of such conscientious religionists concerning the lawfulness of their cause. It is said that a village of six hundred cabins was burnt, and that hundreds of dead and wounded were consumed in the conflagration. A thousand warriors were thought to have lost their lives in this affair, and it was believed that the power of the nation was broken for ever. The sufferers among the colonists themselves were numerous, and mourning came into a vast many families with the tidings of victory.

In this expedition most of the men of the Wish-Ton-Wish had been conspicuous actors, under the orders of Content. They had not escaped with impunity, but it was confidently hoped that their courage was to meet its reward in a long continuance of peace, — a consummation that was the more desirable on account of their remote and exposed situation.

In the mean time, the Narragansetts were far from being subdued. Throughout the whole continuance of the inclement season, they had caused alarms on the frontiers, and in one or two instances their renowned Sachem had taken signal vengeance for the dire affair in which his people had so heavily suffered. As the spring advanced, the inroads became still more frequent, and the appearances of danger so far increased as to require a new call on the colonists to arm. The messenger, introduced in the last chapter, was charged with matter that had a reference to the events of this war, and as the bearer of an especial communication of great urgency he had now demanded his secret audience with the leader of the military force of the valley.

" Thou hast affairs of moment to deal with, Captain

Heathcote," said the hard-riding traveller, when he found himself alone with Content. " The orders of his Honour are to spare neither whip nor spur, until the chief men of the borders shall be warned of the actual situation of the colony."

" Hath aught of moving interest occurred, that his Honour deemeth there is necessity for unusual watchfulness ? We had hoped that the prayers of the pious were not in vain ; and that a time of quiet was about to succeed to the violence of which, bounden by our social covenants, we have unhappily been unwilling spectators. The bloody asault of Pettyquamscott hath exercised our minds severely — nay, it hath even raised doubts of the lawfulness of some of our deeds."

" Thou hast a commendable spirit of forgiveness, Captain Heathcote, or thy memory would extend to other scenes than those which bear relation to the punishment of an enemy so remorseless. It is said on the river, that the valley of Wish-Ton-Wish hath been visited by the savage in its day, and men speak freely of the wrongs suffered by its owners on that pitiless occasion."

" The truth may not be denied, even that good should come thereof. It is certain that much suffering was inflicted on me and on mine, by the inroad of which you speak ; nevertheless, we have ever striven to consider it as a merciful chastisement, inflicted for manifold sins, rather than as a subject that might be remembered in order to stimulate passions that, in all reason as in all charity, should slumber as much as weak nature will allow."

" This is well, Captain Heathcote, and in exceeding conformity with the most received doctrines," returned the stranger, slightly gaping, either from want of rest the previous night, or from disinclination to so grave a subject ; " but it hath little connection with present duties. My charge beareth especial concern with the further destruction of the Indians, rather than to any inward searchings into the condition of our own mental misgivings, concerning any right it may be thought proper to question, that hath a reference to the duty of self-protection. There is no unworthy dweller in the Connecticut Colony, Sir, that hath endeavoured more to cultivate a tender conscience than the wretched sinner who standeth before you; for I have the exceeding happiness to sit under the outpourings of a spirit that hath few mortal superiors in the matter of precious gifts. I now speak of Doctor Calvin Pope, a most worthy and soul-quieting divine; one who spareth not the goad when the conscience needeth pricking, nor hesitateth to dispense consolation to him who seeth his fallen estate; and one that never faileth to deal with charity and humbleness of spirit and forbearance with the failings of friends, and forgiveness of enemies, as the chiefest signs of a renovated moral existence; and, therefore, there can be but little reason to distrust the spiritual rightfulness of all that listen to the riches of his discourse. But when it cometh to be question of life or death, a matter of dominion and possession of these fair lands, that the Lord hath given — why, Sir, then I say that, like the Israelites dealing with the sinful occupants of Canaan, it behoveth us to be true to each other, and to look upon the heathen with a distrustful eye."

"There may be reason in that thou utterest," observed Content, sorrowfully. "Still it is lawful to mourn even the necessity which conduceth to all this strife. I had hoped that they who direct the councils of the colony, might have resorted to less violent means of persuasion to lead the savage back to reason, than that which cometh from the armed hand. Of what nature is thy especial errand?"

"Of deep urgency, Sir, as will be seen in the narration," returned the other, dropping his voice like one habitually given to the dramatic part of diplomacy, however unskilful he might have been in its more intellectual accomplishments. "Thou wast in the Pettyquamscott scourging, and need not be reminded of the manner in which the Lord dealt with our enemies on that favour-dispensing day; but it may not be known to one so remote from the stirring and daily transactions of Christendom in what manner the savage hath taken the chastisement. The restless and still unconquered Conanchet hath deserted his towns, and taken refuge in the open woods; where it exceedeth the skill and usage of our civilised men of war to discover, at all times, the position and force of their enemies. The consequences may be easily conjectured. The savage hath broken in upon, and laid waste, in whole or in part, firstly — Lancaster, on the tenth," counting on his fingers, "when many were led into captivity; secondly, Marlborough, on the twentieth; on the thirteenth ultimo, Groton; Warwick, on the seventeenth; and Rehoboth, Chelmsford, Andover, Weymouth, and divers other places, have been greatly sufferers, between the latter period and the day when I quitted the abode of his Honour. Pierce of Scituate, a stout warrior, and one practised in the wiles of this nature of warfare, hath been cut off with a whole company of followers; and Wadsworth and Brocklebank, men known and esteemed for courage and skill, have left their bones in the woods, sleeping in common among their luckless followers."

" These are truly tidings to cause us to mourn over the abandoned condition of our nature," said Content, in whose meek mind there was no affectation of regrets on such a subject. " It is not easy to see in what manner the evil may be arrested, without again going forth to battle."

" Such is the opinion of his Honour, and of all who sit with him in council; for we have sufficient knowledge of the proceedings of the enemy, to be sure that the master spirit of wickedness, in the person of him called Philip, is raging up and down the whole extent of the borders, awakening the tribes to what he calleth the necessity of resisting further aggression, and stirring up their vengeance, by divers subtle expedients of malicious cunning."

" And what manner of proceeding hath been ordered, in so urgent a strait, by the wisdom of our rulers? "

" Firstly, there is a fast ordained, that we may come to the duty as men purified by mental struggle and deep self-examination; secondly, it is recommended that the congregations deal with more than wonted severity with all backsliders and evil doers, in order that the towns may not fall under the divine displeasure, as happened to them that dwelt in the devoted cities of Canaan; thirdly, it is determined to lend our feeble aid to the ordering of Providence, by calling forth the allotted number of the trained bands; and, fourthly, it is contemplated to counteract the seeds of vengeance, by setting a labour-earning price on the heads of our enemies."

" I accord with the three first of these expedients, as the known and lawful resorts of Christian men," said Content ; " but the latter seemeth a measure that needeth to be entertained with great wariness of manner and with some distrust of purpose."

" Fear not, since all suiting and economical discretion is active in the minds of our rulers, who have pondered sagaciously on so grave a policy. It is not intended to offer more than half the reward that is held forth by our more wealthy and elder sister of the Bay, and there is some acute question about the necessity of bidding at all for any of tender years. And now, Captain Heathcote, with the good leave of so respectable a subject, I will proceed to lay before you the details of the number, and the nature of the force, that it is hoped you will lead in person in the ensuing campaign."

As the result of that which followed will be seen in the course of the legend, it is not necessary to accompany the messenger any further in his communication. We shall therefore leave him and Content busied with the matter of their conference, and proceed to give some account of the other personages connected with our subject.

When interrupted, as already related, by the arrival of the stranger, Faith endeavoured, by a new expedient, to elicit some evidences of a more just remembrance from the dull mind of her brother. Accompanied by most of the dependents of the family, she led him to the summit of that hill which was now crowned with the foliage of a young and thrifty orchard, and placing him at the foot of the ruin, she tried to excite a train of recollections that should lead to deeper impressions, and, possibly, by their aid, to a discovery of the important circumstance that all so much longed to have explained.

The experiment produced no happy result. The place, and indeed the whole valley, had undergone so great a change, that one more liberally gifted might have hesitated to believe them the spots described in our earlier pages. This rapid alteration of objects, which elsewhere know so

little change in a long course of ages, is a fact familiar to
all who reside in the newer districts of the Union. It is
caused by the rapid improvements that are made in the
first stages of a settlement. To fell the forest alone, is to
give an entirely new aspect to the view, and it is far from
easy to see in a village and in cultivated fields, however
recent the existence of the one or imperfect the other, any
traces of a spot that a short time before was known as the
haunt of the wolf, or the refuge of the deer.

The features, and, more particularly, the eye of his sister, had, however, stirred long dormant recollections in the
mind of Whittal Ring ; and though these glimpses of the
past were detached and indistinct, they had sufficed to
quicken the ancient confidence which was partially exhibited
in their opening conference. But it exceeded his feeble
powers to recal objects that would appeal to no very lively
sympathies, and which had themselves undergone so material alterations. Still the witless youth did not look on
the ruin entirely without some stirrings of his nature. Although the sward, around its base, was lively in the brightest verdure of early summer, and the delicious odour of
the wild clover saluted his senses, still there was that in
the blackened and ragged walls, the position of the tower,
and the view of the surrounding hills, shorn as so much of
them now were of the forest, that spoke to his earliest
impressions. He looked at the spot, as a hound gazes at
a master who has been so long lost as even to deaden his
instinct ; and, at times, as his companions endeavoured to
aid his faint images, it would seem as if memory were
likely to triumph, and all those deceptive opinions, which
habit and Indian wiles had drawn over his mind, were
about to vanish before the light of reality. But the al-
lurements of a life in which there was so much of the
freedom of nature, mingled with the fascinating pleasures
of the chase and of the woods, were not to be dispossessed
so readily. When Faith artfully led him back to those
animal enjoyments of which he had been so fond in boyhood, the fantasy of her brother seemed most to waver ;
but whenever it became apparent that the dignity of a
warrior, and all the more recent and far more alluring de-

lights of his later life were to be abandoned, ere his being could return into its former existence, his faculties obstinately refused to lend themselves to a change that, in his case, would have been little short of that attributed to the transmigration of souls.

After an hour of anxious, and frequently, on the part of Faith, of angry efforts to extract some evidences of his recollection of the condition of life to which he had once belonged, the attempt, for the moment, was abandoned. At times it seemed as if the woman were about to prevail. He often called himself Whittal; but he continued to insist that he was also Nipset, a man of the Narragansetts, who had a mother in his wigwam, and who had reason to believe that he should be numbered among the warriors of his tribe ere the fall of another snow.

In the mean time, a very different scene was passing at the place where the first examination had been held, and which had been immediately deserted by most of the spectators, on the sudden arrival of the messenger. But a solitary individual was seated at the spacious board, which had been provided alike for those who owned and presided over the estate, and for their dependents down to the very meanest. The individual who remained had thrown himself into a seat, less with the air of him who consults the demands of appetite, than of one whose thoughts were so occupied as to render him indifferent to the situation or employment of his more corporal part. His head rested on his arms, the latter effectually concealing the face, as they were spread over the plain but exquisitely neat table of cherry wood, which, by being placed at the side of one of less costly material, was intended to form the only distinction between the guests, as, in more ancient times, and in other countries, the salt was known to mark the difference in rank among those who partook of the same feast.

" Mark," said a timid voice at his elbow, " thou art weary with this night-watching, and with the scouting on the hills. Dost not think of taking food before seeking thy rest?"

" I sleep not," returned the youth, raising his head, and gently pushing aside the basin of simple food that was offered by one whose eye looked feelingly on his flushed features, and whose suffused cheek perhaps betrayed there was a secret consciousness that the glance was kinder than maiden diffidence should allow — " I sleep not, Martha, nor doth it seem to me that I shall ever sleep again."

" Thou frightest me by thy wild and unhappy eye. Hast suffered aught in the march on the mountains ?"

" Dost think one of my years and strength unable to bear the weariness of a few hours' watching in the forest ? The body is well, but the mind endureth grievously."

" And wilt thou not say what causeth this vexation ? Thou knowest, Mark, that there are none in this dwelling, — nay, I am certain I might add in this valley, that do not wish thee happiness."

" 'T is kind to say it, good Martha — but thou never hadst a sister !"

" 'T is true I am the only one of my race ; and yet to me it seemeth that no tie of blood could have been nearer than the love I bore to her we have lost."

" Nor mother ! thou never knewest what 'tis to reverence a parent."

" And is not thy mother mine ? " answered a voice that was deeply melancholy, and yet so soft that it caused the young man to gaze intently at his companion, for a moment, ere he again spoke.

" True, true," he said, hurriedly. " Thou must and dost love her who hath nursed thy infancy, and brought thee, with care and tenderness, to so fair and happy a womanhood." The eye of Martha grew brighter, and the colour of her healthful cheek deepened as Mark unconsciously uttered this commendation of her appearance ; but as she shrunk, with female sensitiveness, from his observation, the change was unnoticed, and he continued. " Thou seest that my mother is drooping hourly under this sorrow for our little Ruth ; who can say what may be the end of a grief that endureth so long !"

" 'T is true that there hath been reason to fear much in her behalf, but of late hope hath gotten the better of apprehension. Thou dost not well — nay, I am not assured thou dost not evil — to permit this discontent with Providence, because thy mother yieldeth to a little more than her usual mourning, on account of the unexpected return of one so nearly connected with her that we have lost."

" 'T is not that, girl — 't is not that ! "

" If thou refuseth to say what 'tis that giveth thee this pain, I can do little more than pity."

" Listen, and I will say. It is now many years, as thou knowest, since the savage Mohawk, or Narragansett Pequot, or Wompanoag, broke in upon our settlement and did his vengeance. We were then children, Martha, and 't is as a child that I have thought of that merciless burn_ing. Our little Ruth was, like thyself, a blooming infant of some seven or eight years ; and I know not how the folly hath beset me, but it hath been ever as one of that inno_cence and age that I have continued to think of my sister."

" Surely thou knowest that time cannot stay ; the greater, therefore, is the reason that we should be indus_trious to improve ——"

" 'T is what our duty teacheth. I tell thee, Martha, that at night, when dreams come over me, as they sometimes will, and I see our Ruth wandering in the forest, it is as a playful, laughing child, such as we knew her ; and, even while waking, do I fancy my sister at my knee, as she was wont to stand, when listening to those idle tales with which we lightened our childhood."

" But we had our birth in the same year and month — dost think of me too, Mark, as of one of that childish age ? "

" Of thee ! — that cannot well be. Do I not see that thou art grown into the condition of a woman — that thy little tresses of brown have become the jet black and flow_ing hair that becomes thy years, and that thou hast the stature, and, I say it not in idleness of speech, Martha, for thou knowest my tongue is no flatterer, but do I not see that thou hast grown into all the excellence of a most comely maiden ? but 't is not thus, or rather 't was not thus, with her we mourn ; for till this hour have I ever pic_tured my sister the little innocent we sported with that gloomy night she was snatched from our arms by the cruelty of the savage."

" And what hath changed this pleasing image of our Ruth?" asked his companion, half covering her face to conceal the still deeper glow of female gratification, which had been kindled by the words just heard. " I often think of her as thou hast described ; nor do I now see why we may not still believe her, if she yet live, all that we could desire to see."

" That cannot be — the delusion is gone, and in its place a frightful truth has visited me. Here is Whittal Ring, whom we lost a boy ; thou seest he is returned a man, and a savage ! No, no ; my sister is no longer the child I loved to think her, but one grown into the estate of womanhood."

" Thou thinkest of her unkindly, while thou thinkest of others far less endowed by nature with too much indulgence, for thou rememberest, Mark, she was ever of more pleasing aspect than any that we knew."

" I know not that — I say not that — I think not that. But be she what hardships and exposure may have made her, still must Ruth Heathcote be far too good for an Indian wigwam. Oh! 'tis horrible to believe that she is the bond-woman, the servitor, the wife of a savage !"

Martha recoiled, and an entire minute passed, during which she made no reply. It was evident that the revolting idea for the first time crossed her mind, and all the natural feelings of gratified and maiden pride vanished before the genuine and pure sympathies of a female bosom.

" This cannot be," she at length murmured — " it never can be! Our Ruth must still remember the lessons taught her in infancy. She knoweth she is born of Christian lineage, of reputable name, of exalted hope, of glorious promise !"

" Thou seest by the manner of Whittal, who is of greater age, how little of that taught can withstand the wily savage."

" But Whittal faileth of Nature's gifts ; he hath ever been below the rest of men in understanding."

" And yet to what degree of Indian cunning hath he already attained !"

" But, Mark," rejoined his companion, timidly, as if,

while she felt all its force, she only consented to urge the
argument, in tenderness to the harassed feelings of the
brother, "we are of equal years ; that which hath happened to me, may well have been the fortune of our
Ruth."

" Dost mean that, being unespoused thyself, or that
having at thy years inclinations that are free, my sister
may have escaped the bitter curse of being the wife of a
Narragansett; or, what is not less frightful, the slave of
his humours ? "

" Truly I mean little else than the former."

" And not the latter," continued the young man, with a
quickness that showed some sudden revolution in his
thoughts. " But though, with opinions that are decided,
and with kindness awakened in behalf of one favoured,
thou hesitatest, Martha, it is not like that a girl left in the
fetters of savage life would so long pause to think. Even
here, in the settlements, all are not difficult of judgment as
thou ! "

The long lashes vibrated above the dark eyes of the
maiden, and, for an instant, it seemed as if she had no
intention to reply ; but looking timidly aside, she answered
in a voice so low that her companion scarcely gathered the
meaning of what she uttered, --

" I know not how I may have earned this false character among my friends," she said ; " for to me it ever
seemeth that what I feel and think is but too easily known."

" Then is the smart gallant from the Hartford town,
who cometh and goeth so often between this distant settlement and his father's house, better assured of his success
than I had thought. He will not journey the long road
much oftener alone ! "

" I have angered thee, Mark, or thou wouldst not speak
with so cold an eye to one who hath ever lived with thee
in kindness."

" I do not speak in anger, for 'twould be both unreasonable and unmanly to deny all of thy sex right of
choice ; but yet it doth seem right that, when taste is suited
and judgment appeased, there should be little motive for
withholding speech."

" And wouldst thou have a maiden of my years in haste to believe that she was sought, when haply it may be, that he of whom you speak is in quest of thy society and friendship, rather than of my favour."

" Then might he spare much labour and some bodily suffering, unless he finds great pleasure in the saddle, for I know not a youth in the Connecticut colony for whom I have smaller esteem. Others may see matter of approval in him, but to me he is of bold speech, ungainly air, and great disagreeableness of discourse."

" I am happy that at last we find ourselves of one mind, for that thou sayst of the youth, is much as I have long considered him."

" Thou ! thou thinkest of the gallant thus ! Then why dost listen to his suit ? I had believed thee a girl too honest, Martha, to affect such niceties of deception. With this opinion of his character, why not refuse his company ? "

" Can a maiden speak too hastily ? "

" And if here, and ready to ask thy favour, the answer would be —— "

" No ! " said the girl, raising her eyes for an instant, and bashfully meeting the eager look of her companion, though she uttered the monosyllable firmly.

Mark seemed bewildered. An entirely new and a novel idea took possession of his brain. The change was apparent by his altering countenance and a cheek that glowed like flame. What he might have said most of our readers over fifteen may presume ; but at that moment, the voices of those who had accompanied Whittal to the ruin were heard on their return, and Martha glided away so silently as to leave him for a moment ignorant of her absence.

END OF THE SECOND VOLUME.

VOLUME THE THIRD.

CHAPTER I.

Oh ! — when amid the throngs of men
The heart grows sick of hollow mirth,
How willingly we turn us then
Away from this cold earth ;
And look into thy azure breast,
For seats of innocence and rest.　　BRYANT's *Skies.*

THE day was the Sabbath.　This religious festival, which
is even now observed in most of the States of the
Union with a strictness that is little heeded in the rest of
Christendom, was then reverenced with a severity suited
to the austere habits of the colonists.　The circumstance
that one should journey on such a day had attracted the
observation of all in the hamlet ; but, as the stranger had
been seen to ride towards the dwelling of the Heathcotes,
and the times were known to teem with more than ordinary
interests to the Province, it was believed that he found his
justification in some apology of necessity.　Still none ventured forth to enquire into the motives of this extraordinary
visit.　At the end of an hour, the horseman was seen to
depart as he had arrived, seemingly urged on by the calls
of some pressing emergency.　He had in truth proceeded
further with his tidings, though the lawfulness of dis_
charging even this imperious duty on the Sabbath, had
been gravely considered in the councils of those who had
sent him.　Happily they had found, or thought they had
found, in some of the narratives of the sacred volume, a
sufficient precedent to bid their messenger proceed.

In the mean time, the unusual excitement which had

been so unexpectedly awakened in the dwelling of the
Heathcotes, began to subside in that quiet, which is in so
beautiful accordance with the sacred character of the day.
The sun rose bright and cloudless above the hills, every
vapour of the past night melting before his genial warmth
into the invisible element. The valley then lay in that
species of holy calm, which conveys so sweet and so forci-
ble an appeal to the heart. The world presented a picture
of the glorious handy-work of Him, who seems to invite
the gratitude and adoration of his creatures. To the mind
untainted, there is exquisite loveliness and God-like repose
in such a scene. The universal stillness permits the
softest natural sounds to be heard, and the buzz of the
bee, or the wing of the humming-bird reaches the ear,
like the notes of a sweet anthem. This temporary repose
is full of meaning. It should teach how much of the
beauty of this world's enjoyments, how much of its peace,
and even how much of the comeliness of nature itself, is
dependent on the spirit by which we are actuated. When
man reposes, all around him seems anxious to contribute to
his rest, and when he abandons the contentions of grosser
interests, to elevate his spirit, all living things appear to
unite in worship. Although this apparent sympathy of
nature may be less true than imaginative, its lesson is not
destroyed, since it sufficiently shows that what man chooses
to consider good in this world is good, and that most of its
strife and deformities proceed from his own perversity.

The tenants of the valley of the Wish-Ton-Wish were
little wont to disturb the quiet of the Sabbath. Their
error lay in the other extreme, since they impaired the
charities of life by endeavouring to raise man altogether
above the weakness of his nature. They substituted the
revolting aspect of a sublimated austerity, for that gracious
though regulated exterior, by which all in the body may
best illustrate their hopes or exhibit their gratitude. The
peculiar air of those of whom we write was generated by
the error of the times and of the country, though something of its singularly rigid character might possibly have
been derived from the precepts and example of the individual who had the direction of the spiritual interests of

the parish. As this person will have further connection with the matter of the legend, he shall be more familiarly introduced in its pages.

The Rev. Meek Wolfe was, in spirit, a rare combination of the humblest self-abasement with fierce spiritual denunciation. Like so many others of his sacred calling in the colony he inhabited, he was not only the descendant of a line of priests, but it was his greatest earthly hope that he should also become the progenitor of a race, in whom the ministry was to be perpetuated as severely as if the regulated formula of the Mosaic dispensation were still in existence. He had been educated in the infant college of Harvard, an institution that the emigrants from England had the wisdom and enterprise to found, within the first five-and-twenty years of their colonial residence. Here this scion of so pious and orthodox a stock had abundantly qualified himself for the intellectual warfare of his future life, by regarding one set of opinions so steadily as to leave little reason to apprehend he would ever abandon the most trifling of the outworks of his faith. No citadel ever presented a more hopeless curtain to the besieger, than did the mind of this zealot to the efforts of conviction ; for on the side of his opponents, he contrived that every avenue should be closed by a wall blank as indomitable obstinacy could oppose. He appeared to think that all the minor conditions of argument and reason had been disposed of by his ancestors, and that it only remained for him to strengthen the many defences of his subject, and, now and then, to scatter by a fierce sortie the doctrinal skirmishers who might occasionally approach his parish. There was a remarkable singleness of mind in this religionist, which, while it in some measure rendered even his bigotry respectable, greatly aided in clearing the knotty subject with which he dealt of much embarrassing matter. In his eyes, the strait and narrow path would hold but few besides his own flock. He admitted some fortuitous exceptions, in one or two of the nearest parishes, with whose clergymen he was in the habit of exchanging pulpits, and perhaps, here and there, in a saint of the other hemisphere, or of the more distant towns of the colonies, the brightness of whose faith was something aided, in his eyes, by distance, as this opaque globe of ours is thought to appear a ball of light to those who inhabit its satellite. In short, there was an admixture of seeming charity with an exclusiveness of hope, an unweariness of exertion with a coolness of exterior, a disregard of self with the most complacent security, and an uncomplaining submission to temporal evils with the loftiest spiritual pretensions, that in some measure rendered him a man as difficult to comprehend as to describe.

At an early hour in the forenoon, a little bell that was suspended in an awkward belfry perched on the roof of the meeting-house, began to summon the congregation to the place of worship. The call was promptly obeyed, and ere the first notes had reached the echoes of the hills, the wide and grassy street was covered with family groups, all taking the same direction. Foremost in each little party walked the austere father, perhaps bearing on his arm a suckled infant, or some child yet too young to sustain its own weight: while at a decent distance followed the equally grave matron, casting oblique and severe glances at the little troop around her, in whom acquired habits had yet some conquests to obtain over the lighter impulses of vanity. Where there was no child to need support, or where the mother chose to assume the office of bearing her infant in person, the man was seen to carry one of the heavy muskets of the day; and when his arms were otherwise employed, the stoutest of his boys served in the capacity of armour-bearer. But in no instance was this needful precaution neglected, the state of the Province and the character of the enemy requiring that vigilance should mingle even with their devotions. There was no loitering on the path, no light and worldly discourse by the way, nor even any salutations, other than those grave and serious recognitions by hat and eye which usage tolerated as the utmost limit of courtesy on the weekly festival.

When the bell changed its tone, Meek appeared from the gate of the fortified house, where he resided in quality of castellain, on account of its public character, its additional security, and the circumstance that his studious

habits permitted him to discharge the trust with less waste
of manual labour than it would cost the village, were the
responsible office confided to one of more active habits.
His consort followed, but at even a greater distance than
that taken by the wives of other men, as if she felt the
awful necessity of averting even the remotest possibility of
scandal from one of a profession so sacred. Nine offspring
of various ages, and one female assistant of years too tender
to be a wife herself, composed the household of the divine;
and it was a proof of the salubrious air of the valley that
all were present, since nothing but illness was ever deemed a
sufficient excuse for absence from the common worship. As
this little flock issued from the palisadoes, a female, in whose
pale cheek the effects of recent illness might yet be traced,
held open the gate for the entrance of Reuben Ring and a
stout youth, who bore the prolific consort of the former
with her bounteous gift into the citadel of the village; a
place of refuge that nothing but the undaunted resolution
of the woman prevented her from occupying before, since
more than half of the children of the valley had first seen
the light within the security of its defences.

The family of Meek preceded him into the temple, and
when the feet of the minister himself crossed its threshold,
there was no human form visible without its walls. The
bell ceased its monotonous and mournful note, and the tall
gaunt form of the divine moved through the narrow aisle
to its usual post, with the air of one who had already more
than half rejected the burthen of bodily incumbrance. A
searching and stern glance was thrown around, as if he
possessed an instinctive power to detect all delinquents,
and then seating himself, the deep stillness that always
preceded the exercises reigned in the place.

When the divine next showed his austere countenance
to his expecting people, its meaning was expressive rather
of some matter of worldly import, than of that absence of
carnal interest, with which he usually strove to draw near
to his Creator in prayer.

" Captain Content Heathcote," he said with grave
severity, after permitting a short pause to awaken reverence,
" there has one ridden through this valley, on the Lord's

day, making thy habitation his halting place. Hath the traveller warranty for this disrespect of the Sabbath, and canst thou find sufficient reason in his motive, for permitting the stranger within thy gates to neglect the solemn ordinance delivered on the mount ? "

" He rideth on especial commission," answered Content, who had respectfully arisen when thus addressed by name ; " matter of grave interest to the well-being of the Colony is contained in the subject of his errand."

" There is nought more deeply connected with the well-being of man, whether resident in this colony or in more lofty empires, than reverence to God's declared will," returned Meek, but half appeased by the apology. " It would have been expedient for one, who in common not only setteth so good an example himself, but who is also charged with the mantle of authority, to have looked with distrust into the pretences of a necessity that may be only seeming."

" The motive shall be declared to the people, at a fitting moment ; but it hath seemed more wise to retain the substance of the horseman's errand until worship hath been offered without the alloy of temporal concerns."

" Therein hast thou acted discreetly ; for a divided mind giveth but little joy above. I hope there is equal reason why all of thy household are not with thee in the temple ? "

Notwithstanding the usual self-command of Content, he did not revert to this subject without emotion. Casting a subdued glance at the empty seat, where she whom he so much loved was wont to worship at his side, he said in a voice that struggled to maintain its equanimity —

" There has been powerful interest awakened beneath my roof this day ; and it may be that the duty of the Sabbath has been overlooked by minds so exercised. If we have therein sinned, I hope He that looketh kindly on the penitent will forgive ! She of whom thou speakest hath been shaken by the violence of griefs renewed ; though willing in spirit, a feeble and sinking frame is not equal to support the fatigue of appearing here, even though it be the house of God."

This extraordinary exercise of pastoral authority was

uninterrupted even by the breathings of the congregation. Any incident of an unusual character had attraction for the inhabitants of a village so remote ; but here was deep domestic interest, connected with breach of usage and indeed of law, and all heightened by that secret influence that leads us to listen, with singular satisfaction, to those emotions in others, which it is believed to be natural to wish to conceal. Not a syllable that fell from the lips of the divine, or of Content, not a deep tone of severity in the former, nor a struggling accent of the latter, escaped the dullest ear in that assembly. Notwithstanding the grave and regulated air that was common to all, it is needless to say there was pleasure in this little interruption, which, however, was far from being extraordinary in a community, where it was not only believed that spiritual authority might extend itself to the most familiar practices, but where few domestic interests were deemed so exclusive, or individual feelings considered so sacred, that a very large proportion of the whole neighbourhood might not claim a right to participate largely in both. The Rev. Mr. Wolfe was appeased by the explanation, and after allowing a sufficient time to elapse, in order that the minds of the congregation should recover the proper tone, he proceeded with the regular services of the morning.

It is needless to recount the well known manner of the religious exercises of the Puritans. Enough of their forms and of their substance has been transmitted to us, to render both manner and doctrine familiar to most of our readers. We shall therefore confine our duty to a relation of such portions of the ceremonies, if that which sedulously avoided every appearance of form can thus be termed, as have an immediate connection with the incidents.

The divine had gone through the short opening prayer, had read the passage of holy writ, had given out the verses of the psalm, and had joined in the strange nasal melody with which his flock endeavoured to render it doubly acceptable, and had ended a long and fervent wrestling of the spirit in a colloquial petition of some forty minutes' duration, in which direct allusion had been made not only to the subject of his recent examination, but to divers

other familiar interests of his parishioners, and all without
any departure from the usual zeal, on his own part, or of
the customary attention and a grave decorum, on that of
his people. But when, for the second time, he arose to
read another song of worship and thanksgiving, a form
was seen in the centre or principal aisle, that, as well
by its attire and aspect as by the unusual and irreverent
tardiness of its appearance, attracted general observation.
Interruptions of this nature were unfrequent, and even
the long practised and abstracted minister paused for an
instant ere he proceeded with the hymn, though there
was a suspicion current among the more instructed of his
parishioners that the sonorous version was an effusion of
his own muse.

The intruder was Whittal Ring. The witless young
man had strayed from the abode of his sister, and found
his way into that general receptacle where most of the
village was congregated. During his former residence in
the valley there had been no temple, and the edifice, its
interior arrangements, the faces of those it contained, and
the business on which they had assembled, appeared alike
strangers to him. It was only when the people lifted up
their voices in the song of praise, that some glimmerings
of his ancient recollections were discoverable in his inactive
countenance. Then, indeed, he betrayed a portion of the
delight which powerful sounds can quicken even in beings
of his unhappy mental construction. As he was satisfied,
however, to remain in a retired part of the aisle, listening
with dull admiration, even the grave Ensign Dudley, whose
eye had once or twice seemed ominous of displeasure, saw
no necessity for interference.

Meek had chosen for his text, on that day, a passage
from the book of Judges: " And the children of Israel did
evil in the sight of the Lord; and the Lord delivered
them into the hands of Midian seven years." With this
text the subtle-minded divine dealt powerfully, entering
largely into the mysterious and allegorical allusions then
so much in vogue. In whatever manner he viewed the
subject, he found reason to liken the suffering, bereaved,
and yet chosen dwellers of the colonies, to the race of the

Hebrews. If they were not set apart and marked from all others of the earth, in order that one mightier than man should spring from their loins, they were led into that distant wilderness, far from the temptations of licentious luxury, or the worldly-mindedness of those who built their structure of faith on the sands of temporal honours, to preserve the word in purity. As there appeared no reason on the part of the divine himself to distrust this construction of the words he had quoted, so it was evident that most of his listeners willingly lent their ears to so soothing an argument.

In reference to Midian, the preacher was far less explicit. That the great father of evil was in some way intended by this allusion could not be doubted; but in what manner the chosen inhabitants of those regions were to feel his malign influence, was matter of more uncertainty. At times, the greedy ears of those who had long been wrought up into the impression that visible manifestations of the anger, or of the love of Providence, were daily presented to their eyes, were flattered with the stern joy of believing that the war which then raged around them was intended to put their moral armour to the proof, and that out of the triumph of their victories were to flow honour and security to the church. Then came ambiguous qualifications, which left it questionable whether a return of the invisible powers that had been known to be so busy in the provinces, were not the judgment intended. It is not to be supposed that Meek himself had the clearest mental intelligence on a point of this subtlety, for there was something of misty hallucination in the manner in which he treated it, as will be seen by his closing words.

" To imagine that Azazel regardeth the long-suffering and stedfastness of a chosen people with a pleasant eye," he said, " is to believe that the marrow of righteousness can exist in the carrion of deceit. We have already seen his envious spirit raging in many tragical instances. If required to raise a warning beacon to your eyes, by which the presence of this treacherous enemy might be known, I should say, in the words of one learned and ingenious in this craftiness, that ' when a person, having full reason,

doth knowingly and wittingly seek and obtain of the devil,
or any other god besides the true God Jehovah, an ability
to do or know strange things, which he cannot, by his own
human abilities, arrive unto,' that then he may distrust his
gifts and tremble for his soul. And, oh! my brethren,
how many of ye cling, at this very moment, to those tra_
gical delusions, and worship the things of the world,
instead of fattening on the famine of the desert, which is
the sustenance of them that would live for ever. Lift
your eyes upward, my brethren ————"

" Rather turn them to the earth !" interrupted a voice
from the body of the church ; " there is present need of
all your faculties to save life, and even to guard the tabernacle of the Lord !"

Religious exercises composed the recreation of the
dwellers in that distant settlement. When they met in
companies to lighten the load of life, prayer and songs of
praise were among the usual indulgences of the entertain_
ment. To them, a sermon was like a gay scenic exhibition
in other and vainer communities ; and none listened to the
word with cold and inattentive ears. In literal obedience
to the command of the preacher, and sympathising with
his own action, every eye in the congregation had been
turned towards the naked rafters of the roof, when the un_
known tones of him who spoke broke the momentary delusion.
It is needless to say that, by a common movement, they
sought an explanation of this extraordinary appeal. The
divine became mute, equally with wonder and with indig-
nation.

A first glance was enough to assure all present that new
and important interests were likely to be awakened. A
stranger of grave aspect, and of a calm but understanding
eye, stood at the side of Whittal Ring. His attire was of
the simple guise and homely materials of the country.
Still he bore about his person enough of the equipments of
one familiar with the wars of the eastern hemisphere to
strike the senses. His hand was armed with a shining
broadsword, such as were then used by the cavaliers of
England ; and at his back was slung the short carabine of
one who battled in the saddle. His mien was dignified,

and even commanding; and there was no second look necessary to show that he was an intruder of a character altogether different from the moping innocent at his side.

"Why is one of an unknown countenance come to disturb the worship of the temple?" demanded Meek, when astonishment permitted utterance. "Thrice hath this holy day been profaned by the foot of the stranger, and well may it be doubted whether we live not under an evil agency."

"Arm, men of the Wish-Ton-Wish, arm, and to your defences!—"

A cry arose without that seemed to circle the whole valley, and then a thousand whoops rolled out of the arches of the forest, and appeared to meet in one hostile din above the devoted hamlet. These were sounds that had been too often heard, or too often described, not to be generally understood. A scene of wild confusion followed.

Each man, on entering the church, had deposited his arms at the door, and thither most of the stout borderers were now seen hastening to resume their weapons. Women gathered their children to their sides, and the wails of horror and alarm were beginning to break through the restraints of habit.

"Peace!" exclaimed the pastor, seemingly excited to a degree above human emotion. "Ere we go forth, let there be a voice raised to our heavenly Father. The asking shall be as a thousand men of war battling in our behalf!"

The commotion ceased as suddenly as if a mandate had been issued from that place to which their petition was to be addressed. Even the stranger, who had regarded the preparations with a stern but anxious eye, bowed his head and seemed to join in the prayer with a devout and confiding heart.

"Lord!" said Meek, stretching his meagre arms, with the palms of the hands open, high above the heads of his flock, "at thy bidding we go forth; with thy aid the gates of hell shall not prevail against us; with thy mercy, there is hope in heaven and on earth. It is for thy tabernacle that we shed blood; it is for the word that we contend. Battle in our behalf, King of kings! send thy heavenly legions to our succour, that the song of victory may be incense at thy altars, and a foul hearing to the ears of the enemy.—Amen."

There was a depth in the voice of the speaker — a supernatural calmness in the tones — and so great a confidence in the support of the mighty ally implored, that the words went to the heart. It was impossible that nature should not be powerful within, but a high and exciting enthusiasm began to lift the people above its influence. Thus awakened, by an appeal to feelings that had never 'slumbered, and stimulated by all the moving interests of life, the men of the valley poured out of the temple in defence of person and fireside, and, as they believed, of religion and of God.

There was pressing necessity not only for this zeal, but for all the physical energies of the stoutest of their numbers. The spectacle that met the view, on issuing into the open air, was one that might have appalled the hearts of warriors more practised, and have paralysed the efforts of men less susceptible to the impressions of a religious excitement.

Dark forms were leaping through the fields and on the hill sides; and all adown the slopes that conducted to the valley armed savages were seen pouring madly forward on their path of destruction and vengeance. Behind them the brand and the knife had been already used; for the log tenement, the stacks, and the out-buildings of Reuben Ring, and of several others who dwelt in the skirts of the settlement, were sending forth clouds of murky smoke, in which forked and angry flames were already flashing. But danger pressed most still nearer. A long line of fierce warriors was in the meadows; and in no direction could the eye be turned that it did not meet with the appalling proof that the village was completely surrounded by an overwhelming superiority of force.

" To the garrison!" shouted some of the foremost of those who first saw the nature and the imminency of the danger, pressing forward themselves in the direction of the fortified house. " To the garrison, or we are lost !"

" Hold !" exclaimed that voice which was so strange to the ears of most of those who heard it, but which spoke in

T

a manner that, by its compass and firmness, commanded
obedience. "With this mad disorder we are truly lost!
Let Captain Content Heathcote come to my counsels."

Notwithstanding the tumult and confusion, which had
now in truth begun to rage fearfully around him, the
quiet and self-restrained individual to whom the legal and
perhaps moral right to command belonged, had lost none
of his customary composure. It was plain, by the look of
powerful amazement with which he had at first regarded
the stranger, on his sudden interruption of the service,
and by the glances of secret intelligence and of recognition
they exchanged, that they had met before. But this was
no time for greetings or explanations, nor was that a scene
in which to waste the precious moments in useless contests
about opinions.

"I am here," said he who was called, "ready to lead
whither thy prudence and better experience shall point."

"Speak to the people, and separate the combatants in
three bodies of equal strength. One shall press forward
to the meadows and beat back the savage, ere he encircle
the palisadoed house; the second shall proceed with the
feeble and tender, in their flight to its covers; and with
the third — but thou knowest that which I would do with
the third. Hasten, or we lose all by tardiness."

It was perhaps fortunate that orders so necessary and
so urgent, were given to one little accustomed to superfluity of speech. Without offering either commendation
or dissent, Content obeyed. Accustomed to his authority,
and conscious of the critical situation of all that was dear,
the men of the village yielded an obedience more prompt
and effective, than it is usual to meet in soldiers who are
not familiar with the habits of discipline. The fighting
men were quickly separated in three bodies that contained
rather more than a score of combatants each. One, commanded by Eben Dudley, advanced at quick time towards
the meadows in the rear of the fortress, that the whooping
body of savages, who were already threatening to cut off
the retreat of the women and children, should be checked;
while another departed in a nearly opposite direction,
taking the street of the hamlet, for the purpose of meeting

those who were advancing by the southern entrance of the valley. The third and last of these small but devoted bodies remained stationary, waiting for more definite orders.

At the moment when the first of these little divisions of force was ready to move, the divine appeared in its front, with an air in which spiritual reliance on the purposes of Providence and some show of temporal determination, were singularly united. In one hand he bore a Bible, which he raised on high as the sacred standard of his followers, and in the other he brandished a short broadsword in a way to prove there might be danger in encountering its blade. The volume was open, and at brief intervals the divine read, in a high and excited voice, such passages as accidentally met his eye, the leaves blowing about in a manner to produce a rather remarkable admixture of doctrine and sentiment. But to these trifling moral incongruities both the pastor and his parishioners were alike indifferent; their subtle mental exercises having given birth to the habit of aptly reconciling all seeming discrepancies, as well as of accommodating the most abstruse doctrines to the more familiar interests of life.

" Israel and the Philistines had put their battle in array, army against army," commenced Meek, as the troop he led began its advance.—Then reading at short intervals, he continued,—" Behold, I will do a thing in Israel, at which both the ears of every one that heareth it shall tingle." — " Oh, house of Aaron, trust in the Lord ; he is thy help and thy shield."—" Deliver me, O Lord, from the evil man ; preserve me from the violent man." — " Let burning coals fall upon them ; let them be cast into the fire ; into deep pits, that they rise not again." — " Let the wicked fall into their own nets, whilst that I withal escape." — " Therefore doth my Father love me, because I lay down my life, that I may take it again." — " He that hateth me, hateth my Father also." — " Father, forgive them, for they know not what they do." — " They have heard that it hath been said, An eye for an eye, and a tooth for a tooth." — " For Joshua drew not his hand back wherewith he stretched out the spear, until he had utterly destroyed all the inhabitants of Ai ——" Thus far the words of Meek were intelligible to those who remained, but distance soon confounded the syllables. Then nought was audible but the yells of the enemy, the tramp of the men who pressed in the rear of the priest, with a display of military pomp as formidable as their limited means would allow, and those clear high tones which sounded in the ears and quickened the blood at the hearts of his followers, as if they had been trumpet-blasts. In a few more minutes, the little band was scattered behind the covers of the fields, and the rattling of fire-arms succeeded to the quaint and characteristic manner of their march.

While this movement was made in front, the party ordered to cover the village was not idle. Commanded by a sturdy yeoman, who filled the office of Lieutenant, it advanced with less of religious display, but with equal activity, in the direction of the south, and the sounds of contention were quickly heard, proclaiming both the urgency of the measure and the warmth of the conflict.

In the mean time equal decision, though tempered by some circumstances of deep personal interest, was displayed by those who had been left in front of the church. As soon as the band of Meek had got to such a distance as to promise security to those who followed, the stranger commanded the children to be led towards the fortified house. This duty was performed by the trembling mothers, who had been persuaded, with difficulty, to defer it until cooler heads should pronounce that the proper moment had come. A few of the women dispersed among the dwellings in quest of the infirm, while all the boys of proper age were actively employed in transporting indispensable articles from the village to the cover of the palisadoes. As these several movements were simultaneous, but a very few minutes elapsed between the time when the orders were issued and the moment when they were accomplished.

" I had intended thou shouldst have had the charge in the meadows," said the stranger to Content, when nought remained to be performed but that which had been reserved for the last of the three little bands of fighting men. " But as the work proceedeth bravely in that quarter, we will move in company. Why doth this maiden tarry?"

" Truly I know not, unless it may be of fear. There is an opening for thy passage into the fort, Martha, with others of thy sex."

" I will follow the fighters, that are about to march to the rescue of them that remain in our habitation," said the girl, in a low but steady voice.

" And how know'st thou that such is the service intended for those here arrayed?" demanded the stranger, with a little show of displeasure that his military purposes should have been anticipated.

" I see it in the countenances of them that tarry," returned the other, gazing furtively towards Mark, who, posted in the little line, could with difficulty brook a delay which threatened his father's house, and those whom it held, with so much jeopardy.

" Forward!" cried the stranger. " Here is no leisure for dispute. Let the maiden take wisdom, and hasten to the fort. Follow, men stout of heart! or we come too late to the succour."

Martha waited until the party had advanced a few paces, and then, instead of obeying the repeated mandate to consult her personal safety, she took the direction of the armed band.

" I fear me that 't will exceed our strength," observed the stranger, who marched in front at the side of Content, " to make good the dwelling, at so great distance from further aid."

" And yet the visitation that shall drive us a second time to the fields will be heavy. In what manner didst thou get warning of this inroad?"

" The savages believed themselves concealed in the cunning place, where thou know'st that my eye had opportunity to overlook their artifices. There is a Providence in our least seeming calculations: an imprisonment of weary years hath its reward in this warning!"

Content appeared to acquiesce, but the situation of affairs prevented the discourse from becoming more minute.

As they approached the dwelling of the Heathcotes,

better opportunity of observing the condition of things, in
and around the house, was of course obtained.   The position of the building would have rendered any attempt, on
the part of those in it, to gain the fort ere the arrival of
assistance, desperately hazardous, since the meadows that
lay between them were already alive with the warriors of
the enemy.   But it was evident that the Puritan, whose
infirmities kept him within doors, entertained no such
design ; for it was shortly apparent that those within were
closing and barring the windows of the habitation, and
that other provisions for defence were in the course of
active preparation.   The feelings of Content, who knew
that the house contained only his wife and father, with one
female assistant, were excited to agony, as the party he
commanded drew near on one side, at a distance about
equal to that of a band of the enemy, who were advancing
diagonally from the woods on the other.   He saw the
efforts of those so dear to him, as they had recourse to the
means of security provided to repel the very danger which
now threatened, and, to his eyes, it appeared that the
trembling hands of Ruth had lost their power, when haste
and confusion more than once defeated the object of her
exertions.

   " We must break and charge, or the savage will be too
speedy," he said, in tones that grew thick from breathing
quicker than was wont for one of his calm temperament.
" See ! they enter the orchard : in another minute they
will be masters of the dwelling !"

   But his companion marched with a firmer step and
looked with a cooler eye.   There was in his gaze the understanding of a man practised in scenes of sudden danger,
and in his mien the authority of one accustomed to
command.

   " Fear not," he answered ; " the art of old Mark
Heathcote hath departed from him, or he still knoweth
how to make good his citadel against a first onset.   If we
quit our order, the superiority of concert will be lost, and,
being few in numbers, defeat will be certain ; but with
this front and a fitting steadiness, our march may not be
repulsed.   To thee, Captain Content Heathcote, it need

not be told that he who now counsels thee hath seen the strife of savages ere this hour."

" I know it well; but dost not see my Ruth labouring at the ill-fated shutter of the chamber ? The woman will be slain in her heedlessness; for, hark, there beginneth the volley of the enemy!"

" No, 'tis he who led my troop in a far different warfare!" exclaimed the stranger, whose form grew more erect, and whose thoughtful and deeply furrowed features assumed something like the stern pleasure which kindles in the soldier as the sounds of contention increase: " 'tis old Mark Heathcote, true to his breeding and his name! — he hath let off the culverin upon the knaves! Behold, they are already disposed to abandon one who speaketh so boldly, and are breaking through the fences to the left, that we may taste something of their quality! Now, bold Englishmen, strong of hand and stout of heart, you have training in your duty, and you shall not be wanting in example! You have wives and children at hand looking at your deeds; and there is One above that taketh note of the manner in which you serve in his cause! Here is an opening for your skill: scourge the cannibals with the hand of death!—On, on! to the onset and to victory!"

CHAPTER II.

Hect. — Is this Achilles ?
Achil. — I am Achilles.
Hect. — Stand fair, I pray thee : let me look on thee.
Troilus and Cressida.

It may now be necessary to take a rapid glance at the state of the combat, which had begun to thicken in different parts of the valley. The party led by Dudley, and exhorted by Meek, had broken its order on reaching the meadows behind the fort, and, seeking the covers of the stumps and fences, it threw in its fire with good effect on the irregular band that pressed into the fields. This promptitude caused a change in the manner of the advance. The Indians took to covers in their turn, and the struggle assumed that desultory but dangerous character, in which the steadiness and resources of the individual are put to the severest trial. Success appeared to vacillate; the white men at one time widening the distance between them and their friends in the dwelling, and at another falling back, as if disposed to seek the shelter of the palisadoes. Although numbers were greatly in favour of the Indians, weapons and skill supported the cause of their adversaries. It was evidently the wish of the former to break in upon the little band that opposed their progress to the village, in and about which they saw that scene of hurried exertion which has already been described — a spectacle but little likely to cool the ardour of an Indian onset : but the wary manner in which Dudley conducted his battle rendered this an experiment of exceeding hazard.

However heavy of intellect the Ensign might appear on other occasions, the present was one every way adapted to draw out his best and most manly qualities. Of large and powerful stature, he felt, in moments of strife, a degree of confidence in himself that was commensurate with the amount of physical force he wielded. To this hardy assurance was to be added no trifling portion of the sort of enthusiasm that can be awakened in the most sluggish bosoms, and which, like the anger of an even-tempered man, is only the more formidable from the usually quiet habits of the individual. Nor was this the first, by many, of Ensign Dudley's warlike deeds. Besides the desperate affair already related in these pages, he had been engaged in divers hostile expeditions against the Aborigines in early youth, and on all occasions he had shown a cool head and a resolute mind.

There was pressing necessity for both these essential qualities in the situation in which the Ensign now found himself. By properly extending his little force, and yet keeping it at the same time perfectly within supporting distance, by emulating the caution of his foes in using the covers, and by reserving a portion of his fire throughout the broken and yet well-ordered line, the savages were finally beaten back, from stump to stump, from hillock to hillock, and fence to fence, until they were fairly driven within the margin of the forest. Further, the experienced eye of the borderer saw he could not follow. Many of his men were bleeding and growing weaker as their wounds still flowed. The protection of the trees gave the enemy too great an advantage for their position to be forced, and destruction would have been the inevitable consequence of the close struggle which must have followed a charge. In this stage of the combat, Dudley began to cast anxious and enquiring looks behind him. He saw that support was not to be expected, and he also saw with regret that many of the women and children were still busy transporting necessaries from the village into the fort. Falling back to a better line of covers, and to a distance that materially lessened the danger of the arrows, the weapons used by quite two-thirds of his enemies, he awaited in sullen silence the proper moment to effect a further retreat.

While the party of Dudley stood thus at bay, a fierce yell rung in the arches of the forest. It was an exclamation of pleasure, uttered in the wild manner of those people, as if the tenants of the woods were animated by some sudden and general impulse of joy. The crouching yeomen regarded each other in uneasiness; but seeing no sign of wavering in the steady mien of their leader, each man kept close, awaiting some further exhibition of the devices of their foes. Ere another minute had passed, two warriors appeared at the margin of the wood, where they stood apparently in contemplation of the different scenes that were acting in various parts of the valley. More than one musket was levelled with intent to bring them down; but a sign from Dudley prevented attempts that would most probably have been frustrated by the never slumbering vigilance of a North American Indian.

There was something in the air and port of these two individuals, that had its share in producing the forbearance of Dudley. They were evidently both chiefs, and of far more than usual estimation. As was common with the military leaders of the Indians, they were also men of

large and commanding stature. Viewed at the distance
from which they were seen, one seemed a warrior who had
reached the meridian of his days, while the other had the
lighter step and more flexible movement of youth. Both
were well armed, and, as was usual with people of their origin
on the war-path, they were clad only in the usual scanty
covering of waist-cloths and leggings. The former, however, were of scarlet, and the latter were rich in fringes in
the bright colours of Indian ornaments. The elder of the
two wore a gay belt of wampum around his head in the
form of a turban ; but the younger appeared with a shaven
crown, on which nothing but the customary chivalrous
scalp-lock was visible.

The consultation, like most of the incidents that have
been just related, occupied but a very few minutes. The
eldest of the chiefs issued some orders. The mind of
Dudley was anxiously endeavouring to anticipate their
nature, when the two disappeared together. The Ensign
would now have been left entirely to vague conjectures,
had not the rapid execution of the mandates that had been
issued to the youngest of the Indians, soon left him in no
doubt of their intentions. Another loud and general shout
drew his attention towards the right, and when he had
endeavoured to strengthen his position, by calling three or
four of the best marksmen to that end of his little line,
the youngest of the chiefs was seen bounding across the
meadow, leading a train of whooping followers to the
covers that commanded its opposite extremity. The
position of Dudley was completely turned, and the stumps
and angles of the fences which secreted his men, were
likely to become of no further use. The emergency demanded decision. Collecting his yeomen, ere the enemy
had time to profit by his advantage, the Ensign ordered a
rapid retreat towards the fort. In this movement he was
favoured by the formation of the ground, a circumstance
that had been well considered on the advance, and in a
very few minutes the party found itself safely posted under
the protection of a scattering fire from the palisadoes,
which immediately checked the pursuit of the whooping
and exulting foe. The wounded men, after a stern or

rather sullen halt, that was intended to exhibit the unconquerable determination of the whites, withdrew into
the works for succour, leaving the command of Dudley
reduced by nearly one half of its numbers. With this
diminished force, however, he turned his attention towards
the assistance of those who combated at the opposite extremity of the village.

Allusion has already been made to the manner in which
the houses of a new settlement were clustered near each
other, at the commencement of the colonial establishments.
In addition to the more obvious and sufficient motive,
which has given rise to the same inconvenient and un-
picturesque manner of building over nine tenths of the
continent of Europe, there had been found a religious
inducement for the inconvenient custom. One of the
enactments of the Puritans said, that, " No man shall set
his dwelling house above the distance of half a mile, or a
mile at farthest, from the meeting of the congregation,
where the church doth usually assemble for the worship of
God."—" The support of the worship of God, in church
fellowship," was the reason alleged for this arbitrary provision of the law, but it is quite probable that support
against danger of a more temporal character was another
motive. There were those within the fort who believed
the smoking piles that were to be seen, here and there, in
the clearings on the hills, owed their destruction to a disregard of that protection which was thought to be yielded
to those who leaned with the greatest confidence, even in
the forms of earthly transactions, on the sustaining power
of an all-seeing and all-directing Providence. Among this
number was Reuben Ring, who submitted to the loss of
his habitation, as to a merited punishment for the light-
mindedness that had tempted him to erect a dwelling at
the utmost limits of the prescribed distance.

As the party of Dudley retreated, that sturdy yeoman
stood at a window of the chamber in which his prolific
partner with her recent gift were safely lodged ; for in
that moment of confusion, the husband was compelled to
discharge the double duty of sentinel and nurse. He had
just fired his piece, and he had reason to think with

success, on the enemies that pressed too closely on the
retiring party, and as he reloaded the gun, he turned a
melancholy eye on the pile of smoking embers, that now
lay where his humble but comfortable habitation had so
lately stood.

" I fear me, Abundance," he said, shaking his head with
a sigh, " that there was error in the measurement between
the meeting and the clearing. Some misgivings of the
lawfulness of stretching the chain across the hollows, came
over me at the time ; but the pleasant knoll, where the
dwelling stood, was so healthful and commodious, that, if
it were a sin, I hope it is one that is forgiven. There doth
not seem so much as the meanest of its logs, that is not now
melted into white ashes by the fire !"

" Raise me, husband," returned the wife, in the weak
voice natural to her feeble situation ; " raise me with thine
arm, that I may look upon the place where my babes first
saw the light."

Her request was granted, and for a minute the woman
gazed in mute grief at the destruction of her comfortable
home. Then as a fresh yell from the foe rose on the air
without, she trembled, and turned with a mother's care
towards the unconscious beings that slumbered at her side.

" Thy brother hath been driven by the heathen to the
foot of the palisadoes," observed the other, after regarding
his companion with manly kindness for a moment, " and
he hath lessened his force by many that are wounded."

An eloquent pause succeeded. The woman turned her
tearful face upwards, and stretching out a bloodless hand,
she answered, —

" I know what thou wouldst do — it is not meet that
Sergeant Ring should be a woman-tender, when the Indian
enemy is in his neighbour's fields ! Go to thy duty, and
that which is to be done, do manfully ! and yet would I
have thee remember how many there are who lean upon
thy life for a father's care."

The yeoman cast a cautious look around him, for this
the decent and stern usages of the Puritans exacted, and
perceiving that the girl who occasionally entered to tend
the sick was not present, he stooped, and impressing his

lips on the cheek of his wife, he threw a yearning look at his offspring, shouldered his musket, and descended to the court.

When Reuben Ring joined the party of Dudley, the latter had just issued an order to march to the support of those who still stoutly defended the southern entrance of the village. The labour of securing necessaries was not yet ended, and it was on every account an object of the last importance to make good the hamlet against the enemy. The task, however, was not as difficult as the force of the Indians might, at first, have given reason to believe. The conflict by this time had extended to the party which was headed by Content, and in consequence the Indians were compelled to contend with a divided force. The buildings themselves, with the fences and out-houses, were so many breast-works, and it was plain that the assailants acted with a caution and concert that betrayed the direction of some mind more highly gifted than those which ordinarily fall to the lot of uncivilised men.

The task of Dudley was not so difficult as before, since the enemy ceased to press upon his march, preferring to watch the movements of those who held the fortified house, of whose numbers they were ignorant, and of whose attacks they were evidently jealous. As soon as the reinforcement reached the Lieutenant, who defended the village, he commanded the charge, and his men advanced with shouts and clamour, some singing spiritual songs, others lifting up their voices in prayer, while a few availed themselves of the downright and perhaps equally effective means of raising sounds as fearful as possible. The whole being backed by spirited and well directed discharges of musketry, the effort was successful. In a few minutes the enemy fled, leaving that side of the valley momentarily free.

Pursuit would have been folly. After posting a few look-outs, in secret and safe positions among the houses, the whole party returned, with an intention of cutting off the enemy who still held the meadows near the garrison. In this design, however, their intentions were frustrated. The instant they were pressed, the Indians gave way, evidently for the purpose of gaining the protection of the woods;

and when the whites returned to their works, they were followed in a manner to show that they could make no further movement without the hazard of a serious assault. In this condition the men in and about the fort, were compelled to be inefficient spectators of the scene that was taking place around the " Heathcote-house," as the dwelling of old Mark was commonly called.

The fortified building had been erected for the protection of the village and its inhabitants, an object that its position rendered feasible ; but it could offer no aid to those who dwelt without the range of musketry. The only piece of artillery belonging to the settlement was the culverin, which had been discharged by the Puritan, and which had served, for the moment, to check the advance of his enemies. But the exclamations of the stranger, and the appeal to his men, with which the last chapter closed, sufficiently proclaimed that the attack was diverted from the house, and that work of a bloody character now offered itself to those he and his companion led.

The ground around the dwelling of the Heathcotes admitted of closer and more deadly conflict, than that on which the other portions of the combat had occurred. Time had given size to the orchards, and wealth had multiplied and rendered more secure the enclosures and outbuildings. The hostile parties met in one of the former, where they came to the issue which the warlike stranger had foreseen.

Content, like Dudley, caused his men to separate, throwing in his fire with the same guarded reservation as had been practised by the other party. Success again attended the efforts of discipline ; the whites gradually beating back their enemies, until there was a probability of forcing them entirely into the open ground in their rear, a success that would have been tantamount to a victory. But at this flattering moment, yells were heard behind the leaping and whooping band that were still seen gliding through the openings of the smoke, resembling so many dark and malignant spectres acting their evil rites. Then, as a chief with a turbaned head, terrific voice, and commanding stature, appeared in their front, the whole of the wavering line received an onward impulse. The yells redoubled; another warrior was seen brandishing a tomahawk on one flank, and the whole of the deep phalanx came rushing in upon the whites, threatening to sweep them away, like the outbreaking torrent carrying desolation in its course.

" Men, to your square!" shouted the stranger, disregarding cover and life, together, in such a pressing emergency; " to your square, Christians, and be firm!"

The command was repeated by Content, and it was echoed from mouth to mouth. But, before those on the flanks could reach the centre, the shock had come. All order being lost, the combat was hand to hand, one party fighting fiercely for victory, and the other knowing that they stood at the awful peril of their lives. After the first discharge of the musket and the twang of the bow, the struggle was maintained with knife and axe; the thrust of the former, or the descent of the keen and glittering tomahawk, being answered by sweeping and crushing blows of the musket's butt, or by throttling grasps of hands clenched in the death-gripe. Men fell on each other in piles, and when the conqueror rose to shake off the bodies of those who gasped at his feet, his frowning eye rested alike on friend and enemy. The orchard rang with the yells of the Indians, but the colonists fought in mute despair. Sullen resolution only gave way with life, and it happened more than once that day, that the usual reeking token of an Indian triumph was swung before the stern and still conscious eyes of the mangled victim from whose head it had just been torn.

In this frightful scene of slaughter and ferocity, the principal personages of our legend were not idle. By a tacit but intelligent understanding, the stranger, with Content and his son, placed themselves back to back, and struggled manfully against their luckless fortune. The former showed himself no soldier of parade, for knowing the uselessness of orders, when each one fought for life, he dealt out powerful blows in silence. His example was nobly emulated by Content; and young Mark moved limb and muscle with the vigorous activity of his age. A first onset of the enemy was repelled, and for a moment there

was a faint prospect of escape. At the suggestion of the
stranger, the three moved, in their order, towards the dwelling, with the intention of trusting to their personal activity,
when released from the throng. But at this luckless instant, when hope was beginning to assume the air of probability, a chief came stalking through the horrible *mêlée,*
seeking on each side some victim for his uplifted axe. A
crowd of the inferior herd pressed at his heels, and a first
glance told the assailed that the decisive moment had come.

At the sight of so many of their hated enemies still living, and capable of suffering, a common and triumphant
shout burst from the lips of the Indians. Their leader,
like one superior to the more vulgar emotions of his followers, alone approached in silence. As the band opened
and divided to encircle the victims, chance brought him,
face to face, with Mark. Like his foe, the Indian warrior
was still in the freshness and vigour of young manhood.
In stature, years, and agility, the antagonists seemed equal ;
and, as the followers of the chief threw themselves on the
stranger and Content, like men who knew their leader
needed no aid, there was every appearance of a fierce and
doubtful struggle. But, while neither of the combatants
showed any desire to avoid the contest, neither was in haste
to give the commencing blow. A painter, or rather a
sculptor, would have seized the attitudes of these young
combatants for a rich exhibition of the power of his art.

Mark, like most of his friends, had cast aside all super-
fluous vestments ere he approached the scene of strife. The
upper part of his body was naked to the shirt, and even this
had been torn asunder by the rude encounters through
which he had already passed. The whole of his full and
heaving chest was bare, exposing the white skin and blue
veins of one whose fathers had come from towards the rising
sun. His swelling form rested on a leg that seemed
planted in defiance, while the other was thrown in front,
like a lever, to control the expected movements. His
arms were extended to the rear, the hands grasping the
barrel of a musket, which threatened death to all who
should come within its sweep. The head, covered with
the short, curling, yellow hair of his Saxon lineage, was a

little advanced above the left shoulder, and seemed placed in a manner to preserve the equipoise of the whole frame. The brow was flushed, the lips compressed and resolute, the veins of the neck and temples swollen nearly to bursting, and the eyes contracted, but of a gaze that bespoke equally the feelings of desperate determination and of entranced surprise.

On the other hand, the Indian warrior was a man still more likely to be remarked. The habits of his people had brought him, as usual, into the field, with naked limbs and nearly uncovered body. The position of his frame was that of one prepared to leap, and it would have been a comparison tolerated by the license of poetry, to have likened his straight and agile form to the semblance of a crouching panther. The projecting leg sustained the body, bending under its load more with the free play of muscle and sinew, than from any weight, while the slightly stooping head was a little advanced beyond the perpendicular. One hand was clenched on the helve of an axe, that lay in a line with the right thigh, while the other was placed, with a firm gripe, on the buckhorn handle of a knife that was still sheathed at his girdle. The expression of the face was earnest, severe, and perhaps a little fierce ; and yet the whole was tempered by the immovable and dignified calm of a chief of high qualities. The eye, however, was gazing and rivetted, and, like that of the youth whose life he threatened, it appeared singularly contracted with wonder.

The momentary pause that succeeded the movement by which the two antagonists threw themselves into these fine attitudes, was full of meaning. Neither spoke, neither permitted play of muscle, neither even seemed to breathe. The delay was not like that of preparation, for each stood ready for his deadly effort, nor would it have been possible to trace in the compressed energy of the countenance of Mark, or in the lofty and more practised bearing of the front and eye of the Indian, any thing like wavering of purpose. An emotion foreign to the scene appeared to possess both, each active frame unconsciously accommodating itself to the bloody business of the hour, while the

inscrutable agency of the mind held them, for a brief interval, in check.

A yell of death, from the mouth of a savage, who
was beaten to the very feet of his chief, by a blow of the
stranger, and an encouraging shout from the lips of the
latter, broke the short trance. The knees of the chief bent
still lower, the head of the tomahawk was a little raised,
the blade of the knife was seen glittering from its sheath,
and the butt of Mark's musket had receded to the utmost tension of his sinews, when a shriek and a yell,
different from any before heard that day, sounded near.
At the same moment, the blows of both the combatants
were suspended, though by the agency of very different
degrees of force. Mark felt the arms of one cast around
his limbs, with a power sufficient to embarrass, though not
to subdue him, while the well known voice of Whittal
Ring sounded in his ears, —

" Murder the lying and hungry pale-faces ! They
leave us no food but air ; no drink but water !"

On the other hand, when the chief turned in anger, to
strike the daring one who presumed to arrest his arm, he
saw at his feet the kneeling figure, the uplifted hands,
and the agonised features of Martha. Averting the blow
that a follower had already aimed at the life of the suppliant, he spoke rapidly in his own language, and pointed
to the struggling Mark. The nearest Indians cast themselves in a body on the already half-captured youth. A
whoop brought a hundred more to the spot, and then a
calm as sudden, and almost as fearful as the previous
tumult, prevailed in the orchard. It was succeeded by the
long drawn, frightful, and yet meaning yell, by which the
American warrior proclaims his victory.

With the end of the tumult in this spot, the sounds of
strife ceased in all the valley. Though conscious of the
success of their enemies, the men in the fort saw the
certainty of destruction, not only to themselves, but to
those feeble ones they should be compelled to leave without
a sufficient defence, were they to attempt a sortie to that
distance from their works. They were therefore compelled
to remain passive and grave spectators of an evil they had
not the means to avert.

CHAPTER III.

Were such things here, as we do speak about ?
Or have we eaten of the insane root,
That takes the reason prisoner ?   *Macbeth.*

An hour later presented a different scene.   Bands of the
enemy, that in civilised warfare would be called parties of
observation, lingered in the skirts of the forest nearest to
the village, and the settlers still stood to their arms, posted
among the buildings, or maintaining their array at the
foot of the palisadoes.   Though the labour of securing the
valuables continued, it was evident that, as the first terrors
of alarm had disappeared, the owners of the hamlet began
to regain some assurance in their ability to make it good
against their enemies.   Even the women were now seen
moving through its grassy street with greater seeming confidence, and there was a regularity in the air of the armed
men, which denoted a determination well calculated to im-
pose on their wild and undisciplined assailants.

But the dwelling, the out-buildings, and all the implements of domestic comfort, which had so lately contributed
to the ease of the Heathcotes, were completely in the possession of the Indians.   The open shutters and doors, the
scattered and half destroyed furniture, the air of devastation
and waste, and the general abandonment of all interest in the
protection of the property, proclaimed the licentious disorder
of a successful assault.   Still the work of destruction and
plunder did not go on.   Although here and there might be
seen some warrior, decorated, according to the humours of
his savage taste, with the personal effects of the former inmates of the building, every hand had been checked; and the
furious tempers of the conquerors had been quieted, seemingly by the agency of some unseen and extraordinary
authority.   The men, who so lately had been moved by
the fiercest passions of our nature, were suddenly restrained,
if not appeased, and instead of that exulting indulgence of
vengeance, which commonly accompanies an Indian

u 2

triumph, the warriors stalked about the buildings and through the adjacent grounds, in a silence which, though gloomy and sullen, was marked by their characteristic submission to events.

The principal leaders of the inroad, and all the surviving sufferers by the defeat, were assembled in the piazza of the dwelling. Ruth, pale, sorrowing, and mourning for others rather than for herself, stood a little apart, attended by Martha and the young assistant whose luckless fortune it was to be found at her post on this eventful day. Content, the stranger, and Mark were near, subdued and bound, the sole survivors of the band they had so recently led into the conflict. The grey hairs and bodily infirmities of the Puritan spared him the same degradation. The only other being present, of European origin, was Whittal Ring. The innocent stalked slowly among the prisoners, sometimes permitting ancient recollections and sympathies to come over his dull intellect, but oftener taunting the unfortunate with the injustice of their race, and with the wrongs done to his adopted people.

The chiefs of the successful party stood in the centre, apparently engaged in some grave deliberation. As they were few in number, it was evident that the council only included men of the highest importance. Chiefs of inferior rank, but of great names in the limited renown of those simple tribes, conversed in knots among the trees, or paced the court, at a respectful distance from the consultation of their superiors.

The least practised eye could not mistake the person on whom the greatest weight of authority had fallen. The turbaned warrior, already introduced in these pages, occupied the centre of the group, in the calm and dignified attitude of an Indian who hearkens to or who utters advice. His musket was borne by one who stood in waiting, while the knife and axe were returned to his girdle. He had thrown a light blanket, or it might be better termed a robe of scarlet cloth, over his left shoulder, whence it gracefully fell in folds, leaving the whole of the right arm free, and most of his ample chest exposed to view. From beneath this mantle, blood fell slowly in drops, dyeing the floor on which he stood. The countenance of this warrior was grave, though there was a quickness in the movements of an ever-restless eye, that denoted great mental activity, no less than the disquiet of suspicion. One skilled in physiognomy might too have thought that a shade of suppressed discontent was struggling with the self-command of habits that had become part of the nature of the individual.

The two companions nearest this chief were, like himself, men past the middle age, and of a mien and expression that were similar, though less strikingly marked, neither showing those signs of displeasure which occasionally shot from organs that, in spite of a mind so trained and so despotic, could not always restrain their glittering brightness. One was speaking, and by his glance, it was evident that the subject of his discourse was the fourth and last of their number, who had placed himself in a position that prevented his being an auditor of what was said.

In the person of the latter chief, the reader will recognise the youth who had confronted Mark, and whose rapid movement on the flank of Dudley had first driven the colonists from the meadows. The eloquent expression of limb, the tension of sinews, and the compression of muscles, as last exhibited, were now gone. They had given place to the peculiar repose that distinguishes the Indian warrior in his moments of inaction. With one hand he leaned lightly on a musket, while from the wrist of the other, which hung loose at his side, depended, by a thong of deer's sinew, a tomahawk from which fell drops of human blood. His person bore no other covering than that in which he had fought, and, unlike his more aged companion in authority, his body had escaped without a wound.

In form and in features, this young warrior might be deemed a model of the excellence of Indian manhood. The limbs were full, round, faultlessly straight, and distinguished by an appearance of extreme activity, without however being equally remarkable for muscle. In the latter particular, in the upright attitude, and in the distant and noble gaze, which so often elevated his front, there was a close affinity to the statue of the Pythian Apollo ;

while in the full, though slightly effeminate chest, there
was an equal resemblance to that look of animal indulgence, which is to be traced in the severe representations
of Bacchus. This resemblance, however, to a deity that is
little apt to awaken lofty sentiments in the spectator, was
not displeasing, since it in some measure relieved the sternness of an eye that penetrated like the glance of the eagle,
and that might otherwise have left an impression of too
little sympathy with the familiar weaknesses of humanity.
Still the young chief was less to be remarked by this
peculiar fulness of chest, the fruit of intervals of inaction,
constant indulgence of the first wants of nature, and a total
exemption from toil, than most of those who either counselled in secret near, or paced the grounds about the building. In him, it was rather a point to be admired than
a blemish, for it seemed to say that notwithstanding the
evidences of austerity which custom, and perhaps character,
as well as rank, had gathered in his air, there was a heart
beneath that might be touched by human charities. On
the present occasion, the glances of his roving eye, though
searching and full of meaning, were weakened by an expression that betrayed a strange and unwonted confusion
of mind.

The conference of the three was ended, and the warrior
with a turbaned head advanced towards his captives, with
the step of a man whose mind had come to a decision. As
the dreaded chief drew near, Whittal retired, stealing to
the side of the younger warrior in a manner that denoted
greater familiarity and perhaps greater confidence. A
sudden thought lighted the countenance of the latter. He
led the innocent to the extremity of the piazza, spoke low
and earnestly, pointing to the forest, and when he saw that
his messenger was already crossing the fields at the top of
his speed, he moved with dignity into the centre of the
group, taking his station so near his friend, that the folds
of the scarlet blanket brushed his elbow. Until this movement the silence was not broken. When the great chief
felt the passage of the other, he glanced a look of hesitation
at his friends, but resuming his former air of composure,
he spoke.

" Man of many winters," he commenced, in an English that was quite intelligible, while it betrayed a difficulty of speech we shall not attempt imitating, " why hath the Great Spirit made thy race like hungry wolves; why hath a pale-face the stomach of a buzzard, the throat of a hound, and the heart of a deer? Thou hast seen many meltings of the snow: thou rememberest the young tree a sapling. Tell me, why is the mind of a Yengeese so big, that it must hold all that lies between the rising and the setting sun? Speak, for we would know the reason why arms so long are found on so little bodies?"

The events of that day had been of a nature to awaken all the latent energies of the Puritan. He had lifted up his spirit with the morning, with the warmth with which he ever hailed the Sabbath; the excitement of the assault had found him sustained above most earthly calamities, and while it quickened feelings that can never become extinct in one who has been familiar with martial usages, it left him stern in his manhood, and exalted in his sentiments of submission and endurance. Under such influences, he answered with an austerity that equalled the gravity of the Indian.

" The Lord hath delivered us into the bonds of the heathen," he said, " and yet his name shall be blessed beneath my roof! Out of evil shall come good, and from this triumph of the ignorant shall proceed an everlasting victory!"

The chief gazed intently at the speaker, whose attenuated frame, venerable face, and long locks, aided by the hectic of enthusiasm that played beneath a glazed and deep-set eye, imparted a character that seemed to rise superior to human weakness. Bending his head in superstitious reverence, he turned gravely to those who, appearing to possess more of the world in their natures, were more fitting subjects for the designs he meditated.

" The mind of my father is strong, but his body is like a branch of the scorched hemlock!" was the pithy declaration with which he prefaced his next remark. " Why is this?" he continued, looking severely at the three who had so lately been opposed to him in deadly contest.

U 4

" Here are men with skins like the blossom of the dog-
wood, and yet their hands are so dark that I cannot see
them !"

" They have been blackened by toil beneath a burning
sun," returned Content, who knew how to discourse in the
figurative language of the people in whose power he found
himself. " We have laboured that our women and children might eat."

" No — the blood of red men hath changed their
colour."

" We have taken up the hatchet, that the land which
the Great Spirit hath given might still be ours, and that
our scalps might not be blown about in the smoke of a
wigwam. Would a Narragansett hide his arms, and tie
up his hands, with the war-whoop ringing in his ears ?"

When allusion was made to the ownership of the valley,
the blood rushed into the cheek of the warrior in such a
flood, that it deepened its natural swarthy hue ; but clench-
ing the handle of his axe convulsively, he continued to
listen, like one accustomed to self-command.

" What a red man does may be seen," he answered,
pointing with a grim smile towards the orchard, exposing,
by the movement of the blanket, as he raised his arm, iwo
of the reeking trophies of victory attached to his belt.
' Our ears are open wide. We listen to hear in what
manner the hunting grounds of the Indian have become
the ploughed fields of the Yengeese. Now let my wise
men hearken, that they may grow more cunning. The
pale-men have a secret to make the black seem white !"

" Narragansett ———"

" Wompanoag !" interrupted the chief, with the lofty
air with which an Indian identifies himself with the glory
of his people ; then glancing a milder look at the young
warrior at his elbow, he added hastily, and in the tone of
a courtier — " 'T is very good — Narragansett or Wompanoag — Wompanoag or Narragansett. The red men are
brothers and friends. They have broken down the fences
between their hunting grounds, and they have cleared the
paths between their villages of briars. What have you to
say to the Narragansett ; he has not yet shut his ear ?"

" Wompanoag, if such be thy tribe," resumed Content,
" thou shalt hear that which my conscience teacheth is
language to be uttered.   The God of an Englishman is
the God of men of all nations, and of all time." His
listeners shook their heads doubtingly, with the exception
of the youngest chief, whose eye never varied its direction
while the other spoke, each word appearing to enter deep
into his mind.   " In defiance of these signs of blasphemy,
do I still proclaim the power of Him I worship !"   Content continued : " My God is thy God ; and he now
looketh equally on the deeds, and searcheth with inscrutable knowledge into the hearts of both.   This earth is his
footstool ; yonder heaven his throne !   I pretend not to
enter into his sacred mysteries, or to proclaim the reason
why one half of his fair work hath been so long left in that
slough of ignorance and heathenish abomination in which
my fathers found it ; why these hills never before echoed
the songs of praise, or why the valleys have been so long
mute.   These are truths hid in the secret designs of his
sacred purpose, and they may not be known until the last
fulfilment.   But a great and righteous Spirit hath led
hither men filled with the love of truth, and pregnant with
the designs of a heavily burdened faith, inasmuch as their
longings are for things pure, while the consciousness of
their transgressions bend them, in deep humility, to the
dust.   Thou bringest against us the charge of coveting
thy lands, and of bearing minds filled with the corruption
of riches.   This cometh of ignorance of that which hath
been abandoned, in order that the spirit of the godly
might hold fast to the truth.   When the Yengeese came
into this wilderness, he left behind him all that can delight
the eye, please the senses, and feed the longing of the
human heart, in the country of his fathers : for fair as is
the work of the Lord in other lands, there is none that is
so excellent as that from which these pilgrims in the wilderness have departed.   In that favoured isle, the earth
groaneth with the abundance of its products ; the odours
of its sweet savours salute the nostrils, and the eye is never
wearied in gazing at its loveliness.   No — the men of the
pale-faces have deserted home, and all that sweeteneth life

that they might serve God ; and not at the instigations of craving minds, or of evil vanities !"

Content paused, for as he grew warm with the spirit by which he was animated, he had insensibly strayed from the closer points of his subject. His conquerors maintained the decorous gravity with which an Indian always listens to the speech of another, until he had ended ; and then the great chief, or Wompanoag as he had proclaimed himself to be, laid a finger lightly on the shoulder of his prisoner, and demanded, —

" Why have the people of the Yengeese lost themselves on a blind path ? If the country they have left is pleasant, cannot their God hear them from the wigwams of their fathers ? See ; if our trees are but bushes, leave them to the red man ; he will find room beneath their branches to lie in the shade. If our rivers are small, it is because the Indians are little. If the hills are low and the valleys narrow, the legs of my people are weary with much hunting, and they will journey among them the easier. Now what the Great Spirit hath made for a red man, a red man should keep. They whose skins are like the light of the morning should go back towards the rising sun, out of which they have come to do us wrong."

The chief spoke calmly, but it was like a man much accustomed to deal in the subtleties of controversy, according to the fashion of the people to whom he belonged.

" God hath otherwise decreed," said Content. " He hath led his servants hither that the incense of praise may arise from the wilderness."

" Your Spirit is a wicked Spirit. Your ears have been cheated. The counsel that told your young men to come so far, was not spoken in the voice of the Manitou. It came from the tongue of one that loves to see game scarce, and the squaws hungry. Go — you follow the mocker or your hands would not be so dark."

" I know not what injury may have been done the Wompanoags, by men of wicked minds, for some such there are, even in the dwellings of the well-disposed ; but wrong to any hath never come from those that dwell within my doors. For these lands, a price hath been paid ; and what is now seen of abundance in the valley, hath been wrought by much labour. Thou art a Wompanoag, and must know that the hunting grounds of thy tribe have been held sacred by my people. Are not the fences standing which their hands placed that not even the hoof of colt should trample the corn ; and when was it known that the Indian came for justice against the trespassing ox, and he did not find it ? "

" The moose doth not taste the grass at the root ; he liveth on the tree ! He doth not stoop to feed on that which he treadeth under foot. Does the hawk look for the musquito ? His eye is too big. He can see a bird. Go — when the deer have been killed, the Wompanoags will break down the fence with their own hands. The arm of a hungry man is strong. A cunning pale-face hath made that fence ; it shutteth out the colt and it shutteth in the Indian. But the mind of a warrior is too big ; it will not be kept at grass with the ox."

A low murmur of satisfaction from the mouths of his grim companions succeeded this reply.

" The country of thy tribe is far distant," returned Content, " and I will not lay untruth to my soul, by presuming to say whether justice or injustice hath been done them in the partition of the lands. But in this valley hath wrong never been done to the red-man. What Indian hath asked for food, and not got it ? If he hath been a-thirst, the cider came at his wish ; if he hath been a-cold there was a seat by the hearth : and yet hath there been good reason why the hatchet should be in my hand, and why my foot should be on the war-path ! For many seasons we lived on lands which were bought of both red and white man, in peace. But though the sun shone clear so long, the clouds came at last. There was a dark night fell upon this valley, Wompanoag, and death and the brand entered my dwelling together. Our young men were killed, and —— our spirits were sorely tried."

Content paused, for his voice became thick, and his eye had caught a glimpse of the pale and drooping countenance of her who leaned on the arm of the still excited and frowning Mark for support. The young chief listened with a charmed ear. As Content proceeded, his body had inclined a little forward, and his whole attitude was that which men unconsciously assume, when intensely occupied in listening to sounds of the deepest interest.

" But the sun rose again !" said the great chief, pointing at the evidences of prosperity which were every where apparent in the settlement, casting at the same time an uneasy and suspicious glance at his youngest companion. " The morning was clear, though the night was so dark. The cunning of a pale-face knows how to make corn grow on a rock. The foolish Indian eats roots, when crops fail and game is scarce."

" God ceased to be angry," returned Content meekly, folding his arms in a manner to show he wished to speak no more.

The great chief was about to continue, when his younger associate laid a finger on his naked shoulder, and, by a sign, indicated that he wished to hold communication with him apart. The former met the request with respect, though it might be discovered that he little liked the expression of his companion's features, and that he yielded with reluctance, if not with disgust. But the countenance of the youth was firm, and it would have needed more than usual hardihood to refuse a request seconded by so steady and so menacing an eye. The elder spoke to the warrior nearest his elbow, addressing him by the name of Annawon, and then by a gesture so natural and so dignified that it might have graced the air of a courtier, he announced his readiness to proceed. Notwithstanding the habitual reverence of the Aborigines for age, the others gave way for the passage of the young man, in a manner to proclaim that merit, or birth, or both, had united to purchase for him a personal distinction which far exceeded that shown in common to men of his years. The two chiefs left the piazza in the noiseless manner of the moccasined foot.

The passage of these dignified warriors towards the grounds in the rear of the dwelling, as it was characteristic of their habits, is worthy of being mentioned. Neither spoke, neither manifested any womanish impatience to pry into the musings of the other's mind, and neither failed in those slight but still sensible courtesies, by which the path was rendered commodious and the footing sure. They had reached the summit of the elevation so often named, ere they believed themselves sufficiently retired to indulge in a discourse which might otherwise have enlightened profane ears. When beneath the shade of the fragrant orchard which grew on the hill, the senior of the two stopped, and throwing about him one of those quick, nearly imperceptible, and yet wary glances, by which an Indian understands his precise position, as it were by instinct, he commenced the dialogue. The discourse was in the dialect of their race, but as it is not probable that many who read these pages would be much enlightened were we to record it in the precise words in which it has been transmitted to us, a translation into English, as freely as the subject requires, and the geniuses of the two languages will admit, shall be attempted.

" What would my brother have ?" commenced he with the turbaned head, uttering the guttural sounds in the soothing tones of friendship, and even of affection. " What troubles the great Sachem of the Narragansetts? His thoughts seem uneasy ; I think there is more before his eye than one whose sight is getting dim can see. Doth he behold the spirit of the brave Miantonimoh, who died like a dog beneath the blows of cowardly Pequots, and false-tongued Yengeese ? Or does his heart swell with longing to see the scalps of treacherous pale-faces hanging at his belt ? Speak, my son, the hatchet hath long been buried in the path between our villages, and thy words will enter the ears of a friend."

" I do not see the spirit of my father," returned the young Sachem ; " he is afar off, in the hunting grounds of just warriors. My eyes are too weak to look over so many mountains, and across so many rivers. He is chasing the moose in grounds where there are no briars ; he needeth not the sight of a young man to tell him which way the trail leadeth. Why should I look at the place where the Pequot and the pale-face took his life ! The fire which scorched this hill hath blackened the spot, and I can no longer find the marks of blood."

" My son is very wise ; cunning beyond his winters !

That which hath been once revenged is forgotten. He looks no further than six moons. He sees the warriors of the Yengeese coming into his village, murdering his old women, and slaying the Narragansett girls ; killing his warriors from behind, and lighting their fires with the bones of red men. I will now stop my ears, for the groans of the slaughtered make my soul feel weak."

" Wompanoag," answered the other, with a fierce flashing of his eagle eye, and laying his hand firmly on his breast, " the night the snows were red with the blood of my people is here ! My mind is dark : none of my race have since looked upon the place where the lodges of the Narragansetts stood, and yet it hath never been hid from our sight. Since that time have we travelled in the woods, bearing on our backs all that is left but our sorrow ; which we carry in our hearts."

" Why is my brother troubled ? There are many scalps among his people ; and see, his own tomahawk is very red ! Let him quiet his anger till the night cometh, and there will be a deeper stain on the axe. I know he is in a hurry, but our councils say it is better to wait for darkness, since the cunning of the pale-faces is too strong for the hands of our young men."

" When was a Narragansett slow to leap after the whoop was given, or unwilling to stay when men of grey heads say 't is better ? I like your council ; it is full of wisdom. Yet an Indian is but a man ! Can he fight with the God of the Yengeese ? He is too weak. An Indian is but a man, though his skin be red ! "

" I look into the clouds, at the trees, among the lodges," said the other, affecting to gaze curiously at the different objects he named, " but I cannot see the white Manitou. The pale-men were talking to him when we raised the whoop in their fields, and yet he has not heard them. Go — my son has struck their warriors with a strong hand ; has he forgotten to count how many dead lie among the trees with the sweet-smelling blossoms ? "

" Metacom," returned he who has been called the Sachem of the Narragansetts, stepping cautiously nearer to his friend and speaking lower, as if he feared an invisible auditor,

" though hast put hate into the bosoms of the red men, but canst thou make them more cunning than the Spirits? Hate is very strong, but cunning hath a longer arm. See," he added, raising the fingers of his two hands before the eyes of his attentive companion, " ten snows have come and melted since there stood a lodge of the pale-faces on this hill. Conanchet was then a boy. His hand had struck nothing but deer ; his heart was full of wishes. By day he thought of Pequot scalps, at night he heard the dying words of Miantonimoh. Though slain by cowardly Pequots and lying Yengeese, his father came often at night into his wigwam to talk to his son. ' Does the child of so many great Sachems grow big ?' would he say; ' is his arm getting strong, his foot light, his eye quick, his heart valiant ? Will Conanchet be like his sires ? When will the young Sachem of the Narragansetts become a man ? '—Why should I tell my brother of these visits ? Metacom hath often seen the long line of Wompanoag chiefs in his sleep. The brave Sachems sometimes enter into the heart of their son."

The lofty-minded, though wily, Philip struck his hand heavily on his naked breast, as he answered,—

" They are always here. Metacom has no soul but the soul of his fathers !"

" When he was tired of silence, the murdered Mian-tonimoh spoke aloud," continued Conanchet, after permit-ting the customary courteous pause to succeed the emphatic words of his companion. " He bade his son arise, and go among the Yengeese, that he might return with scalps to hang in his wigwam ; for the eyes of the dead chief liked not to see the place so empty. The voice of Conanchet was then too feeble for the council fire ; he said nothing — he went alone. An evil spirit gave him into the hands of the pale-faces. He was a captive many moons. They shut him in a cage, like a tamed panther : it was here. The news of his ill-luck passed from the mouths of the young men of the Yen-geese to the hunters ; and from the hunters it came to the ears of the Narragansetts. My people had lost their Sachem, and they came to seek him. Metacom, the boy had felt the power of the God of the Yengeese. His mind began to grow weak ; he thought less of revenge — the spirit of his

father came no more at night. There was much talking
with the unknown God, and the words of his enemies were
kind. He hunted with them. When he met the trail of
his warriors in the woods his mind was troubled, for he
knew their errand. Still he saw his father's spirit and
waited. The whoop was heard that night : many died,
and the Narragansetts took scalps. Thou seest this lodge
of stone over which fire has passed ; there was then a cunning place above, and in it the pale-men went to fight for
their lives ; but the fire kindled and then there was no hope.
The soul of Conanchet was moved at that sight, for there
was much honesty in them within. Though their skins
were so white, they had not slain his father. But the
flames would not be spoken to, and the place became like
the coals of a deserted council fire. All within were turned
to ashes. If the spirit of Miantonimoh rejoiced, it was well;
but the soul of his son was very heavy. The weakness
was on him, and he no longer thought of boasting of his
deeds at the war-post."

" That fire scorched the stain of blood from the Sachem's
plain !"

" It did. Since that time I have not seen the marks
of my father's blood. Grey heads and boys were in that
fire, and when the timbers fell, nothing was left but
coals. Yet they who were in the blazing lodge now stand
there !"

The attentive Metacom started, and glanced a hasty look
at the ruin.

" Does my son see spirits in the air ?" he asked, hastily.

" No, they live ; they are bound for the torments.
The white head is he who talked much with his God.
The elder chief, who struck our young men so hard, was
then also a captive in this lodge. He who spoke, and she
who seems even paler than her race, died that night ; and
yet they are now all here ! Even the brave youth that
was so hard to conquer looks like a boy that was in the fire.
The Yengeese deal with unknown gods ; they are too cunning for an Indian !"

Philip heard this strange tale as a being educated in superstitious legends would be apt to listen ; and yet it was with

a leaning to incredulity, that was generated by his fierce and indomitable desire for the destruction of the hated race. He had prevailed in the councils of his nation over many similar signs of the supernatural agency that was exercised in favour of his enemies, but never before had facts so imposing come so directly, and from so high a source, before his stubborn mind. Even the proud resolution and far-sighted wisdom of this sagacious chief were shaken by such testimony, and there was a single moment when the idea of abandoning a league that seemed desperate took possession of his brain. But, true to himself and his cause, second thoughts and a firmer purpose restored his resolution, though they could not remove the perplexity of his doubts.

"What does Conanchet wish?" he said. "Twice have his warriors broke into this valley, and twice have the tomahawks of his young men been redder than the head of the woodpecker. The fire was not good fire; the tomahawk will kill surer. Had not the voice of my brother said to his young men, ' Let the scalps of the prisoners alone,' he could not say, ' Yet do they now stand here!'"

"My mind is troubled, friend of my father. Let them be questioned artfully, that the truth be known."

Metacom mused an instant; then smiling, in a friendly manner, on his young and much moved companion, he made a sign to a youth who was straying about the fields to approach. This young warrior was made the bearer of an order to lead the captives to the hill, after which the two chiefs stalked, to and fro, in silence, each brooding over what had passed, in a humour that was suited to his particular character and more familar feelings.

x

CHAPTER IV.

No withered witch shall here be seen,
No goblins lead their nightly crew;
The female fays shall haunt the green,
And dress thy grave with pearly dew.   COLLINS.

IT is rare indeed that the philosophy of a dignified Indian is so far disturbed, as to destroy the appearance of equanimity. When Content and the family of the Heathcotes appeared on the hill, they found the chiefs still pacing the orchard with the outward composure of men unmoved, and with the gravity that was suited to their rank. Annawon, who had acted as their conductor, caused the captives to be placed in a row, choosing the foot of the ruin for their position, and then he patiently awaited the moment when his superiors might be pleased to renew the examination. In this habitual silence, there was nothing of the abject air of Asiatic deference. It proceeded from the habit of self-command, which taught the Indian to repress all natural emotions. A very similar effect was produced by the religious abasement of those whom Fortune had now thrown into their power. It would have been a curious study, for one interested in the manners of the human species, to note the difference between the calm, physical, and perfect self-possession of the wild tenants of the forest, and the ascetic, spiritually sustained, and yet meek submission to Providence, that was exhibited by most of the prisoners. We say of most, for there was an exception. The brow of young Mark still retained its frown, and the angry character of his eye was only lost, when by chance it lighted on the drooping form and pallid features of his mother. There was ample time for these several and peculiar qualities to be thus silently exhibited, many minutes passing before either of the Sachems seemed inclined to recommence the conference. At length Philip, or Metacom, as we shall indifferently call him, drew near and spoke.

" This earth is a good earth," he said ; " it is of many colours, to please the eyes of Him who made it. In one part it is dark, and as the worm taketh the colour of the leaf on which he crawls, there the hunters are black ; in another part it is white, and that is the part where pale men were born, and where they should die, or, they may miss the road which leads to their happy hunting grounds. Many just warriors, who have been killed on distant war-paths, still wander in the woods because the trail is hid, and their sight dim. It is not good to trust so much to the cunning of ——"

" Wretched and blind worshipper of Appollyon !" in_terrupted the Puritan, " we are not of the idolatrous and foolish minded ! It hath been accorded to us to know the Lord ; to his chosen worshippers all regions are alike. The spirit can mount, equally, through snows and whirlwinds ; the tempest and the calm ; from the lands of the sun, and the lands of frosts ; from the depths of the ocean, from fire, from the forest ——"

He was interrupted in his turn. At the word fire, the finger of Metacom fell meaningly on his shoulder ; and when he had ceased, for until then no Indian would have spoken, the other gravely asked, —

" And when a man of a pale skin hath gone up in the fire, can he again walk upon earth ? Is the river between this clearing and the pleasant fields of a Yengeese so nar-row, that the just men can step across it when they please? "

" This is the conceit of one wallowing in the slough of heathenish abominations ! Child of ignorance ! know that the barriers which separate heaven from earth are im-passable ; for what purified being could endure the wicked-ness of the flesh ? "

" This is a lie of the false pale-faces," said the wily Philip ; " it is told that the Indian might not learn their cunning, and become stronger than a Yengeese. My father, and those with him, were once burnt in this lodge, and now he standeth here ready to take up the tomahawk !"

" To be angered at this blasphemy, would ill denote the pity that I feel," said Mark, more excited at the charge of necromancy than he was willing to own ; " and yet to suffer so fatal an error to spread among these deluded vic-tims of Satan, would be a neglect of duty. Thou hast

x 2

heard some legend of thy wild people, man of the Wompanoags, which may heap double perdition on thy soul, lest
thou shouldst happily be rescued from the fangs of the
deceiver. It is true, that I and mine were in exceeding
jeopardy in this tower, and that to the eyes of men without, we seemed melted with the heat of the flames : but
the Lord put it into our spirits to seek refuge, whither fire
could not come. The well was made the instrument of
our safety, for the fulfilment of his own inscrutable designs.

Notwithstanding the long practised and exceeding subtlety of the listeners, they heard this simple explanation of
that which they had deemed a miracle, with a wonder that
could not readily be concealed. Delight at the excellence
of the artifice was evidently the first and common emotion of both ; nor would they yield implicit faith, until
assured, beyond a doubt, that what they heard was true.
The little iron door which had permitted access to the
well, for the ordinary domestic purposes of the family, was
still there, and it was only after each had cast a look down
the deep shaft, that he appeared satisfied of the practica-
bility of the deed. Then a look of triumph gleamed in
the swarthy visage of Philip, while the features of his
associate expressed equally his satisfaction and his regret.
They walked apart, musing on what they had just seen
and heard, and when they spoke, it was again in the language of their people.

" My son hath a tongue that cannot lie," observed
Metacom, in a soothing flattering accent. " What he hath
seen, he tells ; and what he tells, is true. Conanchet is
not a boy, but a chief whose wisdom is grey while his
limbs are young. Now, why shall not his people take the
scalps of these Yengeese, that they may never go any more
into holes in the earth, like cunning foxes ? "

" The Sachem hath a very bloody mind," returned the
young chief, quicker than was common for men of his
station. " Let the arms of the warriors rest, till they meet
the armed hands of the Yengeese, or they will be too tired
to strike heavily. My young men have done nothing but
take scalps since the sun came over the trees, and they are

well satisfied. Why does Metacom look so hard? What does my father see?"

"A dark spot in the middle of a wide plain. The grass is not green; it is red as blood. It is too dark for the blood of a pale-face. It is the rich blood of a great warrior. The rains cannot wash it out; it grows darker every sun. The snows do not whiten it; it hath been there many winters. The birds scream as they fly over it; the wolf howls; the lizards creep another way."

"Thine eyes are getting old; fire hath blackened the place, and what thou seest is coal."

"The fire was kindled in a well; it did not burn bright. What I see, is blood."

"Wompanoag," rejoined Conanchet, fiercely, "I have scorched the spot with the lodges of the Yengeese. The grave of my father is covered with scalps taken by the hand of his son. Why does Metacom look again? What does the chief see?"

"An Indian town burning in the midst of the snow. The young men struck from behind; the girls screaming; the children broiling on coals, and the old men dying like dogs! It is the village of the cowardly Pequots — No, I see better; the Yengeese are in the country of the great Narragansett, and the brave Sachem is there, fighting! I shut my eyes, for smoke blinds them!"

Conanchet heard this allusion to the recent and deplorable fate of the principal establishment of his tribe, in sullen silence; for the desire of revenge, which had been so fearfully awakened, seemed now to be slumbering, if it were not entirely quelled, by the agency of some mysterious and potent feeling. He rolled his eyes gloomily from the apparently abstracted countenance of his artful companion, to those of the captives, whose fate only awaited his judgment, since the band which had that morning broken in upon the Wish-Ton-Wish, was, with but few exceptions, composed of the surviving warriors of his own powerful nation. But, while his look was displeased, faculties that were schooled so highly could not easily be mistaken in what passed, even in the most cursory manner, before his sight.

" What sees my father next ? " he asked with an interest he could not control, detecting another change in
the features of Metacom.

" One who is neither white nor red. A young woman
that boundeth like a skipping fawn ; who hath lived in a
wigwam, doing nothing ; who speaks with two tongues ;
who holds her hands before the eyes of a great warrior,
till he is blind as the owl in the sun — I see her —— "

Metacom paused, for at that moment a being that singularly resembled this description appeared before him,
offering the reality of the imaginary picture he was drawing with so much irony and art.

The movement of the timid hare is scarce more hurried,
or more undecided, than that of the creature who now suddenly presented herself to the warriors. It was apparent,
by the hesitating and half retreating step, that succeeded
the light bound with which she came in view, that she
dreaded to advance, while she knew not how far it might
be proper to retire. For the first moment, she stood in a
suspended and doubting posture, such as one might suppose a creature of mist would assume ere it vanished, and
then meeting the eye of Conanchet, the uplifted foot re-
touched the earth, and her whole form sunk into the modest
and shrinking attitude of an Indian girl, who stood in the
presence of a Sachem. As this female is to enact no mean
part in that which follows, the reader may be thankful for
a more minute description of her person.

The age of the stranger was under twenty. In form
she rose above the usual stature of an Indian maid, though
the proportions of her person were as light and buoyant,
as at all comported with the fulness that properly belonged
to her years. The limbs, seen below the folds of a short
kirtle of bright scarlet cloth, were just and tapering, even
to the nicest proportions of classic beauty ; and never did
foot of higher instep, and softer roundness, grace a feathered moccasin. Though the person, from the neck to
the knees, was hid by a tightly fitting vest of calico and
the bright short kirtle, enough of her shape was visible to
betray outlines that had never been injured either by the
mistaken devices of art, or by the baneful effects of toil

The skin was only visible at the hands, face, and neck. Its lustre having been a little dimmed by exposure, a rich rosy tint had usurped the natural brightness of a complexion that had once been fair, even to brilliancy. The eye was full, sweet, and of a blue, that emulated the sky of evening; the brows soft and arched; the nose, straight, delicate, and slightly Grecian; the forehead fuller than that which properly belonged to a girl of the Narragansetts, but regular, delicate, and polished; and the hair, instead of dropping in long straight tresses of jet black, broke out of the restraints of a band of beaded wampum, in ringlets of golden yellow.

The peculiarities that distinguished this female from the others of her tribe, were not confined alone to the indelible marks of nature. Her step was more elastic; her gait more erect and graceful; her foot less inwardly inclined, and her whole movements freer and more decided than those of a race doomed, from infancy, to subjection and labour. Though ornamented by some of the prized inventions of the hated race to which she evidently owed her birth, she had the wild and timid look of those with whom she had grown into womanhood. Her beauty would have been remarkable in any region of the earth, while the play of muscle, the ingenuous beaming of the eye, and the freedom of limb and action, were such as seldom pass beyond the years of childhood, among people who, in attempting to improve, so often mar the works of nature.

Although the colour of the eye was so very different from that which generally belongs to one of Indian origin, the manner of its quick and searching glance, and of the half alarmed and yet understanding look with which this extraordinary creature made herself mistress of the more general character of the assemblage before which she had been summoned, was like the half instinctive knowledge of one accustomed to the constant and keenest exercise of her faculties. Pointing with her finger towards Whittal Ring, who stood a little in the back ground, a low sweet voice was heard asking, in the language of the Indians, —

" Why has Conanchet sent for his woman from the woods.? "

The young Sachem made no reply; an ordinary spectator could not have detected about him even a consciousness
of the speaker's presence. On the contrary, he maintained
the lofty reserve of a chief engaged in affairs of moment.
However deeply his thoughts might have been troubled, it
was not easy to trace any evidence of the state of his
mind, in the calmness of features that appeared habitually
immovable. For a single treacherous instant only, was a
glance of kindness shot towards the timid and attentive
girl, and then throwing the still bloody tomahawk into the
hollow of one arm, while the hand of the other firmly
grasped its handle, he remained unchanged in feature, as he
was rigid in limb. Not so with Philip. When the intruder first appeared, a dark and lowering gleam of discontent gathered at his brow. It quickly changed to a
look of sarcastic and biting scorn.

" Does my brother again wish to know what I see ? "
he demanded, when sufficient time had passed to show that
his companion was not disposed to answer the question of
the female.

" What does the Sachem of the Wompanoags now behold ? " returned Conanchet, proudly ; unwilling to show
that any circumstance had occurred to interrupt the subject
of their conference.

" A sight that his eyes will not believe. He sees a
great tribe on the war-path. There are many braves,
and a chief whose fathers came from the clouds. Their
hands are in the air ; they strike heavy blows; the arrow
is swift and the bullet is not seen to enter, but it kills.
Blood runs from the wounds that is of the colour of water.
Now he does not see, but he hears ! 'T is the scalp-whoop,
and the warriors are very glad. The chiefs in the happy
hunting grounds are coming, with joy, to meet Indians
that are killed ; for they know the scalp-whoop of their
children."

The expressive countenance of the young Sachem involuntarily responded to this description of the scene through
which he had just passed, and it was impossible for one so
tutored to prevent the blood from rushing faster to a heart
that ever beat strongly with the wishes of a warrior.

" What sees my father next ? " he asked, triumph insensibly stealing into his voice.

" A messenger : and then he hears — the moccasins of
a squaw ! "

" Enough ; — Metacom, the women of the Narragansetts have no lodges.   Their villages are in coals, and they
follow the young men for food."

" I see no deer.   The hunter will not find venison in a
clearing of the pale-faces.   But the corn is full of milk ;
Conanchet is very hungry ; he hath sent for his woman that
he may eat ! "

The fingers of that hand which grasped the handle of
the tomahawk appeared to bury themselves in the wood ;
the glittering axe itself was slightly raised ; but the fierce
gleam of resentment subsided, as the anger of the young
Sachem vanished, and a dignified calm again settled on his
countenance.

" Go, Wompanoag," he said, waving a hand in disdain,
as if determined to be no longer harassed by the language
of his wily associate.   " My young men will raise the
whoop, when they hear my voice ; and they will kill deer
for their women.   Sachem, my mind is my own."

Philip answered the look which accompanied these words,
with one that threatened vengeance ; but successfully smothering his anger he left the hill, assuming an air that
affected more of commiseration than of resentment.

" Why has Conanchet sent for a woman from the
woods ? " repeated the same soft voice nearer the elbow of
the young Sachem, and which spoke with less of the timidity of the sex, now that the troubled spirit of the Indians
of those regions had disappeared.

" Narra-mattah, come near," returned the young chief,
losing the excited tones in which he had addressed his
restless and bold companion in arms, in those which better
suited the gentle ear for which his words were intended.
" Fear not, daughter of the Morning, for those around us
are of a race used to see women at the council fires.   Now
look with an open eye : is there any thing among these
trees that seemeth like an ancient tradition ?   Hast ever
beheld such a valley in thy dreams ?   Have yonder pale-

faces, whom the tomahawks of my young men spared," been led before thee by the Great Spirit in the dark night?"

The female listened attentively. Her gaze was wild and uncertain, and yet it was not absolutely without gleamings of a half-reviving intelligence. Until that moment, she had been too much occupied in conjecturing the subject of her visit, to regard the natural objects by which she was surrounded: but with her attention thus directly turned upon them, her organs of sight embraced each and all with the discrimination that is so remarkable in those whose faculties are quickened by danger and necessity. Passing from side to side, her swift glances run over the distant hamlet with its little fort; the buildings in the near grounds; the soft and verdant fields; the fragrant orchard, beneath whose leafy shades she stood, and the blackened tower, that rose in its centre, like some gloomy memorial placed there to remind the spectator not to trust too fondly to the signs of peace and loveliness that reigned around. Shaking back the ringlets that had blown about her temples, the wondering girl returned thoughtfully and in silence to her place.

" 'T is a village of the Yengeese!" she said, after a long and expressive pause. " A Narragansett woman does not love to look at the lodges of the hated race."

" Listen. — Lies have never entered the ears of Narramattah. My tongue hath spoken like the tongue of a chief. Thou didst not come of the sumach, but of the snow. This hand of thine is not like the hands of the women of my tribe; it is little, for the Great Spirit did not make it for work; it is of the colour of the sky in the morning, for thy fathers were born near the place where the sun rises. Thy blood is like spring water. All this thou knowest, for none have spoken false in thy ear. Speak; dost thou never see the wigwam of thy father? Does not his voice whisper to thee in the language of his people?"

The female stood in the attitude which a sibyl might be supposed to assume, while listening to the occult mandates of the mysterious oracle, every faculty absorbed and entranced.

" Why does Conanchet ask these questions of his wife ?
He knows what she knows ; he sees what she sees ; his
mind is her mind. If the Great Spirit made her skin of
a different colour, he made her heart the same. Narra-
mattah will not listen to the lying language ; she shuts
her ears, for there is deceit in its sounds. She tries to forget it. One tongue can say all she wishes to speak to Conanchet ; why should she look back in dreams, when a great
chief is her husband ? "

The eye of the warrior, as he looked upon the ingenuous
and confiding face of the speaker, was kind to fondness.
The firmness had passed away, and in its place was left the
winning softness of affection, which, as it belongs to nature,
is seen at times in the expression of an Indian's eye, as
strongly as it is ever known to sweeten the intercourse
of a more polished condition of life.

" Girl," he said, with emphasis, after a moment of
thought, as if he would recall her and himself to more important duties, " this is a war-path ; all on it are men.
Thou wast like the pigeon before its wing opens, when I
brought thee from the nest ; still the winds of many winters had blown upon thee. Dost never think of the warmth,
and of the food of the lodge, in which thou had passed so
many seasons ? "

" The wigwam of Conanchet is warm ; no woman of
the tribe hath as many furs as Narra-mattah."

" He is a great hunter ! when they hear his moccasin
the beavers lie down to be killed ! But the men of the
pale-faces hold the plough. Does not ' the Driven-Snow'
think of those who fenced the wigwam of her father from
the cold, or of the manner in which the Yengeese live ? "

His youthful and attentive wife seemed to reflect ; but
raising her face with an expression of content that could
not be counterfeited, she shook her head in the negative.

" Does she never see a fire kindled among the lodges,
or hear the whoops of warriors as they break into a settlement ? "

" Many fires have been kindled before her eyes. The
ashes of the Narragansett town are not yet cold."

" Does not Narra-mattah hear her father speaking to

the God of the Yengeese? Listen, he is asking favour for his child!"

" The Great Spirit of the Narragansett has ears for his people."

" But I hear a softer voice! 'T is a woman of the pale-faces among her children; cannot the daughter hear?"

Narra-mattah, or " the Driven-Snow," laid her hand lightly on the arm of the chief, and she looked wistfully and long into his face without an answer. The gaze seemed to deprecate the anger that might be awakened by what she was about to reveal.

" Chief of my people," she said, encouraged by his still calm and gentle brow to proceed, " what a girl of the clearings sees in her dreams shall not be hid. It is not the lodges of her race, for the wigwam of her husband is warmer. It is not the food and clothes of a cunning people, for who is richer than the wife of a great chief! It is not her fathers speaking to their Spirit, for there is none stronger than Manitou. Narra-mattah has forgotten all; she does not wish to think of things like these. She knows how to hate a hungry and craving race. But she sees one that the wives of the Narragansetts do not see. She sees a woman with a white skin; her eye looks softly on her child in her dreams; it is not an eye, it is a tongue! It says, What does the wife of Conanchet wish?—Is she cold? here are furs—Is she hungry? here is venison—Is she tired? the arms of the pale woman open that an Indian girl may sleep. When there is silence in the lodges, when Conanchet and his young men lie down, then does this pale woman speak. Sachem, she does not talk of the battles of her people, nor of the scalps that her warriors have taken, nor of the manner in which the Pequots and Mohicans fear her tribe. She does not tell how a young Narragansett should obey her husband, nor how the women must keep food in the lodges for the hunters that are wearied; her tongue useth strange words. It names a mighty and just Spirit; it telleth of peace and not of war; it soundeth as one talking from the clouds; it is like the falling of the water among rocks. Narra-mattah loves to listen, for the words seem to her like the Wish-Ton-Wish when he whistles in the woods."

Conanchet had fastened a look of deep and affectionate interest on the wild and sweet countenance of the being who stood before him. She had spoken in that attitude of earnest and natural eloquence, that no art can equal; and when she ceased, he laid a hand in kind but melancholy fondness on the half inclined and motionless head, as he answered, --

" This is the bird of night singing to its young ! The Great Spirit of thy fathers is angry that thou livest in the lodge of a Narragansett. His sight is too cunning to be cheated. He knows that the moccasin, and the wampum, and the robe of fur are liars ; he sees the colour of the skin beneath."

" Conanchet, no," returned the female, hurriedly, and with a decision her timidity did not give reason to expect. " He seeth farther than the skin, and knoweth the colour of the mind. He hath forgotten that one of his girls is missing."

" It is not so. The eagle of my people was taken into the lodges of the pale-faces. He was young, and they taught him to sing with another tongue. The colours of his feathers were changed, and they thought to cheat the Manitou. But when the door was open, he spread his wings and flew back to his nest. It is not so. What hath been done is good, and what will be done is better. Come ; there is a straight path before us."

Thus saying, Conanchet motioned to his wife to follow towards the group of captives. The foregoing dialogue had occurred in a place where the two parties were partially concealed from each other by the ruin ; but as the distance was so trifling, the Sachem and his companion were soon confronted with those he sought. Leaving his wife a little without the circle, Conanchet advanced, and taking the unresisting and half unconscious Ruth by the arm, he led her forward. He placed the two females in attitudes where each might look the other full in the face. Strong emotion struggled in a countenance which, in spite of its fierce mask of war-paint, could not entirely conceal its workings.

" See," he said, in English, looking earnestly from one to the other, " the Good Spirit is not ashamed of his work. What he hath done, he hath done ; Narragansett nor Yengeese can alter it.   This is the white bird that came from the sea," he added, touching the shoulder of Ruth lightly with a finger, " and this the young that she warmed under her wing."

Then folding his arms on his naked breast, he appeared to summon his energy, lest, in the scene that he knew must follow, his manhood might be betrayed into some act un- worthy of his name.

The captives were necessarily ignorant of the meaning of the scene which they had just witnessed.   So many strange and savage-looking forms were constantly passing and repassing before their eyes, that the arrival of one more or less was not likely to be noted.   Until she heard Conanchet speak in her native tongue, Ruth had lent no attention to the interview between him and his wife.   But the figurative language, and no less remarkable action of the Narragansett, had the effect to arouse her suddenly, and in the most exciting manner, from her melancholy.

No child of tender age ever unexpectedly came before the eyes of Ruth Heathcote without painfully recalling the image of the cherub she had lost.   The playful voice of infancy never surprised her ear, without the sound con- veying a pang to the heart ; nor could allusion, ever so remote, be made to persons or events that bore resemblance to the sad incidents of her own life, without quickening the never-dying pulses of maternal love.   No wonder, then, that when she found herself in the situation, and under the circumstances described, that nature grew strong within her, and that her mind caught glimpses, however dim and indistinct they might be, of a truth that the reader has already anticipated.   Still a certain and intelligible clue was wanting.   Fancy had ever painted her child in the innocence and infancy in which it had been torn from her arms ; and here, while there was so much to correspond with reasonable expectation, there was little to answer to the long and fondly cherished picture. The delusion, if so holy and natural a feeling may thus be termed, had been too deeply seated to be dispossessed at a glance. Gazing long, earnestly, and with features that varied with every changing feeling, she held the stranger at the length of her two arms, alike unwilling to release her hold, or to admit her closer to a heart which might rightfully be the property of another.

"Who art thou?" demanded the mother, in a voice that was tremulous with the emotions of that sacred character. "Speak, mysterious and lovely being; who art thou?"

Narra-mattah had turned a terrified and imploring look at the immovable and calm form of her husband, as if she sought protection from him at whose hands she had been accustomed to receive it. But a different sensation took possession of her mind when she heard sounds which had too often soothed the ear of infancy ever to be forgotten. Struggling ceased, and her pliant form assumed the attitude of intense and entranced attention. Her head was bent aside, as if the ear were eager to drink in a repetition of the tones, while her bewildered and delighted eye still sought the countenance of her husband.

"Vision of the woods, wilt thou not answer?" continued Ruth. "If there is reverence for the Holy One of Israel in thine heart, answer, that I may know thee!"

"Hist, Conanchet!" murmured the wife, over whose features the glow of pleased and wild surprise continued to deepen. "Come nearer, Sachem; the spirit that talketh to Narra-mattah in her dreams is nigh."

"Woman of the Yengeese!" said the husband, advancing with dignity to the spot, "let the clouds blow from thy sight. Wife of a Narragansett, see clearly. The Manitou of your race speaks strong. He telleth a mother to know her child."

Ruth could hesitate no longer; neither sound nor exclamation escaped her, but, as she strained the yielding frame of her recovered daughter to her heart, it appeared as if she strove to incorporate the two bodies into one. A cry of pleasure and astonishment drew all around her.

Then came the evidence of the power of nature, when strongly awakened.   Age and youth alike acknowledged its potency, and recent alarms were overlooked, in the pure joy of such a moment.   The spirit of even the lofty minded Conanchet was shaken. Raising the hand at whose wrist still hung the bloody tomahawk, he veiled his face, and, turning aside, that none might see the weakness of so great a warrior, he wept.

CHAPTER V.

One sees more devils than vast hell can hold ;
That is, the madman.   *Midsummer Night's Dream.*

On quitting the hill, Philip summoned his Wompanoags, and, supported by the obedient and fierce Annawon, a savage that might, under better auspices, have proved a worthy lieutenant to Cæsar, he left the fields of Wish-Ton-Wish.   Accustomed to see these sudden outbreakings of temper in their leaders, the followers of Conanchet, who would have preserved their air of composure under far more trying circumstances, saw him depart equally without question and without alarm.   But when their own Sachem appeared on the ground which was still red with the blood of the combatants, and made known his intention to abandon a conquest that seemed more than half achieved, he was not heard without murmuring.   The authority of an Indian chief is far from despotic ; and though there is reason to think it is often aided, if not generated, by the accidental causes of birth and descent, it receives its main support in the personal qualities of him who rules.   Happily for the Narragansett leader, even his renowned father, the hapless Miantonimoh, had not purchased a higher name for wisdom or for daring, than that which had been fairly won by his still youthful son.   The savage humours, and the rankling desire for vengeance in the boldest of his subalterns, were made to quail before the menacing glances of an eye that seldom threatened without performance; nor was there one of them all, when challenged to come forth to brave the anger or to oppose the eloquence of his chief, who did not shrink from a contest which habitual respect had taught them to believe would be too unequal for success. Within less than an hour after Ruth had clasped her child to her bosom, the invaders had disappeared. The dead of their party were withdrawn and concealed with the usual care, in order that no scalp of a warrior might be left in the hands of his enemies.

It was not unusual for the Indians to retire satisfied with the results of their first blow. So much of their military success was dependent on surprise, that it oftener happened the retreat commenced with the failure of the onset, than that victory was obtained by perseverance.

So long as the battle raged, their courage was equal to all its dangers; but, among people who made so great a merit of artifice, it is not at all surprising that they seldom put more to the hazard than was justified by the most severe discretion. When it was known, therefore, that the foe had disappeared in the forest, the inhabitants of the village were more ready to believe the movement was the result of their own manful resistance, than to seek motives that might not prove so soothing to their self-esteem. The retreat was thought to be quite in rule; and though prudence forbade pursuit, able and well-limbed scouts were sent on their trail, as well to prevent a renewal of the surprise, as to enable the forces of the colony to know the tribe of their enemies, and the direction which they had taken.

A scene of solemn ceremonies, and of deep affliction, followed. Though the parties led by Dudley and the Lieutenant had been so fortunate as to escape with a few immaterial wounds, the soldiers headed by Content, with the exception of those already named, had fallen to a man. Death had struck, at a blow, twenty of the most efficient individuals out of that isolated and simple community. Under circumstances in which victory was so barren, and so dearly bought, sorrow was a feeling stronger than rejoicing. Exultation took the aspect of humility; and

Y

while men were conscious of their well deserving, they were the most sensible of their dependence on a power they could neither influence nor comprehend. The characteristic opinions of the religionists became still more exalted, and the close of the day was quite as remarkable for an exhibition of the peculiarly exaggerated impressions of the colonists, as its opening had been frightful for vio‐ lence and bloodshed.

When one of the more active of the runners returned with the news that the Indians had retired through the forest with a broad trail, a sure sign that they meditated no further concealment near the valley, and that they had already been traced many miles on their retreat, the vil‐ lagers returned to their habitations. The dead were then distributed among those who claimed the nearest right to the performance of the last duties of affection ; and it might have been truly said, that mourning had taken up its abode in nearly every dwelling. The ties of blood were so general in a society thus limited, and, where they failed, the charities of life were so intimate and so natural, that not an individual of them all escaped without feeling that the events of the day had robbed him, for ever, of some one on whom he was partially dependent for comfort or happiness.

As the day drew towards its close, the little bell again summoned the congregation to the church. On this solemn occasion but few of those who still lived to hear its sounds were absent. The moment when Meek arose for prayer was one of general and intense feeling. The places so lately occupied by those who had fallen were now empty, and they resembled so many eloquent blanks in the de‐ scription of what had passed, expressing more than lan‐ guage could impart. The appeal of the divine was in his usual strain of sublimated piety, mysterious insights into the hidden purposes of Providence being strangely blended with the more intelligible wants and passions of man. While he gave Heaven the glory of the victory, he spoke with a lofty and pretending humility of the instruments of its power ; and although seemingly willing to acknowledge that his people abundantly deserved the heavy blow which had alighted on them, there was an evident impatience of the agents by which it had been inflicted. The principles of the sectarian were so singularly qualified by the feelings of the borderer, that one subtle in argument would have found little difficulty in detecting flaws in the reasoning of this zealot; but as so much was obscured by metaphysical mists, and so much was left for the generalities of doctrine, his hearers, without an exception, made such an application of what he uttered, as apparently rendered every mind sa-tisfied.

The sermon was as extemporaneous as the prayer, if any thing can come extempore from a mind so drilled and fortified in opinion. It contained much the same matter, delivered a little less in the form of an apostrophe. The stricken congregation, while they were encouraged with the belief that they were vessels set apart for some great and glorious end of Providence, were plainly told that they merited far heavier affliction than this which had now be-fallen; and they were reminded that it was their duty to desire even condemnation, that He who framed the heavens and the earth might be glorified! Then they heard com-fortable conclusions, which might reasonably teach them to expect that, though in the abstract such were the obligations of the real Christian, there was good reason to think that all who listened to doctrines so pure would be remembered with an especial favour.

So useful a servant of the temple as Meek Wolfe did not forget the practical application of his subject. It is true, that no visible emblem of the cross was shown to excite his hearers, nor were they stimulated to loosen blood-hounds on the trail of their enemies; but the former was kept suffi-ciently before the mind's eye by constant allusions to its merits, and the Indians were pointed at as the instruments by which the great father of evil hoped to prevent " the wilderness from blossoming like the rose," and " yielding the sweet savours of godliness." Philip and Conanchet were openly denounced by name, some dark insinuations being made that the person of the former was no more than the favourite tenement of Moloch; while the hearer was left to devise a suitable spirit for the government of the

physical powers of the other, from among any of the more
evil agencies that were named in the Bible.   Any doubts
of the lawfulness of the contest, that might assail tender
consciences, were brushed away by a bold and decided
hand.   There was no attempt at justification, however, for
all difficulties of this nature were resolved by the imper_
ative obligations of duty.   A few ingenious allusions to the
manner in which the Israelites dispossessed the occupants
of Judea were of great service in this particular part of
the subject, since it was not difficult to convince men, who
so strongly felt the impulses of religious excitement, that
they were stimulated rightfully.   Fortified by this advan_
tage, Mr. Wolfe manifested no desire to avoid the main
question.   He affirmed that if the empire of the true faith
could be established by no other means — a circumstance
which he assumed it was sufficiently apparent to all under-
standings could not be done — he pronounced it the duty
of young and old, the weak and the strong, to unite in
assisting to visit the former possessors of the country with
what he termed the wrath of an offended Deity.   He spoke
of the fearful slaughter of the preceding winter, in which
neither years nor sex had been spared, as a triumph of the
righteous cause, and as an encouragement to persevere.
Then by a transition, that was not extraordinary in an age
so remarkable for religious subtleties, Meek returned to the
more mild and obvious truths which pervade the doctrines
of Him whose church he professed to uphold.   His hearers
were admonished to observe lives of humility and charity,
and were piously dismissed, with his benediction, to their
several homes.

The congregation quitted the building with the feelings
of men who thought themselves favoured by peculiar and
extraordinary communications with the Author of all truth ;
while the army of Mahomet itself was scarcely less influenced by fanaticism, than these blinded zealots.   There
was something so grateful to human frailty in reconciling
their resentments and their temporal interests to their religious duties, that it should excite little wonder, when we
add that most of them were fully prepared to become
ministers of vengeance in the hands of any bold leader.

While the inhabitants of the settlement were thus struggling between passions so contradictory, the shades of evening gradually fell upon their village, and then came darkness with the rapid strides with which it follows the setting of the sun in a low latitude.

Some time before the shadows of the trees were getting the grotesque and exaggerated forms which precede the last rays of the luminary, and while the people were still listening to their pastor, a solitary individual was placed on a giddy eyrie, whence he might note the movements of those who dwelt in the hamlet, without being the subject of observation himself. A short spur of the mountain projected into the valley, on the side nearest to the dwelling of the Heathcotes. A little tumbling brook, which the melting of the snows, and the occasionally heavy rains of the climate periodically increased into a torrent, had worn a deep ravine in its rocky bosom. Time and the constant action of water, aided by the driving storms of winter and autumn, had converted many of the different faces of this ravine into wild-looking pictures of the residences of men. There was one spot in particular, around which a closer inspection than that which the distance of the houses in the settlement offered, might have detected more plausible signs of the agency of human hands, than any that were afforded by the fancied resemblances of fantastic angles and accidental formations.

Precisely at the point where a sweep of the mountain permitted the best view of the valley, the rocks assumed the wildest, the most confused, and consequently the most favourable appearance for the construction of any residence which it was desirable should escape the curious eyes of the settlers, at the same time that it possessed the advantage of overlooking their proceedings. A hermit would have chosen the place as a spot suited to distant and calm observation of the world, while it was every way adapted to solitary reflection and ascetic devotion. All who have journeyed through the narrow and water-worn vineyards and meadows which are washed by the Rhone, ere that river pours its tribute into the Lake of Leman, have seen some such site, occupied by one who has devoted his life to seclusion and

the altar, overhanging the village of St. Maurice, in the can_
ton of Valais. But there is an air of obtrusiveness in the
Swiss hermitage that did not belong to the place of which
we write, since the one is perched upon its high and narrow
ledge as if to show the world in what dangerous and circumscribed limits God may be worshipped, while the other
sought exemption from absolute solitude, while it courted
secrecy with the most jealous caution. A small hut had
been erected against the side of the rock, in a manner to
present an oblique angle to the front. Care had been taken
to surround it with such natural objects, as left little reason
to apprehend that its real character could be known by any
who did not absolutely mount to the difficult shelf on
which it stood. Light entered into this primitive and
humble abode by a window that looked into the ravine, and
a low door opened on the side next the valley. The con_
struction was partly of stone and partly of logs, with a roof
of bark, and a chimney of mud and sticks.

One, who, by his severe and gloomy brow, was a fit
possessor of so secluded a tenement, was, at the hour named,
seated on a stone at the most salient angle of the mountain,
and at the place where the eye commanded the widest and
least obstructed view of the distant abodes of man. Stones
had been rolled together, in a manner to form a little
breast-work in his front, so that had there been any wan_
dering gaze sweeping over the face of the mountain, it was
far from probable that it would have detected the presence
of a man whose whole form, with the exception of the
head and shoulders, was so effectually concealed.

It would have been difficult to say whether this secluded
being had thus placed himself, in order to indulge in some
habitual and fancied communication with the little world
of the valley, or whether he sat at his post in watchfulness.
There was an appearance of each of these occupations in
his air ; for at times his eye was melancholy and softened,
as if his spirit found pleasure in the charities natural to
the species, and at others, the brows contracted with sternness, while the lips became more than usually compressed,
like those of a man who threw himself on his own innate
resolution for support.

The solitude of the place, the air of universal quiet which reigned above, the boundless leafy carpet, which he over-looked from that elevated point, and the breathing stillness of the bosom of the woods, united to give grandeur to the scene. The figure of the tenant of the ravine was as im-movable as any other object of the view. It seemed, in all but colour and expression, of stone. An elbow was leaning on the little rampart in front, and the head was supported by a hand. At the distance of an arrow's flight, he might readily have been supposed no more than another of the accidental imitations which had been worn in the rock by the changes of centuries. An hour passed, and scarce a limb was changed or a muscle relieved. Either contemplation, or the patient awaiting of some looked-for event appeared to suspend the ordinary functions of life. At length an interruption occurred to this extraordinary inaction. A rustling, not louder than that which would have been made by the leap of a squirrel, was first heard in the bushes above; it was succeeded by a crackling of branches, and then a fragment of a rock came bounding down the precipice, until it shot over the head of the still motionless hermit, and fell, with a noise that drew a suc-cession of echoes from the caverns of the place, into the ravine beneath.

Notwithstanding the suddenness of this interruption, and the extraordinary fracas with which it was accompanied, he who it might be supposed would have been most affected by it, manifested none of the usual symptoms of surprise. He listened intently, until the last sound had died away, but it was with expectation rather than with alarm. Arising slowly, he looked warily about him, and then, walking with a quick step along the ledge which led to his hut, he disappeared through its door. In another minute, how-ever, he was again seen at his former post; a short carabine, such as was then used by mounted warriors, lying across his knee. If doubt or perplexity beset the mind of this individual, at so palpable a sign that the solitude he courted was in danger of being interrupted, it was not of a nature sufficiently strong to disturb the equanimity of his aspect. A second time the branches rustled, and the sounds pro-

ceeded from a lower part of the precipice, as if the foot
that caused the disturbance was in the act of descending.
Though no one was visible, the nature of the noise could
no longer be mistaken. It was evidently the tread of a
human foot, for no beast of a weight sufficient to produce
so great an impression, would have chosen to rove across
a spot where the support of hands was nearly as necessary
as that of the other limbs.

" Come forward !" said he, who, in all but the accessories of dress and hostile preparation, might so well be
termed a hermit — " I am here."

The words were not given to the air, for one suddenly
appeared on the ledge at the side next the settlement, and
within twenty feet of the speaker. When glance met
glance, the surprise which evidently took possession of the
intruder and of him who appeared to claim a better right
to be where they met, seemed mutual. The carabine of
the latter, and a musket carried by the former, fell into
the dangerous line of aim at the same instant, and in a
moment they were thrown upwards again, as if a common
impulse controlled them. The resident signed to the other
to draw nigher, and then every appearance of hostility
disappeared in that sort of familiarity which is begotten
by confidence.

" How is it," said the former to his guest, when both
were calmly seated behind the little screen of stones, " that
thou hast fallen upon this secret place ? The foot of
stranger hath not often trod these rocks, and no man before
thee hath ever descended the precipice."

" A moccasin is sure," returned the other, with Indian
brevity. " My father hath a good eye. He can see very
far from the door of his lodge."

" Thou knowest that the men of my colour speak often
to their Good Spirit, and they do not love to ask his favour
in the highways. This place is sacred to his holy name."

The intruder was the young Sachem of the Narragansetts, and he who, notwithstanding this plausible apology,
so palpably sought secrecy rather than solitude, was the
man that has often been introduced into these pages under
the shade of mystery. The instant recognition, and the

mutual confidence, require no further explanation, since enough has already been developed in the course of the narrative, to show that they were not strangers to each other. Still the meeting had not taken place without uneasiness on the one part, and great, though admirably veiled, surprise on the other. As became his high station and lofty character, the bearing of Conanchet betrayed none of the littleness of a vulgar curiosity. He met his ancient acquaintance with the calm dignity of his rank, and it would have been difficult for the most enquiring eye to have detected a wandering glance, a single prying look, or any other sign that he deemed the place at all extraordinary for such an interview. He listened to the little explanation of the other with courtesy, suffering a short time to elapse before he made a reply.

" The Manitou of the pale men," he then said, " should be pleased with my father. His words are often in the ears of his Great Spirit! The trees and the rocks know them."

" Like all of a sinful and fallen race," returned the stranger with the severe air of an ascetic, " I have much need of my askings. But why dost thou think that my voice is so often heard in this secret place ? "

The finger of Conanchet pointed to the worn rock at his feet, and his eye glanced furtively at the beaten path which led between the spot and the door of the lodge.

" A Yengeese hath a hard heel, but it is softer than stone. The hoof of the deer would pass many times to leave such a trail."

" Thou art quick of eye, Narragansett, and yet thy judgment may be deceived. My tongue is not the only one that speaketh to the God of my people."

The Sachem bent his head slightly, in acquiescence, as if unwilling to press the subject. But his companion was not so easily satisfied, for he felt the consciousness of a fruitless attempt at deception goading him to some plausible means of quieting the suspicions of the Indian.

" That I am now alone may be matter of pleasure or of accident," he added ; " thou knowest that this hath been a busy and a bloody day among the pale men, and there are dead and dying in their lodges. One who hath no wigwam of his own may have retired to worship by himself."

" The mind is very cunning," returned Conanchet; " it can hear when the ear is deaf; it can see when the eye is shut. My father hath spoken to the Good Spirit with the rest of his tribe."

As the chief concluded, he pointed significantly towards the distant church, out of which the excited congregation we have described was at that moment pouring into the green and little trodden street of the hamlet. The other appeared to understand his meaning, and at the same instant, to feel the folly, as well as the uselessness, of attempting any longer to mislead one that already knew so much of his former mode of life.

" Indian, thou sayest true," he rejoined, gloomily: " the mind seeth far, and it seeth often in the bitterness of sorrow. My spirit was communing with the spirits of those thou seest, when thy step was first heard; besides thine own, the feet of man never mounted to this place, except it be of those who minister to my bodily wants. Thou sayest true; the mental sight is keen; and far beyond those distant hills, on which the last rays of the setting sun are now shining so gloriously, doth mine often bear me in spirit. Thou wast once my fellow-lodger, youth, and much pleasure had I in striving to open thy young mind to the truths of our race, and to teach thee to speak with the tongue of a Christian; but years have passed away — Hark! There cometh one up the path. Hast thou dread of a Yengeese?"

The calm mien with which Conanchet had been listening, changed to a cold smile. His hand had felt for the lock of the musket some time before his companion betrayed any consciousness of the approaching footstep; but until questioned, no change of his countenance was visible.

" Is my father afraid for his friend?" he asked, pointing in the direction of him who approached. " Is it an armed warrior?"

" No; he cometh with the means of sustaining a burden that must be borne, until it pleaseth Him, who knoweth what is good for his creatures, to ease me of it. It may be the parent of her thou hast this day restored to her friends, or it may be the brother; for, at times, I owe this kindness to different members of that worthy family.

A look of intelligence shot across the swarthy features of the chief. His decision appeared taken. Arising, he left his weapon at the feet of his companion, and moved swiftly along the ledge, as if to meet the intruder. In another instant he returned, bearing a little bundle closely enveloped in belts of richly beaded wampum. Placing the latter gently by the side of the old man, for time had changed the colour of the solitary's hair to grey, he said, in a low, quick voice, pointing with significance at what he had done,—

" The messenger will not go back with an empty hand. My father is wise; he will say what is good."

There was little time for explanation. The door of the hut had scarcely closed on Conanchet before young Mark Heathcote appeared at the point where the path bent around the angle of the precipice.

" Thou knowest what has passed, and wilt suffer me to depart with brief discourse," said the young man, placing food at the feet of him he came to seek. " Ha! what hast here?—didst gain this in the fray of the morning?"

" It is booty that I freely bestow; take it to the house of thy father: it is left with that object. Now tell me of the manner in which death hath dealt with our people, for thou knowest that necessity drove me from among them, so soon as leave was granted."

Mark showed no disposition to gratify the other's wish. He gazed on the bundle of Conanchet, as if his eye had never before looked on a similar object, and keenly contending passions were playing about a brow that was seldom as tranquil as suited the self-denying habits of the times and country.

" It shall be done, Narragansett!" he said, speaking between his clenched teeth; " it shall be done!" then turning on his heel he stalked along the giddy path, with a rapidity of stride that kept the other in fearful suspense for his safety until his active form had disappeared.

The recluse arose, and sought the occupant of his humble abode.

" Come forth," he said, opening the narrow door for the passage of the chief.   " The youth hath departed with thy burden, and thou art now alone with an ancient associate."

Conanchet re-appeared at the summons, but it was with an eye less glowing, and a brow less stern, than when he entered the little cabin.

As he moved slowly to the stone he had before occupied, his step was arrested for a moment, and a look of melancholy regret seemed to be cast at the spot where he had laid the bundle.   Conquering his feelings, however, in the habitual self-command of his people, he resumed his seat with the air of one that was grave by nature, while he appeared to exert no effort in order to preserve the admirable equanimity of his features.   A long and thoughtful silence succeeded, and then the recluse spoke.

" We have made a friend of the Narragansett chief," he said, " and his league with Philip is broken ? "

" Yengeese," returned the other, " I am full of the blood of Sachems."

" Why should the Indian and the white do each other this violence ?   The earth is large, and there is place for men of all colours and of all nations on its surface."

" My father hath found but little," said the other, bestowing such a cautious glance at the narrow limits of his host as at once betrayed the sarcastic purport of his words, while it equally bespoke the courtesy of his mind.

" A light-minded and vain prince is seated on the throne of a once godly nation, chief ; and darkness has again come over a land, which, of late, shone with a clear and shining light !   The just are made to flee from the habitations of their infancy, and the temples of the elect are abandoned to the abominations of idolatry.   Oh, England ! England ! when will thy cup of bitterness be full — when shall this judgment pass from thee — my spirit groaneth over thy fall — yea, my inmost soul is saddened with the spectacle of thy misery and thy downfall ! "

Conanchet was too delicate to regard the glazed eye and

flushed forehead of the speaker, but he listened in amazement and in ignorance. Such expressions had often met his ear before, and though his tender years had probably prevented their producing much effect, now that he again heard them in his manhood, they conveyed no intelligible meaning to his mind. Suddenly laying a finger on the knee of his companion, he said,—

" The arm of my father was raised on the side of the Yengeese to-day ; yet they give him no seat at their council-fire ! "

" The sinful man, who ruleth in the island whence my people came, hath an arm that is as long as his mind is vain. Though debarred from the councils of this valley, chief, time hath been when my voice was heard in councils that struck heavily at the power of his race. These eyes have seen justice done on him, who gave existence to the double-tongued instrument of Belial, that now governeth a rich and glorious realm ! "

" My father's hand hath taken the scalp of a great chief ! "

" It helped to take his head ! " returned the other, a ray of exultation gleaming through the habitual austerity of his brow.

" Come. The eagle flies above the clouds that he may move his wings freely. The panther leaps longest on the widest plain ; the biggest fish swim in the deep water. My father cannot stretch himself between these rocks. He is too big to lie down in a little wigwam. The woods are wide ; let him change the colour of his skin and be a grey head at the council-fire of my nation. The warriors will listen to what he says, for his hand hath done a strong deed ! "

" It may not be — it may not be, Narragansett. That which hath been generated in the spirit must abide, and it would be ' easier for the blackamoor to become white, or for the leopard to change his spots,' than for one who hath felt the power of the Lord to cast aside his gifts. But I meet thy proffers of amity in a charitable and forgiving spirit. My mind is ever with my people ; yet is there place for other friendships. Break, then, this league with the evil-minded and turbulent Philip, and let the hatchet be for ever buried in the path between thy village and the towns of the Yengeese."

" Where is my village ?   There is a dark place near the islands, on the shores of the Great Lake, but I see no lodges."

" We will rebuild thy towns and people them anew Let there be peace between us."

" My mind is ever with my people," returned the Indian, repeating the other's words with an emphasis that could not be mistaken.

A long and melancholy pause succeeded ; and when the conversation was renewed, it had reference to those events which had taken place in the fortunes of each since the time when they were both tenants of the block-house that once stood amid the habitations of the Heathcotes.   Each appeared too well to comprehend the character of the other, to attempt any further efforts towards producing a change of purpose, and darkness had gathered about the place before they arose to enter the hut.

CHAPTER VI.

Sleep, thou hast been a grandsire, and begot
A father to me ; and thou hast created
A mother and two brothers.   *Cymbeline.*

THE short twilight was already passed, when old Mark Heathcote ended the evening prayer.   The mixed character of the remarkable events of that day had given birth to a feeling, which could find no other relief than that which flowed from the usual zealous, confiding, and exalted outpouring of the spirit.   On the present occasion, he had even resorted to an extraordinary, and, what one less devout might be tempted to think a supererogatory, offering of thanksgiving and praise.   After dismissing the dependents of the establishment, supported by the arm of his son he withdrew into an inner apartment, and there, surrounded only by those who had the nearest claims on his affections, the old man again raised his voice to laud the Being who, in the midst of so much general grief, had deigned to look upon his race with the eyes of remembrance and favour. He spoke of his recovered grandchild by name, and he dealt with the whole subject of her captivity among the heathen, and her restoration to the foot of the altar, with the fervour of one who saw the wise decrees of Providence in the event, and with a tenderness of sentiment that age was far from having extinguished. It is at the close of this private and peculiar worship that we return into the presence of the family.

The spirit of reform had driven those who so violently felt its influence into many usages that, to say the least, were quite as ungracious to the imagination as the customs they termed idolatrous were obnoxious to the attacks of their own unaccommodating theories. The first Protestants had expelled so much from the service of the altar, that little was left for the Puritan to destroy without incurring the risk of leaving it naked of its loveliness. By a strange substitution of subtlety for humility, it was thought pharisaical to bend the knee in public, leat the great essential of spiritual worship might be supplanted by the more attainable merit of form ; and while rigid aspects, and prescribed deportments of a new character, were observed with all the zeal of converts, ancient and even natural practices were condemned, chiefly we believe, from that necessity of innovation which appears to be an unavoidable attendant of all plans of improvement, whether they are successful or otherwise. But though the Puritans refused to bow their stubborn limbs when the eye of man was on them, even while asking boons suited to their own sublimated opinions, it was permitted to assume in private an attitude which was thought to admit of so gross an abuse, inasmuch as it infers a claim to a religious vitality while, in truth, the soul might only be slumbering in the security of mere moral pretension.

On the present occasion, they who worshipped in secret, had bent their bodies to the humblest posture of devotion.

When Ruth Heathcote arose from her knees, her hand
was clasped in that of the child whom her recent devotion
was well suited to make her think had been rescued from
a condition far more gloomy than that of the grave.   She
had used a gentle violence to force the wondering being at
her side to join, so far as externals could go, in the prayer;
and now it was ended, she sought the countenance of her
daughter, in order to read the impression the scene had
produced, with the solicitude of a Christain, heightened by
the tenderest maternal love.

Narra-mattah, as we shall continue to call her, in air,
expression, and attitude, resembled one who had a fancied
existence in the delusion of some exciting dream.   Her
ear remembered sounds which had so often been repeated
in her infancy, and her memory recalled indistinct recollections of most of the objects and usages that were so suddenly replaced before her eyes ; but the former now conveyed their meaning to a mind that had gained its strength
under a very different system of theology, and the latter
came too late to supplant usages that were rooted in her
affections, by the aid of all those wild and seductive habits
that are known to become nearly unconquerable in those
who have once been fairly subject to their influence.   She
stood, therefore, in the centre of the grave, self-restrained
group of her nearest kin, like an alien to their blood, resembling some timid and but half-tamed tenant of the air, that
human heart had endeavoured to domesticate by placing it
in the society of the more tranquil and confiding inhabitants
of the aviary.

Notwithstanding the strength of her affections, and her
devotion to all the natural duties of her station, Ruth
Heathcote was not now to learn the manner in which she
was to subdue any violence in their exhibition.   The first
indulgence of joy and gratitude was over, and in its place
appeared the never-tiring, vigilant, engrossing, but regulated
watchfulness, which the events would naturally create.   The
doubts, misgivings, and even fearful apprehensions that
beset her, were smothered in an appearance of satisfaction; and something like gleamings of happiness were again

seen playing about a brow that had so long been clouded with an unobtrusive but corroding care.

"And thou recallest thine infancy, my Ruth?" asked the mother, when the respectful period of silence, which ever succeeded prayer in that family, was passed; "thy thoughts have not been altogether strangers to us, but nature hath had its place in thy heart. Tell us, child, of thy wanderings in the forest, and of the sufferings that one so tender must have undergone, among a barbarous people. There is pleasure in listening to all thou hast seen and felt, now that we know there is an end to thy unhappiness."

She spoke to an ear that was deaf to language like this. Narra-mattah evidently understood her words, while their meaning was wrapped in an obscurity that she neither wished to comprehend, nor was capable of comprehending. Keeping a gaze, in which pleasure and wonder were powerfully blended, on the soft look of affection which beamed in her mother's eye, she felt hurriedly among the folds of her dress, and drawing a belt that was gaily ornamented after the most ingenious fashion of her adopted people, she approached her half-pleased, half-distressed parent, and, with hands that trembled equally with timidity and pleasure, she arranged it around her person, in a manner to show its richness to the best advantage. Pleased with her performance, the artless being eagerly sought approbation in eyes that bespoke little else than regret. Alarmed at an expression she could not translate, the gaze of Narra-mattah wandered, as if it sought support against some sensation to which she was a stranger. Whittal Ring had stolen into the room, and missing the customary features of her own cherished home, the looks of the startled creature rested on the countenance of the witless wanderer. She pointed eagerly at the work of her hands, appealing by an eloquent and artless gesture to the taste of one who should know whether she had done well.

"Bravely!" returned Whittal, approaching nearer to the subject of her admiration:—"'t is a brave belt, and none but the wife of a Sachem could make so rare a gift!"

The girl folded her arms meekly on her bosom, and appeared satisfied with herself and with the world.

z

" Here is the hand of him visible who dealeth in all
wickedness," said the Puritan. " To corrupt the heart
with vanities, and to mislead the affections, by luring them
to the things of life, is the guile in which he delighteth.
A fallen nature lendeth but too ready aid. We must deal
with the child in fervour and watchfulness, or better that
her bones were lying by the side of those little ones of thy
flock, who are already inheritors of the promise."

Respect kept Ruth silent; but while she sorrowed over
the ignorance of her child, natural affection was strong at
her heart. With the tact of a woman, and the tenderness
of a mother, she both saw and felt that severity was not
the means to effect the improvement they desired. Taking
a seat herself, she drew her child to her person, and first,
imploring silence by a glance at those around her, she
proceeded in a manner that was dictated by the mysterious
influence of nature, to fathom the depth of her daughter's
mind.

" Come nearer, Narra-mattah," she said, using the name
to which the other would alone answer. " Thou art still
in thy youth, my child, but it hath pleased Him whose
will is law, to have made thee the witness of many changes
in this varying life. Tell me if thou recallest the days of
infancy, and if thy thoughts ever returned to thy father's
house, during those weary years thou wast kept from our
view ? "

Ruth used gentle force to draw her daughter nearer
while speaking, and the latter sunk into that posture, from
which she had just arisen, kneeling as she had often done
in infancy, at her mother's side. The attitude was too
full of tender recollections not to be grateful, and the half
alarmed being of the forest was suffered to retain it, during
most of the dialogue that followed. But while she was
thus obedient in person, by the vacancy or rather the
wonder of an eye that was so eloquent to express all the
emotions and knowledge of which she was the mistress,
Narra-mattah plainly manifested that little more than the
endearment of her mother's words and manner was intelligible. Ruth saw the meaning of her hesitation, and

smothering the pang it caused, she endeavoured to adapt her language to the habits of one so artless.

" Even the grey heads of thy people were once young," she resumed ; " and they remember the lodges of their fathers. Does my daughter ever think of the time when she played among the children of the pale-faces ? "

The attentive being at the knee of Ruth listened greedily. Her knowledge of the language of her childhood had been sufficiently implanted, before her captivity, and it had been too often exercised by intercourse with the whites, and more particularly with Whittal Ring, to leave her in any doubt of the meaning of what she now heard. Stealing a timid look over a shoulder, she sought the countenance of Martha, and studying her lineaments for near a minute, with intense regard, she laughed aloud in the contagious merriment of an Indian girl.

" Thou hast not forgotten us ! That glance at her who was the companion of my infancy assures me, and we shall soon again possess our Ruth in affection, as we now possess her in the body. I will not speak to thee of that fearful night, when the violence of the savage robbed us of thy presence, nor of the bitter sorrow which beset us at thy loss ; but there is One who must still be known to thee, my child ; He who sitteth above the clouds, who holdeth the earth in the hollow of his hand, and who looketh in mercy on all that journey on the path to which his own finger pointeth. Hath He yet a place in thy thoughts ? Thou rememberest his holy name, and still thinkest of his power ? "

The listener bent her head aside, as if to catch the meaning of what she heard, the shadows of deep reverence passing over a face that had so lately been smiling. After a pause she murmured the word,—

" Manitou."

" Manitou, or Jehovah ; God, or King of kings and Lord of lords! it mattereth little which term is used to express his power. Thou knowest him, then, and hast never ceased to call upon his name ? "

" Narra-mattah is a woman. She is afraid to speak to

z 2

the Manitou aloud. He knows the voices of the chiefs,
and opens his ears when they ask help."

The Puritan groaned, but Ruth succeeded in quelling
her own anguish, lest she should disturb the reviving confidence of her daughter.

" This may be the Manitou of an Indian," she said,
" but it is not the Christian's God. Thou art of a race
which worships differently, and it is proper that thou
shouldst call on the name of the Deity of thy fathers.
Even the Narragansett teacheth this truth ! Thy skin is
white, and thy ears should hearken to the traditions of the
men of thy blood."

The head of the daughter dropped at this allusion to
her colour, as if she would fain conceal the mortifying
truth from every eye ; but she had not time for answer,
ere Whittal Ring drew near, and pointing to the burning
colour of her cheeks, that were deepened as much with
shame as with the heats of an American sun, he said,—

" The wife of the Sachem hath begun to change. She
will soon be like Nipset, all red. — See," he added, laying
a finger on a part of his own arm where the sun and the
winds had not yet destroyed the original colour, " the evil
spirit poured water into his blood too, but it will come out
again. As soon as he is so dark that the evil spirit will
not know him, he will go on the war-path ; and then the
lying pale-faces may dig up the bones of their fathers, and
move towards the sunrise, or his lodge will be lined with
hair of the colour of a deer ! "

" And thou, my daughter, canst thou hear this threat
against the people of thy nation — of thy blood — of thy
God — without a shudder ? "

The eye of Narra-mattah seemed in doubt ; still it regarded Whittal with its accustomed look of kindness. The
innocent, full of his imaginary glory, raised his hand in
exultation, and by gestures that could not easily be mis-
understood, he indicated the manner in which he intended
to rob his victims of the usual trophy. While the youth
was enacting the disgusting but expressive pantomime,
Ruth watched the countenance of her child, in nearly
breathless agony. She would have been relieved by a

single glance of disapprobation, by a solitary movement
of a rebellious muscle, or by the smallest sign that the
tender nature of one so lovely, and otherwise so gentle,
revolted at this unequivocal evidence of the barbarous
practices of her adopted people. But no empress of
Rome could have witnessed the dying agonies of the hapless gladiator, no consort of a more modern prince could
read the bloody list of the victims of her husband's triumph,
nor any betrothed fair listen to the murderous deeds of
him her imagination had painted as a hero, with less indifference to human suffering, than that with which the wife
of the Sachem of the Narragansetts looked on the mimic
representation of those exploits, which had purchased for
her husband a renown so highly prized. It was but too
apparent that the representation, rude and savage as it was,
conveyed to her mind nothing but pictures in which the
chosen companion of a warrior should rejoice. The varying features and answering eye too plainly proclaimed the
sympathy of one taught to exult in the success of the
combatant'; and when Whittal, excited by his own exertions, broke out into an exhibition of a violence more
ruthless even than common, he was openly rewarded by
another laugh. The soft, exquisitely feminine tones of
this involuntary burst of pleasure, sounded in the ears of
Ruth like a knell over the moral beauty of her child. Still
subduing her feelings, she passed a hand thoughtfully over
her own pallid brow, and appeared to muse long on the
desolation of a mind that had once promised to be so pure.

The colonists had not yet severed all those natural ties
which bound them to the eastern hemisphere. Their
legends, their pride, and, in many instances, their memo-
ries, aided in keeping alive a feeling of amity, and it might
be added of faith, in favour of the land of their ancestors.
With some of their descendants, even to the present hour,
the *beau ideal* of excellence, in all that pertains to human
qualities and human happiness, is connected with the
images of the country from which they sprung. Distance
is known to cast a softening mist, equally over the moral
and physical vision. The blue outline of mountain which
melts into its glowing back ground of sky, is not more

pleasing than the pictures which fancy sometimes draws of less material things, but, as he draws near, the disappointed traveller too often finds nakedness and deformity, where he so fondly imagined beauty only was to be seen. No wonder, then, that the dwellers of the simple provinces of New England blended recollections of the country they still called home, with most of their poetical pictures of life. They retained the language, the books, and most of the habits of the English. But different circumstances, divided interests, and peculiar opinions, were gradually beginning to open those breaches which time has since widened, and which promises soon to leave little in common between the two people, except the same forms of speech and a common origin, though it is to be hoped that some remains of charity may still be blended with these ties.

The singularly restrained habits of the religionists throughout the whole of the British provinces, were in marked opposition to the mere embellishments of life. The arts were permitted only as they served its most useful and obvious purposes. With them, music was confined to the worship of God, and, for a long time after the original settlement, the song was never known to lead the mind astray from what was conceived to be the one great object of existence. No verse was sung, but such as blended holy ideas with the pleasures of harmony, nor were the sounds of revelry ever heard within their borders. Still words adapted to their particular condition had come into use ; and though poetry was neither a common, nor a brilliant property of the mind, among a people thus disciplined in ascetic practices, it early exhibited its power in a quaint versification, that was intended, though with a success it is almost pardonable to doubt, to redound to the glory of the Deity. It was but a natural enlargement of this pious practice to adapt some of these spiritual songs to the purposes of the nursery.

When Ruth Heathcote passed her hand thoughtfully across her brow, she felt the painful conviction that her dominion over the mind of her child was sadly weakened, if not lost for ever. But the efforts of maternal love are not easily repulsed. An idea flashed upon her brain, and she proceeded to try the efficacy of the experiment it suggested. Nature had endowed her with a melodious voice, and an ear that taught her to regulate sounds in a manner that seldom failed to touch the heart. She possessed the genius of music, which is melody, unweakened by those exaggerated affectations with which it is often encumbered by what is pretendingly called science. Drawing her daughter nearer to her knee, she commenced one of the songs then much used by the mothers of the colony, her voice scarcely rising above the whispering of the evening air, in its first notes, but gradually gaining as she proceeded, the richness and compass that a strain so simple required.

At the first low breathing notes of this nursery song, Narra-mattah became as motionless as if her rounded and unfettered form had been wrought in marble. Pleasure lighted her eyes, as strain succeeded strain, and ere the second verse was ended, her look, her attitude, and every muscle of her ingenuous features were eloquent in the expression of delight. Ruth did not hazard the experiment without trembling for its result. Emotion imparted feeling to the music, and when for the third time in the course of her song, she addressed her child, she saw the soft blue eyes that gazed wistfully on her face, swimming in tears. Encouraged by this unequivocal evidence of success, nature grew still more powerful in its efforts, and the closing verse was sung to an ear that nestled near her heart, as it had often done during the early years of Narra-mattah while listening to the melancholy melody.

Content was a quiet but an anxious witness of this touching evidence of a reviving intelligence between his wife and child. He best understood the look that beamed in the eyes of the former, while her arms were, with extreme caution, folded around her who still leaned upon her bosom, as if fearful one so timid might be frightened from her security by any sudden or unaccustomed interruption. A minute passed in the deepest silence. Even Whittal Ring was lulled into quiet, and long and sorrowing years had passed, since Ruth enjoyed moments of happiness so pure and unalloyed. The stillness was broken by a heavy step in the outer room ; a door was thrown open by a hand more violent than common, and then young Mark appeared, his face flushed with exertion, his brow seemingly retaining the frown of battle, and with a tread that betrayed a spirit goaded by some unwelcome passion. The burden of Conanchet was on his arm. He laid it upon a table; then pointing, in a manner that appeared to challenge attention, he turned and abruptly left the room.

A cry of joy burst from the lips of Narra-mattah the instant the beaded belts caught her eye. The arms of Ruth relaxed their hold in surprise; and before amazement had time to give place to more connected ideas, the wild being at her knee had flown to the table, returned, resumed her former posture, opened the folds of the cloth, and was holding before the bewildered gaze of her mother, the patient features of an Indian babe.

It would exceed the powers of the unambitious pen we wield, to convey to the reader a just idea of the mixed emotions that struggled for mastery in the countenance of Ruth. The innate and never-dying sentiment of maternal joy was opposed by all those feelings of pride that prejudice could not fail to implant, even in the bosom of one so meek. There was no need to tell the history of the parentage of the little suppliant, who already looked up into her face with the peculiar calm which renders his race so remarkable. Though its glance was weakened by infancy, the dark glittering eye of Conanchet was there; there were also to be seen the receding forehead, and the compressed lip of the father; but all these marks of his origin were softened by touches of that beauty which had rendered the infancy of her own child so remarkable.

" See !" said Narra-mattah, raising the infant still nearer to the rivetted gaze of Ruth; "'tis a Sachem of the red men ! The little eagle hath left his nest too soon."

Ruth could not resist the appeal of her beloved. Bending her head low, so as entirely to conceal her own flushed face, she imprinted a kiss on the forehead of the Indian boy. But the jealous eye of the young mother was not to be deceived. Narra-mattah detected the difference between the cold salute, and those fervent embraces she had herself received, and disappointment produced a chill about her own heart. Replacing the folds of the cloth with quiet dignity, she arose from her knees, and withdrew in sadness to a distant corner of the room. There she took a seat, and with a glance that might almost be termed reproachful, she commenced a low Indian song to her infant.

" The wisdom of Providence is in this, as in all its dispensations," whispered Content over the shoulder of his nearly insensible partner. " Had we received her as she was lost, the favour might have exceeded our deservings. Our daughter is grieved that thou turnest a cold eye on her babe."

The appeal was sufficient for one whose affections had been wounded rather than chilled. It recalled Ruth to recollection, and it served at once to dissipate the shades of regret that had been unconsciously permitted to gather round her brow. The displeasure, or it would be more true to term it sorrow, of the young mother was easily appeased. A smile on her infant brought the blood back to her heart in a swift and tumultuous current; and Ruth herself soon forgot that she had any reason for regret, in the innocent delight with which her own daughter now hastened to display the physical excellence of the boy. From this scene of natural feeling, Content was too quickly summoned by the intelligence that some one without awaited his presence on business of the last importance to the welfare of the settlement.

CHAPTER VII.

It will have blood : they say, blood
Will have blood.   *Macbeth.*

THE visiters were Dr. Ergot, the Rev. Meek Wolfe, Ensign Dudley, and Reuben Ring. Content found these four individuals seated in an outer room, in a grave and restrained manner, that would have done no discredit to the self-command of an Indian council. He was saluted with those staid and composed greetings which are still much used in the intercourse of the people of the eastern states of this republic, and which have obtained for them a reputation, where they are little known, of a want of the more active charities of our nature. But that was peculiarly the age of sublimated doctrines, of self-mortification, and of severe moral government, and most men believed it a merit to exhibit, on all occasions, the dominion of the mind over the mere animal impulses. The usage, which took its rise in exalted ideas of spiritual perfection, has since grown into a habit, which, though weakened by the influence of the age, still exists to a degree that often leads to an erroneous estimate of character.

At the entrance of the master of the house, there was some such decorous silence as that which is known to precede the communications of the Aborigines. At length Ensign Dudley, in whom matter, most probably in consequence of its bulk, bore more than an usual proportion to his less material part, manifested some signs of impatience that the divine should proceed to business. Thus admonished, or possibly conceiving that a sufficient concession had been made to the dignity of man's failing nature, Meek opened his mouth to speak.

" Captain Content Heathcote," he commenced, with that mystical involution of his subject which practice had rendered nearly inseparable from all his communications, — " Captain Content Heathcote, this hath been a day of awful visitations, and of gracious temporal gifts. The heathen hath been smitten severely by the hand of the believer, and the believer hath been made to pay the penalty of his want of faith, by the infliction of a savage agency. Azazel hath been loosened in our village, the legions of wickedness have been suffered to go at large in our fields, and yet the Lord hath remembered his people, and hath borne them through a trial of blood as perilous as was the passage of his chosen nation through the billows of the Red Sea. There is cause of mourning and cause of joy in this manifestation of his will ; of sorrow that we have merited his anger, and of rejoicing that enough of redeeming grace hath been found to save the Gomorrah of our hearts. But I speak to one trained in spiritual discipline, and schooled in the vicissitudes of the world, and further discourse is not necessary to quicken his apprehension. We will therefore turn to more instant and temporal exercises. Have all of thy household escaped unharmed throughout the strivings of this bloody day?"

" We praise the Lord that such hath been his pleasure," returned Content. " Except as sorrow hath assailed us through the mourning of friends, the blow hath fallen lightly on me and mine."

" Thou hast had thy season; the parent ceaseth to chastise while former punishments are remembered; but here is Sergeant Ring, with matter to communicate, that may still leave business for thy courage and thy wisdom."

Content turned his quiet look upon the yeoman, and seemed to await his speech. Reuben Ring, a man of many solid and valuable qualities, would most probably have been exercising the military functions of his brother-in-law, at that very moment, had he been equally gifted with a fluent discourse. But his feats lay rather in doing than in speaking, and the tide of popularity had, in consequence, set less strongly in his favour than might have happened had the reverse been the case. The present, however, was a moment when it was necessary to overcome his natural reluctance to speak, and it was not long before he replied to the enquiring glance of his commander's eye.

" The Captain knows the manner in which we scourged the savages at the southern end of the valley," the sturdy yeoman began, " and it is not necessary to deal with the particulars at length. There were six and twenty red skins slain in the meadows, besides as many more that left the ground in the arms of their friends. As for the people, we got a few hurts, but each man came back on his own limbs."

" This is much as the matter hath been reported."

" Then there was a party sent to brush the woods on the trail of the Indians," resumed Reuben, without appearing to regard the interruption. " The scouts broke off in pairs, and finally men got to searching singly, of which number

I was one. The two men of whom there is question ——"

" Of what men dost speak ?" demanded Content.

" The two men of whom there is question," returned the other, continuing the direct course of his own manner of relating events, without appearing to see the necessity of connecting the threads of his communication ; " the men of whom I have spoken to the minister and the Ensign——"

" Proceed," said Content, who understood his man.

" After one of these men was brought to his end, I saw no reason for making the day bloodier than it already was, the more especially as the Lord had caused it to begin with a merciful hand, which shed its bounties on my own dwelling. Under such an opinion of right doing, the other was bound and led into the clearings."

" Thou hast made a captive ?"

The lips of Reuben scarce severed as he muttered a low assent; but the Ensign Dudley took upon himself the duty of entering into further explanations, which the point where his kinsman left the narrative enabled him to do with sufficient intelligence.

" As the Sergeant hath related," he said, " one of the heathen fell, and the other is now without, awaiting a judgment in the matter of his fortune."

" I trust there is no wish to harm him," said Content, glancing an eye uneasily around at his companions. " Strife hath done enough in our settlement this day. The Sergeant hath a right to claim the scalp-bounty for the man that is slain, but for him that liveth, let there be mercy."

" Mercy is a quality of heavenly origin," replied Meek Wolfe, " and it should not be perverted to defeat the purposes of heavenly wisdom. Azazel must not triumph, though the tribe of the Narragansetts should be swept with the besom of destruction. Truly we are an erring and a fallible race, Captain Heathcote, and the greater, therefore, the necessity that we submit, without rebellion, to the inward monitors that are implanted, by grace, to teach us the road of our duty ——"

" I cannot consent to shed blood, now that the strife hath ceased," hastily interrupted Content. " Praised be

Providence, we are victors; and it is time to lean to councils of charity."

" Such are the deceptions of a short-sighted wisdom ! " returned the divine, his dim, sunken eye shining with the promptings of an exaggerated and subtle spirit. " The end of all is good, and we may not, without mortal danger, presume to doubt the suggestions of heavenly gifts. But there is no question here concerning the execution of the captive, since he proffereth to be of service in far greater things than any that can depend on his life or death. The heathen rendered up his liberty with little struggle, and hath propositions that may lead us to a profitable conclusion of this day's trials."

" If he can aid in aught that shall shorten the perils and wantonness of this ruthless war, he shall find none better disposed to listen than I."

" He professeth ability to do that service."

" Then, of Heaven's mercy, let him be brought forth, that we may take counsel on his proposals."

Meek made a gesture to Sergeant Ring, who quitted the apartment for a moment, and shortly after returned, followed by his captive. The Indian was one of those dark and malignant looking savages that possess most of the sinister properties of their condition, with few or none of the redeeming qualities. His eye was lowering and distrustful, bespeaking equally apprehension and revenge; his form of that middling degree of perfection which leaves as little to admire as to condemn, and his attire such as denoted him one who might be ranked among the warriors of a secondary class. Still, in the composure of his mien, the tranquillity of his step, and the self-possession of his movements, he displayed that high bearing his people rarely fail to exhibit, ere too much intercourse with the whites begins to destroy their distinctive traits.

" Here is the Narragansett," said Reuben Ring, causing his prisoner to appear in the centre of the room : " he is no chief, as may be gathered from his uncertain look."

" If he effect that of which there hath been question, his rank mattereth little. We seek to stop the currents of

blood that flow like running water in these devoted colonies."

" This will he do," rejoined the divine, " or we shall
hold him answerable for a breach of promise."

" And in what doth he profess to aid in stopping the
work of death ? "

" By yielding the fierce Philip, and his savage ally, the
roving Conanchet, to the judgment. Those chiefs destroyed, our temple may be entered in peace, and the voice
of thanksgiving shall again rise in our Bethel, without the
profane interruption of savage shrieks."

Content started, and even recoiled a step, as he listened
to the nature of the proposed peace-offering.

" And have we warranty for such a proceeding, should
this man prove true ? " he asked, in a voice that betrayed
his own doubts of the propriety of such a measure.

" There is the law, the necessities of a suffering nature,
and God's glory for our justification," dryly returned the
divine.

" This out-steppeth the discreet exercise of a delegated
authority. I like not to assume so great power, without
written mandates for its execution."

" The objection hath raised a little difficulty in my own
mind," observed Ensign Dudley ; " and as it hath set
thoughts at work, it is possible that what I have to offer
will meet the Captain's good approbation."

Content knew that his ancient servitor was, though
often uncouth in its exhibition, at the bottom a man of
humane heart. On the other hand, while he scarce admitted the truth to himself, he had a secret dread of the
exaggerated sentiments of his spiritual guide, and he consequently listened to the interruption of Eben, with a
gratification he scarcely wished to conceal.

" Speak openly," he said ; " when men counsel in a
matter of this weight, each standeth on the surety of his
proper gifts."

" Then may this business be despatched without the
embarrassment the Captain seems to dread. We have the
Indian, who offers to lead a party through the forests to

the haunts of the bloody chiefs, therein bringing affairs to
the issue of manhood and discretion."

" And wherein do you propose any departure from the
suggestions that have already been made ?"

Ensign Dudley had not risen to his present rank without acquiring a suitable portion of the reserve which is so
often found to dignify official sentiments. Having ventured the opinion already placed, however vaguely, before
his hearers, he was patiently awaiting its effects on the
mind of his superior, when the latter, by his earnest and
unsuspecting countenance, no less than by the question
just given, showed that he was still in the dark as to the
expedient the subaltern wished to suggest.

" I think there will be no necessity for making more
captives," resumed Eben, " since the one we have appears
to create difficulties in our councils. If there be any law
in the colony which says that men must strike with a
gentle hand in open battle, it is a law but little spoken of
in common discourse ; and, though no pretender to the
wisdom of legislators, I will make bold to add, it is a law
that may as well be forgotten until this out-breaking of the
savages shall be quelled."

" We deal with an enemy that never stays his hand at
the cry of mercy," observed Meek Wolfe ; " and though
charity be the fruit of Christian qualities, there is a duty
greater than any which belongeth to earth. We are no
more than weak and feeble instruments in the hands of
Providence, and as such our minds should not be hardened
to our inward promptings. If evidence of better feeling
could be found in the deeds of the heathen, we might raise
our hopes to the completion of things ; but the powers of
darkness still rage in their hearts, and we are taught to
believe that the tree is known by its fruits."

Content signed to all to await his return, and left the
room. In another minute he was seen leading his daughter
into the centre of the circle. The half alarmed young
woman clasped her swaddled boy to her bosom, as she
gazed timidly at the grave faces of the borderers, and her
eye recoiled in fear, when its hurried glance met the sunken,

glazed, excited, and yet equivocal-looking organ of the Rev. Mr. Wolfe.

" Thou hast said that the savage never hearkens to the cry of mercy," resumed Content ; " here is living evidence that thou hast spoken in error. The misfortune that early befell my family is not unknown to any in this settlement ; thou seest in this trembling creature the daughter of our love, — her we have so long mourned. The wept of my household is again with us. Our hearts have been oppressed, they are now gladdened. God hath returned our child !"

There was a deep, rich pathos in the tones of the father that affected most of his auditors, though each manifested his sensibilities in a manner suited to his particular habits of mind. The nature of the divine was touched, and all the energies of his severe principles were wanting to sustain him above the manifestation of a weakness that he might have believed derogatory to his spiritual exaltation of character. He therefore sat mute, with hands folded on his knee, betraying the struggles of an awakened sympathy only by a firmer compression of the interlocked fingers, and an occasional and involuntary movement of the stronger muscles of the face. Dudley suffered a smile of pleasure to lighten his broad open countenance ; and the physician, who had hitherto been merely a listener, uttered a few low syllables of admiration of the physical perfection of the being before him, with which there was mingled some evidence of natural good feeling.

Reuben Ring was the only individual who openly betrayed the whole degree of the interest he took in the restoration of the lost female. The stout yeoman arose, and moving to the entranced Narra-mattah, he took the infant into his large hands, and for a moment the honest borderer gazed at the boy, with a wistful and softened eye. Then raising the diminutive face of the infant to his own expanded and bold features, he touched its cheek with his lips, and returned the babe to its mother, who witnessed the whole proceeding, in some such tribulation as the startled wren exhibits when the foot of the urchin is seen to draw too near the nest of its young.

" Thou seest that the hand of the Narragansett hath been stayed," said Content, when silence succeeded this little movement, speaking in a tone which betrayed hopes of victory.

" The ways of Providence are mysterious !" returned Meek ; " wherein they bring comfort to the heart, it is right that we exhibit gratitude : and wherein they are charged with present affliction, it is meet to bow with humbled spirits to their orderings. But the visitations on families are merely———"

He paused, for at that moment a door opened, and a party entered, bearing a burden which they deposited, with decent and grave respect, on the floor, in the very centre of the room. The unceremonious manner of the entrance, the assured and the common gravity of their air, proclaimed that the villagers felt their errand to be a sufficient apology for the intrusion. Had not the business of the past day naturally led to such a belief, the manner and aspects of those who had borne the burden would have announced it to be a human body.

" I had believed that none fell in this day's strife, but those who met their end near my own door," said Content, after a long, respectful, and sorrowing pause. " Remove the face-cloth, that we may know on whom the blow hath fallen."

One of the young men obeyed. It was not easy to recognise, through the mutilations of savage barbarity, the features of the sufferer. But a second and steadier look showed the gory and still agonised countenance of the individual who had that morning left the Wish-Ton-Wish on the message of the colonial authorities. Even men as practised as those present in the horrible inventions of Indian cruelty, turned sickening away from a spectacle that was calculated to chill the blood of all who had not become callous to human affliction. Content made a sign to cover the miserable remnants of mortality, and hid his face with a shudder.

It is not necessary to dwell on the scene that followed. Meek Wolfe availed himself of this unexpected event to press his plan on the attention of the commanding officer of

A A

the settlement, who was certainly far better disposed to listen to his proposals than before this palpable evidence of the ruthless character of their enemies was presented to his view. Still Content listened with reluctance : nor was it without the intention of exercising an ulterior discretion in the case, that he finally consented to give orders for the departure of a body of men, with the approach of the morning light. As much of the discourse was managed with those half intelligible allusions that distinguished men of their habits, it is probable that every individual present had his own particular views of the subject ; though it is certain one and all faithfully believed that he was solely influenced by a justifiable regard to his temporal interest, which was in some degree rendered still more praiseworthy by a reference to the service of his Divine Master.

As the party returned, Dudley lingered a moment alone with his former master. The face of the honest-meaning Ensign was more than usually significant, and he even paused a little, after all were beyond hearing, ere he could muster resolution to propose the subject that was so evidently uppermost in his mind.

" Captain Content Heathcote," he at length commenced, " evil or good come not alone in this life. Thou hast found her that we sought with so much pain and danger, but thou hast found with her more than a Christian gentleman can desire. I am a man of humble station, but I may make bold to know what should be the feelings of a father whose child is restored, replenished by such an over-bountiful gift."

" Speak plainer," said Content, firmly.

" Then I would say, that it may not be grateful to one who taketh his place among the best in this colony, to have an offspring with an Indian cross of blood, and over whose birth no rite of Christian marriage hath been said. Here is Abundance, a woman of exceeding usefulness in a newly-settled region, hath made Reuben a gift of three noble boys this very morning. The accession is little known, and less discoursed of, in that the good wife is accustomed to such liberality, and that the day hath brought forth still greater events. Now a child, more or less, to such a woman, can neither raise question among the neighbours, nor make any extraordinary difference to the household. My brother Ring would be happy to add the boy to his stock; and should there be any remarks concerning the colour of the younker at a future day, it should give no reason of surprise had the whole four been born, on the day of such an inroad, red as Metacom himself!"

Content heard his companion to the end without interruption. His countenance, for a single instant, as the meaning of the Ensign became unequivocal, reddened with a worldly feeling to which he had long been a stranger; but the painful expression as quickly disappeared, and in its place reigned the meek submission to Providence that habitually characterised his mien.

" That I have been troubled with this vain thought, I shall not deny," he answered; " but the Lord hath given me strength to resist. It is his will that one sprung of a heathen lineage shall come beneath my roof, and let his will be done! My child, and all that are hers, are welcome."

Ensign Dudley pressed the point no further, and they separated.

CHAPTER VIII.

Tarry a little; — there is something else. *Merchant of Venice.*

WE shift the scene. The reader will transport himself from the valley of the Wish-Ton-Wish, to the bosom of a deep and dark wood.

Such scenes have been too often described to need a repetition. Still, as it is possible that these pages may fall into the hands of some who have never quitted the older parts of the Union, we shall endeavour to give them a faint impression of the appearance of the place to which it has become our duty to transfer the action of the tale.

Although it is certain that inanimate, like animate nature, has its period, the existence of the tree has no fixed
and common limit.　The oak, the elm, and the linden, the
quick-growing sycamore, and the tall pine, has each its
own laws for the government of its growth, its magnitude,
and its duration.　By this provision of nature, the wilderness, in the midst of so many successive changes, is always
maintained at the point nearest to perfection, since the ac-
cessions are so few and gradual as to preserve its general
character.

The American forest exhibits in the highest degree the
grandeur of repose.　As nature never does violence to her
own laws, the soil throws out the plant which it is best
qualified to support, and the eye is not often disappointed
by a sickly vegetation.　There is a generous emulation in
the trees, which is not to be found among others of different families, when left to pursue their quiet existence
in the solitude of the fields.　Each struggles towards the
light, and an equality in bulk and a similarity in form are
thus produced, which scarce belong to their distinctive
characters.　The effect may easily be imagined.　The
vaulted arches beneath are filled with thousands of high
unbroken columns, which sustain one vast and trembling
canopy of leaves.　A pleasing gloom and an imposing
silence have their interminable reign below, an outer and
a different atmosphere seeming to rest on the cloud of
foliage.

While the light plays on the varying surface of the tree
tops, a sombre hue colours the earth.　Dead and moss-
covered logs ; mounds covered with decomposed vegetable
substances, the graves of long past generations of trees ;
cavities left by the fall of an uprooted trunk ; dark fungi,
that flourished around the decayed roots of those about to
loose their hold, with a few slender and delicate plants of a
minor growth, and which best succeed in the shade, form
the principal features of the scene beneath.　The whole is
tempered, and in summer it is rendered grateful, by a freshness which equals that of the subterranean vault, without
possessing its chilling dampness.　In the midst of this
gloomy solitude the foot of man is rarely heard.　An

occasional glimpse of the bounding deer or trotting moose is almost the only interruption on the earth itself; while the heavy bear or the leaping panther is, occasionally, met seated on the branches of some venerable tree. There are moments, too, when troops of hungry wolves are encountered on the trail of the deer; but these are met rather as exceptions to the stillness of the place, than as accessories that should properly be introduced into the picture. Even the birds are, in common, mute; or when they do break the silence, it is in a discordance that suits the character of their wild abode.

Through such a scene, two men were industriously journeying on the day which succeeded the inroad last described. They marched, as wont, one after the other; the younger and more active leading the way through the monotony of the woods, as accurately and as unhesitatingly as the mariner directs his course by the aid of the needle, over the waste of waters. He in front was light, agile, and seemingly unwearied; while the one who followed was a man of heavy mould, whose step denoted less practice in the exercise of the forest, and possibly some failing of natural vigour.

" Thine eye, Narragansett, is an unerring compass by which to steer, and thy leg a never-wearied steed," said the latter, casting the butt of his musket on the end of a mouldering log, while he leaned on the barrel for support. " If thou movest on the war-path with the same diligence as this thou usest in our errand of peace, well may the colonists dread thy enmity."

The other turned, and without seeking aid from the gun which rested against his shoulder, he pointed at the several objects he named, and answered,—

" My father is this aged sycamore — it leans against the young oak. Conanchet is a straight pine. There is great cunning in grey hairs," added the chief, stepping lightly forward, until a finger rested on the arm of Submission; " can they tell the time when we shall lie under the moss like a dead hemlock?"

" That exceedeth the wisdom of man. It is enough, Sachem, if, when we fall, we may say with truth that the

land we shadowed is no poorer for our growth. Thy bones
will lie in the earth where thy fathers trod, but mine may
whiten in the vault of some gloomy forest."

The quiet of the Indian's face was disturbed. The
pupils of his dark eyes contracted, his nostrils dilated, and
his full chest heaved; and then all reposed, like the sluggish ocean after a vain effort to heave its waters into some
swelling wave during a general calm.

" Fire hath scorched the prints of my father's moccasins
from the earth," he said, with a smile that was placid,
though bitter, " and my eyes cannot find them. I shall die
under that shelter," pointing through an opening in the
foliage to the blue void ; " the falling leaves will cover
my body."

" Then hath the Lord given us a new bond of friendship. There is a yew tree and a quiet churchyard in a
country afar, where generations of my race sleep in their
graves. The place is white with stones that bear the name
of ——."

Submission suddenly ceased, and when his look was raised
to that of his companion, it was just in time to detect the
manner in which the curious interest of the latter changed
suddenly to cold reserve, and to note the high courtesy of
the air with which the Indian turned the discourse.

" There is water beyond the little hill," he said : " let
my father drink and grow stronger, that he may live to lie
in the clearings."

The other bowed, and they proceeded to the spot in
silence. It would seem, by the length of time that was
now lost in taking the required refreshment, that the travellers had journeyed long and far. The Narragansett ate
more sparingly, however, than his companion, for his
mind appeared to sustain a weight that was far more grievous than the fatigue which had been endured by the body.
Still his composure was little disturbed outwardly, for
during the silent repast he maintained the air of a dignified
warrior, rather than that of a man whose air could be
much affected by inward sorrow. When nature was
appeased, they arose and continued their route through the
pathless forest.

For an hour after quitting the spring the progress of our adventurers was swift, and uninterrupted by any passing observation or momentary pause. At the end of that time, however, the speed of Conanchet began to slacken; and his eye, instead of maintaining its steady and forward direction, wandered with some appearance of indecision.

" Thou hast lost those secret signs by which we have so far threaded the woods," observed his companion; " one tree is like another, and I see no difference in this wilderness of nature; if thou art at fault, we may despair of our object."

" Here is the nest of the eagle," returned Conanchet, pointing at the object he named perched on the upper and whitened branches of a dead pine; " and my father may see the council tree in this oak — but there are no Wompanoags!"

" There are many eagles in this forest, nor is that oak one that may not have its fellow. Thine eye hath been deceived, Sachem; some false sign hath led us astray."

Conanchet looked at his companion attentively. After a moment, he quietly asked, —

" Did my father ever mistake his path in going from his wigwam to the place where he looked upon the house of his Great Spirit?"

" The nature of that often travelled path was different from this, Narragansett. My foot hath worn the rock with many passings, and the distance was a span. But we have here journeyed through leagues of forest, and our route hath lain across brook and hill, through brake and morass, where human vision hath not been able to detect the smallest sign of the presence of man."

" My father is old," said the Indian respectfully. " His eye is not as quick as when he took the scalp of the great chief, or he would know the print of a moccasin: — see," making his companion observe the mark of a human foot that was barely discernible by the manner in which the dead leaves had been displaced, " his rock is worn but it is harder than the ground. He cannot tell by its signs who passed, or when."

" Here is truly that which ingenuity may portray as
the print of man's foot ; but it is alone, and it may be
some accident of the wind."

" Let my father look on every side, he will see that a
tribe hath passed."

" This may be true, though my vision is unequal to
detect that thou wouldst show.   But if a tribe hath passed,
let us follow."

Conanchet shook his head, spreading the fingers of his
two hands in a manner to describe the radii of a circle.

" Hugh !" he said, starting while he was thus significantly answering by gestures, — " a moccasin comes !' "

Submission, who had so often and so recently been
arrayed against the savages, involuntarily sought the lock
of his carabine.   The look and action were menacing,
though he could see no object to excite alarm.

Not so Conanchet.   His quicker and more practised
vision soon caught a glimpse of the warrior who was approaching, occasionally concealed by the trunks of trees,
and whose tread on the dried leaves had first betrayed his
proximity.   Folding his arms on his naked bosom, the
Narragansett awaited the coming of the other, in an attitude of dignity.   Neither did he speak nor suffer a muscle
to play, until a hand was placed on one of his arms, and
he who had drawn near said in tones of amity and respect, —

" The young Sachem hath come to look for his brother ? "

" Wompanoag, I have followed the trail, that your ears
may listen to the talk of a pale-face."

The third person in this interview was Metacom.   He
shot a haughty and fierce glance at the stranger, and then
turned calmly to his companion.

" Has Conanchet counted his young men lately ?" he
asked, in the language of the Aborigines.   " I saw many
go into the fields that never came back.   Let the white
man die."

" Wompanoag, he is led by the wampum of a Sachem.
I have not counted my young men ; but I know that
they are strong enough to say, that what their chief hath
promised, shall be done."

" If the Yengeese is a friend of my brother, he is wel_
come.   The wigwam of Metacom is open ; let him enter."

Philip made a sign for the others to follow, and he led
the way to the place he had named.

The spot chosen by Philip for his temporary encamp_
ment was suited to such a purpose.   There was a thicket,
denser than common, on one of its sides ; a steep and high
rock protected and sheltered its rear ; a swift and wide
brook dashed over fragments that had fallen with time
from the precipice in its front, and towards the setting
sun, a whirlwind had opened a long and melancholy glade
through the forest.   A few huts of brush leaned against
the base of the hill, and the scanty implements of their
domestic economy were scattered among the habitations
of the savages.   The whole party did not number twenty ;
for, as has been said, the Wompanoag had acted latterly
more by the agency of his allies, than with the materials
of his own proper force.

The three were soon seated on a rock whose foot was
washed by the current of the tumbling water.   A few
gloomy_looking and fierce Indians watched the conference
in the back ground.

" My brother hath followed my trail that my ears may
hear the words of a Yengeese," Philip commenced, after a
sufficient period had elapsed to escape the imputation of
curiosity ; " let him speak."

" I have come singly into the jaws of the lion, restless
and remorseless leader of the savages," returned the bold
exile, " that you may hear the words of peace.   Why hath
the son seen the acts of the English so differently from the
father ?   Massassoit * was a friend of the persecuted and
patient pilgrims, who have sought rest and refuge in this
Bethel of the faithful ; but thou hast hardened thy heart
to their prayers, and seekest the blood of those who wish
thee no wrong.   Doubtless thy nature is one of pride and
mistaken vanities, like that of all thy race, and it hath
seemed needful to the vain-glory of thy name and nation

---

* Massassoit was the father of Metacom, or Philip as he was called by
whites, and as stanch a friend of the English as his son proved to be their
enemy.

to ba'tle against men of a different origin.   But know there
is One who is Master of all on earth, as he is King of
heaven !   It is his pleasure that the sweet savour of his
worship should arise from the wilderness.   His will is
law, and they that would withstand do but kick against
the pricks.   Listen, then, to peaceful counsels, that the
land may be parcelled justly to meet the wants of all, and
the country be prepared for the incense of the altar."

This exhortation was uttered in an almost unearthly
voice, and with a degree of excitement that was probably
increased by the intensity with which the recluse had
lately been brooding over his peculiar opinions, and the
terrible scenes in which he had so recently been an actor.
Philip listened with the high courtesy of an Indian prince.
Unintelligible as was the meaning of the speaker, his coun_
tenance betrayed no gleaming of impatience, his lip no
smile of ridicule.   On the contrary, a noble and lofty gravity reigned in every feature ; and ignorant as he was of
much of what the other wished to say, his attentive eye and
bending head expressed every wish to comprehend.

" My pale friend hath spoken very wisely," he answered.
" But he doth not see clearly in these woods ; he sits too
much in the shade.   His eye is better in a clearing.   Metacom is not a fierce beast.   His claws are worn out ; his
legs are tired with travelling ; he cannot jump far.   My
pale friend wants to divide the land.   Why trouble the
Great Spirit to do his work twice ?   He gave the Wompanoags their hunting grounds, and places on the salt lake
to catch their fish and clams*, and he did not forget his
children the Narragansetts.   He put them in the midst of
the water, for he saw that they could swim.   Did he forget
the Yengeese ? or did he put them in a swamp, where they
would turn into frogs and lizards ? "

" Heathen, my voice shall never deny the bounties of
my God !   His hand hath placed my fathers in a fertile
land, rich in the good things of the world, fortunate in position, sea-girt and impregnable.   Happy is he who can
find justification in dwelling within its borders !"

---

* A shell-fish resembling the oyster that abounds on the coast of North
America, and which is much esteemed for its nourishment and flavour.

An empty gourd lay on the rock at the side of Metacom. Bending over the stream, he filled it to the brim with water, and held the vessel before the eyes of his companions.

" See," he said, pointing to the even surface of the fluid : " so much hath the Great Spirit said it shall hold. Now," he added, filling the hollow of the other hand from the brook, and casting its contents into the gourd, " now my brother knows that some must flow over. It is so with his country. There is no longer room in it for my friend."

" Did I attempt to deceive thine ears with this tale, I should lay falsehood to my soul. We are many, and sorry am I to say that some among us are like unto them that were called ' Legion.' But to say that there is not still place for all to die where they are born, is to utter damning untruth."

" The land of the Yengeese is then good — very good," returned Philip ; " but their young men seek one that is better."

" Thy nature, Wompanoag, is not equal to comprehend the motives which have led us hither, and our discourse is getting to be vain."

" My brother Conanchet is a Sachem. The leaves that fall from the trees of his country, in the season of frosts, blow into my hunting grounds. We are neighbours and friends," slightly bending his head to the Narragansett. " When a wicked Indian runs from the islands to the wigwams of my people, he is whipped and sent back. We keep the path between us open for honest red-men only."

Philip spoke with a sneer that his habitual loftiness of manner did not conceal from his associate chief, though it was so slight as entirely to escape the observation of him who was the subject of his sarcasm. The former took the alarm, and for the first time during the dialogue, he broke silence.

" My pale father is a brave warrior," said the young Sachem of the Narragansetts, reproachfully. " His hand took the scalp of the great Sagamore of his people !"

The countenance of Metacom changed instantly. In place of the ironical sneer that was gathering about his lip, its expression became serious and respectful. He gazed steadily at the hard and weather-beaten features of his ascetic guest, and it is probable that words of higher courtesy than any yet used would have fallen from him, had not, at that moment, a signal been given, by a young Indian set to watch on the summit of the rock, that one approached. Both Metacom and Conanchet appeared to hear this cry with some uneasiness. Neither however arose, nor did either betray such evidence of alarm as denoted a deeper interest in the interruption, than the circumstances might very naturally create. A warrior was shortly seen entering the encampment from the side of the forest which was known to lie in the direction of the Wish-Ton-Wish.

The moment Conanchet saw the person of the newly arrived man, his eye and attitude resumed their former repose, though the look of Metacom still continued gloomy and distrustful. The difference in the manner of the chiefs was not, however, sufficiently strong to be remarked by Submission, who was about to resume the discourse, when the new comer moved past the cluster of warriors in the encampment, and took his seat near them, on a stone so low that the water laved his feet. As usual there was no greeting between the Indians for some moments, the three appearing to regard the arrival as a mere thing of course. But the uneasiness of Metacom prompted a communication sooner than common.

" Mohtucket," he said, in the language of their tribe, " hath lost the trail of his friends. We thought the crows of the pale men were picking his bones!"

" There was no scalp at his belt, and Mohtucket was ashamed to be seen among the young men with an empty hand."

" He remembered that he had too often come back without striking a dead enemy," returned Metacom, about whose firm mouth there lurked an expression of contempt. " Has he now touched a warrior?"

The Indian, who was merely a man of the inferior class, held up the trophy which hung at his girdle to the examination of his chief. Metacom looked at the disgusting object with the calmness, and nearly with the interest, that a virtuoso would have lavished on an antique memorial of some triumph of former ages. His finger was thrust through a hole in the skin, and then, while he resumed his former position, he observed dryly, —

" A bullet hath hit the head. The arrow of Mohtucket doth little harm !"

" Metacom hath never looked on his young man like a friend since the brother of Mohtucket was killed."

The glance that Philip cast at his underling, though it was not unmingled with suspicion, was one of princely and savage scorn. Their white auditor had not been able to understand the discourse, but the dissatisfaction and uneasiness of the eyes of both, were too obvious not to show that the conference was far from amicable.

" The Sachem hath discontent with his young man," he observed ; " from this may he understand the nature of that which leadeth many to quit the land of their fathers beneath the rising sun, to come to this wilderness in the west. If he will now listen, I will touch further on the business of my errand, and deal more at large with the subject we have but so lightly skimmed."

Philip manifested attention. He smiled on his guest, and even bowed his assent to the proposal ; still his keen eye seemed to read the soul of his subordinate through the veil of his gloomy visage. There was a play of the fingers of his right hand, when the arm fell from its position across his bosom to his thigh, as if they itched to grasp the knife whose buck-horn handle lay within a few inches of their reach. Yet his air to the white man was composed and dignified. The latter was again about to speak, when the arches of the forest suddenly rang with the report of a musket. All, in and near the encampment, sprang to their feet at the well known sound, and yet all continued as motionless as if so many dark but breathing statues had been planted there. The rustling of leaves was heard, and then the body of the young Indian, who had been posted on the rock, rolled to the edge of the precipice, whence it fell like a log, on the yielding roof of one of the lodges beneath. A shout issued from the forest behind, a volley roared among the trees, and whistling lead was glancing

through the air, cutting twigs from the undergrowth on
every side. Two more of the Wompanoags were rolling
on the earth in the death-agony.

The voice of Annawon was heard in the encampment,
and at the next instant the place was deserted.

During this startling and fearful moment, the four individuals near the stream were inactive. Conanchet and
his Christian friend stood to their arms ; but it was rather
as men cling to the means of defence, in moments of great
jeopardy, than with any intention of offensive hostilities.
Metacom seemed undecided. Accustomed to receive and
inflict surprises, a warrior so experienced could not be disconcerted ; still he hesitated as to the course he ought to
take. But when Annawon, who was nearer the scene,
sounded the signal of retreat, he sprang towards the returned straggler, and with a single blow of his tomahawk
brained the traitor. Glances of fierce revenge, and of in-
extinguishable though disappointed hatred, were exchanged
between the victim and his chief, as the former lay on the
rock gasping for breath, and then the latter turned in his
tracks, and raised the dripping weapon over the head of
the white man.

" Wompanoag, no !" said Conanchet, in a voice of
thunder. " Our lives are one."

Philip hesitated. Fierce and dangerous passions were
struggling in his breast, but the habitual self-command of
the wily politician of those woods prevailed. Even in that
scene of blood and alarm, he smiled on his powerful and
fearless young ally ; then pointing to the deepest shades of
the forest, he bounded towards them with the activity of a
deer.

CHAPTER IX.

But, peace be with him!
That life is better life, past fearing death,
Than that which lives to fear.   *Measure for Measure.*

COURAGE is both a comparative and an improvable virtue.
If the fear of death be a weakness common to the race, it
is one that is capable of being diminished by frequent
exposure, and even rendered extinct by reflection. It was
therefore with sensibilities entirely changed from their
natural course, that the two individuals who were left alone
by the retreat of Philip, saw the nature and the approach
of the danger that now beset them. Their position near
the brook had so far protected them from the bullets of
the assailants, but it was equally obvious to both, that in a
minute or two the colonists would enter an encampment
that was already deserted. Each, in consequence, acted
according to those opinions which had been fostered by the
habits of their respective lives.

As Conanchet had no act of vengeance to occupy him
like that which Metacom had performed immediately before his eyes, at the first alarm he had given all his faculties
to the nature of the attack. The first minute was sufficient
to understand its character, and the second enabled him to
decide.

" Come," he said, hastily, but with perfect self-possession, pointing as he spoke to the swift running stream at
his feet, " we will go with the water ; let the marks of
our trail run before."

Submission hesitated. There was something like haughty
military pride in the stern determination of his eye, which
seemed reluctant to incur the disgrace of a flight so unequivocal, and as he might have believed, so unworthy of
his character.

" No, Narragansett," he answered ; " flee for thy life ;
leave me to reap the harvest of my deeds. They can but

leave my bones by the side of those of this traitor at my feet."

The mien of Conanchet was neither excited nor displeased. He quietly drew the corner of his light robe over a shoulder, and was about to resume his seat on the stone from which he had but a minute before arisen, when his companion again urged him to fly.

" The enemies of a chief must not say that he led his friend into a trap, and that when his leg was fast, he ran away himself like a lucky fox. If my brother stays to be killed, Conanchet will be found near him."

" Heathen, heathen !" returned the other, moved nearly to tears by the loyalty of his guide, " many a Christian man might take lessons from thy faith. Lead on ; I will follow at the utmost of my speed."

The Narragansett sprang into the brook, and took its downward course, a direction opposite to that which Philip had chosen. There was wisdom in this expedient, for though their pursuers might see that the water was troubled, there was no certainty as to the direction of the fugitives. Conanchet had foreseen this little advantage, and with the instinctive readiness of his people, he did not fail to make it of service. Metacom had been influenced by the course taken by his warriors, who had retired under shelter of the rocks.

Ere the two fugitives had gone any great distance, they heard the shouts of their enemies in the encampment, and soon after, scattering shot announced that Philip had already rallied his people to resistance. There was an assurance of safety in the latter circumstance which caused them to relax their speed.

" My foot is not as active as in days that are past," said Submission ; " we will therefore recover strength while we may, lest we be yet taken at emergency. Narragansett, thou hast ever kept thy faith with me, and come of what race, or worship in what manner thou may'st, there is One to remember it."

" My father looked with the eye of a friend on the Indian boy that was kept like a young bear in a cage. He taught him to speak with the tongue of a Yengeese."

" We passed weary months together in our prison, chief, and Apollyon must have been strong in a heart, to resist the opportunity of friendship in such a situation. But even there, my confidence and care were repaid, for without thy mysterious hints, gathered from signs thou hadst gleaned thyself during the hunt, it would not have been in my power to have warned my friends that thy people contemplated an attack the unhappy night of the burning. Narragansett, we have done each other many acts of kindness, each in our several fashions, and I am ready to confess this last not to be the least of thy favours. Though of white blood and of Christian origin, I can almost say that my heart is Indian."

" Then die an Indian's death !" shouted a voice, within twenty feet of the spot where they were wading down the stream.

The menacing words were rather accompanied than seconded by a shot, and Submission fell. Conanchet cast his musket into the water and turned to raise his companion.

" It was merely age dealing with the slippery stones of the brook," said the latter, as he recovered his footing. " That had well nigh been a fatal discharge ! but God, for his own purpose, averted the blow."

Conanchet did not speak. Seizing his gun, which lay at the bottom of the stream, he drew his friend after him to the shore, and plunged into the thicket that lined its banks. Here they were momentarily protected from missiles. But the shouts that succeeded the discharge of the muskets, were accompanied by yells that he knew to proceed from Pequots and Mohegans, tribes that were in deadly hostility to his own people. The hope of concealing their trail from such pursuers was not to be indulged, and for his companion to escape by flight he knew to be impossible. There was no time to lose. In such emergencies, with an Indian thought takes the character of instinct. The fugitives stood at the foot of a sapling, whose top was completely concealed by masses of leaves which belonged to the underbrush that clustered around its trunk. Into this tree he assisted Submission to ascend, and then, with-

B B

out explaining his own views, he instantly left the spot,
rendering his own trail as broad and perceptible as possible, by beating down the bushes as he passed.

The expedient of the faithful Narragansett was completely successful. Before he had got a hundred yards
from the place, he saw the foremost of the hostile Indians
hunting like blood-hounds on his footsteps. His movement was slow until he saw that, having his person in
view, all of the pursuers had passed the tree. Then the
arrow parting from the bow was scarce swifter than his
flight.

The pursuit had the exciting incidents and ingenious
expedients of an Indian chase. Hunted from his cover,
Conanchet was soon obliged to trust his person in the
more open parts of the forest. Miles of hill and ravine, of
plain, of rocks, of morass and stream, were crossed, and
still the trained warrior held his way, unbroken in spirit,
and scarce wearied in limb. The merit of a savage in
such an employment, rests more on his bottom than on his
speed. The three or four colonists, who had been sent
with the party of amicable Indians to intercept those who
might attempt to escape down the stream, were early
thrown out, and the struggle was now entirely between
the fugitive and men equally practised in limb, and ingenious in expedient.

The Pequots had a great advantage in their number.
The frequent doublings of the fugitive kept the chase
within the circle of a mile, and as each of his enemies
tired, there were always fresh pursuers to take his place.
In such a contest the result could not be questionable.
After more than two hours of powerful exertion, the foot
of Conanchet began to fail, and his speed to flag. Exhausted by efforts that had been nearly supernatural, the
breathless warrior cast his person prostrate on the earth,
lying for several minutes as if he were dead.

During this breathing time, his throbbing pulses grew
more calm, his heart beat less violently, and the circulation
was gradually returning to the tranquil flow of nature in
a state of rest. It was at this moment, when his energies
were recruited by rest, that the chief heard the tread of

We shall not detain the narrative to dwell on the parti‑
culars of the council. The question was gravely considered,
and it was decided with a deep and conscientious sense of
the responsibility of those who acted as judges. Several
hours were passed in deliberation, Meek opening and
closing the deliberations by solemn prayers. The judg‑
ment was then announced to Uncas, by the divine himself.

" The wise men of my people have consulted together,
in the matter of this Narragansett," he said, " and their
spirits have wrestled powerfully with the subject. In
coming to their conclusion, if it wear the aspect of time‑
serving, let all remember that the Providence of Heaven
hath so interwoven the interests of man with its own
good purposes, that to the carnal eye they may outwardly
seem to be inseparable. But that which is here done, is
done in good faith to our ruling principles, which is good
faith to thee, and to all others who support the altar in
this wilderness. And herein is our decision : We commit
the Narragansett to thy justice, since it is evident that
while he is at large, neither thou, who art a feeble prop to
the church in these regions, nor we, who are its humble
and unworthy servitors, are safe. Take him, then, and
deal with him according to thy wisdom. We place limits
to thy power in only two things. It is not meet that any
born of humanity, and having human sensibilities, should
suffer more in the flesh than may be necessary to the ends
of duty; we therefore decree that thy captive shall not die
by torture ; and for the better security of this our charitable
decision, two of our number shall accompany thee and
him to the place of execution : it being always supposed it
is thy intention to inflict the pains of death. Another
condition of this concession to a fore‑ordered necessity, is
that a Christian minister may be at hand, in order that the
sufferer may depart with the prayers of one accustomed
to lift his voice, in petitions, to the footstool of the
Almighty." *

The Mohegan chief heard the sentence with deep atten‑

* The conduct of the Rev. Mr. Wolfe and his coadjutors on this occasion is
historically true.

tion. When he found he was to be denied the satisfaction of proving, or perhaps of overcoming the resolution of his enemy, a deep cloud passed across his swarthy visage. But the strength of his tribe had long been broken, and to resist would have been as unprofitable, as to repine would have been unseemly. The conditions were therefore accepted, and preparations were accordingly made, among the Indians, to proceed to judgment.

These people had few contradictory principles to appease, and no subtleties to distract their decision. Direct, fearless, and simple in all their practices, they did little more than gather the voices of the chiefs, and acquaint their captive with the result. They knew that fortune had thrown an implacable enemy into their hands, and they believed that self-preservation demanded his life. To them it mattered little whether he had arrows in his hands, or had yielded himself an unarmed prisoner. He knew the risk he run in submitting, and he had probably consulted his own character, rather than their benefit, in throwing away his arms. They therefore pronounced the judgment of death against their captive, merely respecting the decree of their white allies, which had commanded them to spare the torture.

So soon as this determination was known, the commissioners of the colony hastened away from the spot, with consciences that required some aid from the stimulus of their subtle doctrines, in order to render them quiet. They were, however, ingenious casuists, and as they hurried along their return path, most of the party were satisfied that they had rather manifested a merciful interposition, than exercised any act of positive cruelty.

During the two or three hours which were passed in these solemn and usual preparations, Conanchet was seated on a rock, a close, but apparently an unmoved, spectator of all that passed. His eye was mild, and at times melancholy ; but its brightness and its steadiness remained unimpaired. When his sentence was announced, it exhibited no change, and he saw all the pale men depart, with the calmness he had maintained throughout. It was only as Uncas, attended by the body of his party, and the two white superintendents, who had been left, approached, that his spirit seemed to awaken.

"My people have said that there shall be no more wolves in the woods," said Uncas; "and they have commanded our young men to slay the hungriest of them all."

"It is well," coldly returned the other.

A gleaming of admiration, and perhaps of humanity, came over the grim countenance of Uncas, as he gazed at the repose which reigned in the firm features of his victim. For an instant his purpose wavered.

"The Mohicans are a great tribe!" he added; "and the race of Uncas is getting few. We will paint our brother so that the lying Narragansetts shall not know him, and he will quit the islands to be a warrior on the main land."

This relenting of his enemy had a corresponding effect on the generous temper of Conanchet. The well-sustained pride deserted his eye, and his look became milder and more human. For a minute, intense thought brooded around his brow; the firm muscles of his mouth played a little, though scarcely enough to be seen, and then he spoke.

"Mohican," he said, "why should your young men be in a hurry? My scalp will be the scalp of a great chief to-morrow as well as to-day. They will not take two, should they strike their prisoner now."

"Hath Conanchet forgotten any thing that he is not ready?"

"Sachem, he is always ready. But"— he paused, and his voice faltered —"does a Mohican live alone?"

"How many suns doth the Narragansett ask?"

"One: when the shadow of that pine points towards the brook, Conanchet will be ready. He will then stand in its shade with naked hands."

"Go," said Uncas, with dignity; "I have heard the words of a Sagamore."

Conanchet turned, and passing swiftly through the silent crowd, his person was soon lost in the surrounding forest.

CHAPTER X.

Therefore, lay bare your bosom.   *Merchant of Venice.*

THE night that succeeded was wild and melancholy. The moon was nearly full, but its place in the heavens was only seen as the masses of vapour, which drove through the air, occasionally opened, suffering short gleams of fitful light to fall on the scene below. A south-western wind rather moaned, than sighed, through the forest, and there were moments when its freshness increased, till every leaf seemed a tongue, and each low plant appeared to be endowed with the gift of speech. With the exception of these imposing, and not unpleasing natural sounds, there was a solemn quiet in and about the village of the Wish-Ton-Wish. An hour before the moment when we resume the action of the legend, the sun had settled into the neighbouring forest, and most of its simple and laborious inhabitants had already sought their rest.

The lights, however, still shone through many of the windows of the "Heathcote House." There was the usual stirring industry in and about the offices, and the ordinary calm was reigning in the superior parts of the habitation. A solitary man was on its piazza. It was young Mark Heathcote, who paced the long and narrow gallery, as if impatient of some interruption to his wishes.

The uneasiness of the young man was of short continuance, for ere he had been many minutes at his post, a door opened, and two light and timid forms glided out of the house.

" Thou hast not come alone, Martha," said the youth, half-displeased. " I told thee that the matter I had to say was for thine own ear."

" It is our Ruth. Thou knowest, Mark, that she may not be left alone, for we fear her return to the forest. She is like some ill-tamed fawn, that would be apt to leap

" There is a pale-face in these woods who is a burrowing fox. He hides his head from the Yengeese. When his people were on the trail, barking like hungry wolves, this man trusted to a Sagamore. It was a swift chase, and my father is getting very old. He went up a young hickory, like a bear, and Conanchet led off the lying tribe. But he is not a moose. His legs cannot go like running water for ever ! "

" And why did the great Narragansett give his life for a stranger ? "

" The man is a brave," returned the Sachem, proudly : " he once took the scalp of a Sagamore ! "

Narra-mattah was silent. She brooded, in nearly stupid amazement, on the frightful truth.

" The Great Spirit sees that the man and his wife are of different tribes," she at length ventured to rejoin. " He wishes them to become the same people. Let Conanchet quit the woods, and go into the clearings with the mother of his boy. Her white father will be glad, and Mohican Uncas will not dare to follow."

" Woman, I am a Sachem, and a warrior among my people ! "

There was a severe and cold displeasure in the voice of Conanchet, that his companion had never before heard. He spoke in the manner of a chief to his woman, rather than with that manly softness with which he had been accustomed to address the scion of the pale-faces. The words came over her heart like a withering chill, and affliction kept her mute. The chief himself sate a moment longer in a stern calmness, and then rising in displeasure, he pointed to the sun, and beckoned to his companions to proceed. In a time that appeared to the throbbing heart of her who followed his swift footsteps but a moment, they had turned a little eminence, and in another minute, they stood in the presence of a party that evidently awaited their coming. This grave group consisted only of Uncas, two of his fiercest-looking and most athletic warriors, the divine, and Eben Dudley.

Advancing rapidly to the spot where his enemy stood, Conanchet took his post at the foot of the fatal tree.

Pointing to the shadow, which had not yet turned towards
the east, he folded his arms on his naked bosom, and assumed an air of haughty unconcern. These movements
were made in the midst of a profound stillness.

Disappointment, unwilling admiration, and distrust,
struggled through the mask of practised composure, in the
dark countenance of Uncas. He regarded his long hated
and terrible foe, with an eye that seemed willing to
detect some lurking signs of weakness. It would not have
been easy to say whether he most felt respect or regret at
the faith of the Narragansett. Accompanied by his two
grim warriors, the chief examined the position of the shadow with critical minuteness, and when there no longer
existed a pretext for affecting to doubt the punctuality of
their captive, a deep ejaculation of assent issued from the
chest of each. Like some wary judge, whose justice is
fettered by legal precedents, as if satisfied there was no flaw
in the proceedings, the Mohegan signed to the white men
to draw near.

" Man of a wild and unreclaimed nature !" commenced
Meek Wolfe, in his usual admonitory and ascetic tones,
" the hour of thy existence draws to its end ! Judgment
hath had rule ; thou hast been weighed in the balances, and
art found wanting. But Christian charity is never weary.
We may not resist the ordinances of Providence, but we
may temper the blow to the offender. That thou art here
to die, is a mandate decreed in equity, and rendered awful
by mystery ; but further, submission to the will of Heaven
doth not exact. Heathen, thou hast a soul, and it is about
to leave its earthly tenement for the unknown world——"

Until now, the captive had listened with the courtesy of
a savage when unexcited. He had even gazed at the quiet
enthusiasm, and singularly contradictory passions, that
shone in the speaker's face, with some such reverence as he
might have manifested at an exhibition of one of the pre-
tended revelations of a prophet of his tribe. But when the
divine came to touch upon his condition after death, his
mind received a clear, and to him, an unerring clue to the
truth. Laying a finger suddenly on the shoulder of Meek,
he interrupted him, by saying,—

" My father forgets that the skin of his son is red. The path to the happy hunting grounds of just Indians lies before him."

" Heathen, in thy words hath the master spirit of delusion and sin uttered his blasphemies !"

" Hist !—did my father see that which stirred the bush ? "

" It was the viewless wind, idolatrous and idle minded infant in the form of adult man !"

" And yet my father speaks to it," returned the Indian, with the grave but cutting sarcasm of his people. " See," he added haughtily, and even with ferocity, " the shadow hath passed the root of the tree. Let the cunning man of the pale-faces stand aside ; a Sachem is ready to die !"

Meek groaned audibly, and in real sorrow ; for notwithstanding the veil which exalted theories and doctrinal subtleties had drawn before his judgment, the charities of the man were grounded in truth. Bowing to what he believed to be a mysterious dispensation of the will of Heaven, he withdrew to a short distance, and kneeling on a rock, his voice was heard during the remainder of the sad ceremonies, lifting its tones in fervent prayer for the soul of the condemned.

The divine had no sooner quitted the place, than Uncas motioned to Dudley to approach. Though the nature of the borderer was essentially honest and kind, he was, in opinions and prejudices, but a creature of the times. If he had assented to the judgment which committed the captive to the mercy of his implacable enemies, he had the merit of having suggested the expedient that was to protect the sufferer from those refinements in cruelty, which the savages were known to be so ready to inflict. He had even volunteered to be one of the agents to enforce his own expedient, though, in so doing, he committed no little violence to his natural inclinations. The reader will therefore judge of his conduct in this particular, with the degree of lenity that a right consideration of the condition of the country, and of the usages of the age, may require. There was even a relenting and a yielding of purpose in the countenance of this witness of the scene, that was favourable to the safety of the captive, when he spoke. His address was first to Uncas.

" A happy fortune, Mohegan, something aided by the power of the white men, hath put this Narragansett into thy hands," he said." It is certain that the Commissioners of the Colony have consented that thou shouldst exercise thy will on his life ; but there is a voice in the breast of every human being, which should be stronger than the voice of revenge, and that is the voice of mercy. It is not yet too late to hearken to it. Take the promise of the Narragansett for his faith—take more, take a hostage in this child, which, with its mother, shall be guarded among the English, and let the prisoner go."

" My brother asketh with a big mind !" said Uncas, dryly.

" I know not how, nor why it is I ask with this earnestness," resumed Dudley ; " but there are old recollections and former kindnesses in the face and manner of this Indian ! And here, too, is one in the woman, that I know is tied to some of our settlements, with a bond nearer than that of common charity. Mohegan, I will add a goodly gift of powder and of muskets, if thou wilt listen to mercy, and take the faith of the Narragansett."

Uncas pointed with ironical coldness to his captive as he said —

" Let Conanchet speak !"

" Thou hearest, Narragansett. If the man I begin to suspect thee to be, thou knowest something of the usages of the whites. Speak ; wilt swear to keep peace with the Mohegans, and to bury the hatchet in the path between your villages ? "

" The fire that burnt the lodges of my people, turned the heart of Conanchet to stone," was the answer.

" Then can I do no more than see the treaty respected," returned the disappointed Dudley. " Thou hast thy nature, and it will have way. The Lord have mercy on thee, Indian, and render thee such judgment as is meet for one of savage opportunities."

He made a gesture to Uncas that he had done, and fell back a few paces from the tree, his honest features express-

sence, and both have departed for the world of spirits in a manner to prove the inscrutableness of Providence. But dost not see here, in the face of her who looketh like a form of stone, traces of a countenance that is familiar?"

" Thou hast allusion to the consort of Captain Content Heathcote?"

" Truly, to her only. Thou art not, reverend sir, of sufficient residence at the Wish-Ton-Wish, to remember that lady in her youthfulness. But to me, the hour when the Captain led his followers into the wilderness, seemeth but as a morning of the past season. I was then active in limb, and something idle in reflection and discourse; it was in that journey, that the woman who is now the mother of my children and I first made acquaintance. I have seen many comely females in my time, but never did I look on one so pleasant to the eye, as was the consort of the Captain, until the night of the burning. Thou hast often heard the loss she then met, and from that hour her beauty hath been that of the October leaf, rather than its loveliness in the season of fertility. Now look on the face of this mourner, and say if there be not here such an image as the water reflects from the overhanging bush. In verity, I could believe it was the sorrowing eye and be-reaved look of the mother herself!"

" Grief hath struck its blow heavily on this unoffending victim," uttered Meek, with great and subdued softness of manner. " The voice of petition must be raised in her behalf, or ——"

" Hist! — there are some in the forest; I hear the rustling of leaves!"

" The voice of Him who made the earth whispereth in the winds; his breath is the movement of nature!"

" Here are living men! — But, happily, the meeting is friendly, and there will be no further occasion for strife. The heart of a father is sure as ready eye and swift foot."

Dudley suffered his musket to fall at his side, and both he and his companion stood in attitudes of decent com-posure, awaiting the arrival of those who approached. The party that drew near arrived on the side of the tree oppo-site to that on which the death of Conanchet had occurred.

The enormous trunk and swelling roots of the pine concealed the group at its feet ; but the persons of Meek and
the Ensign were soon observed. The instant they were
discovered he who led the new comers bent his footsteps
in that direction.

 " If, as thou hast supposed, the Narragansett hath
again led her thou hast so long mourned into the forest,"
said Submission, who acted as guide to those who followed,
" here are we at no great distance from the place of his
resort. It was near yon rock that he gave the meeting
with the bloody-minded Philip ; and the place where I
received the boon of an useless and much afflicted life from
his care, is within the bosom of that thicket which borders
the brook. This minister of the Lord, and our stout friend
the Ensign, may have further matter to tell us of his movements."

The speaker stopped within a short distance of the two
he named, but still on the side of the tree opposite to that
where the body lay. He had addressed his words to Content, who also halted to await the arrival of Ruth, who
came in the rear, supported by her son, and attended by
Faith and the physician, all equipped like persons engaged
in a search through the forest. A mother's heart had
sustained the feeble woman for many a weary mile ; but
her steps had begun to drag, shortly before they so happily fell upon the signs of human beings near the spot
where they now met the two agents of the colony.

Notwithstanding the deep interest which belonged to
the respective pursuits of the individuals who composed
these two parties, the interview was opened with no lively
signs of feeling on either side. To them a journey in the
forest possessed no novelties ; and, after traversing its mazes
for a day, the newly arrived encountered their friends as men
meet on more beaten tracks in countries where roads un-
avoidably lead them to cross each other's paths. Even the
appearance of Submission in front of the travellers, elicited
no marks of surprise in the unmoved features of those who
witnessed his approach ; indeed, the mutual composure of
one who had so long concealed his person, and of those
who had more than once seen him in striking and mys-

terious situations, might well justify a belief that the secret of his presence near the valley had not been confined to the family of the Heathcotes. This fact is rendered still more probable by the recollection of the honesty of Dudley, and of the professional characters of the two others.

" We are on the trail of one fled, as the truant fawn seeketh again the covers of the woods," said Content. " Our hunt was uncertain, and it might have been vain, so many feet have lately crossed the forest, were it not that Providence hath cast our route on that of our friend here, who hath had reason to know the probable situation of the Indian camp. Hast seen aught of the Sachem of the Narragansetts, Dudley? and where are those thou ledst against the subtle Philip? That thou fell upon his party, we have heard; though further than thy general success we have yet to learn. The Wompanoag escaped thee?"

" The wicked agencies that back him in his designs profited the savage in his extremity, else would his fate have been that which, I fear, a far worthier spirit hath been doomed to suffer."

" Of whom dost speak?—but it mattereth not. We seek our child; she whom thou hast known, and whom thou hast so lately seen, hath again left us. We seek her in the camp of him who hath been to her — Dudley, hast seen aught of the Narragansett Sachem?"

The Ensign looked at Ruth as he had once before been seen to gaze on the sorrowing features of the woman, but he spoke not. Meek folded his arms on his breast and seemed to pray inwardly. There was, however, one who broke the silence, though his tones were low and menacing.

" It was a bloody deed!" muttered the innocent. " The lying Mohican hath struck a great chief from behind; let him dig the prints of his moccasin from the earth with his nails, like a burrowing fox, for there'll be one on his trail before he can hide his head. Nipsett will be a warrior the next snow!"

" There speaks my witless brother!" exclaimed Faith

rushing ahead — she recoiled, covered her face with her
hands, and sunk upon the ground under the violence of the
surprise that followed.

Though time moved with his ordinary pace, it appeared,
to those who witnessed the scene which succeeded, as if
the emotions of many days were collected within the brief
compass of a few minutes. We shall not dwell on the first
harrowing and exciting moments of the appalling discovery.

A short half hour served to make each person acquainted
with all that it was necessary to know. We shall therefore
advance the narrative to the end of that period.

The body of Conanchet still rested against the tree.
The eyes were open, and, though glazed in death, there
still remained about the brow, the compressed lips, and the
expansive nostrils, much of that lofty firmness which had
sustained him in the last trial of life. The arms were
passive at its sides, but one hand was clenched, in the
manner with which it had so often grasped the tomahawk,
while the other had lost its power, in a vain effort to seek
the place in the girdle where the keen knife should have
been. These two movements had probably been involuntary, for in all other respects the form was expressive of
dignity and repose. At its side, the imaginary Nipsett still
held his place, angry discontent betraying itself through
the ordinary dull fatuity of his countenance.

The rest were collected around the mother and her
stricken child. It would seem that all other feelings were,
for the moment, absorbed in apprehensions for the latter.
There was much reason to dread that the recent shock had
suddenly deranged some of that fearful machinery which
links the soul to the body. This dreaded effect, however,
was more to be apprehended by a general apathy and failing of the system, than by any violent and intelligible
symptom.

The pulses still vibrated, but it was heavily, and like the
irregular and faltering evolutions of the mill which the
dying breeze is ceasing to fan. The pallid countenance
was fixed in its expression of anguish. Colour there was
none ; even the lips resembling the unnatural character
which is given by images of wax. Her limbs, like her

burning. There was another, which bore, in deep letters, the name of the Puritan. His death occurred in 1680. At its side, there was a humble stone, on which, with great difficulty, was traced the single word " Submission." It was impossible to ascertain whether the date was 1680, or 1690. The same mystery remained about the death of this man, as had clouded so much of his life. His real name, parentage, or character, further than they have been revealed in these pages, was never traced. There still remains, however, in the family of the Heathcotes, an orderly book of a troop of horse, which tradition says had some connection with his fortunes. Affixed to this defaced and imperfect document, is a fragment of some diary or journal, which has reference to the condemnation of Charles I. to the scaffold.

The body of Content lay near his infant children, and it would seem that he still lived in the first quarter of the last century. There was an aged man, lately in existence, who remembers to have seen him, a white-headed patriarch, reverend by his years, and respected for his meekness and justice. He had passed nearly, or quite, half a century unmarried. This melancholy fact was sufficiently shown by the date on the stone of the nearest mound. The inscription denoted it to be " the grave of Ruth, daughter of George Harding, of the colony of Massachusetts Bay, and wife of Capt. Content Heathcote." She died in the autumn of 1675, with, as the stone reveals, " a spirit broken for the purposes of earth, by much family affliction, though with hopes justified by the covenant, and her faith in the Lord."

The divine who lately officiated, if he do not now officiate, in the principal church of the village, is called the Rev. Meek Lamb. Though claiming a descent from him who ministered in the temple at the period of our tale, time and intermarriages have produced this change in the name, and happily some others in doctrinal interpretations of duty. When this worthy servant of the church found the object which had led one born in another state, and claiming descent from a line of religionists who had left the common country of their ancestors to worship

in still another manner, had an interest in the fortunes of
of those who first inhabited the valley, he found a pleasure
in aiding the enquiries.   The abodes of the Dudleys and
Rings were numerous in the village, and its environs.   He
showed a stone, surrounded by many others that bore these
names, on which was rudely carved, "I am Nipsett, a Narragansett ; the next snow I shall be a warrior !"   There is a
rumour, that though the hapless brother of Faith gradually returned to the ways of civilised life, he had frequent glimpses of those seducing pleasures which he had
once enjoyed in the freedom of the woods.

Whilst wandering through these melancholy remains of
former scenes, a question was put to the divine concerning
the place where Conanchet was interred.   He readily
offered to show it.   The grave was on the hill, and distinguished only by a head-stone that the grass had concealed
from former search.   It merely bore the words " The
Narragansett."

" And this at its side ? " asked the enquirer.   " Here
is one also, before unnoted."

The divine bent in the grass, and scraped the moss
from the humble monument.   He then pointed to a line,
carved with more than usual care.   The inscription simply
said,—

" The Wept of Wish-Ton-Wish."

THE END.

LONDON :
Printed by A. SPOTTISWOODE,
New-Street-Square.